THE TELL-TALE
STONE

A TWIST OF POE MYSTERY

Also By

VELDA BROTHERTON

TWIST OF POE MYSTERIES

The Purloined Skull

The Tell-Tale Stone

The Pit and the Penance

Masque of the Rising Moon

THE VICTORIANS

Wilda's Outlaw

Rowena's Hellion

Tyra's Gambler

THE MONTANA SERIES

Montana Promises

Montana Treasures

Montana Dreams

Montana Fire

Montana Destiny

Montana Legacy

OTHER TITLES

Beyond The Moon

A Savage Grace

Once There Were Sad Songs

Stoneheart's Woman

Wolf Song

Remembrance

THE TELL-TALE STONE

A TWIST OF POE MYSTERY

VELDA BROTHERTON

LAGAN

OGHMA CREATIVE MEDIA

www.oghmacreative.com

Library of Congress Control Number: 2018944184

ISBN: 978-1-63373-291-9

Interior Design by Casey W. Cowan
Editing by Staci Troilo

Lagan Press
Oghma Creative Media
Bentonville, Arkansas
www.oghmacreative.com

This book is dedicated to my favorite publisher,
who has opened up new opportunities for so many writers
who deserve to have their work published.

Thank you, Casey Cowan, for being who you are.
I will always be grateful.

ACKNOWLEDGEMENTS

I would like to acknowledge several people who were with me along the way from the beginning of my writing career. These *Twist of Poe* mysteries are based in a large part on the nine years I spent as a feature author and city editor for *The Washington County Observer*. Though we never investigated a murder, like Jessie West and Dal Starr, we met so many marvelous characters who now walk through the pages of this series.

I worked with so many good people, a few who have now gone on. In particular, Parker Rushing, my editor and the owner of the paper, who hired me though I never had a day's training as a journalist. He guided me through every facet of my job from photography—we still used black and white film developed in a darkroom on site, and 35mm cameras—to conducting interviews and telling the stories. He gave me opportunities I'll never forget and was with me when I learned my first book, *Goldspun Promises*, was to be published by Penguin.

Judy Housley, our super receptionist who did everything at the newspaper to keep it going from dealing with disgruntled callers and visitors to typing all those column submissions, some handwritten in what could appear to be a foreign language. She befriended me and taught me so much about the newspaper business.

Lori Ericson, who came to work several years after I did. A real pro, Lori was loved by everyone unless she got on their case and dug deep to find the truth surrounded by their cover-ups. I learned a lot from her about writing exciting news stories and turning a good interview into a fantastic story.

And a special thank you to Boyce Davis, who bought the paper a few years later, and kept me on, disregarding my lack of journalistic training. He made me City Editor when I protested, and I certainly learned a lot during those years. Lessons that have helped me immensely in editing my own work. He gave me a full page on which to write a feature historical column every week, and was patient with my questions.

To them and all the others I worked with over the years, I want to say thank you for being kind and understanding with me and guiding me through a magnificent nine years in the best job I ever had.

1
CHAPTER

The moment Jessie settled down to draft an article about the book drive for the library, the police scanner sputtered to life. A body found in a pond. So much for a quiet day at the office. On the remote chance it was a human body, she reached for her reporter's survival kit.

The phone played "Dragnet." Her friend Tinker at Grace County Sheriff's Office probably calling to tell her the same thing the scanner had. With a rueful smile, she answered.

Sure enough. Same message, followed by, "Thought you might like to join Deputy Dal, maybe write something clever about the current crime wave. This is three floaters in two weeks."

"Yeah, well, after a dead deer half-eaten by coyotes and a child-sized doll some kid tossed into an open well, it's hard to imagine what this one might be."

"But just think. You have an excuse to spend some time in the boonies with our hot deputy."

"There is that. Thanks, Tink." The idea had a certain appeal, and given ten minutes, she could finish this library story. "What's that address out there?"

Tinker told her. She jotted it down, crammed her notebook in the backpack with her other necessary gear, and left, locking the door behind her. No one else would be in the office till tomorrow when they started putting the paper together for the following week.

It had been ten days or more since she'd seen Dal. The second anniversary of his wife's death was coming up, and she worried about him. Afraid he would go on a bender. He still had a hard time dealing with the way she had died—with a needle hanging out of her arm—and him a narc. The media tore him a new one for that. A few months later, he was shot and disabled while undercover for the Dallas Narcotics Unit, whereby the fickle media turned him into a hero.

Slightly the worse for wear, the sexy Cherokee lawman showed up a year ago in Cedarton, burned out and carrying a lot of baggage. Grace County Sheriff Mac Richards, admirer of the downtrodden, had hired him to fill the new position of crime scene investigator with the small department when he learned of his special talent.

And her friend Tinker was right. He was hotter than fire, and she'd already been singed a few times. Each time, after she and Dal came together like an explosion, they both backed off to cool down. But he couldn't stay away from her for long, and the feeling was mutual. They walked on the edge, risking their careers and damage to their personal lives.

She hopped in the Jeep, clipped her long hair back, opened the window, and pulled out. On the opposite side of the square, a narrow gravel road left town headed northwest and climbed steeply around Sugar Mountain through a series of S curves. In about ten minutes, she reached the mailbox labeled "J. Norton," that and the address painted in black.

Dal's patrol unit, a deep blue Ford SUV, was parked near a pond behind the house and barn. It was hot for March, and she slipped out of her sweatshirt before hiking across the pasture to see what he was up to. Tiny insects clouded the air heavy with the smell of damp soil and new growth. Dried weed stalks slapped against the legs of her jeans.

Dallas hunkered on the other side of the vehicle, hidden from sight, his sexy butt resting on his good leg. Fishing something out of the pond with a long stick, he paused, glanced over his shoulder straight at her. Dang Cherokee mind reader could sense her coming half a mile off. Unless she was furious with him, in which case he picked up her vibes a mile away.

She slipped her camera from the backpack and snapped a few shots. Whatever he had hooked on the end of the stick slithered off and back into the water.

"Lose your fish, deputy?" She lowered the camera and smiled.

His slight grin sent a happy shiver through her. "Guess I should have known you'd get word of the latest mystery floater. How you doing, Jess?"

"Lonely. You okay?" He wasn't. Dark circles under his eyes told her so. She touched him on the shoulder, and he tensed. "What you got there?"

"Looks like a dead alligator, but never saw one in the Ozarks before." He went to poking at it with the stick again.

"Maybe you need a bigger pole." She took another few shots.

"Think this might turn into the story of the week?" Dal resented reporters and didn't mind letting it show on occasion. That only added more burn to their relationship.

He wiggled his snakeskin cowboy boots firmly into the grassy bank, and made another try at dragging the mystery animal out of the water. Mud coiled up and over one leather toe and he began to slip. She wrapped her arms around his waist to steady him, his thigh muscles hard against her.

Nice addition to her day.

Together they managed to keep him from sliding into the water so he could drag the dripping burden onto the shore.

"Too bad someone wasn't here with a camera to get that picture." She rested her head briefly against his back without turning loose. His heart thumped in her ear, the heat of his body zinged through her.

"Jess, not that you don't feel mighty good, but you'd better let me go. Wouldn't want to put on a show for our audience." He gestured toward the back yard of the house where the Nortons stood peering toward the pond.

"Mmm, I was just beginning to enjoy it."

"Another time." His voice was gruff with warning, and she took heed. "Now, let's see what we've got ourselves here. Maybe a new breed of Arkansas gator." Again he squatted, and she stood over him, camera at the ready.

Pulling a pair of leather gloves from his pocket, he slipped them on, and with two fingers turned the critter over on its back. "Damn, it does look like a gator. Something's been at its insides, though."

"It's not very big. You think maybe one of their kids had it for a pet and turned it loose when it got bigger than they thought it would?"

He rose with a grimace. "Wouldn't surprise me. I'm going up to talk to them. Might as well invite you to come, 'cause that's what you'll do anyway."

"Yep." She strode along beside him. "Did the gator's spirit impart any thoughts to you?"

"Funny. Got any other clever questions, Miss Reporter?"

"Just thought, if the poor critter met a violent death, his spirit might be hanging around to commune with you about it 'cause you usually go all weird-eyed and don't sound like yourself."

He snorted. "Weird-eyed? Exactly what does that mean?"

"You stare off into space like there's something out there. Guess you can see the dead, after all." Instead of replying, he lifted a hand to the Nortons. "Ma'am. Mr. Norton, you have a son?"

"Yeah, but he's upstairs, so it ain't him." Norton hitched his britches up, crinkled his eyes, and waited for a response to his joke.

A breeze blew the woman's faded dress around her thin legs. She scowled at her husband. "James Edward, shame."

Dal chuckled. "Did he have a pet alligator? Maybe a baby?"

"Well, yes. Got it down in Florida when we took him to Disneyland last summer, but he claimed it run off." That from Mrs. Norton.

"That's possible, but if it did it headed right for the pond and has been living out there. These critters are found in low densities, but normally the presence of alligators in Arkansas is limited to more suitable habitat. That sure doesn't include the Boston Mountains here in Northwest Arkansas. Don't know what killed it, or maybe it froze over the winter. Anyway, it's dead."

Dal was always doing that. Quoting some fact about animals like it came right out of a book. Could be it was some Cherokee thing.

The woman glared at her husband, obviously blaming him for the entire episode. "Sure sorry to bother you, Sheriff."

"Deputy," Dal said. "Deputy Dallas Starr."

"Right, right," Jim Norton said. "You're that feller up from Dallas. We thank you for coming out. Ruby here could have swore it was a body, and I wasn't about to go poking around on it, just in case she was right. She watches them shows on teevee, and says to me that you're not supposed to disturb a crime scene. Me, I don't care too much for them. The teevee shows, that is, not crime scenes. Ain't got no opinion 'bout them, one way or the other."

"Uh-huh. You can go ahead and bury that carcass." Dal touched the underside brim of his Stetson and aimed a killer smile at Ruby Norton. She patted her graying hair and allowed a tight grin in return.

To keep his company longer, Jessie walked beside him to his patrol car.

"A hard day's work over and done with." She stood on her tiptoes and kissed him under his jaw line. "You charmer, you. Every woman in the county's in love with you. Call me. You look like you could use some sleep, and I could help with that."

"Or keep me up all night." He touched her cheek with the tip of his thumb. "Not very good company. Some other time."

"Dal?" She craved more from him. Waited.

"Gotta go, Jess."

"Me, too. You take care of yourself, you hear? See you."

Without answering, he climbed into the Ford and was gone by the time she reached the Jeep.

Back at *The Observer,* she hadn't typed more than ten lines in the story of the alligator floater before the scanner crackled again. A police call from dispatch to Mac. She listened a moment. A body? Could it be a real one this time? Not much chance. They ought to take to identifying these bodies to save wear and tear on everyone. Maybe add a number to the code call that said human.

Probably a coon or possum this time. Still, it was her job to follow up on stuff like this. As down as he was, Dal might not have turned on his police radio, so she gave him a quick call. Who was she kidding? This time she had a plan to maybe spend more time with him.

When he answered, she launched right into the subject. "You heard? Reckon it's the real thing this time?"

"There's always a chance."

"Give me a ride? You home yet?"

"Just got here. Was fixing to turn around. Your Jeep not running all of a sudden?"

"Truth is, I'm trying to save on gas. You get yours paid for. Besides, do you know how to get to that address? I'm on your way, and I can keep you from wandering around for a couple of hours."

Get real. What she wanted was to be with him. Besides, the way he was acting he could use the company. And he still did get lost when he got too far off the beaten track.

"We'll see. Where is it?"

Because he sounded reluctant, she said, "It's okay if you want to drive out by yourself. Remember how Dogtown Road curves around the mountain to River Road then heads to Harrison? Well, you make sure not to take any of the left forks, not even that teeny weenie track that goes to Theron's place. Once you go past SEFOR, then it's the second right, just past that old red barn where that old horse, well you know... ?"

"Shit, never mind. I'll pick you up. Be there in ten."

With a chuckle, she hung up before he could change his mind. No point in trusting GPS in this remote county. Nine times out of ten the friendly voice deposited you either on a road with a fallen tree blocking it, or one that dead-ended at a bridge that had fallen in or been washed away. "You have reached your destination" often became an old logging road, an empty clearing, or a river bank.

"Not much info about the body on the scanner, except it is a human," he said when she hopped in with him.

"You could radio Mac and ask the circumstances."

"No need, he's got his hands full. We'll know when we get there."

Dal parked as close as he could to the gathering of deputies, the sheriff among them, glad to see the ground was fairly level. Easy to get around on.

A slight breeze carried the scent of death. All six deputies gathered around the center of attraction. He made his careful way to the gravesite, the damned leg giving him hell. Jess strolled along beside him, keeping her hands off. He grunted in appreciation. She knew good and well he'd swell all up like an angry toad frog if she made a big deal out of the limp.

Traipsing through the woods wasn't always easy, so he'd taken a pill before picking her up. It hadn't helped a whole lot yet.

The body had been buried in a shallow grave then dug up, probably by coyotes, and scattered out like a feast for other smaller animals. Crows then fed on the face. Looked like they'd already removed the eyeballs and a couple of them had worked on the tongue until the gaggle of humans arrived. Several of the black birds perched in tree limbs, others circled above, cawing in anger, their wings slapping at the wind.

"Good Heavens," Jess declared with disgust.

Assailed by the cacophony of lingering violence, and a voice that battered at him as if floating up from the bones, Dal halted about ten feet from the cluster of lawmen. Dammit to hell. Sometimes this so-called gift was nothing but a curse. His body language, tone of voice. And reactions to what he experienced often frightened anyone looking on. He couldn't say as he blamed them. One reason he preferred to investigate a crime scene on his own. Too bad it wasn't usually possible.

A couple of deputies were clearing earth and debris, but when they spotted him, they eyed each other and stepped back. As the only crime scene investigator in the county, he was responsible for gathering evidence. But that wasn't the real reason the uniformed men backed off and formed a loose circle to watch. In truth, they all thought him a bit weird.

Squinting against a shattering attack from what he thought of as the spirit world, he hissed through gritted teeth and swayed. Made a sound down in his throat as if he'd been slugged in the gut.

She grabbed his arm, but he pulled away. Best she didn't get caught up in the attack from those dark places while he did his thing. Something neither he nor anyone else could fully explain. His muscles went tight as cables, and he shuddered, tightened his fists, and squeezed his eyes tight, as if he could see more in the shadows of his imagination than in the reality before him. In truth, he often did. Too often, he existed in both worlds at one time.

An abnormal stillness settled over the circle of deputies who knew better than to say anything. Or were too scared to do so. He never was sure which. He wasn't the easiest to work with, and for the most part, they kept their distance. Suited him just fine. He never made friends easily, and didn't really give a damn. Wished they weren't even around to witness his unusual interrogation.

Finally, he relaxed. Recited in a monotone which Mac Richards recorded. Something they'd agreed upon after the first murder and his lone investigation.

"Two men, both alive when they got here. They know each other, maybe even related. Killer is bigger, stronger, younger. This one wiry." He gestured toward the shallow grave. "Both are angry, viciously so. Words spat at each other. Look for a rock, baseball-sized. It'll have blood and brains on it. He threw it, so you'll have to scour the perimeter. Something I'd usually do, but can't right now." He took a deep breath, sweat beading on his forehead and upper lip. "Older one is angry at the other over a secret, a discovery, something vague. No names yet." He shuddered, dragged in another deep breath, and jerked loose from the swarm of fury.

"Mac could've taken care of this." Jess took his arm again, couldn't just leave him the hell alone. "You should have stayed home and gotten some sleep. It's been a bad time for you. We all realize that."

Though she spoke under her breath so no one else could hear, her bringing up the anniversary of Leann's death like that stirred a deep-set anger in him which he reined in before speaking. She was only trying to help. He didn't appreciate it, though. Came too close to pity.

"We found out something about the killer we wouldn't have known had I not been out here. I can't gather that stuff out of thin air."

"You did with the killings at the Norville house. That scene was more than thirty years old."

"There was a lot of blood soaked into the floor boards. Here that would all be soaked into the ground. And rain would wash away any hints of blood left in the soil. I had to come." He glanced around. The men strained to hear the private discussion. "Back off, Jess. Let me get this done."

"Sure, you old bear. Don't you go changing your cranky self for me."

"Don't expect you'll be changing your Miss Nosy self, either. You go on over there and get your photos and make your notes. Leave me be."

Casting him a squint-eyed look, Jess grabbed her bag and lugged it closer to the crime scene to do her thing, being careful where she stepped.

After she snapped the prerequisite photos she would share with Mac, she moved away from the body and snapped a few of the deputies at work. No one wanted to look at dead people on the front page of the paper, especially not one gnawed on this bad.

Doc Cramer probably wouldn't come up with anything, because he wasn't a real medical examiner. Dal preferred to sit in on the cursory examination before Doc sent the body down to Little Rock, but Jess drew the line at being present for that. She'd puke on the evidence. While she finished taking notes, he went to sit in his patrol car. No doubt he'd have this figured out before the ME in Little Rock drew his final conclusions. She headed his direction, and he slid from the seat, went back toward the scene.

"What are you doing?"

"I need to give it another try. I missed something I ought to have read from what was going on."

"Well, I'm going with you, and I'm going to get Mac at your side, too. Big as you are, you start toppling, I can't catch you all by myself."

"What makes you think I'm going to topple? I'm fine."

"You were fine, then you turned into some sort of exorcist."

His eyebrows crawled upward. "Exorcist? Couldn't have been all that bad. I know I didn't spew green goo."

"I almost did when I saw that tongue half-ripped out of that poor guy's face." She puckered her lips.

"Crows like to take something away with them. Eyeballs being their favorite, but the tongue would be a juicy treat."

Her face drained of color, and she punched him on the shoulder. "Stop that."

"Then don't come to a crime scene." The words were light and teasing, but he meant them.

Spotting the sheriff, she raised a hand and beckoned to him.

Mac showed up, and they approached the body one more time. She wouldn't remain near him while he did his thing, and he didn't blame her. It was more than a tad scary. His voice changed when he described what he was feeling, deepened and lost its lyrical quality.

On this second approach, he went deeper into the head of the man doing the killing. The victim's fear often overrode thoughts of the killer, and he wanted to sort them out.

"Something is hidden by someone the killer's close to, maybe his grandfather or father. He makes the mistake of telling the vic, who wants to hunt for it. They don't know precisely where it is. Or what it is. The killer says not now. Victim accuses him of wanting it all for himself. Killer does not set out to kill the victim, but when the fight grows violent, he grabs the rock and hits him in the head." Dal sucked in a ragged breath, continued in a controlled monotone. "Scares the ever-loving shit out of him. He panics. If he'd stopped with one blow, he probably wouldn't have killed him, but he loses his temper, bad temper. In a rage, he hits him over and over after he goes down, beats his brains out. Then he goes one more step and attempts to bury the body. His voice. Think I'll know his voice."

"That's all I get now." Dal hunched his shoulders in a huge sigh, relieved to let go the spirits.

Mac supported him by the elbow, but he shook loose.

"I'm okay. I was hoping I could get a name. Individual thoughts were blurred by the fury of the fight that led to the killing. Strange how rarely people think of their own names or those of the ones they're with. The older one, the vic, did think of something he didn't say out loud. Something to do with a crow, or someone named Crow. Hard to tell."

The black birds resting like sentinels along the tree branches set up a cawing. "Could be I was getting it all mixed up with those crows crowding around to divvy up the remains. Might not be a name at all. Hell, I don't know." He shook his head, and watched as one of the birds grew bold and darted in to peck at the ragged tongue. A deputy waved his hat and hollered till the bird rejoined the others in the trees. They all settled as if waiting for everyone to leave them to their feast.

Mac scratched under his hat. "There is a woman by the name of Crowe lives here on the mountain. At least, I think she's still around. Lots of folks come into the Ozarks to begin a new lifestyle and they pretty much remain invisible. Don't believe in electricity, or phones, or socializing much."

Dal glanced up once more at branches black with the noisy birds, cawing and calling to others who moved in until the bare limbs bent with their weight.

"Maybe it was just them messing with me," he joked. Wasn't very funny, but a few deputies chuckled nervously. Probably to relieve their heebee jeebees over the messed-with corpse and this weird deputy who visited with spirits.

After he dropped Jess back at *The Observer*, Dal headed home. He was on call, but sometimes he went home early, especially when he had a headache coming on, which usually happened after one of these visitations. He should be thinking about the case, but he was so damned tired. If he could get more sleep, it would help. The past few nights he'd been startled awake by bad dreams of gloomy alleys and his own blood dark in the moonless night, smearing over visions of his dead wife, Leann.

Awakening, he would crawl out of bed and wander around the rest of the night, too uneasy to risk going back into that nightmare land. Two years now, and he couldn't get past the anniversary of Leann's death without the wild ass dreams that jerked him awake with the sweats. After a while, the lack of sleep made him feel like a zombie.

Seeing Jess today hadn't been good for him either. On the one hand, he couldn't keep his hands off her. On the other, he got the guilts over their relationship. Leann was gone, he couldn't be untrue to a ghost. Still, that whole mess haunted him. The two-faced reporters hating him one minute, turning him into some kind of hero the next. Courting him to the point of distraction. Thinking about Leann and all that shit so much lately had made him question his attraction to Jess. How the hell could he now take up with a reporter? None of them could be trusted, including the country-lovely Jessie West. Talk about weak minded.

At the entrance to Hidden Holler Trailer Park, Ina Mae waved to him. He tamped down the memories and waved back. She was a tough but sweet old lady who'd come through some hard times, what with losing her husband a few years back. Even so, she greeted him with a cheerful grin. Always let it be known he was her favorite tenant. But she kept an eye on all her folks, as she called the renters of the dozen or so mobile homes in her park. He drove slowly past her tidy little cottage, the lane skirting her garden where neat rows of delicate green shoots poked through the rich dark earth. His new home sat on the bank of the creek at the end of a long line of aging trailers spaced out on well-kept lots.

Some called them mobile homes, but that was a bit ridiculous. They were trailers of varying descriptions, his ninety feet long and twelve feet wide, maybe a dozen years old. The size offered him a space that closed him up good and tight and he liked that. Open spaces were fine when he could tune in to his surroundings, but when he wanted to sleep or have some privacy, he needed a cocoon of sorts to shut out the world.

The phone was ringing when he opened the door to a lingering aroma of the morning's coffee. Must be someone without his cell number. One of those automated sales pitches. Not Sheriff Mac Richards. He'd use the walkie. He let voicemail take the call and unstrapped his .45, draping it over the back of the only kitchen chair. Pulled out his cell and plugged it in. A beer would be good, but he delayed that to grab a frozen dinner and stick it in the microwave. Put something in his stomach first.

His throat ached, his stomach clenched at the thought of food, his eyes burned, and he felt like he was going to fly apart. Damn it all, he wasn't going to get past this. A grown man and he was about to bust out crying. He carried a gun, for God's sake. He came from warrior stock—his grandfather, Lone Bear Stands, was a Cherokee shaman.

Wonder if he ever cried, that grandfather from whom he had inherited this cursed ability to converse with spirits, especially victims of violence. What the Cherokee called asgi`na, ghosts, and anasgi`na, evil spirits.

This is why he left the Dallas PD and came here? So he could hide out in his cave and come apart every few months? Well, it wasn't going to happen. Not this time. He opened the cupboard, took down a bottle of Jack Daniels Black, and poured four fingers. Knocked it back and refilled the glass. Stared through the amber drink toward the creek and beyond, seeing only the ghost that haunted his mind in the golden beauty of late afternoon sunlight. Leann in her happier days, before the drugs. Life before the loneliness and bitterness ripped them apart.

The microwave beeped and he ignored it, went into the living space and sprawled into the man-sized recliner, the only new piece of furniture in the otherwise shabby room. Stretched out his long legs and waited for the whisky to do its job. For a long while, he held up the glass, finally set it down on the small table next to his chair, leaned his head back, and closed his eyes. Fought against the desire to toss down more of the fiery stuff.

Wouldn't do to have a call and be drunk. Not only was he the only criminal investigator with the sheriff's department, he could be called out for just about anything when no other deputy was available. And he liked his job a lot because the county was small and pretty much peaceful. Little squabbles over property or someone's wife, for the most part. Some pot and meth. This was the first murder this year, would probably be the only one. And that was the reason he'd come here in the first place. To find some sort of peace.

Being around Jess was tough because he wanted her. It was good for the same reason. He'd immediately felt a stirring in his nether parts when she laid her hand on his shoulder. They'd worked together a few times when she had a story and he had the call out to investigate. Hard to get used to working hand in hand with a reporter, when in Dallas it had always been just the opposite. Reporters there got in the way, wrote shit they didn't know anything about, made up half their stories, and didn't hesitate to cut him off at the knees when Leann died.

Okay, he hadn't meant to get around to that. But there it was.

The phone ringing in the middle of the night. Her voice, broken by deep breaths and sobs.

"I can't do this anymore. I hate it. I hate living this way."

And then the phone hitting the floor, the circuit remaining open so he heard her slapping at a vein, the silence of the needle going in, gasping her last breath from way too much of the contaminated shit, crumpling to the floor. Dying and he couldn't do a damn thing but shout 'No!' at her, like that might help. Like he hadn't already told her to stop, put her in a program, policed her and the apartment daily.

You couldn't keep shit away from dopers.

Dal dragged in a deep breath, picked up the drink, and slugged down the Jack. It joined the first shot to hit his empty stomach like napalm. God help him if he got a call this night, 'cause he was in no shape to handle it.

Head tipped back, he tried to catch some sleep. Maybe the drinks would keep away the dreams.

Darkness surrounded him, so black that when he reached out at arm's length he couldn't see his hand. Worse than that, he didn't know where he was or how he got there. Someone was with him. Close. Breathing rasped into the silence, a heartbeat that wasn't his, thumping loud as drums.

"Who is that?" Even as he asked, he didn't want to know.

Whoever or whatever it was walked by him so close the air quivered. And then he caught the odor of tanned hides.

"Grandfather?"

"She treads close to the edge, my grandson. If you don't catch her, she will fall." The voice pitched low.

"Who you talking about?"

"The one you care for. You will know when it is time."

"Time for what? Stop speaking in riddles."

No reply. No breathing. No heartbeat. Nothing but black and more black, and the only aroma the liquor on his own breath.

Gone.

He was gone. "Don't leave. Explain. Tell me."

He awoke with those last words on his lips. Darkness beyond the open windows. Despite the cool night air, he sweated. A cryptic message delivered not in a dream, but by the *asgi'na* of his grandfather. A vision that unnerved him. Though he could touch anyone's mind, he normally only dealt with those spirits who had been involved in violence. Both the victims and the perps. The dead and the living. So why this? And why at this particular time? Grandfather could not have been warning him about Leann, she was gone. Someone else he cared for? Had to be Jess. He cared for no one else. Surely the warning was a dream, but a voice told him different. A warning voice he shut out. All he wanted was to get through this, come out on the other side, and be back to normal.

As normal as he ever could be considering he dealt with dark specters.

Car lights swept across the front windows, then went out. Who the hell was coming here in the middle of the night? He checked his watch. Nine-thirty. Well, it really wasn't all that late, but still....

A rap on the door. He hadn't turned on any lights. Thought about not answering. But his unit was parked outside. They'd probably just keep knocking. Again a rap. Soon it would be pounding, then hollering and waking old Mr. Jenson next door, who'd come outside in his long white night shirt—a sight not easily beheld by the faint of heart—and shout curses even he had never heard. Hell, he might as well answer and get it over with.

Now that he seldom drank, the whisky had hit him hard, and he staggered a bit before getting the door open. Jess stood there in the glow from the nearby security light Ina Mae insisted on, and he squinted at her.

"Jess, what the hell?"

"Good to see you too, Dal. Can I come in?"

"Go home."

"You look terrible."

"And you came to do what? Sympathize? Nurse me back to health?"

"You've been drinking."

"Holy shit, it's my mother. Please go away." He backed up, intending to shut her out, but she ducked under his arm and stood behind him by the time he closed the door.

When he turned around, she stepped close, put her arms around him, and laid her head on his chest.

Her hug went through him like a warm wind, and he let out a

noise, not sure what it was. Surely not a sob. He gathered her close, laying his cheek against the top of her head. She smelled so good, like lilacs and sweet breezes. Like woman.

Dammit to hell.

He lifted her, slammed her up against the wall, and pulled at the sweats she wore, dragging them down so he could shove a hand between her legs. She wasn't wearing panties. No surprise. And she was hot and wet.

"Is this what you came for?" He spoke the words under his breath, his mouth against the soft flesh of her throat which he then sucked on.

"Yes. No. Yes. Is it what you want?" She didn't fight him. She never did. Whatever he did to her, she accepted. But he'd never hurt her, not this way. Not with his hands, not with sex. And she knew it. He hurt her a lot otherwise, though. Turning from her. Sending her away.

He let go, supported her against him till she found her balance. "I'm sorry, Jess. I just…."

"I know. I know what day it is. I wasn't going to come, but I didn't want you to be alone. You shouldn't be alone. You're so self-destructive." She pushed away, tugged her pants up. "Did you eat? Let me fix you something."

He gestured toward the kitchen. "In the microwave. I forgot about it."

She touched his face, traced along his mouth and jaw line. He closed his eyes, but all he could see was that needle sticking out of Leann's arm when he busted down the door to the hovel where she was staying that week. The week she died.

"Fuck it," he said and collapsed in the recliner.

Without another word, Jess went into the kitchen. Rewarmed the dinner, dragged a fork out of the drawer, found a paper towel to serve as a napkin, and brought him the food.

"Here. Eat. Want a beer with that or what?"

"Better not. Too much already. How about a Pepsi, or whatever's in there?"

She brought two cans of Pepsi Max, opened and set one down beside him on the table. Kept the other one and dropped onto the couch to drink it.

The dinner was flat, tasteless, but he choked it all down. She wouldn't leave till he ate, so eat he would. Like most women, Jess had a need to nurture and had picked him for the task. Most times, he didn't resent it. She meant well, and besides, he liked her in spite of what she did for a living. Liked her, hell. It was something a lot more than that. Like maybe his crazy world was a bit better for having her in it. Making sure he didn't give in to the darkness.

"Feeling better?" she asked when he set aside the empty tray.

"Not really. I may throw up."

She reached over, squeezed his arm. "Anything I can do?"

"Yep, but we probably ought not do it tonight. I'm feeling guilty enough as it is."

She shot him a puzzled glance. "Having sex with me adds to your guilt? You never told me that before."

"I'm surprised. I've told you everything else." Sarcasm didn't go very far with her. She could shoot it right back at him.

"Yeah, I tend to bring that out in my men. But I'd rather not be causing you guilt."

"Don't worry about it. Your men? How many you got?"

"Only one at a time, Dal. One at a time. And I'm with that one at the moment."

"Well, thank goodness. I'm pleased we're so close."

She jumped up and went to stand behind him, placing her fingers at his temples rubbing gently. "Sarcasm will get you nowhere."

"Oh, God, that feels good."

"Just relax, honey. Relax."

Slowly, his body uncoiled, went limp.

When he awoke in the recliner, it was dawn, Jess was asleep on the couch, and his headache was gone. Best of all, he couldn't remember having a bad dream. For a long time he remained where he was, watching her sleep. She was sexy as hell, even in sweats. A real country girl with a natural flush to her cheeks, healthy skin, and slightly muscled arms and legs. Sun-streaked hair she didn't torture with spray or dye. No extra padding, but not skin and bones either. For the thousandth time, he wondered what was wrong with him that he couldn't accept what she wanted to give him? She got too close, he shoved her firmly away. Yet when they coupled, it was like they were possessed by mad, uncontrollable lust.

Maybe that was the problem.

They often were thrown together on cases and fought over how to proceed like badgers at a kill. That only brought about a romp in bed. Strangest relationship he'd ever had, and one he would not give up. Ever. Still, he could not make that final commitment. The one that would turn their savage lust to love. Why ruin a good thing?

Coffee was in order so he climbed to his feet, massaged his bad leg till it decided to halfway work, then limped four steps away into the kitchen to put on a pot.

While he stood at the cupboard taking down two cups, she came up behind him and snaked her arms around his waist, laid her cheek against his back.

Felt so damned good. "Morning. Sleep okay on that lumpy couch?"

"I could sleep on a pile of rocks in the woods. How about you? Still have that headache?"

"Nope. Thanks, Miss Magic Fingers."

"You're welcome. Coffee smells good."

"Let me go, I'll pour us some."

In companionable silence they drank coffee and ate two Honey Buns he found in the cabinet. They were slightly stale.

"Big man. Smart man." She slapped her chest and he laughed.

"If I don't get myself to work, I'll be looking for a job." He stood, gazed down at her a minute. "Like your hair in the morning," he said, and mussed the tangles with a splayed hand.

"Thanks so much. Yours is pretty cool, too." For a moment she leaned close, rubbed her palm over the cropped black mass, not a buzz but short enough it couldn't tangle, then sighed. "I have to get going. Have a reunion to go to. See you later?"

He leaned down and kissed her on the mouth, tasted the crumbs from the sweet roll and caffeine and her. Best of all, her. "Tomorrow's Friday. Want to go dancing?"

"Love to. The slow stuff suits me just fine, old man."

"I'll show you old man. Later."

"Brag on."

He grabbed the cell and walkie, strapped on the gun and utility belt, and opened the door. "Lock up for me, will you?"

"Sure thing. When you gonna learn? You're in Arkansas now, you don't need to lock the doors."

"Yeah, sure." He let the screen bang shut behind him. "Arkies don't commit crimes."

He climbed in the SUV and glanced through the windshield. She stood on the porch, arms crossed under her breasts, watching him leave.

Times like this he thought he probably loved her as much as he'd ever loved anyone… before or since Leann. Maybe one day he'd get past that and he could tell her so.

Maybe not.

2
CHAPTER

Jessie peered through a drifting fog and steered slowly along the winding mountain road. Heck of a day to hold a family reunion, but then no one could guess the weather here in the Ozarks. Up ahead, back in the trees that had grown up around it, was the old Boston school building. Cars, pickups, and SUVs angled into spaces forming a brightly colored necklace for the dilapidated building. A scattered growth of persimmon saplings, brambles, and wild roses blocked the circle lane that once allowed access to the school and would soon engulf the sagging structure.

She parked the Jeep, nose in the shallow ditch, grabbed her survival bag, and crawled out. The crowd, originally scheduled to meet outside at tables placed behind the building, had sought refuge inside away from the light rain. The uneven floor sagged and creaked, but it had been there for centuries, and no one appeared worried it would collapse. Some gathered in bunches, laughing and sharing pictures. Others set out their dishes of fragrant casseroles, breads, and desserts, filling the tables that had been carried in. Outside, hunkered under the porch roof, a few men sucked on cigarettes and passed a bottle disguised in a paper sack. Smoke and laughter hung around them in the damp air.

She had come to interview Malburn Ortho. He was the eldest member of the clan and had served as sheriff of Grace County before she was born. She worked her way through the crowd, spotted an elderly man relaxing in a chair by the window. Had to be Mr. Ortho. She took a seat next to him and introduced herself.

"From *The Observer*, huh?" he cawed. "You can call me Mal. Don't have no idea what you could write about me."

"Well, I'll just ask you some questions, and I'll bet we'll come up with something everyone would like to read."

The interview began pretty ordinary, and once past where he was born, how many kids in the family, and when they settled on the mountain, he reminisced about some of the crimes out of the past. Told a most extraordinary story about a cache of diamonds hidden by two men who stole them from a store in Harrison over in Boone County. As the old man put it, 'more'n thirty years ago.'

"Did they ever find them?" She glanced at her electronic recorder to make sure the red light was on, but scribbled notes all the same.

"Nope, never did. Them ole boys wouldn't tell where they were or nothing about 'em. After the robbery, the two showed up big as you please in Cedarton looking for gas. They stopped at ole Herb Nolan's station, and he called it in cause they was acting weird, according to his notion." He chuckled and she joined him.

"Tell you a secret," he said, bending toward her to whisper. "Ole Herb thought anyone not borned and raised right here in Cedarton was weird. Reckon in that case, he was right." They both chuckled some more.

"After we got the call, we lit out after 'em, and they ended up hiding out in a place a bit like this one." He gestured around at the sagging one room structure. "And when we tracked 'em down on horseback, rode up on them, they come out without a fight."

"But they didn't have the diamonds?"

"Nope. They went to prison, down to McAlester, without saying a word. I reckoned at the time they figgered to return once they got out of jail and get 'em."

"Well, when would they get out?"

"Oh, turned out they never did. They was killed in a riot in 1982, that was a couple years after they was incarcerated, I believe."

Jessie smiled at his use of incarcerated when most of his language consisted of heavily accented country words. "So you suspect the diamonds are hidden somewhere in this part of Grace County?"

"Well, somewheres between Cedarton and where we caught 'em."

"And where was that?"

"You know that old school house up on Dyer Creek? One that washed away in the high water back in 2001, I think it was. About that time, anyways."

"Okay." She didn't know that particular school, but could find out more about it and where it was located.

The aroma of fried chicken distracted her, and she glanced toward the table to see a platter piled high with crusty brown drumsticks, thighs, and breasts. Definitely had to have some of that. The Honey Bun eaten on the run at eight that morning had worn thin.

Back to her business though. She chewed on the end of her pen a minute. "Well, didn't you look for them? You and your deputies."

Again his chuckle that sounded like he was gagging. "Why, all we had was a few part-time deputies who was on call from their regular jobs, farmers mostly, plus me and Jefferson Davis on full time. I reckon he took a few turns around where they was caught, but where in the thunder would you begin to look for a little ole poke of diamonds?

"Leastways, they hightailed it off through the woods when they cottoned to old Herb calling us in. We got us up a posse and rode in after them. Some rough country in there."

She scribbled down everything including the name of the store they had robbed in Harrison which wasn't in business any more, and drew a box around a notation of her own. Car? It soon became clear that she had gotten all she was going to get about the diamond heist, so she brought up another subject to get Mal talking about life as a lawman fifty years earlier. After several stories, he began to run down, and she eyed the platter of chicken, decreased in size by more than half. Time she got herself some.

Bonnie Lou Reed, a distant relative, sidled up to meet her, and they strolled about speaking to a few others and working their way to the heavily laden table.

"Child, I hadn't seen you in so long. You need to get you a plate. Looks like you could use some fattening up. I read your stories in *The Observer* every week. We're so happy to have you writing about how it was living around here in the early days."

By the time Bonnie finished, she'd led Jessie to the heavily laden table, stuck a plate in her hand, and moved on to speak to someone else.

Jessie left an hour or so later, with notes enough for a couple of weeks' worth of columns for her historical page, plus some dandy photos. If she didn't miss her guess, Parker would want the diamond story Mal had told her on the front page. Along with the news of the body turning up, of course. That would lead. And she had this crazy but familiar itch in the back of her brain. A story in the making. Tracking down those diamonds would make for an exciting article.

All the way back to the newspaper office, she alternated over worrying about Dal and mulling the story of the diamonds. Wouldn't it be something if they could be found after all this time? Better if she found them. Was Dal having nightmares again? Who would the diamonds belong to? Probably an insurance company had paid off on the loss of the stones, and technically they would be theirs. Maybe she ought to go by and see Dal before she went home this evening. No. Best if she let him be to work it out himself.

She arrived back at the office about four o'clock, deposited the heavy bag on her desk, and sat down to make some calls. People who had been here when the diamond thieves were caught would have something to say about it so she could fluff out the piece with some choice quotes. A few phone calls handled that.

After she finished the story, she printed out a copy for her boss. Old fashioned as he was, he liked a hard copy to edit, even though the newspaper had gone to computers some ten years earlier. Then she went to work on a historical piece from the stories Mal had told about his time as sheriff. Besides the photos she'd taken of him, he said his grandson would be able to email her copies of some he had from the old days.

Finished with the column, she printed it, left it with the other draft on Parker's desk, and hurried to the library. There she asked for microfiche copies of the newspapers from the time of the diamond heist, curious to read the entire story for herself. Those she copied and headed for her cabin south of town, still worrying over Dal.

Sometimes she wanted to smack him upside the head, other times she wanted to gather him close and hug him till he healed. She would do neither. Instead, she would continue to mind her own business, mostly, and be his friend and lover when he allowed it. He wouldn't welcome company right now, and so she wouldn't visit him out at the trailer park where he'd settled in quite comfortably. Said it was quiet there, and he'd grown fond of his landlady, Ina Mae Carter, a lonely widow who liked to bake pies for him but kept a shotgun handy. If he got in real trouble, Ina Mae would see to him. She was a tough old bird with a kind heart, and she liked a lawman living in the park. If Dal wanted to see Jess, he'd come to the cabin. Besides, they were going dancing tomorrow night.

At home, she stripped out of her jeans and tee shirt, took a quick shower, donned a sleep shirt, and made herself a salad. She carried it, a glass of iced tea, and copies of the diamond stories into the small front room and spread the pages out on the couch and coffee table. Beyond the sliding glass doors and out across the valley to the mountains beyond, the setting sun spread a golden glow over trees fuzzy with early spring green. Creamy dogwood blossoms and redbud blooms laced the hills. The new highway, still unfinished, spanned the valley high above Cedar Creek and the railroad tracks like some gigantic monster from outer space poised to yank them up and haul them off to some unknown planet.

By eight o'clock, she had highlighted several important facts in the news stories that would be good additions to her own. They also gave clues that could lead to locating the hiding place. Amused that she would consider going treasure hunting, she stacked the work neatly on one corner of the table and went into the bathroom to brush her teeth and get ready for bed.

She was still mulling over the possibility of a treasure hunt when she pulled a light blanket over herself and fell asleep. Sometime during the night, she awoke with a start. Maybe an owl called or something moved through the dry leaves. Stars glittered in the endless black of space, and night critters sang. Nothing stirred, yet it was a long time before she finally went back to sleep.

By the time she arrived at work the next morning, Parker had blue-penciled both drafts. A bit bedraggled because she'd worn her wrinkled jeans and tee shirt from the day before, she half-expected a wry comment. But he raised an eyebrow and said nothing. He wouldn't dare. This man who wandered in and out at all hours with his shirt tail hanging out and red sneakers on his feet. Don't even mention the variety of pants. When it came to a dress code, he probably figured, 'What the heck?'

She fixed the edits and started building her column page. Wendy tapped away at her computer, copying the local columnists' submissions, some typewritten, others handwritten, that came in from the small settlements around Cedarton. Once Wendy finished, Jessie checked them for typos and then laid out the pages.

Friday was not her favorite day at the office, but she started editing what Wendy had already sent to her folder. The best part of this day would be going dancing tonight with Dal, if he didn't cancel on her. He had a bad habit of doing that. Massaging away his headache and staying with him Wednesday night might earn her the promise of an evening out, but by today, he could suffer from guilt and have a change of heart.

The back of her neck tingled and she turned to see Parker standing in the door to his cubicle of an office watching her. His dark wavy hair had grown back in after chemo last fall, and he had put on a few of the lost pounds. She smiled and wiggled her fingers at him.

"The diamond story." He waited.

"Yes? Front page, right? I sent some additions from home after I picked up background at the library. Did you get them?"

"Yes. Good job. You want to add or shall I? Mac didn't give us much in the release on the body, so both for the front page will fill it better. Good photos, by the way."

"Thanks. You can add whatever, I'm busy with edits here."

He hadn't finished worrying the diamond story yet. "Did you ever hear about the theft before? From one of your relatives?"

"No, why?"

"Odd, don't you think? That no one has tried to find those stones, the way so many folks around here like to hunt for lost treasure."

She had continued to type while he talked, but now she paused, twisted her chair around to face him. "I didn't think of it, but yeah, you're right. I don't know though, it was a long time ago. Maybe all the excitement finally died down when no one found them. Folks I called didn't have much to add. Some didn't even recall the robbery."

"How do you know that?"

"What? That no one found them? If they had I'm sure that would have been a topic of conversation for a long time."

"Not if whoever found them never said anything." He grinned.

Should she tell him that she planned to get Dal to help her see if they could trace the lost stones? Parker might be right. Someone could've found them and kept quiet about it. But would anyone living around here have the knowledge to turn stones like that into cash?

"Where are you going with this?" She smiled up at him.

"Oh, nowhere, I guess. Just a thought. When this goes on the front page, if someone did find them they're apt to get mighty nervous. If no one did, have you thought that we may be overrun with treasure hunters? Either way, it might be fun to watch."

"And it'll also make for some more stories for the paper."

"That's true. I'm getting ready to set the front page. I've got some ideas for making sure no one misses the story."

"I'll just bet you do." Her laughter trailed his. She knew Parker. He liked nothing better than starting something in town, then sitting back and watching with glee as reactions unfolded. He preferred to write the headlines for most stories, especially those she wrote, because he had a knack for piquing curiosity and she was lousy at it.

Without saying anymore, he nodded and went back in his office.

Once he wrote a front page story about two boys, eleven and thirteen, who were apprehended eating a stolen ice cream bar and smoking pilfered cigarettes behind the very store they'd taken them from. He managed two two-inch columns plus a huge headline that read *'Crime wave eliminated.'* That ought to scare the pants off the city council members.

The remainder of the day passed like most Fridays. Hectic last minute writing and editing, phones ringing every few minutes, and people dropping by with ads and photos. Monday noon was the deadline, so Friday began the rush to finish up. Parker liked to come in on Saturday when no one else was there and look over the pages, make final additions, and shoot the bull with people who dropped by. After a late Monday night, the paper went to Harrison over in Boone County for printing Tuesday morning, and on the stands and in the mail to subscribers on Wednesday. Then the week began all over again for the following weekly edition.

By the end of a hectic day, Jessie was good and ready to go out and have some fun. No call from Dal should mean they were still on. No calls on the police scanner either, so he'd had a light day. Since she hadn't taken time off for lunch, just grabbed a yogurt at noon and ate at her desk, on her way home to change she called him to ask if they could go early and eat. He didn't answer his cell or his landline, so she called Tinker.

"Seen Dal?" she asked after their usual pleasantries.

"He hasn't been in today. Mac said he was taking some personal time."

"Oh? Well, he's not answering either of his phones." Something was going on she didn't like.

"Got me. Want to get a movie tonight?"

"Mmm. Some other time. I've got plans. Or I did have. Could I get back to you?"

"Oh, you and Deputy Dal getting together?"

"Well, last I heard we were. Only trouble is now I'm not hearing anything. I'll go by his place. He wasn't feeling real good when he left for work Thursday morning."

Silence from Tinker and Jessie realized what she'd just said. "Uh, okay. Say it."

Tinker laughed. "Me? Why should I say anything but go girl? Hot damn. On again, off again with you two. Glad you're on again."

"That remains to be seen. Gotta go. I'll call you back."

Now what was he up to? If he wasn't at home and not at work, not answering either phone, then where the heck could he be? And what should she do? She wasn't his keeper, but since they did have a date, maybe he'd forgive her looking for him.

She tried his landline again, just in case he was at home and for some reason didn't have his cell on. Sometimes he didn't get a good signal out there. But the phone rang four times and went to voicemail.

"Dammit, where are you? And what are you doing? Mostly, are you okay?" Leaving that message probably wouldn't do any good, but she did it anyway, then clicked off her cell, tossed it in the console and started home. It rang before she arrived, and it was him.

"Hey, was starting to worry about you." She tried to keep her voice light.

"That's why I'm calling. Something came up." His voice sounded stressed.

She waited and when he didn't say more, asked, "And so?"

"Jess, I... could you come out to my place?"

Without waiting for her reply, he clicked off.

"Well, dammit, Dal."

She made a three-point U turn and headed toward Hidden Holler. Something was definitely wrong, and her heart skittered around a bit before she finally arrived. She'd seen him go off the rails a couple of times. Once he tore his hands up fighting a barbed wire fence, so she wasn't exactly at ease at the moment.

When she drove through to his trailer, Ina Mae was standing on her front porch and old Mr. Jenson was out in his yard staring toward Dal's trailer, thankfully fully dressed. The patrol car sat at an odd angle, the lights flashing and the door open. What the hell?

She skidded to a stop, leaped out and bounded up on the porch and inside without knocking. Dal sat on the floor against the sliding glass door, eyes closed, legs splayed in front of him and blood all over his shirt front.

Dropping to her knees, she cupped his face, smelled liquor on his breath. "Dal, look at me. What happened here? *Dal.*"

His eyes fluttered open. "Jess. I... dammit, I feel so stupid."

"What is this?" She ripped his blood-soaked shirt open. There was a bullet hole through the muscle of his upper right arm, seeping blood. "Why didn't you call 9-1-1 instead of me? Who did this to you?" She remembered she'd left her cell in the car, found his cordless, and punched in the numbers.

"No, put that down. Don't." He knocked the phone from her hand. It skidded across the floor and he gripped her wrist.

"You've been shot. You have to go to the hospital."

"Shit, Jess. Shit."

"What happened here?"

"I shot myself."

"You what?"

"I need you to help me before we call anyone. Jess, come on, dammit."

The look in his pain-filled eyes and the desperation in his voice did it. "Okay, relax. Tell me what I need to do."

"I took the damn thing out of the holster to check the clip. Been out doing some practice shooting." He stopped, closed his eyes and grimaced, then went on. "Had a round in the chamber and the damned thing went off."

"Oh, Dal. I don't know what I can do. You've been drinking. If—"

"Don't think I don't know it. Drinking while on duty. Messing with my gun. I could lose my job, and I can't let that happen." He shuddered and clenched his teeth against the pain.

She went to the kitchen and found some Tylenol in the cupboard, shook out three, and ran a glass of water. All the while, her mind ran in furious circles. She had a way out, but he'd probably pitch a fit.

"Here, honey. Take these. I've got an idea. Where's the gun?"

"Kitchen floor, why?"

Without replying, she spotted the weapon on the floor, picked it up, found the clip on the table and slapped it in place, racked a shell into the chamber.

He said her name but she didn't reply, just stepped to the back door and fired it once into the creek bank across the way.

"What are you doing?"

"It was me. We were talking and you took out your gun, laid it on the table to clean it. I picked it up, and it went off. Hit you in the arm. I've got GSR on my hand."

"No, Jess. No, I can't let you do that." He struggled to get up, but couldn't. "I thought maybe I came home, found someone here, got my gun and—"

"No, too many variables. Too much investigation. Someone could be blamed. It's done. This will work. No one else involved. Did Ina Mae come up when she heard the shot?"

"Nope, I'd been practice shooting out back, so she didn't."

"Why is your car sitting out there like that?"

"I'm not sure. I don't remember."

"Okay, I'll take care of that too. Stay put, I'm calling the police and an ambulance for you. You keep your mouth shut, Dal. Just keep it shut. I gave you a drink afterward."

"Dammit, Jessie, don't do this." His chin tilted to his chest and she checked. He'd passed out. She'd have to think of a reason she hadn't called right away. It was clear from the coagulating blood that the shot had been a while ago.

She was searching for the phone he'd knocked out of her hand when Ina Mae came busting through the door, shotgun hanging at her side.

"What in thunder is going on?"

Jess came up with the phone. "I'm gonna call 9-1-1, then I'll explain."

The woman nodded, raked splayed fingers through her hair so it stood on end, and dropped into a kitchen chair. Waited while Jessie dialed.

She took several deep breaths and when the dispatcher answered, said in a panicky voice, "I've shot him. I didn't mean to, but I shot him.

Please hurry." Then she hung up. The dispatcher in Cedarton had the address. It would've come up the minute she answered Jessie's call.

"Speak, girl. I heard a shot after you come up." Ina Mae had waited all she could.

"Listen to me. You have to help me... help Dal. Other than his target shooting earlier, you only heard one shot and that was mine, but not just now. It was a while ago that I arrived. Ina Mae, please. He needs you to help. Could you go outside, shut off his car and the lights, close the door?"

The woman skittered off, and Jess sank to the floor next to him holding back tears. Upset about what he'd been going through the last couple of years, she prayed to God he wouldn't say anything. By the time the first responders arrived, she had her story ready to explain the delay in calling and the alcohol on his breath. And Ina Mae had returned to sit in the kitchen chair, shotgun on the floor beside her.

Ina Mae would keep her word, of that Jess had no doubt.

Mac Richards arrived, followed by two more deputies and the ambulance. She threw herself into his arms, hating that she had to deceive this man who had been so good to her since her return from Los Angeles.

"I didn't know what to do, Mac. I guess I just panicked. I couldn't believe I'd been so stupid and shot him. I think I wandered around in a fog trying to make up a story to explain me being so dumb. He was out for a while, then he came to. I gave him a drink. He was hurting, kept begging me not to call, said he'd think of something so I wouldn't get blamed. He was afraid I'd get in trouble. But then he passed out again and so I was able to call. It's not too serious, is it? I don't think it is." She stopped babbling.

He seated her firmly on the couch and turned to Ina Mae. "What can you tell me?"

"Deputy Starr was doing some practice shooting earlier. I heard them shots." With a glance at Jess, she added, "I heard one shot after Jess arrived, and that was a while ago. I can't be sure how long, didn't look at the clock. Came running to see what had happened, been sitting right here in this chair ever since." She clenched her lips together and glared at the sheriff.

He turned back to Jess. "Settle down, now. You two weren't fighting or anything, were you?"

"No. No. He'd been upset because, well, you know, his wife died two years ago yesterday, and I spent the night here keeping him calmed down. Then we were going to go dancing tonight, so I came back over from work. That's when it happened, but we weren't fighting, I swear we weren't."

Ina Mae backed her up. "Didn't hear no fighting." Her gaze caught Jessie's, then slid away.

As for Mr. Jenson, wandering around outside talking to himself, bare legs white in the moonlight, no one ever paid him much mind, since he was half crazy anyway. Jess dismissed him as a problem and tried to relax.

The EMTs carried Dal out on a stretcher, him objecting that he didn't need to go to the hospital, it was just a flesh wound, all the way out to the ambulance.

Oh, Dal, please, please keep your mouth shut. "Can't I go with him?" she yelled and jumped to her feet.

"Sit down," Mac ordered. "We ain't through here yet. You know that."

Numb with dread, she nodded and sat at the table near Ina Mae. With their crime scene investigator on his way to the hospital, Mac would test her hands for GSR, just to go by the book. With fists clenched, she retold the story much as she had told it the first time, submitted to the test, and blew into his damned contraption to prove she hadn't been drinking. What a mess, but this was much better than Dal going through it. Even if he didn't lose his job, he'd be suspended if the truth came out, and he didn't need that. Not after all that had happened in Dallas. Because he was Dal, and she had admitted to shooting him, no one would bother to check his liquor intake or his hands. Even if they did, her story would explain everything. And he had been target shooting earlier.

By the time they finished with her, she was more than ready to go home. Too late to get in to see about Dal at the hospital, but first thing in the morning she'd be there. The wound wasn't serious, and they'd probably release him if someone was there to take him home. That would be her. She wasn't about to give him the chance to blurt out the truth to one of his cronies in the department. If Burt Sample or Les Howard showed up, the only two in the department who had befriended him, he might tell them in confidence.

He occasionally had a beer with them after shift. The two deputies were as different as night and day. Dal didn't take up with people easily, kept to himself a lot, but Burt was young and green, and Dal had taken him to raise. Les, on the other hand, was forty-six, and had come to the sheriff's department after twenty-five years in the Army. He had three adult children and a pretty little wife named Belinda who put up with his crazy hours by doing volunteer work. Jess never quite figured out why Les took up with Dal, or the other way around, for that matter.

At the cabin, she peeled out of the jeans and tee shirt splotched with Dal's blood while she crossed the living room. The landline rang and she glanced at the Caller ID. Parker. Uh oh. Word of the shooting had raced through the grapevine. She picked it up.

He began with no preamble. "So you shot our favorite deputy? How in the hell did you manage that?"

"It was an accident."

"Didn't figure you'd turned into Belle Starr. Not fighting, you two?"

"No, Parker. Not fighting. A stupid accident, that's all. He's okay. Isn't going to press charges or sue me. Nothing like that."

"You know I don't believe you, don't you?"

She paused, stared across the room. "I know. Leave it be, Parker. Please."

He was the one who paused then, cleared his throat. "Be careful, Jessie. Just be real careful. That deputy is a bubble off center."

Her heart leaped in her chest and she swallowed hard. "He's okay, just different. Besides, I'm always careful."

"I don't think so. You know how I feel about you. He hurts you, he's in a world of hurt himself."

"I know. I'll be careful. Besides he won't hurt me."

He hung up without a goodbye.

She threw the bloody shirt in the trash, dropped the jeans in the sink and ran cold water over them. Tears spilled down her cheeks and, with no idea why she was crying, she moved to the bathroom, turned on the shower, and stepped in.

The phone started ringing while she stood under the hot water.

Dammit. Stumbling water-slick naked to pick it up, getting a dial tone. The number, his cell. She fumbled around, replayed the message.

Dal's voice. "I'm not staying here. Come get me. I'm breaking out."

Crap. Dressing while wet wasn't easy, but she stuffed herself into clean jeans and tee shirt, carried the sneakers while she ran to the Jeep. Leaped in and made the hospital in record time. Let out a breath when she saw him sitting outside the entrance on one of the benches supplied for smokers. Arm in a sling, wearing his bloody shirt, knees splayed, staring between them at the ground.

She hit the horn and when he didn't look up, left the Jeep idling and jumped out in her bare feet. Even though she said his name, he didn't look up till she touched his arm. Then he jumped.

"Dal, come on. You okay? I'm sorry, I didn't think they'd let you out till tomorrow."

He looked right through her seeing something or someone else entirely. Damn, he was taking this hard.

Dear God, what if he shot himself on purpose? No, not possible. He'd have done a better job of it had that been the case. That realization scared the hell out of her.

Last year she hadn't known him so well, so he got through this horrid anniversary of his wife's death alone. That in itself was sad. No one should have to do that. At that point, he'd already been through hell. Leann's death and reporters raking him over the coals. The shooting, doctors telling him he might never walk again. Six months proving them wrong. Then leaving Dallas to come here. What a nightmare.

She put her arm around him. "Come on, hon. Let's get you home."

"Huh? Yeah, sure. Home."

Back at the trailer he didn't move when she parked, just sat there like he was waiting for something else to happen. So she went around and wrestled him out of the seat, literally dragging him to his feet and walking him inside then across the living room into the bedroom that consisted mostly of a king-sized bed and a narrow space to get around it. Clearly, the doc had doped him up good.

Dal sat on the edge of the bed, conscious that he was home, not sure how he got there. He stared down at the floor. Jess knelt in front of him, and he reached out to touch her. Opened his mouth to speak, but no words came out

Back turned to him, she straddled his legs, one at a time, and pulled off his boots, tugged off his socks. She turned around and knelt between his legs to undo his belt and zipper. Like a helpless child, he allowed her to pull off his jeans, remove the sling, unbutton and ease the shirt off. In its pocket, a prescription for pain meds. She laid it on the nightstand. He wouldn't need those till tomorrow.

"Get up so I can turn the covers back."

Dal obeyed, then crawled in and moved over. With a feeling of panic, he clamped her wrist in one hand. "Don't go."

Her eyes, gleaming in a stream of light from the other room, stared down at him.

She straightened, pulled off her tee shirt, and slipped out of her jeans. Naked underneath. Beneath the covers, she snuggled close, slipped an arm around him. Breasts warm and soft. She smelled so good. Like something sweet he'd like to taste. His arm hurt, but to hell with that. Desperately, he searched for her mouth with his, found it, devoured her. Going deep, deeper still, making love to her as if he hadn't had a woman in months. Overriding the pain with pleasure. She responded in kind, one's need feeding the other's until they were both spent, exhausted, satisfied.

Holding on to her, he fell back and slept.

And dreamed. But it was good, soothing, peaceful in that dream, and when he awoke, she was still in his arms, sleeping. He slipped out of bed, the arm throbbing, his head pounding. How could he have been so damned stupid? And her doing what she did. He stood over her studying her face, sweet in repose.

Good God, now she'd have something more to hold over him. Something so big it could ruin his life. Even now, after she'd kept some of his darker secrets, he didn't fully trust her. A reporter, for God's sake. What a story this would make. Still, she'd have some tall explaining to do herself.

Aw, what the hell?

He managed to put on his jockey shorts, then padded barefoot to the kitchen and started the coffee, awkwardly handling the pot and the grounds. His arm was useless. His right arm, at that. He could go in for some rehab, get it loosened up a bit, or he could just do it himself. Shit, what a fuck-up this was. He opened the cabinet, reached for the Jack. Stopped.

Yeah, asshole, have another drink. See where that gets you. He slammed the cabinet door shut.

While he waited for the coffee to brew, she came silently into the kitchen. Not naked now, but dressed. Gave him a half-grin. "Like your outfit. How's the arm? Sorry I had to shoot you."

"It's okay. Hurts a bit. I didn't intend to get you involved this way. Didn't know anyone else to call. Thought you would just patch me up and let that be the end of it."

"You couldn't keep something like getting shot from Mac. How would you explain not being able to use your right arm?"

"I could have made up a story. All the same, I wish to hell you hadn't done what you did. What did Mac say? Are you gonna be in trouble?"

"Not unless you sue me." She grinned big then and rubbed a hand over his bare chest. "You won't do that, will you?"

"Of course not." He poured two cups of coffee, not at all what he had in mind with her touching him like that.

She moved away, put the cups on the small table. "Any more stale Honey Buns?"

"Nope, guess I need to shop."

"Want me to help you get dressed?"

"Why, can't resist me this way?" He struck a silly pose, then dropped into the chair. "I need this coffee more than I need clothes. I still can't believe you did what you did."

"A simple thank you, then let's forget it."

"Thank you. I mean it."

"I know you do. How's your head?"

"It's okay. I'm okay. Can we just forget the whole thing?"

"Diamonds. Let's talk about diamonds."

Good God. Now *what had he done or said?* Surely they weren't engaged and he'd missed it. Just because she'd done him a favor didn't mean he'd marry her. Frantic, he peered at her over the rim of his mug. "Diamonds?" The word came out like a croak.

"Oh, I forgot to tell you. I met an old retired sheriff at the reunion I covered and…." she proceeded to tell him the story from start to finish.

Relieved, he almost dropped the mug and spilled hot liquid over the back of his hand. "Damn." He sucked at his knuckles.

"You okay? Here." She reached for him, and he jerked away, poured more coffee out on the table.

"What in the world is wrong with you?"

While she mopped at the puddle with a wad of paper towels, he did his best to calm down. "Nothing, really. Just a bit nervous about that whole shooting thing."

"I thought we were going to forget that. I wonder if you and I could find those diamonds if we set our combined clever detecting minds to it."

"You serious?"

"Why not? It'll be fun."

Finally able to forget about engagement rings, he considered her idea for a while. "Mac put me on disability till this arm heals some, so I guess I can lend a hand. I'll be helping him investigate the murder, but not in the field."

"I almost forgot about that. Okay, tell me, where would you hide diamonds around here if you knew the law was coming to get you?"

"Heck if I know. If I help you with this diamond thing, maybe you'll stay out of my way and let me solve the murder."

"Wait a minute. That's no fair."

"What is? Fair or not, that's the deal. Where would I hide diamonds? Tell me where was I last?" He put his fingertips on both temples, closed his eyes.

"Stopping for gas at the old abandoned station on Twenty-Three. Well, it wasn't abandoned then, of course."

After a moment of silence. "I'm getting nothing."

She laughed. "Fool. You know, Parker suggested someone might already have found them and never said anything."

"Could be. Look for someone living above their means."

"Oh, yeah? Wouldn't they have to have some inkling where to go to turn them into cash without getting caught? Not very likely around here. I'm going to talk to the people who live in that area, the ones who were there in the eighties. Maybe one of them will remember seeing something. I'll tell them it's for an article for the paper."

"Doubtful after thirty years. You want me to just sit here and try to commune? I need someone doing something violent. Shooting, fighting, killing, something like that."

"I don't think there was anything like that. How about the store owner who got robbed? Suppose he's still alive? Or would it be better if he was dead? Then you could talk to him."

51

"Not funny." But he laughed anyway.

She did too. "Let's drive over to Harrison and see. It's a pretty day."

"I'll call Mac. Even though I'm on the disabled list, he should know where I'm gonna be, in case he needs me for something."

After telling Mac he was okay three times, he told him where he and Jess were going and why. He hung up chuckling. "Mac says I'm taking my life in my hands, seeing as how I'm going with Two-Gun Gert."

"I'm never going to live this down. Think I'll get me a gun and start carrying it on my hip. Might as well."

"Jess, I'm so damned sorry."

She patted his arm. "Forget it. Let everyone have their fun. It's sure not hurting anyone. What else did Mac say?"

"Thinks we're on a wild goose chase, but to have fun anyway. Says it's a good idea for me to keep busy. You ready?"

"Think maybe you ought to put on some pants before we leave?"

"Oh, yeah. Wanna help?"

"Sure, why not?"

Sometime later, fully dressed this time, he made a bee line for the patrol unit still sitting slantwise. After she reminded him he'd been shot the day before, he gave in and let her drive the Jeep. She rolled down the rag top. The trip into the next county proved uneventful, something unusual when they were together. Creamy dogwood petals fell like snow in the soft spring air. His mind settled. At rest, he relaxed in the passenger seat and listened to her chatter. Shooting himself had been a hell of a wake-up call, but it appeared to have brought him out of his yearly funk.

Leaning his head back, he watched the scenery, stared at the bluffs soaring above one side of the highway, beneath his door at the stream chuckling over rocks and gravel. He filled his lungs with country air, rubbed her leg with the flat of his hand, smiled when she glanced over at him looking pleased with herself.

"Glad we came?" she asked.

"Oh, yeah. It's a good day. Say, I've been meaning to ask you. Have you talked to your boss since the… uh, the shooting?"

"Sure. He called first thing, soon as he heard. Word got around town like a wildfire. He didn't believe me, but he won't say anything. He's that way. I trust him."

He nodded, not at all sure he trusted Parker, a newspaperman who would do anything to sell papers. "Don't let him hassle you too much about it. Damn, I hate that I got you involved."

"Aw, quit your bitchin'. I thought we already got that out of the way. I'll handle Parker and anyone else who gives me a hard time. I wear big girl drawers, you know. Now, let's drop it, okay?"

She drove directly to Harrison City Hall. They went in and identified themselves, then he asked for any records of past businesses available.

"Not on our computers," the elderly clerk said. "But we do have records. I can take you back to the file room and show you where to look. Can't spare anyone to do it for you."

Jess glanced at him and waggled her eyebrows. He laughed, knowing what she was remembering. The day she'd followed him into the bowels of the old county courthouse when they were working the lost skull case, and they ended up having a grand time together while shrouded in cobwebs, the light bulb swinging back and forth, their tangled shadows leaping over the walls.

"What was the name of the store?" The clerk had taken them into the underbelly of the building and left them there amid bank boxes, labels scrawled on them by black markers. Not much room to have a go at each other.

"Hamilton's, but I don't know when it closed. Not long after the robbery. Let's look in the H drawer." She pulled open a few drawers to get a handle on the filing system. "Alphabetically, not by year."

It didn't take long to find all the legal information available on Hamilton's Jewelry Store, including its locale, names of owners, and that the year of closing was 1981. Once they had a name, they returned to the city clerk.

"Could you tell us if Lawrence Hamilton is still alive?" Dal asked. She looked like an Alma or a Mabel. In his head, he settled on the former.

"I could check the tax rolls." Alma was at least seventy, her white hair thinning on top, and she remained standing there as if waiting for further instructions.

He smiled patiently. "Would you mind?"

She rose, shuffled to a bookcase holding large, black tomes.

"No computer?" Jess whispered.

"There's one over there by the phone." He gestured with a nod.

Alma returned in a few minutes. "Sorry it took so long. I've never learned how to look these things up on that dad-blamed computer. Now, if you'd have been a half hour earlier, Melody would have been here and she could have found it quicker than I did. However, they let me keep working here so I can do stuff she doesn't like to do. Girl has no patience at all, but I'll look for something till I find it if it takes me all day."

"Well, how did you do it then—finding this, I mean?" Dal asked, using his nice voice.

In reply to his grin, she smiled sweetly up at him. "Ah, well, you see, I didn't find him on the tax rolls for this year. Would you like me to look and see how far back I have to go before I find him? That would tell you when he passed."

Jess interrupted before he could speak. "Did you find any Hamiltons, perhaps relatives of his?"

"Oh, my. That could take some time. Not every Hamilton is related to him. Some arrived here much later. So many of 'em I've lost track, or I could help you more. Come to think of it, I do recall him dying the year we had that dreadful hail storm. Now, when was that?"

Dal drew in a long breath, reminded himself she was old and he ought to be patient. "Perhaps if we could look? Would that be okay?"

"Well, I'm not sure…."

He reached for his badge, pulled it out, flashed it and a grin he'd been told by Jess was a winner. Because of the damned dimples. Indians were supposed to be stoic, severe looking, she often added with a smirk.

Alma simpered. "Oh, well, then, I guess it would be okay. Come with me. Is she a detective, too?"

He glanced at Jess who nodded her head. Without correcting the woman as to his own status, he added to the lie. "Yes, ma'am, she's my partner."

Jess trailed along behind him, and Alma soon had them both seated at a small table with several large books stacked there.

"I could've found them all in my iPhone." She took his hand. "You feeling all right?"

He leaned his head against hers. "Yep, I'm good. That damned thing lists every Hamilton in the county. Can't tell for sure which ones are actual residents of Harrison. Besides, I like spending time with you in dark, quiet places."

There, he'd done it again. Before he could think of taking it back, she'd kissed his cheek, which led to mouth-to-mouth resuscitation and her magnetic world once again enticed him. He'd do anything she pleased. Damned scary, but oh so enjoyable.

Her fingers grappled with the zipper of his pants, slid it down, reached inside and gripped his erection while her tongue continued to explore his mouth. He groaned and gave in totally. Whatever it was that made her enjoy having sex in places where they could get caught, he'd never figured out. Her explanation had always been, 'what are they gonna do, put us in jail? Maybe we'll get the same cell.'

At this point, what the hell did he care? After some adjusting of her own clothing, she straddled him and came down hard, muffling his cry with her hungry lips.

From beyond the wall, someone laughed and conversation began. Coffee break was over, and Jess moved off his lap and back into the chair. For a few moments he took deep breaths, head spinning. Could be from the gunshot wound, but he doubted it.

"Good God, Jess." He took some deep breaths and zipped up.

Her only reply was a soft and very satisfied chuckle.

It took another two hours to make a list of Hamiltons residing in and around Harrison. Jess pulled out her iPhone and punched in the white pages for their phone numbers

"Jess, I'm starving," Dal said. "Couldn't we eat while you do that? Remember, I've been shot, I need to keep up my strength."

She dropped the phone in her purse. "Poor baby. I'll ask about a good place. Come on, my wounded hero."

She took his hand and he liked that, idiot that he was. Jess asked about eating and he spaced out, not bothering to listen to the directions. In truth, he was feeling a bit woozy and found it necessary to concentrate to keep from staggering. Jess thanked the clerk and she waved like they were leaving on a train or something.

He bumped up against Jess.

"You okay?"

"Fine, thank you." He put an arm around her waist to steady himself all the same.

By the time Jess found the restaurant, he was feeling better, but just in case, he wrapped an arm around her again. A fella couldn't be too careful. Besides she felt so damned good, her fine parts snugged up close like that. This woman was going to drive him around the bend if he wasn't careful. Maybe she already had.

He'd about become resigned to his idiocy. Hell, he was half drunk on those damned pills she'd picked up at the pharmacy before they left Cedarton. He'd swallowed three, a regular dosage for him.

While they waited for their meal to arrive, she read off the phone numbers of those on the list they'd made, and he jotted them down. Hoped he could read the scrawls later.

"We can call them from the office." She studied him closely. "You don't look so good, and besides it would take forever to knock on all the doors and talk to them. Once we find someone who is related, we can make contact face to face. If there's a son or daughter, or grandkids here, they'll surely know the story better than the papers told it."

"Considering how reporters are," he said.

"Don't start with that," she said, keeping her tone light.

"Sorry." He glanced at her to judge her mood.

She reached across the table and covered his hand with hers. "I'm the one who's sorry. You feeling any better?"

He fiddled with his silverware for a moment. "I'll be okay. Thanks."

The waitress arrived with two steaming plates piled high with fried chicken, mashed potatoes drowning in white gravy, not that brown stuff like was served at fast food joints, corn, and a basket of rolls.

Dal perked right up. "Looks like we came to the right place to eat. Smells good, looks better." He dug in and they ate in silence, her chuckling when he mopped his empty plate with half of the last roll.

"What? Don't you do that here in Arkansas? In Texas, we always mop our plate clean with our bread. Want me to teach you how?"

With a hearty laugh, she followed his example.

"Okay, smart-ass, so you already know how. And there you were pretending ignorance." Damn, he was high as a kite. What were in those pills, anyway?

She leaned back, regarding him so he felt her stare and glanced up.

"I've had fun today, Dal."

"Well, don't act so surprised. I can be nice when I put my mind to it." He covered her hand with his. "Sorry about the dance date. Maybe next time."

"Maybe. If you're done, I guess we'd better get back."

When she pulled the Jeep into the space near his trailer, she left the engine idling. He started to open the door, then looked over at her. "I'm feeling a little woozy. Don't suppose you'd consider spending the night, just in case I need you?"

"Don't push it, Dal."

He shrugged and climbed out. "It was worth a try." He was halfway to the trailer when the engine stopped running. He didn't look back, but when he finally poked the damned key where it belonged and tussled the door open, he stepped inside and held it for her.

3

CHAPTER

Sunday morning Jess awoke, butt snugged against Dal's belly, his legs wound around hers. Spending the whole night together could get to be an enjoyable habit. She lay still, listening to him breathe. After a few moments, his hand crept under her arm and cupped her breast. That felt pretty good, too, so she let him leave it there, as if she might still be asleep.

He blew in her ear. She wiggled her bottom against him.

"You can do that again. Trying to stir something up?"

"Sort of feels like I did."

And indeed, she had. Half an hour or so later they climbed out of bed, took a shower together, and dressed.

"Time to get busy." He was on his third cup of coffee, but moving carefully. "I've had enough downtime."

"Sore?" She sipped at her mug.

"More than yesterday. Not too bad. I only took one of those pills."

"Well, then. Let's divide the names and start calling."

"It's Sunday. We're not going to find people at home till after dinner."

She looked at her phone to check the time. He didn't seem to need clocks. Eleven-thirty. "Okay, let's go to Grandma's and get breakfast. Time we get back, we can begin."

"Do you ever just sit still and enjoy the day? Look out there. Spring is springing. It smells like earth and green stuff and clean air."

"I thought it was women who were supposed to be romantic. So what are you thinking?" She tilted her head from the papers, enjoying a long look at his copper-toned regal looks, his shorn hair black as a raven's wing. She imagined it long and thick, blowing in the wind. Oh, God. War paint. Sleek naked bodies.

Chill, woman.

"I don't know. A picnic down on the creek bank. Sitting on a big rock eating sandwiches or something."

Shaking away the visions, she managed to reply without choking. "Have you looked in your refrigerator? You like mustard and butter sandwiches?"

"Well, what's in yours?"

"Uh, yogurt and... wait a minute, let me think."

"Sour milk is better than mustard and butter?"

She laughed. It was a plumb silly discussion, but her mind moved back where it belonged. "If we keep this up a bit longer, everyone will be home from church, and we can start making our calls."

"You know, we're both pathetic." He finished off his coffee.

She drank hers without replying, 'cause he was right. She just didn't know what to do about it. So they went to Grandma's on the square and ate breakfast.

All afternoon they called the Hamilton names from the list, finished off the pot of coffee, and chatted. Finally, around four o'clock, she found the grandson of the owner of the jewelry store in the 1980s, James Hamilton. When the robbery took place, his father, who had passed away, was working in the store with his father, owner Lawrence Hamilton, who was also gone.

She put him on speaker and gestured at Dal, who disconnected from his call and scooted over close to her.

"Dad did tell me about the robbery," James said. "It was the most exciting thing that ever happened in our family. He said that two men wearing Halloween masks, those scary monster kind, came in just at closing time. It was a Friday evening and they asked expressly for the Vandergriff diamonds. Grandpa thought it was odd because he had just received the delivery the day before. Over two dozen stones, several more than two carats, for a necklace he had designed for the couple's fiftieth anniversary. I reckon they were a bit ostentatious for around here. Anyway, Grandpa couldn't think who had told these guys about the necklace. Normally, he would never have had such large diamonds in the store."

"That was never in the newspaper," Jess said.

"I wouldn't know about that," James said. "Ole Doc Vandergriff was not one to keep his mouth closed, and he would surely have bragged about it to friends. Anyone buying diamonds that big was bound to be doing it so's they could brag about 'em. It's a cinch lots of folks knew about the surprise for Doc's wife."

"He still alive?"

"No. Neither is Mrs. Doc. Both gone on to their reward years ago."

Dal spoke up. "Did your Dad ever tell you any more, like which direction the men went, if they were on foot or if they had a car? Did either of them say anything that he could remember? Maybe about where they were going?"

So Dal had also wondered what happened to the crooks' car.

"You know they were caught, don't you?" James asked.

"Yes, but we're trying to figure out where they might have stashed these stones before they were arrested in Cedarton."

"I don't reckon I can help you there. At the time, Sheriff Ortho said he and his deputy scoured the countryside trying to find them stones. Dad never said anything... wait. He did remember that granddad ran outside to watch them drive away, and they almost ran over Annie Lincoln turning on River Road while she was crossing there."

Jess started to ask about the car, but Dal spoke first. "This Annie Lincoln, she still live there in Harrison?"

"Man, I don't know. Let me look in the phone book here." A pause and the sound of pages turning, then he came back on. "There's an A. Lincoln here." He gave them the number.

Jess thanked him and disconnected, stared at Dal a moment. "It's possible that whoever told these guys about the diamonds could still be alive. And what do you suppose happened to the car?"

"I don't know to both."

He punched numbers in his phone. Listened a while, then said, "Mrs. Lincoln?" He nodded at Jess, told the woman who he was and why he was calling. Put it on speaker and laid the phone down on the coffee table so they could both listen.

"Why, goodness gracious," she said. "That was so long ago, I'm not sure I even remember it. Why in the world you checking on this now? I thought them fellers got caught."

It turned out she had nothing further to add, but did remember they definitely turned left on River Road. Though she kept trying to remember what make and color the car was, the best she could do was that it might have been blue or gray or maybe green. One of them little scrunched up cars, nothing like the big Olds her husband drove.

Dal finally thanked her and hung up.

"Do you have a county map?" Jess picked up her empty mug and his. "Want more?"

"Sure. Map's in the car. I still get lost about half the time running around these back roads called one thing and signed another. Why?"

"'Cause, River Road in Harrison intersects with Dogtown Road the other side of Sugar Mountain. Pretty rough, mostly unpaved back roads. But after the robbery, they could've taken it all the way into Cedarton instead of following the main highway. They'd have come out in Cedarton near Herb Nolan's station. We could go drive it. There's time yet today. You feel up to it?"

"Why not? Better than sitting around here."

"Okay, then let's do it. Maybe we can get some idea of the places they might've hidden those stones. And what happened to the car."

"Fine with me, but I'll bet the lawmen back then thought of that. Probably drove it and searched the area on foot. Horseback, too. And that long ago. Brush will have grown up. Hell, by now trees could've grown right through a little ole bag of rocks. I don't think we stand a chance of finding those diamonds."

She handed him his mug, steaming with coffee. "A bag of rocks? Wait, we need to talk to that guy again. Find out if he knows what they put the diamonds in. A bag, a box, their pockets?"

Dal dialed James Hamilton back and asked him.

"Why, that's interesting you asked. Dad said they insisted his father put them in a black velveteen bag that was laying on a shelf behind the counter. I hadn't thought of that till just now you asked me. I'll be blamed."

Dal thanked him and hung up. Raised his eyebrows in her direction.

She shrugged. "I don't know, I just thought it might be important, that's all. A car is bigger than a bag of diamonds. What do you suppose happened to it?"

Dal shrugged, and she went on. "You know, Ortho told me he only had one fulltime deputy and they mainly searched around Old 41 School where they caught the guys. But it'd be fun. You're the one who wanted to get out and sniff the air and sit on a big rock. You feel like driving with that arm, or shall I?"

He made a fist, grimaced. "You drive, I'll look."

They went out the door carrying mugs of coffee and two bottles of water. "Get the map," she said, and climbed in the driver's side of the Jeep.

Jess was right about the route, so she went through Cedarton and headed up Sugar Mountain on Dogtown Road, driving at a leisurely pace.

"Good thing all the leaves aren't on yet. We can still see through the woods."

"Yeah, but see what? A handful of diamonds aren't going to jump up and holler at us."

Drinking the last of her coffee, she put the cup in the console. "A fancy black bag of stones. If there was a car, it would've probably been found and dragged away by now. But just maybe not. They would've been coming from the other way, so chances are the passenger would've been the one to decide where to stash their loot. That'd make it on my side going back this way. And they'd want a landmark of some kind that wouldn't be cut or tore down if they got caught and sent to prison."

Dal laughed. "Tell me, is this the way you write your stories? By guess and by golly? We don't have one single thing to go on. Might as well be driving blind."

"Well, this is just a fishing trip. After I get through interviewing some of the folks who live along this route, then we'll be able to pinpoint where to search. Soon as we get the paper out Monday night, then I'll be free Tuesday to come on out here and talk to some folks."

Dal pointed through the trees at an odd rust-parched ball that stuck up above the tree line. Several low-slung buildings crouched around it. "What is that? I've seen it before. Always wondered but never could remember to ask."

Jess stopped. "Oh, that's SEFOR."

"What the hell is a sefor?"

"It's Southwest Experimental Fast Oxide Reactor."

"Oh, sure. Feel dumb I didn't know that."

She laughed. "It's a breeder reactor to produce electricity."

"What's it doing off out here in the middle of nowhere? Breeder reactor? Does that mean it's radioactive? Looks sort of dead. Damn, you never know what you'll find in the woods nowadays."

"Maybe it's a little hot. It was shut down in the eighties."

"Couldn't find anyone who wanted its product? How come they didn't tear it down?"

"Well, a quick Infogram. The nuclear material was removed in 1972, but the site's plagued by residual radiation and chemicals. Some claim that junk is going into the water table. The feds want it decommissioned and decontaminated, but there's no funding available. Last I read, it would cost about sixteen million dollars to clean it up and return the area to its former condition. But that was a couple years ago. What with inflation, it's probably way more than that by now."

"Good God almighty. You mean if I go hiking and come upon this thing I could lose all my hair and my balls would shrivel up?"

"You can't come upon it. There's a high fence around it with warning signs to keep out."

"And there it sits, counting on all who approach to pay attention to a goofy sign. Hell, look at the warning on cigarettes. Doesn't keep some people from smoking. What makes anyone think a stupid sign will keep dumb asses out? This is a very bad idea, very bad indeed. Who owns it, the government?"

"Nope, CJC owns it. Cedarton Junior College. Where Dave and Kathy Spacey teach."

"Oh, sure, your friends who like to feed us on Sundays sometimes. The forensic twins? You know what, Jess? Drive on, just keep right on driving. I don't like even being this close to that place."

"Worried about your boys, I guess."

"Damn right I am." He clasped his hands in his lap. "What are you waiting for?"

She put the Jeep in gear and headed on down the road.

"Would you write down the names from mailboxes along the route so Tuesday I can begin interviews? There's a pad and pen in the outside pocket of my bag. I like to call them first and make an appointment. Some of these people are suspicious of anyone who just shows up at their door."

"Some of the boxes only have the number and some are blank, but I'll do my best."

"That'll be fine. I can double check on those Tuesday." Hopefully, in the process she would uncover stories that would fit well in her historical column so she could kill two birds with one stone, or 'multi-task' as everyone was fond of calling it now.

After a few miles of driving in silence, she asked, "What should we do if we spot a likely place to hide diamonds?"

"Do? You mean put up little flags or hang ribbons in trees?"

"Goofy. We need to have a plan so we don't just run around willy-nilly trying to find what we're looking for."

"Oh, sure. Mustn't run around willy-nilly." He settled for drawing a map, marking large black Xs at possible treasure sites, and singing 'Yo Ho Ho and a Bottle of Rum.' Easy to see he was humoring her and had no intention of tromping merrily through the woods in search of the long-ago stolen gems.

When they entered Harrison on River Road, the afternoon sun hung low, spilling a golden glow over the peaks and valleys and glittering on ribbons of creeks that cut the greening pastures. Not only had they not found the diamonds, they hadn't spotted an abandoned car either. Disappointment tainted her hopes.

"I don't know about you, but I could eat," he said.

She drummed her fingers on his tee-shirted flat belly. "Where do you put all this food?"

"Got me a storage pack. No kidding. I've been shot and I need some nutrients."

She pulled into a Sonic. "Will this do?"

"Perfect. They've got these huge hot dogs smothered in chili and cheese and onions. That's what I want. And some onion rings and a large Coke. You order French fries and share them with me."

"An honest to God gourmet." Laughing, she pushed the red button and placed his order, adding a strawberry milkshake and a large order of French fries.

"That's all you're going to eat?" He lifted his butt and took out his wallet, removing a twenty. "Here, it's on me."

She fanned herself with one hand. "I may faint. You're finally taking me out to supper. I've waited a long time for this. Should've ordered me one of those hot dogs."

"Well, you paid for breakfast. That's equality of a sort."

"Of a sort? You ate enough for three people."

"That reminds me. I was supposed to take you dancing Friday. Sorry."

"You've already apologized once, but you were high on pain killers and probably don't remember. Don't you think it was sort of overkill, to shoot yourself to get out of our dance date?" He glared at her, and she held up a palm. "Sorry, shouldn't have joked about it. It isn't at all funny."

His stony gaze told her to drop the subject.

A young man skated up to the car with their order, she handed him the twenty and told him to keep the change.

"Hey, you gave him a seven dollar tip."

She passed him the bag giving off the aroma of chili and onions and grinned. "Yeah, I did, didn't I? You get paid big bucks, you can afford it. Not that anyone could tell it by looking at how you live. Besides, I thought you'd want to splurge, finally taking me out to supper and all."

While she talked, he removed the large hot dog, unwrapped one end, and took a big bite. His mouth was full, so he couldn't reply to her teasing. But his deep green eyes flashed at her in mischief. She laughed and handed him a French fry. Sometimes it made her heart ache that she didn't dare let go and fall in love with this guy. It would be so damned easy.

Darkness lay along the edges of the woods when she dropped him off at his place. Out back, the creek sparkled in the last rays of daylight.

"You could come in." Outside the car door, he leaned down and gave her one of his smoldering looks.

"Better not. It could get to be habit forming."

"There are worse things."

If he touched her, especially if he kissed her, she wouldn't be able to resist the invitation.

Before he could do either, she said goodbye and drove off. Something about him built fires inside her, but something else warned her he could be as dangerous as those persistent flames. She could be burned badly. This business of communing with spirits, something she hadn't believed until she saw it happen when they were at a crime scene together at the Norville house, scared the bejezus out of her. It wasn't natural. And that mind reading was a definite turn-off.

At the cabin, she parked under the security light, hopped out, and went inside. It was too early to go to bed, so she plopped down on the couch and studied the names on the list Dal had made from mailboxes on the route they'd driven today. A couple of them were familiar, but that wasn't unusual, as those on this side of Sugar Mountain traded in Cedarton, and no doubt subscribed to *The Observer*. There wasn't a Crowe there, but plenty of boxes didn't have names, just numbers. So that didn't mean much. Someone along the road may have seen those guys scamper through the woods and hide those diamonds all those years ago. Or at least seen two men doing something unusual way back then. Perhaps one or two might even recall something specific. Some folks were just naturally nosy, and if anyone remembered anything, she was going to dig it out of them. But thirty-four years was a long time back.

Tuesdays and Wednesdays were her usual days to go out on interviews, or follow up stories, so she'd soon be doing just that. This time she would have a hidden agenda. By Thursday, everyone who took the paper or bought it off the stand would've read her story about the diamond heist. It might stir up more memories. Wouldn't it be something if she found those stones?

Dal watched her leave then poured himself a cup of coffee and stood at the back window staring out into the darkness. When he finished, he rinsed the mug, set it on the counter, left the trailer, climbed in the patrol unit, and headed for county jail. If anyone would remember the eighties, it would be retired deputy Samuel Watson, who worked the night shift at the jail at odd times when the younger guys wanted time off. Sunday night was one of those times. Old Sam hated being retired because he didn't have anything else in his life. No family, no farm or ranch to look after, no hobbies. Just the law, that was all. And no one liked to jaw more than Sam. Especially about past crimes.

Dal hadn't gotten well acquainted with the old man, only knew him in passing. It wasn't in his nature to seek out friends. Yet it was a good bet Sam would feel like talking to him about the long ago robbery. He parked, crawled out, and made his way a bit painfully to the side door. The damned bullet hole ached in unison with his bad leg, and the two together called for either a drink or a double dose of Tylenol. Since the painful bullet hole was the roundabout result of too much drinking, he settled for Tylenol which he carried in his pocket alongside the Tramadol. A duo for the bad times.

At the water fountain inside the long hall, he tossed three pills in his mouth and sucked in the icy liquid, raising to swallow. Boots echoing eerily on the tile floor, he approached the closed door of Sam's office and tapped, then stepped in. The old deputy sat behind a desk where three monitors showed sections of the jail proper. From there he could see the men in their cells, the intake room, and dispatch. Jessie's best friend Tink was on duty tonight. She was a cute little thing with lots of wild red hair and a sunshine disposition. Tiny as she was, he'd once seen her deck a perp who got rowdy when he was being signed in.

"Doing?" Sam was a man of few words.

"Off a couple a days." With a grunt, Dal lowered his large frame into the only spare chair.

"Heard."

"Got a question for you."

"Shoot." Sam leaned his shaggy head back to peer closely at Dal. "Hurts, huh?"

"Damn right. Not the first time I've been shot, but the first damn time I've shot myself."

Sam laughed heartily. "Crazy damn Indian."

"Never happened that way. Actually a jealous husband shot me, but it was an accident."

"Gotcha. I don't say much."

"Hell you say." Dal couldn't help grinning broadly. Damned if he wasn't starting to like the old codger, in spite of himself.

"What did you want to know?"

"Back in the eighties a couple of guys robbed a jewelry store over in Harrison. They were arrested here."

Before Dal finished Sam was nodding his head. "Wesley Miller and Mathon Wells, they was. Two fellers from down Hot Springs way. Always wondered how they knew that piddly jewelry store would have unset diamonds worth stealing."

"Were you a deputy then?"

"Naw, I was working for the Cedarton police force. They was only ten of us back then, but that was all we needed. Five on days, five on nights. All on call all the time. Off and on took turns on weekends. I come to the county sheriff's department in nineteen and eighty seven when they started hiring some full-time deputies."

It appeared Sam wasn't always a man of few words. Ask the right question and he got plumb wordy. "So you weren't involved in this case?"

"Naw. Boone County had jurisdiction, even when them ole boys were spotted here in Grace County. I kept up with what was going on."

"You think the file might still be around somewhere?"

"Well, you know. Not on computers."

Dal shook his head. Sighed. The basement of the old courthouse. Boxes stacked to the ceiling all the way around the dungeon-like room. One lone light bulb hanging over a small table. Cobwebs in the corners. Jessie coming in, eyes alight, wearing one of those filmy blouses. Hadn't known her for very long then. And he couldn't keep his hands off her for another minute. Her feeling the same. Damn, she could go wild ass crazy sometimes.

"Suppose I can find it. Eventually." Dal squirmed to get comfortable.

Sam chuckled, rheumy eyes alight. "You might invite that purty reporter to help you. She's bound to be interested in this case." He squinted toward Dal. "Ain't she?"

"Damn, Sam. Is there anything you don't know?"

"Nope."

"Where would you hide diamonds where you could find 'em, even after a few years in prison? They were bound to figure they'd get caught. My guess is they stashed them somewhere they'd be safe. Not down in a hole or under a rock or up in a tree. Those can all be moved or removed."

"By dern, if you haven't hit on something I don't know. What brought this back up?"

"I'm surprised you don't already know. That purty thing interviewed Mal Ortho at a big reunion last week. He told her about it. Got her all stirred up."

"Ole Malburn still alive? I'm damned."

"You don't read the obits, keep up with who's died?"

"One thing I won't do is read who has gone on. It depresses me."

Dal raised to his feet, worked the leg a few times, then remembered he wanted to ask if they'd searched for a car. Before he could ask, Sam lunged from his chair.

"What the hell?" His fist closed around his weapon. "Trouble at intake."

Unarmed, Dal only hesitated a moment before barreling through the door ahead of the old man. Down the hall, through another door in time to see a wall-eyed, bald haired, gigantic tattooed man standing over a deputy with a gun pointed at him. Dal launched himself and hit the guy midsection at the same time Tinker came over her desk. Together they held Baldy down, Dal astraddle of him. Tinker pinned both the guy's arms to the floor above his head.

"Where's the blasted gun?" Sam hollered.

"I'm sitting on it," Dal said, and eased lower along the kicking legs to retrieve the .45, locked and loaded.

"Good God, boy. He coulda shot your balls off."

Dal rolled over and lay on his back taking deep breaths. Damn. That hurt. And for the life of him, he couldn't get up. So he took deep breaths and sucked down the pain.

Sam and Tinker yanked Baldy to his feet, handcuffed him. The deputy who'd lost control of his charge stood by shaking his head.

"What the hell happened here?" Sam yelled into the young deputy's face.

He shrugged and spread his hands in a surprised gesture. "One minute I had him, the next he had my gun."

"Lucky he didn't kill you." Sam turned to look down at Dal on the floor, one arm across his forehead. "You okay, son? Need some help?"

Embarrassed and feeling like a turtle turned on its back, Dal cursed a while before allowing Sam and the deputy to pull him to his feet and seat him on the bench reserved for perps.

While cradling his aching right arm against his chest, he rubbed at the leg that felt like someone had laid a brand on it. Damn, what the hell was going on here? Be damned if he wanted to be helpless again, trapped in a wheelchair the remainder of his life. He wasn't supposed to do what he'd just done. One of the reasons he was no longer a narc on the streets of Dallas.

Sam laid a hand on his heaving back. "You gonna be okay, son?"

"Yeah, thanks Sam. Just give me a few minutes."

Tinker eased over next to him. "Hey, Deputy Dal, you saved the day a minute ago. Thanks. That old boy was gonna shoot that deputy, I could see it in his eyes. And I'd a been next. Too far from him to do anything, till you knocked him down."

He squinted up at her, smiled, and took another deep breath. "Just wait till I get up from here, I'll let you give me a great big hug."

Tinker laughed. "I can do that now." She leaned over and wrapped both arms around him. Said softly in his ear, "Is it true Jessie shot you? I can't believe it."

"Keep it a secret, but it was really a jealous husband."

"Shame on you, Deputy Dal. Lyin' like that. You can bet I'm gonna ask my fine friend what she was thinking, marring such gorgeous man flesh."

Despite the pain, Dal laughed. "You're a caution, young woman. A real caution."

By the time Dal arrived back at the trailer, the pain had settled itself firmly along his back and down his bad leg. He'd have to be more careful.

Inside he took a Tramadol, shed his clothes, stood under a hot shower for a while, them limped to the bed where he lay down and closed his eyes. The opiate took a while to work, but once it did, he was able to go to sleep.

Dallas. 2012. The stinking alley was dark and layered in filth. Alongside the buildings on either side, street people slept in boxes. Earlier, Dal had set up a meet to make a buy from Swinger, a dealer in heroin and meth, both deadly and addictive. He was getting closer to the distributor with each big buy and this one could open the door to the source of the massive shipments of heroin coming into Dallas.

If he had his way, he'd line up every drug dealer, distributor, and source and gun them down without hesitation. Pimps would come next, for most of them controlled their girls by getting them hooked.

Up ahead a black SUV eased in his direction, headlights off, tires crackling on the wet pavement. In his left hand he carried a silver briefcase filled with half a million bucks and a cleverly hidden GPS. His other hand was ready to use the gun tucked inside his jacket if this went south. The vehicle rolled to a stop. A pair of feet lowered to the ground from the passenger side. Each back door swung open to let out two more men. The inner lights were turned off, so all were mere shadows revealed by a dim glow leaking into both ends of the alley from the brightly lit streets. He stopped, spread his legs just a bit, and let them come to him, their shoes grating on the dirty wet pavement. When they got close enough he could make out their shapes, he set the briefcase filled with money on the ground, popped the lid open and took a step back.

"Stay where you are. One of you bring the package, the rest stay put."

From over his shoulder footsteps whispered on the alley's surface. He stiffened, kept his hand inside the jacket, fingers around the grip of the .45. Movement from above. A fire escape rattled.

"Lousy cop," someone shouted.

Made. Good God. His gut clenched, legs ready to propel him away. Before he could move, bullets crawled up his left thigh and zagged across his back, knocking him to his knees, where he got off a few rounds before he was hit from the front.

For a long few seconds, he remained conscious, feeling nothing. One of the men grabbed up the briefcase, another gave him a kick for good measure, a third bent over him. A cold hard something pressed against his temple. Lights strobing, guns firing, nearby backup closed in, and he let it all go. He was dead anyway, so why fight it?

He awoke in the hospital strapped into a rotating bed, where he was told he'd been there two weeks, and oh, by the way, you'll never walk again. Sorry, sir, or something like that, was all he heard in sympathy.

The left leg had been hit twice from the front, once from the back, shredding bone and muscle. But that wasn't the real problem. The shots that hit him from behind all but cut him in two. After four surgeries on his back and six months of intense rehab, he fooled them all by standing on his feet and taking a few stumbling steps. But he'd never work the dark streets again. The press turned him from a supplier of drugs for a wife who'd OD'd the year before into a hero, but by then he was fed up with the entire mess. The force gave him a medal before he climbed out of the wheelchair. It didn't help ease the pain or bitter disappointment.

Dal awoke Monday morning, his leg some better, so after dressing he drove to town for breakfast and coffee. One of these days, he would actually buy some groceries so he could eat at home, but for now he had better things to do. Shopping and cooking weren't high on the list. Peace and quiet was, and that he had most of the time. And, oh yeah, a tumble once in a while with Jess, as long as that didn't get serious.

After he ate, he dropped by the paper to say hi to everyone, most especially Jess. Wendy was a cute plump blonde who liked to gossip. Parker he'd learned to tolerate despite his love of sarcastic prodding of the law, the fire department, all the churches, and anyone else he could think of. Anything he could do to start controversy, he'd do. Nothing or no one was sacred. Jess loved him like a brother. At least that's what she said. Sometimes he wasn't so sure, but he'd learned to tolerate the droll man. She loved Sheriff Mac, too, said he was like her grandfather who had passed while she was in California. Dal felt the same about Mac, who had rescued him from the despair of having nothing to live for.

Inside, he leaned down to peek through the service window and watch them all running around like ants on a bed of hot coals.

"Busy day?"

Jess glanced up from her desk. "Hey, hi Dal. How are you?" She always looked so pleased to see him. The way he treated her sometimes, he couldn't quite figure that out.

"Hi there, Miss Jessie. Looks like you have lots of news this week. Be working late?" Referring to her as *Miss Jessie* in public probably wouldn't keep folks from knowing their relationship, but he stuck to the habit just the same.

"Yeah, maybe midnight or so."

"Was wondering if you want company when you go on your diamond hunt tomorrow."

"No lost dogs to find? No more floaters?"

"Nope, not yet. But you never can tell. Sheriff Mac has me on disability, so I'm available."

"Well, if you have nothing better to do tomorrow, come by the house. We can fight over who drives and who pays for dinner."

He grinned. "Sounds good. So if no bodies turn up, I'm yours for the day. A badge sometimes opens doors that a press card won't."

"And vice versa," she said.

"Better go. See ya. Bye Miss Wendy." He escaped before Parker came out of his office to say something sarcastic.

4
CHAPTER

Jess stared at the door after Dal closed it. That was odd. Usually he'd just call or text if he wanted to meet up. She would do the same. But his dropping in on a Monday morning like that, plus that overly happy persona he used to cover his real feelings, now that was strange. Almost like there was something he wanted to say, but couldn't bring himself to say it.

Then things in the office got frantic, and she let her doubts slip away into the hustle of a wild Monday.

Discovery of the body and her diamond story with all her photos filled the front page. The rush to get the layout finished wound down around eleven and she dragged herself out to the Jeep.

When she got home, Dal's patrol unit was parked in front of the cabin. The security light cast a shadow across the porch so she didn't see him sitting in the swing.

"Ought to leave your porch light on." His deep voice startled her, ran a finger up her spine.

She sat down beside him, touched her foot on the floor to swing.

He remained quiet.

"What's up? Are you okay?" Something was definitely bothering him. Maybe he'd been ruminating over Leann's death. Who could blame him? She found his hand in the dark and covered it with hers. Waited for him to answer.

"I guess. Sorry if I bothered you, I just… I'll get on out of here so you can go to bed. I know you're tired. Wanted to see you, that's all."

"It's dark out here. If you really want to see me, come inside. I'll make us some hot chocolate or something. Have you eaten today?"

He chuckled. "Don't tell me you went shopping and could actually feed me for a change."

"I guess not. I wanted to make sure you're okay. You're acting weird."

"Aw, hell. I am weird, didn't you know that?"

"Dal." She touched his thigh and he jerked.

This big, tough, no-nonsense man only acted this way when he was ready to bolt, like he was running for cover. It had happened before when things between them grew too intense. Like the time he tangled himself in a barbed wire fence to escape her getting too close to him emotionally. She cupped his face with a palm. "Hey, what is it?"

"Better go." He rose with effort, limped across the porch, and took hold of the post for a minute before going down the three steps.

Damn stubborn man. She watched him make his way slowly to the car, climb in, and drive away. There was more going on with him than the gunshot wound in his arm.

Unable to fall asleep, she tossed around and worried about him and what was wrong. He'd be over in the morning, maybe she could find out more then. She fell asleep to the serenade of night creatures.

Tinker called early, waking her. She almost didn't answer the phone, then thought about how Dal had acted the night before and fumbled around till she found it and muttered a hello.

"Sorry, girlfriend. Hate to wake you up. Have you seen Deputy Dal?"

"For a little bit, why? Is something wrong?"

"Whoa, you sound sort of scared. I was just going to tell you about something that happened Sunday night that had me kind of worried."

"With Dal?"

"Yeah. We had an incident while he was here. A guy got hold of a deputy's gun."

By the time Tinker finished telling the story, Jess had crawled out of bed to perch on the edge of the mattress. "And Dal was hurt?"

"I don't see how, but he acted like he was. I thought at first it was just a reaction to having a locked and loaded semi-auto stuck in his nether parts, combined with being shot by you know who, which, by the way, I want a complete re-enactment of, but Sam thought he was hurt. I just wondered if he'd said anything."

"No, but that explains the way he's been acting. Thanks, Tinker. He's such a big strong hunk we think nothing can faze him, but he's been through a hell of a lot, both emotionally and physically, and he sure doesn't want to talk about it. I'll see if I can find out what's going on without him erupting like a volcano."

Tinker was quiet for a minute, "You in love with the guy, Jess?"

It was her turn to be quiet. The question made her feel like she'd been slugged in the gut and the wind knocked out of her. "Of course not," she managed. "No. We're friends, that's all." But was it? Crap if she knew.

"Uh-huh. Friends with sleepover privileges. Okay, whatever you say. Movie night is tomorrow. Gonna make it?"

"Sure. Whose turn is it to pick?"

"Yours."

"Something with that sexy Channing Tatum in it."

"Funny, I thought it was Tatum Channing. Though it doesn't matter, he's still hot. Maybe a Greek gods flick, huh? Well, Tatum it is then."

"Okay, I'll bring popcorn and ice cream."

"Yum."

The next morning, wide awake, Jess made coffee and dressed for a day of traipsing around the countryside interviewing possible witnesses to the diamond heist. When ten o'clock rolled around and Dal hadn't shown, she texted him. No reply, so she called his cell and his landline. Still no reply.

Ordinarily, she'd think he'd simply changed his mind and neglected to let her know, but the way he'd acted the night before, maybe she'd just drive by his place before leaving.

He wasn't home. Ina Mae said she hadn't seen him at all that day.

"Did he come home late last night?"

"Uh, nope, come to think of it, I don't believe he come home at all. Didn't worry though, just thought he was at your place. Course once I'm asleep I'm hard to wake up, so he could've. But if he shows up I'll tell him you're looking for him."

She thanked the woman and left.

One more try, then she'd be on her way. She called Mac and was very careful what she said. Her snooping could get Dal in trouble with his boss if he'd gone out to work on the murder. And that's probably where he was.

"Hey, Mac, have you seen Dal this morning?"

"Nope. As you may remember, he's on disability. Some crazy woman up and shot him you know, so I probably won't. Anything wrong?"

"No, just curious. And thanks for that reminder. Good way to begin my day. I'd better go, got some running to do. Bye." She hung up before he could get too nosy.

The whole thing was odd, but she wasn't Dal's keeper and he didn't have to go with her. So she headed out with her list. The plan—get close to a residence, call on her cell, and ask if she could drop by and talk to them. Then do so before they could get to thinking about it and change their minds. Some people liked to have their name and stories in the paper, others didn't.

The first person she contacted wanted to know if it was about the body, said a deputy had already talked to them about that. So she opened each approach with questioning that had nothing to do with the body. Mac would pitch a fit if she interviewed people about a case under investigation.

On the third visit, she hit pay dirt. A couple in their seventies name of August and Allie Sims told her they had lived in the same house since they married in the late fifties. The reason they recalled the day of the robbery, it was their twenty-fifth anniversary, and they had a barbecue in the yard with several neighbors over that evening.

"It was when we were cleaning up," Allie said. "This car we didn't recognize goes barreling past the house and out of sight around yonder curve, just where the fence for SEFOR corners. We remarked on it, but folks, especially those from out of town, usually drive too fast on these back roads, so we didn't think any more about it."

August chimed in. "Until right at dark. I carried some stuff out to the burn barrel and saw a light moving off in the woods. Yonder." He stepped to the window and pointed in the same direction as the car had been going. "Come to think of it, not far from where them deputies found that body the other day. Someone wandering around in the woods on private property gets my dander up, so I kept watching. But after a while, the light disappears and nothing else happens. I finally come in the house." He turned to his wife. "'Member, I told you about it and you said probably some kids looking for a place to make out?"

"So you remember anything about the car. Color, make, tag number?"

"We both talked about it being blue, and it was one of those little cars. What they called a compact back in those days, but we didn't know what kind and sure couldn't see the tag number."

"Did anyone live on that property at the time?"

Allie nodded in agreement while August did most of the talking. "Aw, no. Been vacant for years. Pretty sure some feller from out of state owns it. Butts right up to SEFOR land, so no one in his right mind would build there. I hear that plant is polluting the water table with whatever filth it is leaks out of a place like that. Wish they'd just tear it down and clean up the site like they said they would a few years back."

Chewing on her pen, Jess nodded in silence. A follow-up on SEFOR would make a good front page story next week, especially if there were no further leads on the body. Time attention was called to the fiasco again. The plant had closed permanently in 1986, so it would still have been open on a part-time basis when the robbery occurred.

"Thank you so much for sharing your story with me. Would you mind, Mr. Sims, showing me about where you saw that light?"

He went out in the front yard with her and pointed just beyond the corner fence line of the SEFOR breeder plant. If Dal came with her, he'd be real upset about having to search so close to the plant that folks said still bled radioactivity into the ground. He might not even do it.

"One more question," she said when Sims insisted on walking her to the Jeep. "Did you tell Sheriff Ortho about this? When he or his deputy came to talk to you?"

"Never. No one come to ask us about anything back then. You're the first to do so."

Good thing Dal wasn't with her. That would make him spitting mad. The thought prompted her to call him again before contacting the next family on her list. Still no answer. She left a message for him to call, but that was all she could do. He must have turned his cell off. He was a private person, but this was beginning to worry her. If he didn't show up soon, she'd get in that trailer and find out why, though it probably wasn't a good idea. Once before she'd broken in and he was peeved at her for so long she thought they'd never make up.

The memory brought a frown. That was when she found out about his past by snooping in a bunch of clippings he had from Dallas. And that was when he caught her. For a while, she'd thought he would arrest her and take her to jail. But he didn't. Just stayed mad at her for a few days. Finally learned to trust her when she didn't tell anyone what she'd found out about him.

Back to business. She located one other person who remembered seeing the car speeding along River Road the day of the robbery. Fred Simmons, an elderly man, said he saw a blue Ford Falcon and reported it to Sheriff Ortho at the time. The rest of the day yielded nothing about the heist, but she did collect a couple of good family stories for her shadows of the past column so the day was fruitful. A dozen or so people weren't home, so she made a note to try again. No mailbox had the name Crowe on it. Still, quite a few boxes only had addresses with no name, and Mac had thought he recalled the name.

By the time she covered the route all the way to Harrison, the sun was setting, so she took the highway back to Cedarton and on to her cabin. She had no intention of taking this to Mac, not until she had a chance to search the woods where Sims had seen the lights. First she had to find out who owned the property, then get permission to poke around. Parker would be unhappy if she got in trouble for trespassing. Folks around here were a might touchy about their privacy being invaded, even if it was just someone walking around on land they didn't even live on.

She'd go to the court house and find out who owned that parcel of land. Without a legal description that would take a while, but Wanda in the tax collector's office would be more apt to help her than anyone. There couldn't be that much land along that road with the taxes being paid by out-of-town owners.

In Cedarton, she picked up a sandwich and some potato salad from Harp's, then drove on home in the dark. Again, she'd not turned on her porch light, so had to approach with only the glow from the security light, which did not reach under the sloping porch roof.

Hands full, she set down the sack to open the door. Shoving it open with her foot, she retrieved the food and someone hit her hard from behind, pushed her roughly to the floor inside the living room. She landed with a thunk on her elbows and knees.

"Leave it be if you know what's good for you." A gruff voice sprayed the scent of chocolate into her face.

By the time she regained her footing and whirled to face her attacker, he was gone, feet scuffing up dry leaves across the yard and into the trees along the southern boundary of her property. Just a dark, fleeing shadow. Probably parked on the old logging road down there.

In Los Angeles, she had more than once been confronted by someone angry at her about something she'd investigated or written. But here? The worst was back when Caveman Jake sent her notes when she and Dal were working on the stolen skull case last fall. And she'd lived through that experience.

What could this be about? She hadn't worked on anything recently that should bring about such a reaction. Things had been relatively quiet all winter. She'd even had to dig deep for front page stories to keep readers interested in the paper. Except for the diamond story.

Could it be that?

She gathered up the contents of her sandwich scattered across the floor and tossed them out for the night critters. The container of potato salad had held up, though, so she poured herself some iced tea and fingered a spoon out of the drawer, then sat down on the couch to eat and drink. Headlights swept across the front of the room.

Now what?

She went to stand in the door, turned on the porch light, and waited for the visitor to approach. The glowing globe on its high pole reflected off a bar of lights across the top of the vehicle, and she thought it was Dal. But Sheriff Mac strolled into view, crossed the yard, and removed his Stetson when he spotted her standing in the doorway.

"Well, good to see you. I was just going to call you. Come on in."

"What about? Dal?"

"Dal? No, not about Dal. Why do you say that?" Too bad she couldn't see if his expression was concerned.

"'Cause no one can find him. He seems to have disappeared. Did he say anything at all to you about going somewhere? I know he's off duty a few more days till that arm heals up, but it ain't like him to just evaporate like fog in the sunlight. Figgered I'd find him here."

"I haven't seen him, Mac. I was going to call you 'cause someone was waiting for me when I got home. They knocked me down right here in my own house and told me to leave it be if I know what's good for me."

"Aw, girl. Are you hurt?" He propelled her into the lighted room and looked her over.

"I'm fine. Landed on my knees and hands. Ruined my sandwich, so I'm not real pleased."

"Leave what be? Have any idea who it was?"

"He didn't say what. And I never got a look at him, didn't recognize his voice. It was a man, though. A bit taller than me."

"Good Lord, girl. What are you sticking your nose into now?"

"Oh, sure. Blame me. Nothing. I…." She stopped and stared at him. "Nothing other than the diamond story."

"Aw, shit. Why would anyone care about that? It's old and done with. No one's gonna find them diamonds, and even if they did, what would they do with them?"

"You're probably right. I wrote the first story, but it won't come out till tomorrow. So who could even know about it yet?"

"Those you're talking to about it have known since the weekend when you began questioning everyone, and all the folks they told about it. That's what I'd suspect. Does Dal know you're looking into it?"

"Sure. He was supposed to go with me today to do some interviews, but he didn't show up. He was here last night, acting kinda funny. Weird, he admitted, but laughed it off and said he was always weird anyway. Then he left. I thought he acted sort of sad, but I put it down to his thinking about his wife's death. You don't think he'd—"

"Naw, gal. Did you go by his place?"

She nodded. "No sign of him, but I didn't go in and look around."

"Maybe it's time someone did. I'll just go on over, see if I can get in. Miss Ina would probably let me check it out."

Exhaustion dragged at Jessie, her eyes hung at half mast, yet she had to ask if she could go with him.

"If you need to. I'd be sure to call you first thing, though."

"I know, but I'd like to go." She already had her bag gathered up. This time she turned on the porch light before they headed out.

At the park, Mac got a key from Ina Mae, then pulled up near the trailer, cut the ignition and asked her to remain in the car. "He's probably not here, unless someone stole his car, but someone could be in there."

"No way. I didn't come along so I could wait out here like a good little girl."

He frowned but said nothing more.

She slid out of the car to a chorus of frog songs along the creek bank and chirpers in the woods. The air was sweet and cool. A sickle moon hung low in the west before slowly abandoning the velvety night sky to star shine.

Mac crept up the steps to the stoop, gun drawn. Her breath caught. He suspected something had happened to Dal, that maybe he lay inside dead or hurt real bad, or else he wouldn't be creeping up armed like that. Heart pounding, she mimicked his approach, and he held out an arm to keep her behind him. There were no lights on inside.

Gun in one hand, he stood to the side of the door and worked the knob. Locked. He stuck the key in the lock and swung the door open slow and quiet. Before he stepped into the darkness, he felt around on the inside wall and flipped a switch. Light flooded both the empty living area and the tiny kitchen.

He moved inside, gun pointed ahead of him. She trailed along. Bathroom too tiny to hide anything, shower curtain half open. Bedroom had sliding closet doors at the foot of the king-sized bed. Mac checked under the bed, then slid open the nearby door to reveal a few shirts, pants, and a spare uniform. On the upper shelf, the box of private things she'd snooped through once a while back and a Stetson hat box.

"Ain't nobody here, nothing looks upset. He's just gone off somewhere to be by hisself, I reckon. He'll show up soon. He's scheduled to go back on light duty Monday."

Jessie laughed nervously. "Most duty around here is light. What does that mean?"

Mac chuckled. "No chasing bad guys, or fist fights, or running over roofs, or sneaking around in the woods looking for lost stuff."

She sank down on the foot of the bed. "You know, Mac. Since the place was locked, we can presume he left of his own volition, but that doesn't make me feel any better."

"Nope, me neither. Let's stop and inquire of Miss Ina. If she don't know anything, then I'm gonna go back to the office and put out an APB on his vehicle and him. He may get mad at me, but dammit, he's got the responsibility of letting someone know when he takes off. We're his friends, not just his co-workers. Damn fool kid."

If it weren't for Mac's usual disregard for what he called 'dang fool doodads,' she'd suggest he track Dal's GPS. Best to not bring it up. Let Mac run his own business. If it came down to it, she'd have Tinker do it.

Dal was hardly a kid, but he must be to Mac, who was easily twenty years older than his new deputy. Which meant Mac thought of her as a kid, too.

They went back to Mac's SUV. He stopped at Miss Ina's to find her on the porch in the glow from the outside light, arms crossed under her breasts, a frown creasing her forehead. He gave her the trailer key and asked about Dal. She hadn't seen him at all. Mac's expression revealed his concern, which added to Jessie's fear that something bad had happened to Dal. Her concern ratcheted up a few notches. Mac took her home where she tossed and turned all night.

The paper hit the newsstands the next morning with the diamond story on the front page along with the discovery of a dead body. The body remained unidentified, so Parker requested that anyone who might know something call *The Observer*. By Friday, after the papers had been delivered by mail to all subscribers, the phone rang every few minutes. Wendy, Parker, and Jess spent so much time speaking to people who thought they might know where the diamonds could be hidden or who the mysterious body might be that they didn't get much work done.

The missing diamonds cold case quickly became a hot topic, almost as important as who the dead body might be. Mac said they'd made no headway on identifying the man or his killer. And Dal was still among the missing. No one in the county could find his vehicle or him any-where. Mac, Jess, and Tinker were frantic, while most everyone else wrote his absence off to 'just the way that weird fella is.'

By that afternoon, Parker was fed up with answering the phone. "Let's see if we can get somebody to come in Monday and take care of these calls so we can get the paper ready to go."

"Who?" Jess asked.

He threw his arms up. "I don't care who. How much sense does it take to answer a phone and write down some information? Then we can sift through for anything that seems important." He beckoned her into his office.

"Where's Dallas Starr?"

She shrugged, studied her toes.

"Jessie, what the hell went on between you two? You shoot him then he turns up missing. Something's going on. Good God, you didn't kill the man, did you? Maybe bury him in the woods?"

"Of course not. I hope you're kidding. I swear the two aren't connected. I don't know where he is or why he didn't say anything to anyone." Her voice broke.

He put his arms around her. Held her in silence and she didn't push away. This good man loved her and she loved him. But it was different, so different from the way she felt about Dal.

"I'm sorry, Parker," she finally said and kissed him on the cheek.

"Yeah. Me, too, Jessie. Me, too." He let her go, turned, and picked up a stack of papers. "He'll turn up. You know how strange he is."

With a silent nod, she watched him for a while. But when he didn't look up, she went back to her desk.

Wendy had a friend who had been laid off her job, so she called her and had her come in to talk to Parker about answering the phones on Fridays and Mondays till things quieted down some. After a few minutes, he brought her out of the office, introduced her as Susan, and showed her to a desk piled high with stacks of newspapers, old black and white photos from the dark room days, and boxes of print and photographic paper. He cleared her a spot, stacking the stuff in a leaning pile against the wall, plugged in a phone, gave her a new yellow legal pad, and put her to work.

By five o'clock, she had filled several pages with notes and contact names and numbers. Jess and Parker divided them up, transferred the phones to the answering service, and took their work home with them.

After a quick supper and two phone calls, one to Dal's cell, the other to his landline, both with no results, Jess shed her clothes, put on a sleep shirt, and sat cross-legged on the bed to start contacting her share of the potential leads from Susan's notes.

One guy saw little gray men running through the woods, so maybe aliens had taken the diamonds to use for some secret project. Bet they'd returned the other night and buried the body of a man they'd kidnapped to probe. Another spotted a black Cadillac, long as a house, so he figured the Chicago mob was involved in both the diamond heist and the killing. She scratched them both off. Then a note caught her eye.

Someone who didn't leave their name suggested getting in touch with Alvin Marcy, who it was rumored had come across an abandoned car back in the woods near the sharp curve on Dogtown Road. It was a blue Falcon, they weren't sure of the year. This had been in 2007. Said he'd talked about it, but they didn't know if anything was ever done. That was twenty-seven years after the diamond heist. The car was all rusty and overgrown with ivy and weeds. For all they knew it was still down there, rust, weeds, and all.

Excited, she circled the neat notes Susan had made and went on reading but didn't come up with anything else that made sense in the thirty or so calls. On the chance that Marcy was home, she dialed the number and a woman answered. She told Jessie that Alvin was out at the moment but would be in by nine or so if she wanted to call back. Asked what it was about. Jessie preferred not to tell her, so she just said she'd call later and hung up.

At which time the phone rang. She grabbed it. "Dal?"

"Who is this?" a low voice said.

"Oh, sorry. Who are you calling?"

"You the woman who wrote that story in the paper? That Jessie West?"

Oh, great. She sighed. "Yes, that's me. You need to call *The Observer* Monday and speak to Susan."

"Why? She didn't write the blamed story. She ain't the one out running around getting folks all stirred up about a robbery that happened more'n thirty year ago. What's wrong with you, lady? You got a death wish or something?"

Her spine prickled, like a spider had climbed up it. "A death wish? Are you threatening me? Because if you are, your phone number will show up on my incoming calls. Idiot."

"Hell, no, I ain't threatening you. I just know for sure that if you keep poking your nose into this, something bad could happen to you. And I ain't calling from my phone. I ain't stupid, and I ain't no idiot, neither."

"Why don't you come in to the office and we can talk? I'd like to hear what you know about this. I could write a story about the person who helps us solve it. You might even get a reward."

"Hell, no. I myself ain't got no death wish." He hung up.

Her hand clenched the phone so tightly it took her a while to disconnect and put it down on the bed. Then she snatched it back up and looked at the incoming call numbers. It was a local area code but she didn't recognize the number. It wasn't Cedarton. The name was blocked but that wasn't unusual.

Immediately she dialed it back. No one answered. She didn't bother to leave a message on voice mail. The caller probably wasn't lying about calling from someone else's phone. Shivering, she went to each window and peered out into the night as if she might spot something threatening out there. Calm down, woman. This wasn't the first time someone had warned her about a story she had written. She went back to the couch.

Too bad Dal wasn't here to bounce this off of. Maybe it was time to try to find him through his GPS. She could imagine how angry he'd be if they ran him down that way. He did like his privacy.

To get him involved officially in her search, they really needed a murder directly connected to the stolen diamonds. Then he'd be here, and he could pick up some vibes. That was a pretty stupid, thought. Damn you, Dallas Starr, where the hell are you? Moreover, why don't you call?

That last phoned threat was enough to prod her to call Mac and tell him what was going on. She dialed his cell, and when he came on told him about the call and gave him the number.

"Two threats ought to be enough, young lady," he said. "Lock your doors and be careful. Want me to, I can send a deputy out."

"No need in that, Mac. You know how this goes. I get a lot of calls about the stories I write. If I panicked every time, I'd be a basket case. Just thought you might want to follow up on this one."

"Will do. And you take care, will you? I'll have a deputy drive by regular-like all night just in case." He paused a moment and she waited. "Don't suppose you've heard from Dal."

"Nope, and when I do he's going to get a good chewing out. If I did this, he'd rake me over the coals for sure."

"Well, he'll turn up. You take care now. Gotta go. Good night."

Noise in the background sounded like an uprising of some sort. He must be at the jail.

After she disconnected, to prove to herself she wasn't frightened, she took a cup of tea out on the deck to enjoy the night air already warm as a summer night. A fingernail moon perched on the peaks to the west, then retired for the night. From out of the woods came the mournful cry of a whippoorwill. As if in reply, from inside came the ringing of the phone.

Holy crap. Why didn't she just once remember to carry the thing around with her? Why did she think they invented cordless phones in the first place? By the time she got inside, her voicemail had taken the call. She gave it time to register, then dialed for a message.

"Hi, Jess. Thought I'd better let you know I'm okay. Sorry. Will call back later."

"Goddammit it, Dal," she screamed into the phone while the thing told her to hit seven to erase the call or nine to save it. She hit nine mostly because she might want to listen to his voice again so she could yell at him some more. Then she went to the phone's screen to check what number he'd called from.

A 417 area code. Not his cell or landline. What the hell was he doing in Missouri?

She threw the cordless onto the couch, then thought about it, picked it up and redialed the number he'd called from. A professional voice answered. "Mercy Hospital. How may I direct your call?"

What in the world was going on? The voice on the other end prompted, "May I help you? If this is an emergency, please dial 9-1-1."

"No, um, do you have a Dallas Starr there?"

"As a patient, ma'am?"

"Yes."

"One moment."

She waited the moment. Finally, "Are you a relative of Mr. Starr?"

Her heart went into her feet, she swore it did. "My God, what's happened to him?"

"I'll connect you with patient care. Just one moment."

Another moment that dragged on and on. God, what did they call a moment? Almost three minutes later, she timed it on her watch, another voice came on. "Ma'am, what is your name, please?"

To hell with this. "I'm Dallas Starr's sister, Jessie. Could you tell me if he's been admitted?"

"One moment."

Holy crap.

"Ma'am?"

"Yes, please. Is he okay?"

"I'll connect you to his room. Please hold."

After five rings, a woman answered.

Surprised, she stammered. "This is… I'm… could I speak to Dallas, please?" By this time, Jessie was biting her nails, a habit she'd broken several years earlier. Had he had an accident? What was he doing in a St. Louis hospital?

Hesitation.

More nail biting. Finally his voice. At least he was alive. "Who is this?" Not very happy, sort of weak sounding.

"Dal, this is Jess. Are you okay? What happened? Please say you're okay. Was there an accident?"

"How the hell did you find me? Stop asking questions so I can answer some of them. I'm fine. No accident. I came in for a checkup. Thought I'd be right back, but there's a small problem. Nothing serious."

She let out a long breath. "Oh, I could smack you. We've all been worried sick about you. Small problem?"

"Oh? Well, I'm sorry. How in hell did you find me?"

"I'm a reporter, that's what I do. You say you're sorry? Big fat deal. When are you coming home? I want to wring your neck. What's wrong?"

"Jess, the doctor just came in. I'll call you back soon as I know something." He hung up.

She stood there holding the phone, staring at it. The man was impossible. She'd known from their first meeting that he was a loner, a man happier sequestered away from everyone, a man who made few friends. A burned out cop often had problems and she understood that. But damn, going off without a word to anyone? How could he think that would be okay?

Just wait till he came back. He'd have another problem, and it might not be so small.

But for now, she had a problem too. She had to get onto that property where the Sims saw the flashlight moving around. But she'd better do it legally or Parker would have nine kinds of fits. So first thing Monday she'd be at the courthouse to see if Wanda could get the name of the owner. Sooner or later she would have to dig out the old records, and that meant a visit to the courthouse basement where the records not yet on computers were stored. But that would have to wait. Monday was too busy at the paper.

If only Dal were here to go down there with her. The place held a special memory for both of them. Did he even remember it? Him and her together, the urge to touch, to be one for the first time. Something they'd both fought for some time. Then locked together in the cobwebby dark confines of the storage rooms.

The pounding increased, tossing her into a wild whirling storm of fury. Of rage. Of uncontrollable dark cravings. And then he came with that same fury, filling her, clutching her, nose and mouth buried against her neck to muffle the deep-throated groan that tore from his throat. More pain than pleasure.

Her body's passion raced to catch up, sent her panting into exhaustion until all she could do was hang on. Shed tears of anguish, of pure joy, of terror. He lowered her to the desk, backed off and asked her if this was what she'd come for. In that voice that rubbed her raw. God, she'd been furious with him. Brushing her off like that when they'd… hell with him.

After they closed that case, he became so distant she could not touch him without him pulling away. Only recently had he begun to allow intimacy between them again. She never knew why he backed off, didn't suppose she ever would. Recently though, that same feeling of withdrawal was growing between them.

She didn't know when or why he would retreat again. That didn't keep her from caring what happened to him. And right now she was worried sick.

5
CHAPTER

Dal felt foolish sitting on the edge of the examining table, long bare legs dangling from under the too-short hospital gown. Doctor Swinton tapped on the door and entered, clipboard in one hand, the other outstretched to shake with him.

"Stay off that leg for a while. You've pulled some ligaments and that can be worse than a break, especially with that leg's history. Let's give it time to heal. Stop behaving like a twenty-year-old." He propped half his butt on the edge of the table, a serious expression on his face. "However, we may have another problem. The MRI shows some fragments from the old injury have moved around in your back. That's of some concern. Hell, man. On top of that you've got a bullet wound in your shoulder and you tackle some guy with a gun?" The doctor paged through the thick medical file. "I don't want to go digging around in your back. Could do more damage than good. You've done a tremendous job just getting back on your feet. But take it easy for a few weeks. Here's a prescription for the pain. It should subside, but I want to keep an eye on you. Make an appointment for next month, and we'll see where we go from there. And no more acrobatics. You ought to stay on disability at least till I see you again. That latest damage is a workplace injury, by the way, so let them know. Sign a release and I can supply your medical records."

To say he was terrified was putting it mildly, but Dal hated to admit that, even to himself. How the hell was he going to keep his job? How much would he have to tell Mac? And Jess? Damn, he'd promised to call her. Lord, the woman was under his skin good. Didn't help to steer clear of her. In fact, it wasn't possible. Now he was beholden to her.

He thanked the doctor and, crutches under his armpits, stumped his way out of the hospital and down the ramp to his patrol car, already hating the damned things. The day was cloudy, the wind moist. St. Louis smelled of car exhaust and bus fumes, the noise outrageous. Felt like he was back in Dallas, and he couldn't get out of there fast enough.

He maneuvered the wooden sticks awkwardly and fell backward onto the seat of the SUV. Hell of a thing, and just what he didn't need. But he was lucky. It could've meant another surgery, and that he had to avoid.

After filling the prescription at the pharmacy near the hospital, he headed for I-44. Damned if he'd spend another night here. All he wanted was his trailer, his own bed, and a good night's sleep in the peace and quiet of Cedarton. He popped a couple of the pain pills, dropped the bottle in the console, and as soon as traffic thinned on the Interstate, kicked the speed up to eighty-five. One of the perks of driving a deputy's unit. Wouldn't have to mess with being stopped by the highway patrol.

Four and a half hours later, he took the exit south that would lead him to Highway 23 and home. Soon the new highway from Tulsa to Branson would be finished. The bridges arched around Cedarton, as if leaving the place to its own devices. But there would be an exit on the outskirts of town, and from there came the expectancy of criminal activity, thus the hiring of someone to investigate those crimes. To solve them. That was him, and he needed this job. Liked it, too.

Alan Jackson sang, and Dal beat a rhythm on the steering wheel. In spite of the concern that outsiders would cause the crime rate to spike, the first killing he'd had to solve was committed by a local resident, Mary Smith. She had been found not guilty and was once again serving on the city council. The jury bought that the shooting of her raging husband was self-defense, and he had, too... after dealing with a couple of visits from the spirit of the dead man and hearing her amazing story.

Still, Mac was right to be worried about outside criminal activity. With easy access comes the criminal element, especially those too dumb to tie their own shoes. Men who want to make a quick score, then get on the highway and run. Hitting residences to steal whatever was small enough to carry off, jacking cars, robbing businesses, stuff like that. And inevitably, an innocent victim got hurt or killed.

Dal's ability to read crime scenes by communing with spirits, dead or alive, who were involved in violence made him extremely valuable to the small department. And he was a good detective, too. The lack of violent crime in the area made the job easy on his soul. He'd gazed at too many young people killed by drugs. The best part was Mac pretty much left him alone when he was working. With such a small pool of deputies, Dal often got called out on family squabbles, lost kids, and the occasional store robbery. Usually nothing too drastic. Mikey's twenty-four hour quick stop out on the highway northwest to Eureka Springs was a favorite target for snatch and grab.

Wildlife was another problem for the small town. This spring, a large herd of deer wandered into the park where mothers took their kids to play. Several deputies were called out to convince the animals to graze elsewhere. Deer are not always docile and fearful of humans, and they can't be herded like cattle or horses. A frightened doe charged Wayne, a slightly-built deputy. Flailing hooves knocked him to his knees, and he came away with a swollen jaw and black eye, lucky he hadn't been stomped.

All in all, working for the small county department offered plenty of variety. It was astonishing what some people would do. Stupid stuff that made him scratch his head and wonder what the hell they were thinking.

Some things were good for a laugh or two. Like the guy who climbed into a tree to cut the top off so it would fall on his neighbor's house after they had a set-to over their fence line. Only he got on the wrong side of the chainsaw and landed on the house along with the huge oak branch and the saw. The owner of the house lit into him, and they had a brawl on what was left of the roof. After both were treated at the clinic, they ended up in jail for thirty days, where they became bosom buddies.

Ruminating over such incidents and listening to country music kept Dal sane during the trip home. With great relief he parked, hopped, and swung his way into the trailer on the unfamiliar walking sticks, ignoring the newspapers on the stoop and his stuffed mailbox. All he wanted was a bed, and he fell face down there, not even bothering to take off his boots.

He knew nothing more until someone touched him, and he emerged from a dream of dark alleys and gunfire, rolling to his back and swinging both fists.

"Dal, it's me. I'm sorry I startled you."

Propped on one elbow he squinted through the gloom to see Jessie's lovely troubled face. Rubbing a hand across his own, he shook his head. "Time is it?"

"Ten o'clock."

"Day or night?"

"Morning. Ina Mae called me when you got home yesterday. I didn't want to bother you 'cause I figured you'd be tired and sleepy, so I waited till this morning."

"Okay, Jess. Enough. My head hurts."

"Not enough, my friend. I'm trying to be considerate, but after what you did, I'm having a lot of trouble with—"

"What the hell did I do? I've been asleep since I got home. Shit, Jess."

"Before that. Do you remember you promised to call me back? From the hospital?"

He'd forgotten all about that. But she never forgot anything. Ever. He massaged his temples and sat on the edge of the bed next to her. Not wanting their thighs to touch like they did, not wanting to inhale her scent, so fresh and bright, like a bouquet of sunflowers and daisies. And most especially not wanting her to touch him the way she was touching him. A hand on his arm, moving ever so slowly over his bicep. He shivered.

Damn, what was wrong with him?

"You disappeared into thin air, that's what you did. Leaving no clue as to where you were or what was wrong. My God, Dal. Everyone thought I shot you, then you're gone? Maybe I made good this time and buried you in the woods."

"Whoa, there, Jess. Don't be ridiculous."

"Ridiculous? What's ridiculous is that you shot yourself in the first place. Then you take off. Crap, what were you thinking?"

He cocked his head with that half grin of his. "I don't know, Jess. What were you thinking when you told everyone you shot me? It wasn't my idea, you know."

"Just a minute. You saying this is all my fault? Anyway, let's get back to the subject at hand. Were you in the hospital in St. Louis because I shot you? That doesn't even make sense."

"Oh, I don't know, Jess. Makes perfect sense to me."

"You're being an asshole, Dallas."

He laughed. She only called him Dallas when she didn't have a good comeback.

"Don't you dare laugh at me." Tears streaked down her cheeks. "How do you think I felt when I found out you were in the hospital?"

He wrapped an arm around her shoulder. "I apologize, Jess, but for what I'm not exactly sure."

She shook him loose. "And I have to run you down in some hospital three hundred miles away. When I do, you say, 'I'll call you back.' Then you don't. What was wrong? What are the crutches for? Did you break your leg? You don't have a cast. And you sure as heck never called me back. I'm beginning to think I ought to have shot you, for real."

Sorry he'd made her cry, he held up a hand. "Come on, Jess. Enough. I just don't understand why you're so upset, but let's drop it. And please don't cry. That's using unfair ammunition."

For that, she sent him a harsh glare and wiped her cheeks with the flat of her hands.

The reaction was so Jess, babbling when she was the least bit hacked off. But crying? Not her at all. Clearly she'd rather hit him over the head with something. He ought to grab her and kiss her so deeply she couldn't speak for ten minutes at least.

Instead, he groaned, planted his elbows on his knees, and leaned his head in both hands. Wrong thing to do. She touched him, cool palm on his forehead in a tender gesture that whammed deep into his gut.

"Damn you, Dallas." The soft tone told him she'd surrendered.

He gripped her upper arms pulled her down onto the bed and lay beside her, hugged her close so he could feel her breath against his neck. Fear of what almost happened to him sent adrenaline coursing through his veins.

"Dear God, Jess." Her sun-streaked hair tumbled over her face, and he fingered it away until her mouth was free. Placed his lips on hers, gently at first to enjoy their inviting softness, then more intense. He tasted her exquisite flavor, sweet and creamy.

She made a humming sound and gave back with an ardor that stirred him to the roots. The anger he sensed in her drained away, replaced by an eager acceptance that fed his desire for more than a kiss.

He tore at her jeans. She unbuckled his belt and unzipped his pants, getting farther than he, slipping both his jeans and jockey shorts down in one swift move.

His fingers fumbled at her zipper. "Get these off, Jess. Come on."

She went to work on her own jeans, slipped them off. He ripped away the dainty underwear, gripped her thighs, and kissed her belly. That earlier fear drove a passion he couldn't stop.

Nibbling upward, he teased one breast then the other with lips and tongue, fitted their bodies together, approached her mouth with his, and slipped inside her like their separate parts were at last where they belonged. Long and sweet turned to hard and fast, and he cried out, entered that special place with her, then slipped down into a fuzzy tranquility and relaxed, held her between his legs while she bucked and uttered those little sounds she made when coming.

Damned if he hadn't done it again. Half-awake, being touched by her, was all it took. They couldn't get near each other without having at it like rabbits. And him inside her mind 'cause he couldn't stop it in those moments. It doubled his enjoyment and he was addicted to being there, hearing her think how he made her feel. A tender pleasure only a woman could experience.

Dear God, but he felt loved more than he deserved. He petted her face and touched her lips with his fingertips. She opened her mouth and sucked at his thumb, pinched his nipple, licked along his jawbone sending shudders through him. She'd once told him that after-play was as much fun as foreplay. He hadn't believed her till he'd been with her and she started this strange, deeply satisfying ritual. Staying inside her, he relaxed and let her after-play all the hell she wanted to. It felt damned good. Drove away memories of the serious expression he'd seen on the doctor's face. Offered him the possibility of a life he'd not thought possible. Sure as hell couldn't accept.

She finished by branding him with one hell of a hickey where it'd be sure to show above his shirt collar before lying back, separating them but not moving too far away.

"I was so worried about you. We all were. Please don't do that again."

"It was something personal. No need in sharing."

"I know this is a difficult concept, but you have friends here. And friends care for each other. Not because we're being nosy, but because we love you. I love you and—"

"Whoa, there. That word gets tossed around too much. Everyone loves everything. Makes it not mean a hell of a lot."

"Dallas, I'm using it properly right now. You need to be more accepting. How do you feel about Tinker and Mac and your two deputy friends, Burt and Les? Me?"

He grinned at her. "Oh, you're okay, I guess."

"Seriously, Dal. We were all scared something had happened to you. Mac and I came out here to the trailer to make sure you weren't hurt or something."

"You did? Well, my car wasn't here. You had to know I'd gone off somewhere in it."

"Or someone had knocked you in the head and stole it. Maybe your gun, too."

Though the presumption was ridiculous, he hugged her close. "I'm sorry. I truly am. I just never thought anyone would care that I took off for a few days."

"Took off? You went in a hospital. In St. Louis. Don't you think we care that you were sick or hurt or whatever you were?"

"Look, I'll apologize to everyone. I have to take a few weeks off, doctor's orders. I hate like hell to do it, but it's important."

She leaned back, studied his face. "You don't look sick. Fabulous, is what you look. What's wrong?"

"Does it matter?"

"What were we just discussing?"

Shit, this wasn't something he wanted to get into. He figured he'd tell Mac what was up, and he'd be the one to explain it to the others. Didn't look like Jess was going to let him get away with that. Her mind was made up.

"Only you were discussing. I'm just listening." One last shot at distancing himself.

She shot him a dark look he knew better than to ignore.

"Okay, dammit. Short version. When I jumped that guy at the jail, I tore some ligaments in my leg."

"The bad one?"

"Yes. And some fragments from one of the bullets that hit bone when I was shot are still in me. One has worked its way close to my spine and it's trying to paralyze me." He was barely able to utter those last few words, said them against her skin that tasted and smelled so good.

"Oh, my God. I'm so sorry. Sweetheart." She kissed his cheek, then his mouth.

Recovering, he moved away. "It's not a big deal. Don't go all mushy on me. That's why I didn't want to bring it up. Doc thinks if I'm careful and stay off the leg, it'll heal. As for the fragments, I'm not to do anything strenuous for a few weeks, and he thinks scar tissue will continue to grow over it and stop the movement."

"He thinks? Doesn't know? Why doesn't he just take it out?"

"Well, that is an option if it continues to move. We'll see."

She bounced up to sit cross-legged next to him. "You'd better not be lying to me."

He shrugged for effect. "Would I do that?"

"You would." She took a deep breath, and when she continued, her voice was bright, lilting, like she got when she was doing her best to cheer up. "Then you'll need some help for a while. But nothing will keep you from giving me a hand figuring stuff out. I've learned a lot about the diamond heist while you were gone. So when you feel up to it, maybe we can get together and try to make some sense of what I've uncovered so far. It's a whole bunch more than Sheriff Ortho shared with me. He's old, though, so he may have forgotten a lot. We may need to go down in the storeroom below the old courthouse."

She stopped, stared at him till he met the gaze. Knew exactly what she was thinking. "Jess, no. We go down there, you know what will happen."

"Well, yeah. But maybe with you sort of incapacitated, I could be the aggressor this time." Reading her mind wasn't necessary. The look on her face was priceless. Anticipation, delight, an evil desire, all flashed in her cornflower blue eyes, turned up the corners of her mouth, added a flirtatious tilt to her head. "What am I thinking this minute? Hmmm?"

Her lovely eyes trapped him as surely as if they cast a spell on him.

He couldn't help but respond. "Well, it sure hasn't anything to do with this case. You're seeing yourself backing a helpless me into that dark, cobwebby corner, and… Whoa, Jess. Clean it up."

"I don't know how you do that." Evidently all was forgiven, 'cause she laughed and threw her arms around him. "I'm so happy you're home and going to be okay." She skittered off the bed. "Oh, I brought your mail and papers in. All on the kitchen table. And I made a pot of coffee. I'll bring you a cup before I leave. By the way, you didn't ask, but they still don't know much about the dead body. Maybe you can make some suggestions. But I'll be back tomorrow with everything I've found so far on the diamond heist. I really could use your help figuring out what's going on. Do you need anything before I go?"

Numbly he shook his head. There was not much he could do to escape the trap of those eyes, her fresh pretty face, the raw desire that captured him every time he came near her. He fought this attraction. Love like that was destructive, and he wanted no part in it.

After Jess arrived at the office later that day, prepared to finish up some work while it was quiet, she called Mac, told him that Dal had returned, and gave him the short rundown on what had happened. Anything else between the two of them, they could sort it out. All she knew or cared about was that he was back and, if not exactly okay, at least still alive, though not kicking. And they had made love. That she would keep to herself even from Tinker, who couldn't be trusted with a secret.

She ended the call, sat down at her computer and typed up a short summary of the things she had learned from the interviews regarding the diamond heist. Then she shuffled her notes and began an article for her historical column. She didn't see Dal again until later that evening when she drove by to make sure he didn't need anything. Getting around on crutches and being house bound would soon make him an unhappy camper.

"Jess, our dead guy hasn't shown up on NCIC, so if we could get a sketch artist to fill in some of the missing parts of his face, could you get Parker to run a photo of him in the paper next week? Maybe someone would recognize him."

"Sure. Get it to us before we go to press Monday night, and we can put it in somewhere. Parker would get a real kick out of the chance to put a dead guy's picture in the paper and get away with it."

"I'll call Mac and see what he can do. I think one of the artists out at the college does that kind of thing for the department."

"Yep, Sheila Bondardt, I think's her name."

"Yeah, that's it. Couldn't remember. Forget you know what goes on around there better than I do. And by the way, did you find out anything about a family named Crow? Something from the crime scene still keeps bugging me. They probably pay taxes, if nothing else."

"Funny you should ask. There was no mailbox with that name on it. But a lot of folks weren't home. I'm going to call Wanda at the court house to check and see if she could figure out who owns the property where Allie and August Sims saw those strange lights right after the robbery. So I guess we have two things to check out there."

"We?" Dal asked. "Are you butting into my crime scene investigation again?"

"Nope, not at all. I'm looking for diamonds." She shot him a smart-ass grin. "Your crime scene? You are not even officially working. Did you tell Mac your doctor put you on rest for a month?"

Dal glared at her. "Woman, mind your own business."

"Sorry, but some of my business is you, and there's no way around that. You know it as well as I do. You want that shrapnel paralyzing you? Putting you in a wheelchair… again?"

When she brought it up, the old fury emerged. "Keep that to yourself, if you don't mind." It wasn't a begging tone, either. His eyes turned hard as stones. She had learned a lot about his past while going through his trailer not long after he arrived in Cedarton. He'd never quite forgiven her, though he prompted the search when he began an investigation into her past.

"I'm sorry. Truly, I am. It's just that you won't take care of yourself."

Her throat burned, a sign she was about to tear up. Not good at all, especially around this man, who still thought all reporters were designing, manipulating liars.

"Well, that's on me, then, isn't it?"

"If no one gave a shit, it might be. But some of us do, so don't you go hurting yourself, or I'll hurt you worse."

"Okay. I get it. I'm sorry. I'll take better care of myself. I promise. Why don't you go see Wanda when you get a chance, and you can share with me what you get. How's that?" He grinned one of those dimpled smiles that bounced through her like a ping pong ball.

She kissed his chin, missing his mouth on purpose to keep from going all wonky inside. Best to stay angry at him a while longer. Make him pay for being such an ass. "Don't worry, I'll share everything, and I won't reveal anything you don't want known."

He shook his head. "I trust you with this. I can, can't I?"

"You know you can."

He ran a hand down over his face, peered at her. "I don't like the idea of sitting around in my trailer for a month doing nothing."

"Oh, don't worry, you'll have plenty to do. I'd love to solve this, and you can help. Hope you don't mind my company for a while. And I know Mac will keep you in the loop on the dead guy. Just so you don't expect me to cook for you."

It was a standing joke between them if they ever did break down and get together, they'd probably starve or live on frozen dinners and stale Honey Buns. So she laughed to show forgiveness and punched him playfully in the stomach, the only spot she dared punch. It would have to be enough that most of the time they worked together just fine, and made love once in a while, what he stubbornly called having sex or just fucking.

But to hell with that. She knew what it was and so did he.

First thing Monday morning, she went to check on the tax records. The new brick courthouse, built in the center of the square after the old post office there burned, was a square building with a U-shaped hallway that led to various county offices. She made her way down the right leg of the U to the tax collector's office.

Inside the wooden door, Wanda sat at her desk drinking a cup of coffee and chatting with a chubby, smiling man who was obviously smitten with the pixie-like Wanda. Jess caught her eye and the fellow moved off, leaving her after a whispered comment that caused her to giggle.

"Jessie, what can I do for you?" Wanda brought the coffee with her, brown eyes sparkling with enjoyment.

"Mmm, new guy?"

"He's one of our new assessors, Jim Laughton. Interesting, huh?"

Not Jessie's type, but she could see how Wanda would be attracted to him. He was an elf to her pixie. "Looks like. I have a problem we thought you could help with."

"We?"

"Dal is a bit incapacitated right now, so actually it's for the paper and for the law. We're trying to find out who owns a piece of property, but we don't have the legal description. It's someone who lives away, so we can't go to the door, so to speak."

The phone rang and Wanda held up a finger. "Coffee break, so I'll have to get that." She gestured toward the empty desks around her.

Jessie nodded and leaned on the counter till Wanda answered some questions on the phone, then returned to her.

"Well, let's look at the maps. If you can show me where it is we can get the legal description, then I can look it up for you. Freedom of Information Act makes it easy peasy." She opened the door leading behind the counter. "Come on back and grab a seat. Is it located around Cedarton?"

"Yes, on Dogtown Road near the old SEFOR plant."

Wanda pulled a map from a row of pockets holding paper rolls and brought it to the table where she'd seated Jessie. There she spread it out and remained standing while Jessie ran a finger along a dark line that represented Dogtown Road till she reached the property in question. "Right there."

Wanda jotted down the legal description, then went to her desk and pulled out a large black book from several on a wooden shelf at an angle from her desk.

"Looks like that twenty acres, which butts up against SEFOR on the west, is owned by John Reilly."

Jessie jotted down the man's name and address in Kansas City in her notebook. "Now one more question. Is there a family name of Crow in the Cedarton area? They'd pay county taxes probably, wouldn't be in the city limits."

"What's up?" Wanda asked, going through the pages of the book. She glanced up. "You know, I remember a Julie Crowe, went to school with Tink and me and some of the others still living here in town. She does live out there. I remember she got pregnant and quit school. Her son's name is, um…." She tapped her lips with the end of her pen. "Merle, that's it. And his name is Crowe as well. I think they live in a trailer on Mathon Wells's place." She pointed the pen at the property on the map, then checked. "Yep, that's it, and Mathon's widow Sara owns the place. It's cut in two by the road through there, and she and her son Lennie live on one side of the road, Julie and Merle on the other." She glanced up. "What's happening?"

"An ongoing case with the sheriff's department, so I can't say much, but thanks for the help. When the case is closed, I'll reveal all in the paper, but till then you'll have to be happy with what they let me write. Catch this week's edition."

Wanda wiggled her fingers at Jessie and went back to her desk, and probably to the curly-haired pudgy fellow with pointy ears, too. Jessie didn't stick around to see. Back at the office, she called Dal before getting to work. He answered after three rings.

"Hey, whatcha up to?" In the background, the sound of music playing.

"Well, I'm driving along Dogtown Road looking for Crows and listening to The Birds." He chuckled.

"Oh, very funny. Her name is Julie Crowe, with an 'e.' She has a son named Merle. And there isn't a baby-daddy in the picture." She gave him the address. "Across the road from the Wells's place. But she may be at work now. Oh, and something interesting, at least it pushed one of my buttons. Julie Crowe? She rents a trailer from… wait for it. Mathon Wells's widow Sara. I have to ask Tink about her. Turns out they went to school together. Must keep a low profile. Even Mac only vaguely recalled the Crowe name."

"That *is* interesting. Pushes some of my buttons too, if that's possible."

She chuckled. "That I can do."

"Keep it clean. Did you have any luck getting the name of the property owner?"

"Yep, got his name and address. John Reilly. Probably best if you guys contact him."

"What are you wanting to do on this Reilly property?"

"Thought I'd just walk around, see if I can find anything unusual, but I need permission from the owner. Parker would kill me if I got in trouble for trespassing. He's real sticky about that." She hesitated a moment. "Not sure, but I think the body was found on Reilly's land."

"Interesting. But despite Parker, you're not above doing a little trespassing, are you?"

She laughed. "You know me so well. But let's try it the legal way first."

"I can't believe you think you can find those diamonds by just walking around out there."

"Is it a coincidence that the body was found in the same vicinity?"

"Probably. Don't have enough facts yet. Neither the perp nor the victim thought of diamonds during their fight. If the two are connected, then they didn't know what they were looking for. Just that it's worth a lot of money. They'll know now, what with the article in the paper. But the location of the property or the killing may not have a thing in the world to do with the diamond heist. Thirty-four years was a long time ago, these guys seemed younger than that. Still it does seem to be a helluva coincidence." His voice faded during the last of the conversation, became spotty, then died before she could understand anything else he said.

She hung up. If he wanted to say more, he'd call her back when he got a signal again. What would happen if she just went out there to the Reilly property and took a quick look? Not really messing with anything, no real digging, just sort of taking a hike. Reconnoitering, so to speak. It could be days before Dal or Mac got permission to search the property. And she'd just be a citizen taking a stroll.

It was a beautiful day and she was dressed for poking around in the woods. With some time to kill before she had to meet Tinker, why not? What harm could it possibly do? Yeah, but… Parker would have a fit if someone saw her and said something.

Starting up the Jeep, she said aloud, "Who gives a crap? Let's do it," and laughed when a man walking by turned to stare at her as if he thought she were talking to him or crazy. Hard to tell which.

A half hour or so later, she parked alongside the road, hooked her backpack to her shoulders, and stepped onto the property owned by John Reilly. No signs, no tree trunks painted purple to say don't tread near me. Birdsong filled the peaceful woods, critters scurried through dried leaves, a squirrel scolded. Otherwise, it was quiet except for her footfalls scuffing through knee-high weeds. The few people who traveled the road wouldn't pay attention to her Jeep parked there.

Several animal trails curled amidst the scattered underbrush of wild roses and brambles and ivy, then headed into a heavy growth of trees. Leaves fringed the branches and would soon be full to hide much of what might be spotted there. That old familiar feeling struck hard. Her heart thumping in her temples at the idea of a breaking story. She could be the one to uncover the hidden diamonds. After all these years, she was probably kidding herself. Yet the hunt made for an enjoyable afternoon excursion, and it was work, wasn't it? She picked one of the narrow trails, cut by deer and some smaller species like foxes, 'coons, and 'possums, and started down the slight incline toward a creek that flowed along the bottom of the gulley.

Twenty acres. She tried to figure out how much land she was actually looking at, but couldn't. She'd hike down to the creek along the eastern perimeter, then go along its bank north to the western edge and return to the road. It would give her some idea of what sort of terrain there would be to search later. Soon the trail she'd chosen to reach the creek angled to the east, and she was walking parallel to the fence line of the SEFOR nuclear breeder plant. Despite how she'd teased Dal, she didn't believe that simply being near the place put her in danger of radiation.

Inside the fence, a large, flat-topped building sprawled among a few smaller ones, and the reactor, a huge ball of a structure, red paint splotched by rust red smears over rusted white, hunkered up close to them. The buildings were all showing their age and she wondered why the state didn't simply clean it up rather than leaving it to the owners. Nuclear material was removed from the site in 1972. The Cedarton Junior College took over ownership in 1975 and conducted research at the facility until 1986. Because it continued to be plagued by residual radiation and chemicals feared to be leaking into the water table, residents demanded something be done.

Time to do a story. Every few years, *The Observer* ran an update on the possible fate of the plant and the danger it might pose. She'd run across a few articles while looking through the bound copies for background material. It was time for another, what with the adjoining property possibly being the scene of a crime. She squatted, slipped the backpack from her shoulders, and took out her camera. After shooting several angles of the old plant, she snapped a few of the Reilly property, which she would withhold from Parker until permission to be there came through.

A bottle of water tumbled from the pack and she opened it, drank at least half, put everything away, slipped her arms into the straps, and hiked on down to the creek. She had been walking about forty-five minutes when she heard voices. Crap. What was anyone doing down here? The farther she walked, the louder they became. When she drew near enough they might see her, she stopped behind a large cedar tree and peeked around it.

Deputies milled about inside a marked crime scene. Feeling a bit stupid, she got her bearings. Deep in thought, she had walked right up to the spot where the body had been discovered last week. From what she could figure, the corpse was buried on the Reilly property, just as she'd suspected. Throwing back her shoulders and attempting to look nonchalant, she approached them, took a few photos as she strolled around the yellow tape fastened to trees.

She spotted Les Howard. "Thought you were done here."

"Mac wanted us to take one last look around. Make sure we didn't miss anything. What you doing here?"

"Thought I'd get a few more shots. Wanted to take a look around SEFOR. Maybe do an update on what's going on with the cleanup. Still no ID on the victim?"

"Nope. Check with Mac on what you can use in the paper."

"We're going with a sketch made by an artist to see if anyone recognizes him. That was Dal's idea."

"How is he doing? Sorry to hear about his accident. That was a big ole boy he tackled. Probably saved Tinker getting hurt, too."

"Well, he'll be laid up a while. Tore some ligaments in his leg. Doc says those will take a month or so to heal."

"Tell Dal we're not buying it." Les said. "He's just trying to get out of working the hard cases."

She laughed. "I'll do that. He'll be real impressed with your sense of humor, considering how he hates those damned crutches."

After she told the guys so long, she trudged back down the road to her Jeep, shoes kicking up dust alongside the ditch. It was so quiet she could hear herself think, and she wasn't sure she liked what she heard.

6
CHAPTER

Back at the office, Jessie found plenty of technical information online about SEFOR. Along with the photos she'd taken, she soon had a decent article about the nuclear breeder plant. Write the words nuclear fission and most readers gobbled up the story. Parker would be pleased because it would stir up the old controversies and pave the way for tying in the locale to the murder scene. If she located the diamonds there as well, what a story that would make. By six o'clock, she was worn out from the long day and headed for home.

Since the previous year when Caveman Jake came into her cabin a few times to leave cryptic messages about the case they were working on, she'd taken to locking the place. Not something she enjoyed having to do. One of the perks of living in Grace County was never having to lock doors or take keys out of cars. Still, her job did attract a certain lowlife type, and both Mac and Dal convinced her to lock up.

She parked near the front porch and walked across the new spring grass scattered with tiny blue spring beauties. Breathing deeply of the clean warm air, she didn't notice anything was amiss until she ran up the steps, key in one hand.

The door stood open a few inches.

Oh, crap. Now what?

She stopped, dug out her cell phone, and dialed Mac's number. Not about to enter the house where someone might lie in wait, she backed down off the porch and moved around to one side while Mac's phone continued to ring. She hated to call 9-1-1 and get sirens and half the department out here. So when he didn't answer, she punched off, dropped the phone in her pocket, and sneaked to the first side window. Cautiously, she raised her head till she could see inside the living room. It looked undisturbed and empty. The bathroom window was over her head, the one beyond that offered a view of her bedroom. Again, nothing amiss.

What the hell?

If someone was still in there and they came out the front door, they'd see her car and might opt to run out the back door, so she trotted to the far corner and peeked carefully around. Nothing. Nobody. She'd wait a while, and if nothing happened, she'd go on in presuming whoever had been in there was long gone.

Then something fell inside making a loud thump and raising the hairs on her neck. Bravery, or perhaps stupidity, being the stronger part of her personality, she raced to the back door, hollered through the locked screen.

"Hey, you. Get out of there or I'm calling the sheriff. Get out now."

Her approach gave them only one exit if they wanted to avoid a person crazy enough to confront them. And whoever it was made a decision. The front door slammed hard, and by the time she ran around the house, a figure wearing a white tee shirt and jeans ran out of sight into the nearby woods. She caught a glimpse of pale hair that said female, but the figure didn't look like it. So a lanky male with long wispy blond hair. Definitely not the guy who'd knocked her down a few evenings ago.

Heart in her throat, she hurried inside to see if they'd done any damage or left her something disgusting. It wasn't till she reached the bathroom that she found the message. Written with lipstick, of all things, on the bathroom mirror.

LAST WARNING—STAY AWAY OR GET HURT.

What was this with people leaving her notes? It was getting old. Couldn't people pick up a phone anymore?

A large bottle of shampoo lay in the bathtub. The thud of something falling she'd heard from outside. It had been sitting on the rim of the tub. Nothing else anywhere was disturbed. She pulled out her cell and snapped a picture of the lipstick note.

Since she wasn't currently involved with another big story, the warning indicated that someone alive today had been a part of the diamond heist, or at least had knowledge of it and might have an inkling where the stones were hidden. There was an off chance it referred to something else, but what? There might be fingerprints, so she didn't touch anything but called Mac again. This time he answered. She told him briefly what had happened and that he needed someone to come out and dust for prints. Probably useless, but who knew?

Dal was headed home after eating supper at the Red Bird when his radio repeated a request for a deputy to go to Jessie's.

He made a quick U-turn and headed toward her place, muttering a few choice words under his breath. What had she been up to now? Every time he turned around, she was in some kind of deep shit. And he had to get to her fast. Not that she'd see it that way. Before she'd sit still for being rescued, she'd throw herself into a killer's arms.

Accelerator on the floor, he headed for her place. He liked that he could drive like a bat out of hell whenever he wanted to. That was especially fun on the curves and switchbacks of these country roads.

He skidded up the lane to her house before anyone arrived. Not sure what he would find, he bailed out before he remembered the damned crutches. Stood there for a moment, both feet on the ground before the left leg collapsed so all he could do was grab the door to avoid falling flat on his butt. Pain rocketed through his spine and hit the top of his head with an explosive intensity.

Goddamned, he had to stop doing this. Hissing through his teeth, he hopped on one foot holding on to the car until he could get his bearings and see past the stars bursting inside his skull. Jess yelled his name like a distant echo. Strong arms went round him, eased him to sit on the car seat.

"Shit, shit, shit," he muttered and let her hold on to him till he could see again.

"Dal, what were you thinking? What are you doing here? Look at me. Are you all right?"

He said 'shit' a few more times, leaned his head on her shoulder, and took deep breaths. Then he peered at her through slitted lids. "What happened? You okay?"

"I'm fine. It's you who needs an ambulance or doctor."

"Nah, I'm okay. I heard the call. Thought you might be in trouble. Got here as quick as I could."

"And almost fell on your ass, you idiot. Are you sure you're not hurt? You're pale as one of your ghosts."

"I don't have any ghosts. If you're so fine, why did Mac call some-one out here?"

"To take fingerprints. When I got home, someone was in the house. They left me a nice little note."

"Dammit, what've you been up to this time?"

"Just the diamond story, I think. Can I do something for you? A glass of water or something. You look like hell."

"Appreciate it, Jess. Really do. Just leave me be here for another min-ute, and I'll be just a bit better than dead."

"I feel really bad about this. You coming here to rescue me like a su-perhero. I mean, I appreciate your concern. I just feel bad about the rest."

"About me falling on my ass, you mean?"

"Well, that too, but mostly are you sure you didn't, you know, make that thingee move or something? Should you maybe get an x-ray?"

"Enough already. Just for fingerprints? You didn't walk in on them or anything?"

"Nope. I stayed outside when I saw the door had been jimmied."

"Well, at least you've learned something since meeting me."

She wrapped her arms around his shoulders. "I'm sorry. Why don't you come on in and stay awhile? I hate you to drive home yet. You look really shaky."

"So I'll drive slow." He liked the feel of her arms around him, but it was best not to get too comfortable with that. "Gotta go. Let me know what you find out, if anything."

"Could I come over later? Maybe bring you something decent to eat?"

"Not necessary."

"I know that, but just the same, if you won't kick me out I'll be over after they finish printing stuff. Besides, I need to tell you what I did today. You must be bored out of your gourd sitting around drinking beer and staring off into space."

"Hey, I been out doing some stuff, too. Have you know, when I got back from my little drive, I ate supper at the Red Bird and picked up on all the latest gossip. Those ole boys half the time know more about a case than I do. Besides, who says I'm boring company?" He dragged his legs into the car and switched on the ignition. "See you," he said and drove off, leaving her standing there looking scared.

That woman would be the death of him. He fought the attraction successfully only when out of her sight. Then she got in trouble and there he was, Mr. Hero, rushing to her rescue when in truth she seldom needed the help. In real truth, he welcomed any excuse to be around her then beat himself up for being such a stupid fool. Now she was coming over to play nurse, and he absolutely positively knew they'd end up in bed.

That in itself wasn't a bad thing. She was a tiger who could also cuddle and purr, but therein lay the problem. Reporters had ruined his life with lies. So here he was, panting after one who held those same powers. The more she learned about him, the more ammunition she had to use against him should she decide to do so. She might be a tiger in bed, but she was a shark elsewhere.

So why didn't he stay the hell away from her? Hell if he knew. She was everywhere he looked, butting into every investigation with her gentle and polite country girl ways. If he had good sense, he'd leave this town and find a job somewhere he could become anonymous. Trouble was, he liked it here. Liked the people and liked this job because he could do it without hiding what he was. A freak of nature, a man who walked among the dead and worse, talked to them. Sometimes he read the minds of the living. Hell, that even gave him the willies.

By the time he finished ruminating on what his crazy life had become, he'd parked near his trailer, not remembering the drive home. A vehicle was nosed up to the trailer. One he didn't recognize. Cursing, he maneuvered the crutches, got out of the SUV carefully because his leg and back still hurt like the devil, hobbled up the steps, and eased the door open. He'd have his gun out if he could handle it and the damned sticks at the same time. Probably get his dumb ass shot before this was over. As if he hadn't already accomplished that act himself.

"Dal, it's just me." A male voice he couldn't place came from around the corner.

"Well, me, I'd appreciate it if you'd show yourself so I can come on in."

"Hey, don't shoot me or anything. It's Sam Watson."

Dal stumped into the living room to see the white haired retired lawman making himself at home in his recliner. When he saw Dal, he rose.

"What happened, boy? Did you get shot again or something? Here, take your chair, I'll perch on that couch."

"Thanks. No, I didn't get shot, at least not in the past twenty-four hours. That's healing, thank you. Figured you already knew all about this. Besides tearing some ligaments in that fracas at the jail, an old injury has kicked up, that's all." He lowered himself into the recliner and laid the crutches on the floor. Sighed long and deep, hoped he didn't do something so stupid as leap out of his truck again very soon. "What's up?"

"I've been out of touch this week. Had some family business. Hope you can catch me up on stuff, though. Hate being in the dark." The well-groomed older man smiled, gray eyes twinkling.

How in the hell the man got in was anyone's guess. Must've forgot to lock the door when he left earlier. Hell, Jessie's country ways were rubbing off on him.

Dal nodded at Sam. "I'll do my best. What can I do you for?"

"Well, you know we talked about that diamond heist? I thought of something else after you left the other day. I've turned it over and over in my mind. Can't think if this could possibly mean anything or not. You know that Mathon Wells fella involved in the robbery?"

"Sure. What about him?"

"You might want to talk to his son, Lennie. I think he's still around somewhere. They lived down in Hot Springs, but they moved up here sometime before that robbery. Sara is his mom. Lennie was born here, I think. Lost track of lots of folks when I retired. I believe he lives with his mom still yet. Somewhere out on Dogtown Road."

"Yeah, Jessie gave me a lead to the Crowe family and mentioned that Mathon's widow and his son lived out that way. Think I remember seeing that name on a mailbox. We'll see if we can locate Lennie. What about Wesley Miller? Did he have any kin around that you know of? Hell, we don't even have a place to start. Wondering if that body we found last week might be connected. If it isn't, it's one hell of a coincidence, turning up so near where they picked those guys up. Nothing definite there yet, just a possibility. Still… thirty-four years is a long span."

He stopped there, not wanting to tell Sam why they suspected the victim was related to his killer. He wasn't sure how much the old man knew about Dal's odd abilities. Though on second thought, he knew everything else that went on.

Sam rubbed his chin and frowned. "Wesley Miller come in here from somewhere else and took up with Mathon and Sara right off the bat. There was a girl, his sister, I think. Can't recall her name, though. The four of them were birds of a feather, if you'll excuse the expression. Trouble waiting to happen. Nobody knew much of anything about

Miller. No wife I know of. You might get some information at McAl-ester as to who his next of kin is. The sister I think got married and moved up north somewhere."

Dal shrugged. "Probably doesn't make any difference."

"That body you found out near the old reactor plant might be con-nected to the diamond heist? Wish I was involved in crime fighting like in the good old days, where we hunted 'em down and shot 'em for their trouble. Or even back when they had a gallows next to the court house where they hung the sumbitches right after trial."

"I have to say it makes me a bit nervous to poke around at that reac-tor plant for very long at a time." Dal twisted in his chair.

Sam chuckled and rose, adjusting his pants self-consciously. "Know what you mean, there, boy. Reckon I'll get on out of here. You look like you could use some rest. You take 'er easy, and if I think of anything else, I'll give you a holler. Or come on in and visit with me. I'll be on Sunday evening till midnight shift, probably all summer. I'd downright enjoy getting in on this one just to whet my whistle, so to speak."

Dal started to rise and the old man held out a palm. "Stay put. I can see myself out. Found my way in with no trouble."

"Pleasure to see you again, sir." Dal cranked the recliner back so his feet were off the floor.

That's where he was when someone rapped on the door. "Well, god-damn." Beyond the window the sun hung low in the sky, its golden twilight gleaming on the new leaves of the oak and maple.

"It's me. Don't get up." Jess came in carrying a sack in her arms.

"What time is it?" He rubbed at his eyes and jacked the recliner into a sitting position.

"Almost seven. You feeling better? I brought something to eat. Figured if we were going to go over all this stuff, I might starve to death since you never have a snack laying around."

She set the bag on the small table in the kitchen and brought out several containers from Harp's deli. Shedding the heavy backpack in a corner, she opened each one, stuck plastic spoons in them, and produced a package of Styrofoam plates. Back into the sack for a carton of Pepsi Max. "I do hope you have ice, these aren't cold. I did bring cups though." She pulled out a package of red cups.

He started to heave himself out of the chair but she came over to him, put her hands flat on his shoulders. "Stay put. I'll fix you a plate. You don't start taking care of yourself, I'll move in and do it for you. Bet you don't want that, so stay put."

He found that easy to do.

"Okay, good. Now, potato salad?"

He nodded and she went through the list piling his plate full of barbecued chicken, potato salad, greens with dressing, and a couple slices of freshly baked bread, poured Pepsi Max over ice and brought it all to him with a tea towel. "Forgot to buy napkins. Want cookies now or later? They're double stuffed Oreos. I know you like them."

"Later. Thanks." He studied her face, lit with enjoyment in taking care of him. A natural nurturer. Something he found doubly dangerous when combined with her prowess in bed.

She fixed herself a plate, plopped down on the couch, and smiled across at him. His heart kicked, not once but twice. He lowered his head and started shoveling in the food. Damn, he was hungry. With the last bite, he finally glanced at her. She sat cross-legged, watching him.

"Don't look like you ate at the Red Bird this evening. You must have been half-starved. I'm so sorry."

"For what?"

"For not realizing that you were sitting over here all day with nothing in the house to eat. Make me a list of stuff, and I'll do some shopping for you. I haven't been a very thoughtful friend."

"You don't have to do that. I really did eat earlier at the Red Bird."

"Must've been your only meal of the day. You sure can shovel it in for someone who ate supper once already. And so that's what you did today. Want another plate?"

He grinned and nodded. "That was two, three hours ago. Wouldn't mind some more chicken and bread. I was roaming around in the middle of nowhere most of the day with nothing but dust to chew on."

She brought him another plate of chicken and bread plus a stack of Oreos, a cup of coffee which she'd put on to brew while fixing their plates, and a note pad from her backpack. "Make that list while I dig out all the stuff I've learned so far about the diamonds."

"Yes, dear." She was right, he felt like hell and he wouldn't bother going back to the Red Bird or anyplace else for a while. He jotted some stuff down that he could eat without any more than a quick nuke added some fresh fruit and veggies and handed it to her along with his debit card. "Use this. PIN number's on the list." Odd that he trusted her with his money but not his emotions.

She read over it, laid it down, added a few items to the bottom and stuck it in her pocket.

"What was that?"

"Oh, don't worry. You're almost out of coffee, and I thought maybe I'd come over Sunday and fix you a good meal, so I put the fixin's for that on there." She glanced down at him. "Hope you don't mind."

"Would it do me any good?"

"Grouch. You ready to talk about the case now? Or would you rather grumble some more?" Her phone buzzed, and she dragged it from her pocket.

"Tinker? Oh, I'm so sorry. I got tied up with some stuff and forgot all about our movie date. Can we make it another night?" She listened a while, smiling at him and nodding. "Okay, great. Keep the movie. I'll pay the overdue on it. See you then. Bye."

He spread one hand over his eyes and leaned back. "You're a good friend, and you have been since we first met. And all I do is—"

She grinned and inserted, "Bitch."

"Yeah. So I learned some interesting stuff this afternoon. Sam Watson came to see me, you know the retired deputy who mans the desk at the jail odd times?" He proceeded to tell her what Sam had shared while finishing off the remainder of his food.

"I believe you learned as much sitting in that recliner as I did running my butt off."

He picked up an Oreo, split the halves and licked off the white filling, washed it down with a sip of coffee, and squinted at her over the cup's rim. "So, whatcha got?"

She studied him closely. He looked so beat up, so worried. And she didn't blame him. What if that piece of bone or bullet or whatever it was moved and paralyzed him? No one would be happy thinking about that. Still, she needed to distract him 'cause he didn't take compassion very well.

She spread her notes out as if she didn't notice his distress, and began to tell him what she had learned. Which wasn't a heck of a lot. She told him about the strange light the Sims family had witnessed the night of their anniversary party, and the blue Ford Falcon Fred Simmons saw speeding around the curve after the robbery, and of

Alvin Marcy finding one just like that run off the road and rusting in the woods years later.

"So we'll need to see if we can find out who owned that Falcon and talk to them if they're still around," Dal said. "Wouldn't hurt to get a look at it. Maybe it was stolen, though who steals a Falcon? If you're going to steal a car, you'd think it would be at least an Olds or a Buick. Don't guess there were many of these fancy little foreign cars like there are today."

"My bet is it belonged to one of the men involved in the robbery. I intended to call Marcy back. Forgot about it." She bit at the end of her pen and handed him a folded sheet of paper. "I made you a copy of my notes so you don't have to do that. There's also the list of the names on the mailboxes you jotted down when we took our drive. Didn't know if you kept it or not."

"Wish I'd a been able to go with you. Which ones of these were you not able to find at home?"

"See the star before the names or addresses?" She poked a finger at one of the stars. "They weren't home, so maybe they need to be talked to. I can get out again in a few days and check with them. We might learn more, but it was a long time ago. Those who did remember had a specific reason for recalling that particular day. The others I saw looked at me like I had blood running out of my eyes or something."

"Jesus. You say the weirdest things."

"Guess I do. You ought to be used to it by now. Besides, doesn't that make two of us?"

"Well, that one was particularly disturbing. Two of us what?" He cocked an eyebrow at her.

"I apologize. I guess it was a pretty thoughtless thing to say to an ex-cop. Two of us who are weird."

"Ah. Okay. Were those the only three of the people you saw who remembered anything?"

"Actually four, if you count both Sims. But, yep, you can see there were about eight people who weren't home." She rubbed his shoulders till he groaned. "One of 'em might remember something."

"Lord, that feels good. You talked to Mac about this yet?"

"Nope. He doesn't think this is a case, so I wanted to put more together first. Oh, yes, I got the name of the man who owns the land where the Sims saw the lights that night and where the body was found. John Reilly. He bought it back in 1979, never did anything with it. Mac agreed to try to get me permission to go on his land."

"Do you intend to wait for that?"

She paused the massage, stared at the floor for a while.

"Jess?"

"I took a walk." She grinned when he gave her his serious look. "*Only* a walk. I know that look. No digging around, no searching. And if I'd found anything, I'd have left it right where it was till we got permission to mess with it."

He shook his head, then looked at her with a smile she had trouble resisting. Those brilliant green eyes with flecks so dark they looked black. So expressive, they often did her in. Made her want to drag him onto that king sized bed in the other room and do wild things to him. Before she could contemplate that any longer, he spoke.

"We need to see if we can find Lennie Wells. He might remember something or be willing to talk about his dad. About how he and Wes Miller knew about those particular diamonds being at Hamilton's Jewelry on that specific day. It's weak, but worth following up."

"There on the list is the Wells name. Two mailboxes, one only has an address. According to Wanda at the courthouse, Julie Crowe lives across from Sara Wells. As you can see, no one was home. But that's it."

"With me, too. So, the Crowe thoughts might be connected to her?"

"I'd guess so." The backpack lay on the table in front of the couch, and she took a long time folding and stuffing her notes away, then she rose, went to Dal, and held a hand down.

"Let's go to bed. You look whipped."

For a moment or two, she thought he was going to refuse, but then he gave her his hand. "I'll need those," he said.

She picked the crutches up off the floor and tucked them under his arms. After a stop in the bathroom, he followed her into the bedroom where she had turned down the covers.

Hard to get used to him not being totally mobile. Without a word, he dropped to the edge of the mattress. She knelt between his knees, unfastened his belt and zipper, tugged the pants out from under him, and pulled them down around his boots which she then pulled off as well. All the while, he said nothing. Just sat there watching her every move.

"Shirt?"

He lifted his arms and she pulled it off over his head.

She turned up the edge of the bandage peered under it. "Hmm, arm is healing well. Now lay down."

Again, he did as she asked. Odd behavior. By now, he ought to be objecting about her taking care of him like he was sick or something. Instead, he watched her with silent intent when she pulled off her tee shirt and bra, stepped out of her shoes and jeans, then hooked her thumbs in the top of her panties and took them off. His gaze tracked her movements, and when she lifted a leg to crawl over him, he pulled away the covers, took her waist in both hands, and stopped her halfway.

"There, like that," he whispered.

He slipped inside her with a low moan. She wiggled a bit, then settled around him. Gently, easily, she rocked until they came at the same time. With a satisfied sigh, he pulled her down to nestle her head against his shoulder.

For a long while she remained there, his breath fluttering her hair, his hands spread over her behind. He had never treated her with such tenderness. To tell him how she felt would be a bad mistake, so she curled up and snuggled against him. He fell asleep quickly and she kissed his cheek, whispered, "I love you." The most surprising thing of all was she meant it. At least at that very moment. She drifted off to sleep listening to him breathing.

It was still full dark when she crawled carefully off the foot of the bed so as not to disturb him. Carrying her clothes, she took a quick shower in the cramped bathroom, dressed, and went to the kitchen where she made a pot of coffee, found two packages of Honey Buns in the groceries she'd brought, and laid them in a saucer next to a coffee cup with a spoon in it. Then she pulled a paper towel off the roll, grabbed a pen and scrawled on it, 'I'll be back,' without signing it.

Driving home under a canopy of brilliant stars, she began to cry. Why, she had no idea, or maybe she did, but just didn't want to explore the complicated reasons. She and Dal would never fit together perfectly. Both had too much baggage to ignore. Yet they were drawn to each other as if mated from another time.

Working with him, having sex with him, would have to do. Maybe forever. Was she a fool with the sweet and caring Parker waiting in the wings? Probably.

At the cabin, she ran through the dew-sprinkled grass, unlocked the door, and slipped inside. The yard light blinked once and went out, plunging the room into an intense darkness. Into the utter silence, something that sounded like a heartbeat fluttered to life. Slow at first, it sped up to match her own pulse.

Good God, what was that?

Blindly she swiped a hand over the wall switch. No light came on. The weird heartbeat sped up.

Faster and faster till she wanted to scream.

Instead, she did what she should never have done. Rather than getting the hell out of there, she stumbled across the room and into the kitchen where again she tried the lights. Still nothing. Cell in her backpack on her back. Cordless somewhere. On the counter. Nothing. Her searching hand knocked something to the floor. It shattered. Trembling, she shed the pack, pawed around in it. Where was the damned phone?

The heartbeat ceased, leaving silence as loud as thunder. No whirr of the fridge running or the wall clock ticking its peculiar click, yet a roaring in her ears impossible to muffle. She crouched behind the counter that separated the small kitchen from the living room. Like it made a difference. It was so damned dark she couldn't see, but neither could whoever was in there with her.

Clasping her hand over her mouth to keep from making a sound, she swallowed. He'd most surely heard the gulp.

Footsteps. Someone walking through the shards of glass on the floor. Right next to her. She cursed the country darkness. Good God, she could feel the heat from his body, smell something odd. Acrid, so strong it left an ammonia taste on her tongue. Not the same man as before. The thought came, then fear chased it away.

He bent down and looked right into her face, his eyes reflecting what little light there was, his fetid breath washing over her. His voice grating and threatening.

"We warned you to back off. One more chance, just one. Tell me you understand."

She tried, but only croaked.

"Say it." He punched at her, connecting with her chin so her teeth clacked together.

"I... yes, I do."

"Do what?"

Taking a deep breath that sucked in his putrid smell, she muttered, "Unnerstand."

Feet crunched over the glass strewn floor, air from the door being opened, then closed with a bang. Shaking so hard she couldn't move, she imagined herself scrambling to the door to catch a glimpse of someone running away. In the dark? Even if she could move, it would do no good.

Several deep breaths later, she scrambled through the shards of glass toward her backpack, cutting the palms of her hands and her knees. Grabbed the pack.

Phone.

Light.

She would be able to see if only she could find the damned thing.

"I understand, you son of a bitch," she said through gritted teeth. "Doesn't mean I'll do what you said."

Hands stuck to everything she touched. Blood. Blood all over everything. Finally the phone and she punched it on. The screen turned bright. At last, light. At last. She almost hugged the stupid thing. Crouched there with the blessed glow in her face for the longest time before she punched in 9-1-1. No damn way was she letting this guy get away with something so juvenile. Beating hearts and growling voices. Threats in the night. Who the hell did he think he was? Certainly not either of the first two who'd messed with her. A third person involved in this bizarre mess.

A killer, that's who.

In *her* house. Breathing on her. Threatening her.

7
CHAPTER

The 9-1-1 operator came on and Jessie babbled what had happened. The volunteer fire station was only two miles away, the volunteers scattered. Two lived out her road, they'd come straight to her. But they'd be in bed. Five minutes anyway. She sat where she was because her knees were bleeding, and besides, she couldn't move without cutting herself worse. Time on the phone crept. One, two, three minutes and someone hammered on the door.

"Jessie West? First Responders. Are you alone?"

"Yes, yes." Wonder they could hear her, the words buried so deep in her panic.

"We're coming in."

"Please, please, please." All she could say.

A woman knelt beside her. In the gleam from the telephone, she couldn't recognize her. "There's glass everywhere. Be careful." The voice she knew. Clara Jenkins.

"Lights. Where are the lights?" Clara's husband Boyd.

"He turned them all off."

"Where's the box?"

"Back wall. Bedroom." She burst into tears. "Thank you. Thank you."

The lights came on. Four a.m. clicked onto the phone. "Got you all out of bed. I'm sorry."

"Jessie, I'm going to take your blood pressure Just relax." Clara wrapped a cuff around her arm. "Where is all the blood coming from? You're not shot or anything?

"No. Hands. Knees. Cuts. Glass." The words sliced through her sobs.

Clara removed the cuff and checked her hands with gentle fingers. "Glass in the cuts, honey. We'll wait for the EMTs. Okay?"

Sirens in the distance. First responders leading the pack. Mac and the guys, too. An ambulance. All converging on her. Come to protect her.

The more the merrier.

She hiccoughed and continued to cry. "Oh, honey, don't worry." Sweet Clara again.

The door slammed open, feet pounded, huge men everywhere. Testosterone thick in the room. Members of the Grace County Volunteer Fire Department #1 that served Cedarton and environs. Men all over the place. Women, too. These people took their work seriously, and most were trained EMTs as well as firefighters.

They circled around her, speaking softly, finding out what had been done for her, what still needed doing. And then, one by one, they carried out their jobs. Finally two of them lifted her off the floor, supported her into the living room, and sat her in the big recliner, their boots crackling in the shards of glass.

"Cut her jeans off?"

"No, don't. Please. Cost a fortune."

Why couldn't she stop thinking in fragments? Almost like she was taking notes so she could write a story later.

Boyd and Clara chuckled. "Bring her that afghan off the couch," Clara said, then to Jessie, "Just slip them off, honey and cover up with this." She handed her the requested afghan, pulled off Jessie's shoes and the jeans. "Oh, honey. I'm gonna let the guys in the ambulance take care of getting the glass out, and I'll put these in a sink of cold water. Afraid they're ruined, though. Holes all in the legs from the glass."

Jessie's phone started ringing. Peering at the screen, she made out Dal's name. Oh, God, he'd heard the call on his scanner. She connected.

"Goddammit, can't I turn my back a minute? You okay? Shit."

"Yes, I'm okay. I'm shook up, but okay."

"What happened?"

"Not now, please. I just want to sit here and wait for the ambulance."

"Ambulance? I'm coming over."

"No. Don't you dare. You stay right where you are. I'll call you the minute I can explain stuff. Please, don't. Please." Don't you dare hurt yourself because of me. If she said that, he'd blow his stack, so she kept it to herself.

His breath sucked in and out several times, he said shit a few more times, then, "You promise you're all right?"

"I promise."

"And you'll call me the minute you can."

"I promise. Stay put. You promise."

Without promising, he hung up.

The ambulance arrived, one of the EMTs removed all the glass from her hands and knees, cleaned up her wounds and bandaged them. "We can take you in if you want. These aren't life threatening, just painful. But it's up to you."

"No, it's okay. I'll stay here. Silly to go to the hospital for this."

"Not silly if you feel you need to."

She shook her head.

About that time Mac slammed through the door, followed by Burt Sample, Les Howard, and a deputy whose name she couldn't remember.

Oh, God. New testosterone recharging the old.

All the first responders cleared out, with waves and goodbyes and take it easies. The EMTs packed up their equipment and the ambulance pulled away, leaving only Mac, the three deputies, and Jessie sitting in her recliner with an afghan over her lap and bandages on her hands and knees. Stillness settled like a heavy fog after a rain.

"Well, what are you mixed up in this time?" Mac broke the silence and lowered himself to the couch with a sigh.

Alone in the middle of the cramped kitchen, Dal threw one of the crutches down on the floor in the middle of his kitchen and resisted the urge to kick it, which might then cause him to lose his balance and fall over. Goddammit. He needed to go off somewhere where he didn't know what was going on so he wouldn't have to ignore the police calls then worry what the hell was going on. And when he did get his hands on Jess, he was going to tie her to a chair. Or better yet, his bed. Keep her out of trouble. Never met a woman who could get in more scrapes than she could.

In an effort to calm down, he hopped with the aid of one crutch, poured himself a cup of coffee and ripped open a pack of Honey Buns, scarfed them down. Jess's doing, and he thanked her for it, but that didn't ease his irritation at her. She'd stumbled too close to something bad once again. That little innocent hike of hers probably took her near a weed patch or meth lab. Grace County had its share of both. Replaced all the moonshine stills of the old days. No telling what she'd stirred up this time.

Stupid to jump to the conclusion that it had something to do with those diamonds that probably were buried so deep no one would ever find them. If they were even in the county any longer. And everyone dead who knew about it, anyway. More than thirty years. Drugs was more than likely the source of her latest fiasco. And the cause of the dead body, as well.

He cursed his condition once more, bent carefully, retrieved the crutch and made his way to the car. Use common sense, drive to her place, go inside, and find out what happened. Be damned if he'd sit at home waiting for her to call. No matter what happened, she'd make light of it. If someone had hurt her, they would pay.

He met the ambulance going out, signaled with his lights and a blip of the siren, and they stopped. He rolled down his window. "Are you taking her in?"

"Nope. She's back at the house. You doing okay, Dal? Heard about your accident."

"Nah, I'm fine. A few weeks and I'll be back at solving all the big crimes in the county." No sense explaining it hadn't been an accident.

He shared a laugh with the driver, waved goodbye, and drove on.

Mac was at her house, along with three other patrol cars. But as he parked, two of the deputies came out of the house, waved in his direction, got in their units, and drove off. When he went in without knocking, Burt Sample was sweeping glass off the bloody kitchen floor and Mac was sitting on the couch talking to Jess.

Jess in a chair. Bandages on both knees and around her hands, an afghan draped over her lap.

He went to her, stood looking down. Wished like hell he could kneel beside her and take her hands in his. "You okay?"

She nodded. "I asked you not to come."

"Since when do I pay attention to anything you say?"

"Since never. Sit down. I was just fixing to tell Mac about it."

Outside the windows, the sky silvered, then streaked a bright orange fading to pink along the tops of the mountains to the east. Another day coming awake.

Dal dropped to the couch. Jessie shivered a couple of times, then began her tale, stumbling over some of the details. Mac and Dal and Burt, who had dumped the broken glass in the trash can, listened intently, not interrupting until she finished with the man's warning and smack on the chin.

Dal exploded. "The bastard. Did you recognize his voice?"

She gazed at him, and from her thoughts he caught a vision of something she had left out. "He smelled like what?" Dal asked.

Her eyes widened. "Okay, yes, I forgot that. Acrid, almost like ammonia or alcohol or a combination of the two with a little skunk mixed in."

"Meth," Dal and Mac said at the same time.

"I figured this was connected to drugs." Dal studied her a while longer. "Just what did you really find on the Reilly property?"

"You're the mind reader, you tell me." Her lips clamped shut. He'd made her angry. She didn't like him probing around in her head, and he tried not to, but dammit, this was different. She wasn't sure what was going on, but she might have something hidden in there he could use.

Mac stared at Dal, then at Jess. "You went on that property? What were you thinking?"

"Just trying to see how close it was to where the body was found. Just hiked through. Didn't search anything."

"Well someone didn't like you just hiking through. Didn't see a shack or trailer, some place they could be cooking meth?" Mac was pissed, too. Something Dal rarely saw between her and the sheriff.

"I told you, I wasn't looking for anything. Wanted to wait till we got permission. Did you call John Reilly, ask him if we could have access to his land?"

"Left him a message. He was out."

"Did you find out what he does for a living?" Dal asked.

"Woman who answered the phone said Reilly Import/Export, but I didn't ask her any more than that."

Jess eyed Mac for a moment. "Wonder why he's hanging on to twenty acres in the boonies of Arkansas, adjacent to a leaking reactor plant the federal government has requested decommissioned and decontaminated? Could die waiting for land values to go up. You guys may disagree, but there's more here than a meth lab or a marijuana patch. A lot more, even, than a few diamonds. Import/Export. Good grief, what does that suggest? Anyone find out just what those few stones are worth?"

Dal pinched his temples with spread fingers. His head felt like it was going to split apart. "Got any Tylenol, Jess?"

"Sure, I'll get it."

"Stay where you are." Mac rose. "Tell me where it is."

She did, and he returned shortly with the pills and a bottle of water he'd found in the fridge. Dal washed down three pills and drank half the bottle of water.

"I wish you'd stayed home, Dal. You look like hell."

"Appreciate that, Jess. I really do." He was not accustomed to feeling like this, hadn't for a long time, and it made him want to curse and throw things. Which he tried mightily not to do.

"Sorry." She kept her gaze on his for a long while.

He got her message clearly. For once, she hoped he would read her mind, 'cause she wanted to tell him how much she cared for him, how much she wished he wasn't having to go through this after all he'd endured in the past.

He nodded, gave her an understanding grin, and leaned his head back. Damn woman. Always knew how to jerk his chain then smooth out the results. He couldn't think straight on this case Mac insisted wasn't a case. Too much going on to be coincidence, and sure as hell it was all connected. All they had to do was find who was up to what when and where, and they'd have it solved. Simple as that.

The thought made him chuckle in spite of the headache.

"What?" she asked. "You've thought of something. Come on, share."

"It's not much, just enough to make me want to follow through on the diamond heist information, look into this being a drug thing, and connect both to this murder."

"You're on disability for four weeks," Mac reminded him.

"Doesn't keep my mind from working. She or you can bring me what you learn, and I can try to put it all together. I am, after all, a detective first."

She rose from the chair and walked stiffly toward the couch, holding the afghan around her waist so it dragged on the floor behind her. Dal cringed. She had a look in her eyes, something on her mind that he dared not poke into. Sinking down between the two men, she looked first at Dal.

"You take better care of yourself, or you'll find me staying with you to make you behave, and believe me, you don't want that. And you," she turned to Mac. "Couldn't you help us find out what's going on with this diamond thing? I'm convinced my visitors are upset over me looking into that. I didn't see any meth labs or weed, no hidden shacks or overgrown caves or anything like it. They're afraid I'm going to find those diamonds before they do. And it's someone close to Mathon Wells. He had a son by the name of Lennie. Could have told him. Why don't you find out where he's at and stop pooh-poohing me." She turned to Dal. "And don't forget Julie Crowe and her son Merle. I have the address somewhere in my backpack."

He laid a hand on her arm, then took it away because it made him want to touch her somewhere else. "Never mind it now. It'll keep. So, what are you going to be up to that we can't stop, no matter what we say?"

She smiled at him, nose crinkling in that way that made him tingle all over. God, man, get hold of yourself.

"I'm going to find out just what those diamonds are worth, if I can, then I'm going online to find out more about this Reilly Import/Export Company. If I'm going to write another story, I want to have all my ducks in a row, or Parker will skin me."

Dal said as sweetly as he could. "And you will share everything you learn, I presume."

"Of course. You know I will. I'll take it straight to Mac, and he can let you in on it if you need to know."

"Ouch," he said.

Mac stood and rubbed at his back. "This old man is going home to grab an hour's sleep before going to work. Dal, wish you'd do the same."

She took Dal's hand, embarrassed him by kissing the back of it. "Oh, he's going to, aren't you?"

"Yep, soon as I can get up off this couch."

Mac gave him a hand and they both stood over her. "You'd be wise to do the same, young lady," Mac said, "but far be it from me to dare tell you what to do. Just try not to be the feature attraction on the police scanner again anytime soon, would you?"

She held up a hand. "I will do my best. Now get out of here. I have to get dressed and go to the office while my story for next week is fresh in my mind. I'll teach those idiots to try to scare me."

"Oh, good God. Let's get out of here Mac, before I smack her one upside the head."

Dal hobbled out chatting with Burt, Mac following along.

Burt was on duty in the eastern quarter of the county, and he left the two of them, Dal sitting in his SUV, Mac leaning up against the front fender.

The older man squinted his pale blue eyes at Dal. "You gonna be okay, son?"

Dal nodded, tried out a smile that didn't quite form. "I think so." He studied his boots for a minute. "I don't want to lose this job, Mac. I know this is hard, since we don't really have enough men if something bad was to happen. But I'd appreciate it if you'd give me a chance to get back in shape."

"I'd like to do that, son. You got hurt on my watch, so I'll see you're taken care of. But you can understand that if you're gonna be laid up a long while, I'll have to take someone else on to fill in the gap." He held up a hand when Dal started to speak. "I know there ain't anyone around here can do what you do when it comes to solving violent crimes, but I need somebody to help run this county all the rest of the time. I'll do my best to keep your job open, though my budget only allows for so much in outgoing funds."

Dal nodded. "I understand. The doc says four weeks, then we'll see. Can you give me that much time? I can consult on everything, I can drive just fine if you need someone to patrol."

Mac scratched the back of his head, tipping the Stetson forward a bit. "I can do that, but I don't want you doing anything that could get you hurt. If I need some patrolling done that don't involve anything else, I'll give you a call. Otherwise, you do like our little gal says and take good care of yourself. Some of us have took quite a liking to you. We get befuddled on this case, we'll be sure to consult you."

Embarrassed, Dal didn't meet Mac's gaze, instead stared out across the valley toward the mountain peaks, bright in the morning sun. Dammit, he didn't want to lose this job. He'd learned to love this place, and hated the thought he might have to leave it. If he couldn't hold this job, then there weren't any others available he could manage. Especially if things went bad with this sliver of lead moving around inside him.

Bidding him a good morning and telling him to git on home, Mac went to his car.

Dal keyed the ignition and followed the sheriff out the long lane to the highway where he parked out of sight around a curve. He wasn't going home quite yet. Not till Jess came out and he tailed her to the newspaper office.

All that waited for him at home was an empty and lonely trailer. He'd never been lonely before, always preferred the company of silence, but something was going out of whack with that. It was what he felt for Jess. He missed her when she wasn't around, though he hated to admit it. Be damned if he would. He'd concentrate instead on this mystery of the diamond heist. Give him something to do while he was on disability. After he saw her inside the office, he went home, took a Tramadol, made his way to the bed, only taking off his boots before lying back, arm over his eyes. When he awoke, the clock said 11:30, so he pulled himself up, hooked the crutches off the floor and went into the kitchen to make coffee.

Armed with the list Jess had given him and a mug of the fragrant brew, he went over the names slowly. Surely something would key his memory. The crime scene hadn't furnished much. The perp and the victim were related somehow, and there was that thing about a crow. The black birds had been thick in the top of a huge tree, but with this Julie Crowe turning up, it was one hell of a coincidence. Still, it might be a reference to the Crowe woman. He just wasn't sure. He dug out his cell, called Jess. She answered right away.

"Hey," he said. "You okay?"

"I'm doing just fine. How about you. You okay?"

"Sure. You find out anything more about those diamonds? Or our mysterious Lennie?"

She chuckled. "Count on me. I learned some about both. I didn't get to the Reilly company, but I called the Harrison PD this morning, had them look into their records on the heist. I know we have a file, but we're gonna have to dig it out over at the old court house, and I thought this would save us some time."

"And a lot of complications," he added, smiling at the memories of being with her in that dusty old storeroom.

"Yeah, that, too. They're gonna get back to me soon as someone can dig up their files. Seems they have a dusty old store room, too."

"Hmm, wonder if...."

"Best we don't go there."

He didn't say anything for a moment. Then only, "Hmmm," and changed the subject. "This list of people along the route. Gonna go out there again. Would like to find this Crowe woman, just to make sure, but if she works, she won't be home. Still, I thought I could check out some more of the folks, see if they know anything."

"I'm done here and tired of being on this computer. Maybe I could go along?"

"What about your call back from Harrison?"

"I gave them my cell number."

"Jess, what was that?"

"Nothing. I didn't hear anything. Can I go with you?"

He stared out the window a second. Shrugged. Aw, hell. Why not? "I guess I could put up with you, if you really want to go." What the hell was going on? Whispers. Footsteps?

Her reply came over the faint background noise. "Well, it'll be tough, but I suppose I can make it. Kidding. Pick me up whenever. See you."

Before he could say anything, she hung up. From outside came the sound of someone creeping through gravel, followed by and a car door slamming. What the *hell?*

He was scarcely on his feet, without time to think about it when the door burst open and two burly men filled the small kitchen. The violence and hatred of their action swarmed into his subconscious, warned him they weren't there to talk business. He'd have caught it sooner if he hadn't been thinking of Jess. He tried to reach his weapon, hanging in its holster on the back of the chair, but one of them jerked the crutches out from under him and threw them out the door. Flashes of murderous intent swept through his mind before the other slugged him hard enough that he drifted into a heavy darkness.

He came to in the back of a moving car that lurched and swayed over a rough country road. Hands and ankles bound with what was probably Duct tape. Helpless. Two men in the front seat, arguing about some guy named Merle. He'd heard that name, knew it, but it was what they were about to do that concerned him. Nothing else.

For some reason he couldn't read, these men had every intention of beating the shit out of him, and if they did, he would not survive it in one piece. He'd be back where he was after the shooting in Dallas. To go through that again wasn't thinkable. He had no choice but to do something even though he might very well hasten his own death. It was better than what they had in mind.

He lunged forward from the back seat, looped his bound wrists over the passenger's throat and locked his arm in a choke hold.

Gagging and kicking, the guy reached back, trying to defend himself with a .45 semi-auto. The driver beat at Dal's arm with one hand, but the car threatened to leave the narrow rough road, so he clamped both hands on the wheel. By the time the passenger passed out from the hold Dal had around his throat, the driver had slewed the car all over the road instead of stopping. Then he must have changed his mind, decided the best thing to do was pull over and help his buddy.

But he was way too late.

Dal let the limp guy loose, ran taped wrists along one of his arms, fumbled the gun into his fist, and shot the driver, even as the car rolled to a stop.

The throttled one came to, saw his wounded buddy, and chose to grab him and drag him off into the woods.

Even if Dal could peel away the tape, he couldn't get out of the back seat, certainly could not chase the two of them. Breath coming in great gasps, heart slamming in his chest, he crouched down, still holding the gun, and waited for what would happen next. If either one returned, he'd shoot the son of a bitch. Trouble was, his head pounded so hard he saw double. If the second one decided to come back and try to finish him off, he might well accomplish the feat because Dal was about to pass out again. Probably had a concussion, but that didn't worry him so much as that he couldn't feel his legs, twisted into the small space of the cramped back seat. His last realization before darkness closed in. Even if Jess and Mac found him, he might live to wish they hadn't.

Jess checked to make sure she had extra batteries for her recorder, then went out in the sunshine to wait for Dal. She'd arranged for him to pick her up so they could find some more folks at home on Dogtown Road. She waited some more, then dug out her cell to call him. It went to voice mail. She called Mac, filled him in.

"I'm worried he's hurt or something. He was coming right over and that was almost an hour ago."

Mac said he'd go himself since all the deputies were out. "Mac, swing by and pick me up first, would you? Please."

"Sure. No problem."

He was there in five minutes and sped off before she shut the car door. It took only ten minutes to get to the trailer park some fifteen miles away, with her hanging on for dear life.

Ina Mae was standing on the porch when they drove in and Mac slowed down. "Some men came a while ago," she yelled. "They weren't back there long, till they come barreling out like their tails were on fire. Time I got to my shotgun, they was gone plumb out of sight. I run back there and Dal, he ain't nowhere. His crutches was laying just outside the door, like he'd dropped them going down the steps. I was about to call you, sheriff. You gotta hurry. They went north and I think they took him, though I couldn't see him in the car. It's blue and white, a Ford, I think."

Jessie's voice caught in her throat. "Oh, Mac. What if they hurt him bad? What if they...?" She settled for a few choice curse words under her breath to get rid of the tension.

Ordinarily she'd feel sure he would kill at least one of them, but the shape he was in, he'd be helpless, and especially when they could paralyze him with just the right blow.

At noon, Dal had been taken. By 12:30, Mac sent out an APB to the State police. He spent the next few hours patrolling, remaining in touch with his five deputies, and she stayed with him. No blue and white car, no suspicious car at all. Around four that afternoon, a State Trooper radioed Mac. An abandoned blue and white car had been found on Highway 23, fifty miles south in Boone County. There was blood on the front seat.

Jessie started crying.

"Your deputy was in the back seat," the trooper went on. "We've got him. He said he disarmed one of the men and shot him, but they got away when he couldn't get out of the car to go after them."

Jessie leaped up and down in her seat. "Is he hurt?"

"Sounds like our boy," Mac said, pride in his voice. "Where's he now?"

"State headquarters, but we'll bring him home. We've got an APB out on the two men. He described them pretty good. Who is this guy anyway? He ain't no ordinary deputy, more like a wild ass Indian, you ask me. Told us things these guys could only have been thinking. They sure as hell wouldn't have told him."

Mac laughed. "Yeah, well you ought to work with the guy. He'd scare the pants off you, what he can do. But you can't have him. He's all ours." Mac went by Dal's and picked up his crutches before heading for his office in Cedarton.

Silent tears ran down Jessie's cheeks all the way back to the sheriff's office, where she waited till the State Trooper drove up with Dal in the front seat. She was the first to get to the car, Mac right behind her carrying the crutches. Despite her bandaged hands, she yanked the door open and threw herself at him.

"Easy there, Jess," he said, holding on to her as tightly as she did him.

"I was so afraid they'd hurt you."

"Well, I'm fine. Just help me get out of this car." He turned to the trooper. "Hey, thanks for the good job. I really appreciate it. Marines make the best lawmen in the country."

The guy stared at him. "How'd you know I was a Marine?"

"A lucky guess."

Jessie laughed. "You ought to be ashamed."

"Could you get me out of the car? I'm having a bit of a problem and I need you to pull my legs out. Okay?"

Staring into his eyes, heart thudding, she whispered, "Oh, Dal."

"It's okay. Just move 'em out, put my feet on the ground and give me the crutches."

Tears pouring, she did as he asked. He managed to stand with her help then moved very slowly on the crutches toward the office.

"Did they hurt you? Do you need to go to the hospital? Or a doctor? Or—well, *something?*"

"I'm all right. Just stiff. Legs went to sleep after I lay folded up in the back seat most of the day. Stop your crying right now. I mean it."

"Okay. I'm sorry. You tough piece of rawhide. I won't shed another tear for you."

He chuckled and moved easier. "See there, just needed to get the circulation back." But he sounded as relieved as she felt.

He glanced at her bandaged knees. "Between the two of us we've had ourselves quite a day. I think we need to take the night off and watch a movie or something. Got any popcorn at your place?"

"Just so happens I do. You bringing the beer?"

"You were at my place. Did you see any beer?"

"Then I'd better stop somewhere and get some. Oops, we don't either one have our car here. Guess we'll have to get Mac to take us by the office, I'll pick up my car, and we can stop on the way to my place and get some beer." She slanted a look to see how he might take the invite.

"Sounds like a plan to me. Got anything in mind for after the movie?" Those expressive eyes sparked all over the place.

"You better believe I do, big guy. But I'll let you guess what it might be. Oh, I forgot, you read minds, so bet you already know."

"I can see that you want to give me a massage since I've had such a rough day."

She laughed. "Well, we can start with that."

The movie was fun. He sprawled on the couch and she sat on the floor, leaned back, his hand spread on her shoulder. They laughed and she cried at the end of Safe Haven, definitely a chick flick, then she clicked off the remote and stood.

"Massage coming up, on the bed. Too sore or tired to get there?"

"For a massage, I'd crawl."

She went in to turn down the bed and take off her clothes before he made his slow steady way to her.

His eyes flared wide when she greeted him with no clothes on. "Know the bandages don't lend themselves to making this sexy, but I'll do the best I can under difficult circumstances."

He started to sit, but she stopped him, unbuttoned and unzipped his jeans and dragged them and his jockey shorts down to his knees.

"There, now you're as unsexy as I am. A bare assed man with boots, britches and jockeys down around his ankles. Not exactly an inviting sight. You may now sit and I'll finish undressing you."

"Best offer I've had today."

She laughed and after attempting to tug off his boots with her damaged hands, let him toe them off. The jeans she managed. "Arms up and I'll get rid of that shirt."

He obeyed and lay down. "Second time you've undressed me in twenty-four hours."

She picked up the bottle of lotion, started to pour some into her cut palm, and chuckled.

"What? What's so funny?"

"I think I'll have to give you a rain check on that massage."

"Oh, hell. I forgot all about your wounds. Can't have you trying to give me a rub down. You know what, Jess?"

"No. What?"

"There's only one thing left to do."

She crawled over him and stretched out full length, touching him everywhere she could. "What might that be?"

"This is a good start."

He turned over and took her in his arms. She trembled and held on tight. "I was so scared for you."

"Hush that, now. You ought to know I can take care of myself."

"Would you please do so this very minute, then." She fought every urge she had to cry and relaxed into his tight embrace.

8
CHAPTER

Dal kept his eyes open while he held Jess, afraid of what he might see if he closed them. He had come close to buying it or worse that afternoon. And when he went to sleep, he would pay for it with nightmares, no doubt about it.

Both Mac and Jess did exactly what he trusted them to do, and a Statie had found him. So everything was okay. No more thinking about it. Determined to spend most of the night making love to Jess, he got as far as responding to her charms through one mind-blowing orgasm, then while she brushed her fingertips over his face, and followed with a trail of soft kisses in gentle after-play, he fell asleep holding onto her.

In the morning when he awoke, he smelled bacon and eggs. Smiled. No telling what condition breakfast would be in. He gave her credit for trying, though.

He pulled on his jeans and a tee shirt, and made his painful way into the kitchen.

"Oh, good," she said. "Help." Her knees must be feeling better, she was wearing jeans and her favorite tee shirt that said, 'Be careful what you say, I'll put it in the newspaper.'

"I'm not much help when it comes to cooking, but I can do this." He moved to her, fingered her tee shirt aside and kissed her on the back of the neck. "Thank you. I can always count on you to know what's best for me."

"And would that be burnt eggs or undercooked bacon?"

"You know that's not what I meant."

She turned, raised her lips to his, and kissed him. "Yes, I know. Want a Honey Bun with your coffee?"

Laughing with him, she scraped the ruined eggs and bacon out the door for one of the feral cats that wandered through on a regular basis. Together they sat and drank coffee and ate their Honey Buns. He held his up after taking a bite. "At least it smells like bacon in here. Know why I like these so much?"

"No, I could never guess. They're easy?"

"Oh, that's dreadful. But what I was gonna say is, they remind me of another honey bun I know."

"And she's easy."

"That was worse. Feel up to going out and talking to some people, or are your injuries too painful?"

"Can't go today, have to work. But I can take you home so you can do whatever you want."

Her crystal-blue-eyed gaze held his, and he mentally shook himself. He could drown in there, easy. Dammit, he'd vowed not to get involved, not to get all mixed up in a relationship that couldn't go anywhere.

Then quit jumping in bed with her, you danged fool. Trouble was, he couldn't figure out a way to do that. Or not do it, or whatever.

She grinned. "What? What is it? You look so pensive."

"Nothing." He stuffed the last bite of sweet bun in his mouth and washed it down with the rest of his coffee. "Ready?"

She glanced around at the messy kitchen. "Sure, anytime you are. Next time around, it's your kitchen we'll mess up."

See there. Next time. Getting too familiar, taking him for granted. He'd put a stop to this soon as he could figure out how. Every time he tried, he needed something from her or got horny or both. Not any way to treat a woman like her in the first place.

"Dal, are you okay? You've been acting so strange this morning. You sure everything is okay? I mean, you'd tell me, wouldn't you?"

"Don't mess with me, woman." Though half serious, he attempted a light teasing tone and she must've figured it out. She shut up, went to fetch that safari kit she carried around on her back, and returned with an angry look on her face.

"Well, we're not waiting on me." She headed out, leaving him to get the crutches, fumble with the door—opening and closing, making sure it was locked. Served him right. She'd have helped him if he'd kept his big mouth shut. But hell, he didn't need any help. Did he? Big man.

Not one to pout or sull up like a 'possum, she was soon chattering on about one thing, then another, and him half listening, while she drove toward his place to drop him off. He could do some of the interviews that didn't involve traipsing a mile in the woods. Stuff they were supposed to do together the day before. She, however, didn't let it be.

"You know what? If you want me to go with you, tomorrow's Saturday. More people likely to be home, and I have the entire day free."

He was silent, contemplating his earlier vow and this sensible suggestion. Folks who worked all week were the ones they hadn't found so far. Could have more luck catching them on a Saturday.

"Or not," she injected into the silence.

"No, no. I was actually thinking of something else. Sounds like a great idea. We can make a day of it, maybe check all the names off the list and find out more about that Crowe family's connection to this. And I want to learn about our visitors yesterday. Bastards could've hurt or killed either one of us, but that wasn't their intention."

"Oh, is that right? Glad you told me. So we're good to go in the morning?" Relief rang clear in her tone. "The idea of you clomping around, up and down steps, and long rocky walks to some of those houses off in the woods, without me there to look after you. Well, I don't like that much." She glanced at him. "And before you swell all up like a toad frog and tell me you can take care of yourself, look at it this way. If things were reversed, would you want me taking that kind of chance?"

"Hell, no. But that's different."

"Why? Why is it different?"

"Because... well, dammit, just because it is, that's all."

"Cause you're a big lunkhead of a man, stubborn and capable of doing everything without help from anyone, while I'm a helpless, stupid female who can't walk and chew gum?"

His face wrinkled into one big frown. "I never said any of that. You go off taking chances all the time. Pisses me off, but I don't tell you to stop."

"Ha, that's a laugh. You're forever telling me what I should and shouldn't do."

"Only when it involves investigating one of my cases, like maybe you were a detective or something."

"That something being a trained investigative reporter."

He clamped his mouth shut, tired of the argument he wouldn't win anyway, even if he wanted to. Deep down inside, where he filed stuff he didn't want to admit, he felt easy with her, mostly glad to have her along. And now, dammit, no matter how he objected, he felt less than capable with these damned crutches and what the doc was holding over his head. If something happened, it might be much worse than yesterday, and he'd be damned glad to have her along. Still, no matter the danger, he would not sit in that trailer for four weeks doing nothing. He'd just be extra careful, that's all.

Her words interrupted his thoughts. "Why don't you get online and check out those two guys who pulled the robbery? You might find a connection to one of the families on our list. Sam told you Mathon moved here from Hot Springs. You've got their names, plus this Crowe name you heard at the crime scene. The dead guy may have been identified by now, and you could run him down online as well. Didn't you get in their heads and learn either one of your attacker's names or their intent?"

"Too busy getting knocked around. But I'll do some work from home till my babysitter's free."

She punched him hard on the arm, said "Ow," and shook her fist. "Hurt me more than you, you big—"

"Lunkhead," he supplied in a sour voice. "That's assault, by the way. Good thing it wasn't the arm you shot me in. You know the penalty for assaulting a law enforcement officer?"

She mimed 'I shot you?' Rubbed his arm with the tips of her fingers, reached up and tweaked his ear. "No, what is it?" in that soft, bedroom voice that caused his groin to tighten. "You going to handcuff me and do bad things to me?"

"Watch it. By tonight I'm gonna be bored as hell." He said that without thinking, wanted to bite his tongue. He had as much as invited her to spend the night.

"I'll keep that in mind."

She steered around Ina Mae's thriving garden and stopped next to the trailer to let him out.

"Don't forget to charge up your cell," she called before driving off.

Damned woman, determined to take care of him. He smiled, carefully made his way up the steps and into the trailer where he plugged in his cell, lowered himself in the recliner, and opened the laptop.

He began by Googling Reilly Imports, LLC. Why the hell was John Reilly hanging on to twenty acres next to contaminated land and water? Why had he bought the land in the first place? On the home page of the company, he clicked on 'about' and learned that John and his wife Delia Miller Reilly lived in the suburbs of Kansas City, had been married thirty-four years, exactly the time that had passed since the diamond heist, and had two children, both grown and involved with the business. Daughter Claire Reilly Duncan was CFO, son Rand was First VP and unmarried.

Delia Miller? One of the men who took the diamonds was named Wesley Miller. Pretty common name, but since he didn't believe in coincidences, he made quick notes about the possible connection of Delia Miller. Sam had said there was another woman running with the Wells and Miller gang. Said she was Wesley Miller's sister. He grinned at that.

Looking away from the computer through the window, not seeing the creek or surrounding trees, but hearing something one of the men who grabbed him had said while they were arguing. They'd definitely mentioned a Merle, no last name. Julie Crowe's son, according to Jess. Then he checked out Mathon Wells, the other robber, in the 1980 Census online. At the time, Mathon lived with wife Sara and a son named Lennie, age two, in Cedarton.

Julie and Merle Crowe now lived on property listed as owned by Mathon Wells. What the hell? All these people tied together with a pretty bow, but what it meant he wasn't sure yet. Perhaps it was all about something that had nothing to do with the diamond heist in Harrison, but on the other hand, if he stuck to his no coincidences rule, it was all hooked together, including John Reilly, his import business, and the body found a few days ago on his property.

Jasper. Dammit, yes. Jasper somebody was the body. One of the men who took him had thought the name while arguing with the other man. Shit, he wished they hadn't knocked him around so much. It buggered up his memory.

He glanced toward the charging phone on the kitchen table. Trailer was small, but big enough he'd have to get up to get it. He needed a cup of coffee too, so he decided to just hop on one foot the three or four steps to the kitchen, start a pot, and make his phone call.

Coffee perking, he dropped into the only kitchen chair and punched in two on his phone, reaching the sheriff's cell.

Mac picked up, and he asked him if there'd been any results on identifying the body.

"We're circulating his dental x-rays now. Be lucky if that turns up anything. His teeth haven't been worked on in recent years. A couple of fillings that look like they were put in while he was in his early teens, so maybe we'll get lucky. I take it this means you're working on this case."

"Well, yeah, doing what I do. What I can do, that is, sitting in this trailer. Tell you what, Sheriff. You might run the names Jasper no-last-name and Lennie Wells through NCIC. They'd be local, so you could rule a lot of them out. I got me a hunch these old boys have records."

"Don't suppose you'd care to tell me where you got the names?" He paused, and Dal said nothing. "Didn't think so. Reckon you might just be worth your salt, boy. You don't do anything crazy, and I'll see you stay on partial active duty somehow. Would your doc go along with that till your next checkup?"

Dal's heart warmed to the old man. Doing his best to make sure he didn't have to hire someone to replace Dal. "Thanks, Mac. I appreciate that. I'll phone him, get him to write this up as desk duty for four weeks. How would that be?"

"That'll work, but don't you go running around doing nothing dumb."

"Jess and I are going out tomorrow, but she'll do the interviews and I'll just provide a badge and a vehicle. How's that?"

"Sounds okay, but I know how the two of you can get in trouble without even trying. So you tell her for me I said no funny stuff. And keep her blamed hands off your weapon."

Dal cringed. Jess would never be allowed to forget what she hadn't done in the first place. "Okay, and I appreciate this, Mac. I really do."

"Stow it, boy. I'll let you know soon as we find out anything about our Jasper Doe."

Jessie arrived at the newspaper office and entered a bee hive of activity, as was always the case on a Friday. People dropped by with last minute ads and society notes, local gossip columns and engagement and anniversary photos. As usual, Parker shut himself up in his office editing news stories and features and ignoring the phone, leaving the newly hired temp to handle the excess calls. Jess and Wendy typeset and edited everything that came in the mail. Some of the local columnists were seventy and eighty years old and determined to handwrite every word. Parker didn't have the heart to tell them no. Readers loved the columns these folks wrote about the old days and all their visiting kin, so it was up to Wendy and sometimes Jess to decipher the handwriting and get it set and edited. The place was a damned madhouse, and she thrived on it.

When a call came on her cell phone, she let it go to voice mail and didn't check it till they took a quick break at their desks to eat a sandwich and drink a Coke. It was a message from Harrison PD with a cell number and the name of someone to contact.

Up to her ears in work, but anxious to learn what was going on, she punched one and Dal answered on the first ring without so much as a hello. Just launched into the conversation.

"Tell me it's exciting. I'm so tired of Google I could throw something."

"Here's a cell number and name at Harrison PD. They've got something for us, and I don't have time to call them. You'd better share this with me. You got that? 'Cause I dug it up."

"Hey, you know you can trust me."

"Bullshit." She hung up because the small room echoed with the ringing of phones. Wendy talked on one while the temp held one call then spoke to someone else. "Good God, you'd think people wouldn't wait till Friday to get all their business done with."

Wendy laughed, hung up. "You want to stay in the office all week and take care of this stuff? Parker won't, and neither will I."

"I'll take one." Jess punched a flashing button. "*Observer*, may I help you?"

"I need to talk to someone… about the story in the paper." A shaky woman's voice, wispy, frightened.

"This is Jess. You mean the story about the stolen diamonds? Is that why you're calling?" She punched her recorder on.

"I guess… I mean, I think I may have seen something, but I'm afraid."

"Ma'am, what are you afraid of?"

"There's a lot goes on over at that dreadful place. Folks hadn't ought to be messing about over there, but they are. Liable to make all their hair fall out. Since you wrote that blamed story, some nights there's flash-lights all over the place. A long while back pickups came and went at night. In and out, in and out. Stopped a few years ago. Now we've got ghosts wandering around."

"What's your name? Maybe I can come see you, you can tell me all about it."

"Oh, no. You mustn't come here. Someone will see you."

"I could meet you somewhere. Tell me your name."

"Oh, no. You can't put it in the paper. You gotta promise me you won't put none of this in the paper."

"Well, ma'am, you did call me, and I write for the paper. Why did you call if you don't want me to put it in the paper?"

The phone on the other end clicked off. Caller ID didn't help much, but she punched in star sixty-nine. No one answered. She glanced down at the red light on the electronic recorder she kept connected to the desk phone. Folks nowadays pretty much blocked their numbers and names anyway, especially those with something to hide or those with a story they didn't want credited to them. Dal might make something out of the recorded call though. He often could get information from a tone of voice, the words used, the way a caller strung sentences together. She sure wouldn't want to try to keep something from him.

About five-thirty, they wrapped things up and one by one trailed out of the office and headed home. Monday would be worse, and they'd be there till midnight laying out the paper. Actually, they designed and put the pages together on the computer. From there it went down to the daily in Harrison where it was printed on Tuesday. In the Jeep, she dialed

Dal and got his voice mail. He must be talking to someone. He was bad about not taking a call while on another. Said it was rude. So she drove on home, expecting him to return her call. He didn't.

Dammit, had something else happened? This was getting scary. In her living room, while she was stowing the backpack and kicking off her shoes, her cell rang. It was Dal.

Her breath whooshed out in relief.

"Sorry. I was on with Harrison PD for the second time."

"Where are you? I hear traffic."

"I'm on my way back from Harrison."

"Dal."

"Before you get all bent out of shape, I was at the police station. No steps. You gotta hear some of this. Not on the phone. I'm coming to your place. Can I bring something to eat?"

"If you want to eat, you'd better."

"Pizza okay?"

"Sure. When?"

"I'll be another hour or so. Are your doors locked?"

"Why?"

"Is that an answer to my question?"

On her feet, she padded to the front of the house. "I'm locking the door this minute, the rest are locked. What is it?"

"Tell you when I get there."

"Dal?"

He was gone. For a full minute or more, she stared at her cell phone and muttered under her breath words she seldom used aloud. She finished off the tirade with 'the big lunkhead.' Even though she often wanted to shake him till his teeth rattled, if anything bad happened to him she would be fit to be tied. That wasn't something she admitted aloud to anyone, him especially. Most times not even to herself.

She'd ruined the life of one man she loved with her incessant need to dig up a story no matter the consequences. When it came right down to it, she couldn't be trusted. Her deepest fear remained that somewhere, sometime a chance at that big story would come along and she'd run with it. What if she couldn't resist? What if she betrayed Dal after letting herself love him? Despite all her self-assurances that it wouldn't happen, the possibility haunted her nightmares. The worst part of all that? It was much too late because she already loved him. But he wasn't about to trust her or love her. So they were both getting what they wanted from the relationship. Or were they?

Great. She'd become a little nooky on the side.

While waiting, she peeled out of her jeans, shirt, and bra and changed into a sleep shirt. The cuts on her knees were healing, and she now had them plastered with Band Aids. Made her look like a badly patched inner tube. At night, she smeared medication on her palms and slipped on soft white cotton gloves. She dug out the MP3 with the woman's phone call on it and listened to it closely. Nothing else there that she could hear, but she'd bet Dal could. Not creepy enough that he could read crime scenes like they were taking place in front of his eyes, it was like he could crawl inside someone's head and hear what they meant as well as what they said. Even voice recordings.

Creepy. Plus—*weird.*

A bank of thunderclouds rolled in before the sun set, thunder rumbling so loud the house shook. Headlights swept across the front windows while she was in the bedroom. Had to be Dal.

The rain turned loose before he could get out of the car, and she ran across the grass barefoot to carry whatever he'd brought from Harrison. Soaked to the skin, she peered in the car, took the box he handed over.

"Wondered how I was going to handle that." The dome light revealed a grin that turned her heart upside down. "You're wet. Look like a drowned rat."

"Thanks. Put the pizza in this box"

"Yes, ma'am. Appreciate the help."

She hurried toward the house, leaving him to deal on his own. When he reached the door, she handed him a towel. He vigorously rubbed his wet head, peeking out through a gap in the towel. God, he was cute as a rain-drenched puppy.

Eyes flashing with appreciation, he settled his gaze on the soaked shirt clinging to her figure. "I was wrong about the rat thing." Again the smile.

She snapped her fingers in front of his face. "Quit staring at my titties and concentrate, we've got a lot of work to do."

He tossed her the towel. "Sorry, lost control there for a minute. Dry off and relax. It's Friday night. I thought we might kick back, eat pizza, drink beer, and get a little."

"This isn't a romance novel." Even so, she couldn't help but admire his pecs and abs and six pack, all hugged by the drenched tee shirt. If he wasn't a romance cover, she didn't know who was.

God, Jess, get a grip.

To get back at him, she ran a hand down his chest, over his waistband and stopped just short of invading his privacy. "And I thought you were sexy in your uniform."

"Goddammit, Jess."

She danced away, stuck out her tongue. "Your turn, big guy."

"I thought we had work to do."

"First, I'll get out the beer and some plates. I'm starved." Digging the wet pizza box out of the bank box half filled with files and evidence bags, she moved about in the kitchen putting out the food while he poked around removing folders and piling stuff on the coffee table.

"I have something interesting, too. Come on and let's eat this before it gets cold."

He came to the table and lowered himself into a chair, discarding the crutches and stretching his long legs out.

She watched him closely. "How's the head?"

"It's fine. Only hurts when I breathe." He lifted a slice of pizza and took a bite before continuing. "Detective Morris dug up some interesting info. Don't know how much of it will help. He thinks there was a rash of robberies about the time of our heist, and he's been working on the theory that they were committed by the same men who took the diamonds. I'm not sure I agree, but thought we could dig deeper and see what we think. If so, there may be a whole lot more stuff than a handful of sparkly stones. None of it ever turned up, and those two guys died in prison, so...." He shrugged and chomped off another huge bite of pizza. "Mmm, God, I'm hungry."

"So he let you bring the evidence back with you?"

"Oh, hell yeah. The case is so old and the robbers are dead, so there's no reason to worry about chain of evidence or the like."

She chewed thoughtfully, took a sip of beer. "So why is he so intent on solving it?"

"Because of all the loot. He thinks it's been hidden somewhere. And that maybe there was a regular organization working at the time. Probably doesn't matter much about that now, it was so long ago. But it might be fun to find this stash and recover things lost for more than thirty years. Besides, seeing the things people would steal then could be interesting. These guys wouldn't want to go to prison for a few diamonds, but they might be willing to serve their time if, when they got out, they'd have a million or more in contraband stowed away. A million dollars in the eighties was a hell of a lot of money."

"Speak for yourself. It's still a lot to me." She tilted her head. "But with them dead, how can he hope to find their hidey hole?" Something pecked at her memory, but she couldn't quite grasp it. Something she'd heard recently. But what?

"'Cause someone else knows where it is." He glanced at her. "I'm sorry, but I couldn't help it. You think you know something?"

She nodded. "If you're so smart, then what is it? I can't come up with it, but it's driving me nuts. If this someone knows where it is, why hasn't he taken it and run?"

"That is the sixty-four million dollar question. I have a theory." He scooped up a third slice of pizza and attacked it.

"Glad to see you haven't lost your appetite." She meant that sincerely, but he took it as a jibe and gave her a long harsh look.

"Why in hell would I lose my appetite?"

She dropped it with a shrug. Changed the subject. "I have something, too, though I didn't discover it. Just answered the phone." She told him about the call.

"Nothing much there," he said, and drank the rest of his beer in one big long gulp.

"More?"

"No, thanks. What do you think she was talking about?"

"A reach? I think there's been a lot of activity around SEFOR, and I'll bet she lives within eyesight of the place. I think we've got treasure hunters. And I think I know why John Reilly wanted to own that property, after listening to the caller and Allie and August Sims. If you own property, then you can do a lot on it without anyone bothering you. It belongs to someone else, you could get shot for trespassing."

He eyed her closely. "So?"

"Where better to stash stuff till you get it where it's going than that old abandoned plant? And all you have to do is cross your own property to access the place." She snapped her fingers. "Pickup trucks. She said 'bad enough all them pickups in there at night some years back, now we got ghosts, too.' What could that mean? Hauling stuff in. Keeping it there till they moved it."

"Wow, that's a big leap."

"Not so big. Hear what she says about their hair falling out. That tells me she's worried about radioactivity, which means she lives within sight of the reactor plant, ergo John Reilly's property. It's only an educated guess. I recorded the conversation, maybe you can make some more out of it. I'm going to check my list to see if there's someone living close to that place who might've made this call. Then we can talk to them tomorrow."

The lights flickered, lightning flashed, and thunder rattled the windows. Something scraped at a screen in the kitchen, and Jess tensed.

"Just a tree branch," he said. "Let's listen to that recording."

She handed him her MP3 and he stuck in the ear buds. While he listened, she checked her list on the computer till she came to the three mailboxes the closest to SEFOR. Of course, one was August and Allie Sims, the couple who had given her so much information. Two others and then it was a quarter of a mile before more houses and boxes. The Reilly property lay on the opposite side of the road from the Durning's and the Carter's. It had to be someone living at one of those two residences who'd made the call. Because of the curve in the road coming from the south just before SEFOR, it was not possible to see the grounds of the plant from that direction.

Dal listened to the audio a few times, scribbling fast notes while she poked through the stuff from Harrison, separating evidence from files, then poring through the files until he looked up.

"Okay, want to hear what I think about this phone call?"

She dropped a folder and went to where he still sat at the table. "Why don't you come over to the couch where it's more comfortable?"

"Yeah, in a minute. First this. You see here?" He indicated his scribbled notes. "She says about the story, but I'm not sure that's what she really means. It's like she's asking you when she says that. Wanting you to say what she really needs to talk about. That in itself isn't too unusual. A lot of people end a sentence with a question when it really isn't. But she goes on to say she thinks she may have seen something? Again that inflection, that rising of her tone like she's asking. While this is the way some younger people talk, you rarely hear an older person do it unless it is a question."

"Do you think she knows more than she's telling?"

"I do. But she's not sure about revealing it, so she's questioning you. What is it you really need to know? Her question, not mine. Usually age is difficult to tell on the phone in middle aged people, but the very young and the very old are easier to identify. This woman is fairly old. I'd say she sits in a chair by her window and spends a lot of time watching people come and go. We need to find her. That remark about the hair falling out? You're right, she lives near SEFOR. That's where she's seen something unusual. Again, you're right. To get in there, they could easily be coming in from the back part of the twenty acres Reilly owns. And the pickup trucks? Damn, Jess."

She nodded. "Then all these people work for or with John Reilly?"

"Well, only if our theory is right and he's involved in a theft ring. He has a son, could be him up to no good."

"So, John or his son up to their neck in this. I think our caller is either a Durning or a Carter." She showed Dal the map she'd sketched out, pinpointing where some of the families lived around SEFOR.

"Okay, you're right. You're right about this chair, too. I have to get out of it and to the couch. Besides, all our files are there. I believe I'll join you."

She moved to give him easy access to the end nearest the kitchen, and he sank down with a deep sigh of relief. "Dammit, I forgot that last slice of pizza, unless you want it."

"Nope, but I'll get it for you. That's just this once. You know I don't usually tote and carry to a man, unless of course his leg is broken." She jumped to her feet, glanced at him quickly. "Oops, sorry, I didn't mean to make light of it."

"Why not? It's better than crying."

She trailed a hand over his shoulder on her way to fetch the pizza. His muscles tightened under her touch. She wanted to ask more, say more about the headaches he was having. It worried her a lot, but she didn't know how to tell him so. He hated so to be fussed over. So she asked, "Need anything else?" and left it at that.

"Nope, thanks."

Dal would have enjoyed more from Jess than a brief touch, but her desire to nurture him was disturbing. He stiffened in an effort not to react to her fingers moving over him. She touched him a lot, and it usually soothed him, but sometimes it made him horny as hell. This was one of those times. Yet he let it run its course and paged through one of the old files.

Though he itched to work on the murder case, Mac had been firm. Desk duty or else, so he'd have to let the other deputies do the field investigating. They'd bring anything to him he wanted. Since he was now sure the murder was related to the diamond heist, he might be able to get in on some of the investigation if he and Jess could turn up something more definitive than wild suppositions.

"Did you ever see such a variety of stuff being stolen? And all within one summer. I think Detective Morris is right in thinking it was all one gang. That reinforces our theories." She rifled through several files on cases. "We've got coin collections, taken from four different houses in Boone County. Necklaces and rings, mostly gold, silver, or diamonds, rubies, emeralds, some antiques and the like." She picked up another couple of files. "Good grief, collections of ceramics from two different homes in Harrison, valued at tens of thousands of dollars. Hummels, pre-World War II Japanese figurines."

Dal opened another file. "Can go you one better. Belt buckles, but only special ones, like rodeo championships, race drivers', sharpshooters'. Holy shit, I never knew some of this stuff even existed. Question is, how did these guys know it? And how did they figure out who had such shit and that it was worth anything?"

The question had no reply, and so she said nothing.

The storm moved away, quieted down. They continued to pore through the folders. He tossed one down and poked around through the meager evidence collected at the crime scenes. A plain kitchen towel in a plastic bag drew his attention. He ripped off the initialed tape and reached in. The minute his fingers touched the cloth, a violent emotion rattled his teeth. As he often did, he clutched the item tighter, searching for a reason for the terror slamming through him.

The face of a woman with cropped sandy hair, eyes wide with fear, lips moving in a frantic plea. "Here, take it. Take everything. Please don't hurt me, or him. Don't hurt him. He's only a helpless boy."

Moving his hand over the cloth, he becomes one with her, sees what she sees . A man, not too tall, broad and strong, wears a mask. The face of Richard Nixon. A stocking cap covers his hair, gloves on his hands. A black outfit. None of his skin shows anywhere. Dal hovers like a wraith, not replying to her for she can never hear him as he hears her. A strange feeling washes through him. Why is he capable of this mad ability? Yet he can't stop what happened, what will happen.

The woman watches the intruder move toward a young man seated in a wheelchair making pitiful whimpering sounds. She breaks and runs toward the boy, throws herself over him. Her terror so intense Dal lets go the towel, covers his face with both hands, and takes deep breaths.

Jess touched him on the shoulder. Waited. She knew not to bring him out, but once he let go, she frequently touched him, never saying a word for the longest time. He couldn't remember when she had started to do that. At first, he'd frightened her making these spiritual contacts. Now that she knew what was going on she handled it pretty well, considering what he must look like while he walked with the dead.

"Shit. I hope to hell they didn't hurt that kid."

"Which case?" she asked, pawing through the files.

"Reynolds, I think. I don't always get names. Took her ring, a gold one."

"Here it is. Nope. Nothing here about assault. Another thing I'm sure you've noticed already. They're not armed. They just use brute force to frighten people. Or they go in when the house is empty. They don't seem to care, either way. Lucky someone didn't pull out a gun and shoot one of them. Most people being armed like they are."

Dal shook off the last of the reaction with a shudder. "If they get caught, it's not armed robbery. Someone smarter than they are is setting this up. In this case, there was only one perp. How the hell does he control an entire family? If these are all the work of Wells and Miller, then one remains outside, or he's off somewhere else pulling a job. Let's check dates."

She made a chart from the files, including dates and times and what was taken, and they soon learned that out of the twenty-some odd robberies that summer of 1980, four of them were pulled off one after the other in the same time frame as another set of four. Did that mean two men pulling separate jobs, or were there more than the two who were caught for the diamond heist?

He leaned over to take a look at her chart, and she penned in the value of items taken from each score. Whistled. "Christ, no wonder they were willing to spend time in jail. Wouldn't be more than a couple of years actually served, since they never tied them to any of the jobs except the diamond heist, plus no armed robbery. No one actually thought to put them together till Detective Morris got hold of the cold case. Like I said, the one running this wasn't the ordinary stupid criminal type. And I'll bet he never got his hands dirty."

She tapped the pen against her teeth. "So he pulled the strings, arranged the jobs, planned how they'd be carried out. And he must be the someone who could help them get rid of the stuff 'cause he already had a buyer. John Reilly… or his son."

"We'd have to prove it, but it only makes sense if he took care of delivering the stuff while they were away. I have a hunch none of this stuff is around anymore. I think it's long gone to whoever they stole it for. Maybe even the diamonds. He'd have no reason to leave them hidden all these years. Unless he was in jail for something unrelated."

"Or unless the two men who went to jail never told where the diamonds were."

"Once these guys were killed in that riot, why didn't he then… shit, you're right. He didn't know where they hid them. That's why your first story brought them back. Wells and Miller were caught after they hid them and before they told anyone. Had to be. But he figures they used the drop spot at SEFOR."

"If that's true, how come he's still looking?" Brow furrowed, she checked the last few files. "Wait. What if it's not my story but something else that has them crawling out of the woodwork?"

"Like what?"

"Like someone found out where the diamonds are hidden. One of those men, or maybe both of them, were looking for something valuable. That happened before I wrote the diamond heist story." She jotted into her chart what was taken that year, the value, when and where. "Okay, notice how many of these robberies are diamonds, but all in pieces of jewelry except the one? They seem to have an affinity for them."

"Sure, why not? They're the most valuable item, non-breakable, small, and easy to hide. Take the stones out of the settings so they couldn't be identified from police reports. Some of this other stuff almost seems like an afterthought. Took it 'cause they liked the looks of it. And it isn't really worth that much. Maybe our guys weren't so smart after all. Look at this one. Championship cups for golf tournaments. Not gold or silver or platinum. Just pretty and durable. You notice that none of these items are things that would grow mold or rot when hidden away for several years."

"What if…?" She shook her head, scribbled with the pen a moment. "What if these guys were like you said, not smart enough to tie their shoes. But they were sent in for one specific item, say valuable stones, but told they could take anything else they wanted personally. Just don't leave a trace, don't carry a weapon, and don't hurt anyone."

"Okay, that's entirely possible, considering the stuff taken. So what we need to do is identify those items, then we'll be able to pinpoint what sort of person might have arranged these robberies. He had to be someone who knew the victims, their habits, their collections, or items they owned."

"I'm still betting on John Reilly." She glanced his way, and in that moment, wind howled around the eaves with an ungodly sound, and the lights went out.

9
CHAPTER

The room turned black as pitch, without a blink or a warning. Something that happened often during a storm. With all that was going on, though, it could be something else. Someone else. Caught engrossed in studying the files, Dal fumbled about, but his flashlight was with his utility belt, over the back of a kitchen chair with his weapon. Amazing how dark it was in the country when the lights went out. Blinking his eyes, he waited a moment. Sometimes the power came right back on, but not this time.

"Can you see anything?" Jess asked. "Is it… just a power outage?"

"Probably. Maybe. But I can't see any more than you can. I may have some odd talents, but seeing in the dark isn't one of them."

"Then you stay where you are, and I'll feel my way around till I locate a flashlight. I don't want you falling."

The concern she put into those last few words flew all over him. Why did she always have to play the caretaker? Like it was up to her to protect him. "Stay still. At least let me get my gun." The anger left as quickly as it had come, to be replaced by an unexpected emotion. After years of having no one who cared for him, a wife he loved but couldn't save from her addiction, this woman touched him where it mattered. A place he thought no longer existed. And his throat stung until he couldn't say a word.

What the hell was he going to do about her? Despite all his efforts, she had wormed her way into his heart and soul.

"Dal? You okay?"

"Yep," he croaked. "I'm okay. Not really afraid of the dark. You getting closer to finding a flashlight?" If it was any more than the storm taking out the power, they'd have known by now. He relaxed.

"There was one in the drawer here by the stove. Yep, here it is." She flipped it on and it emitted a pale glimmer.

"Damn, you need to light a candle to see that."

"Maybe we ought to just go to bed."

Sounded damned good to him. He'd had enough for the day. His head pounded, his eyes burned. He was so tired of feeling like this. Reminded him of the days he'd spent coming out of recovery after the shooting.

"Crap," she said.

"What is it?"

"Cell phone." A light flashed on from the kitchen. "Cell phones make super flashlights. Funny we neither one thought of that."

She came to him, lay a hand on his leg when he leaned back and closed his eyes. "You can stay over if you want to. I promise I won't jump your bones. You look done in."

"Damn, and here I was wishing you would jump my bones. I know I ought to go home, but the more I think about this guy actually coming in your house to threaten you, the more concerned I am. Think I'll just bed down here tonight." Yeah, best excuse he could come up with for staying with her. Not that he felt much like a bodyguard at the moment.

"In case I need protecting?" She leaned against him and rubbed his chest. "Are you armed and dangerous?"

"I'm armed, but too damned wore out to be dangerous. I'd better just sleep on the couch."

"With your long legs? Come on to bed. I promise I won't bother you. And let me get you some Tylenol."

He stretched out a bit, dug in his pocket. "I've got Tramadol. I need heavy duty shit tonight." Why in the hell did he let himself get into these situations with her?

With the rain hammering against the windows, he climbed to his feet and hobbled into her bedroom, her leading and lighting the way. He dry swallowed the pill and peeled out of his damp clothes, all of them, and lay down, pulled the sheet up to his chin. The bed floated around beneath him, and he whirled off into the dark. Her crawling over him to lie on the other side was the last thing he remembered until he opened his eyes to a bright sunny morning.

The bed was empty, but she rattled around in the other room, attempting to be quiet. The opiate was still hard at work on the pain, so he felt pretty good. When he sat on the edge of the bed and reached for his clothes, they were gone.

"Where's my britches?"

She came in smiling, so pretty with her hair curling around her face and hanging loose down her back, blue eyes bright, and that grin he always felt was just for him.

"In the dryer with mine. Want to go watch them play together?"

"Dammit, how do you do that?"

Wide-eyed, she stared at him in all innocence. "Do what?"

"Make me want to grab you before I even have something to eat."

She moved into the room, close enough for him to span her waist with both hands, which he did. "Now that you've grabbed me, whatcha got in mind, big guy?"

"Well, since we both know there's nothing to eat in this house, how about second choice?"

She kissed him lightly on the forehead, and before he could take it any farther, danced out of his reach. "Second choice, huh? Soon as your britches are dry, I'll be back with them. But just to warn you, I'm staying out of reach. We've got a big day, and we need to get going."

He groaned. "I'm naked. How am I supposed to get to the bathroom to shave and all?"

"Hmm. I'll admit a naked man on crutches is a really silly sight, everything sort of flopping around and all. But it's that or wait till the dryer buzzes. Up to you."

"Everything flopping around? Fine choice of words. Well, I can't wait." He fetched the crutches and hopped right past her and into the bathroom while she laughed.

"Funny. Make fun of a poor cripple. Aren't you ashamed?" he asked through the door.

She cracked it open. "Wasn't that so much as watching what bobbled up and down. Sort of doing a bat and balls dance."

He threw a towel at her, grabbed another from the basket in the corner and wrapped it around his middle before picking up one of his razors. Another bad sign. When had he started leaving his stuff lying around her place? Not exactly a sin or a commitment in this day and age, but still....

By the time he finished showering, which wasn't easy jiggling around on one foot, she'd stacked his folded clothes inside the door. Damn wonder she didn't reach through the curtain and poke him. A bit disappointing.

He was sitting on the toilet putting on his jeans when she tapped on the door. "Need some help in there?"

"That would be nice." He grinned, thinking maybe she'd take pity and come help him into, or out of, his pants, but she only laughed.

"I know you can dress yourself, Dallas Starr. You live alone and manage quite well. Now get cracking."

Within a half hour, they were in his vehicle and on the road. Her too tight to spring for the gas. Couldn't blame her. They probably didn't pay her much at that rinky-dink paper. It would be hard to make ends meet, and he really didn't mind doing the driving. At times, he wondered how a beautiful, sensitive, and intelligent woman like her could've made such a mess out of her life. It wasn't like a situation she couldn't control had arisen. No, she'd been in control the entire time. Getting a story no matter that it ruined her life.

She still was in control, and that's why he would not get serious about her. It didn't matter that he had been attracted to her since the day, new in the department, he piled out of Mac's car and saw her sitting on a boulder waiting to lead them up to their first shared crime scene. A reporter for God's sake. At a crime scene. Sunlight splashed her streaked hair and highlighted her features. He'd heard of love at first sight, but that was a crock. Lust at first sight was a better description of how he'd felt that day. Like he'd been socked low in the gut so hard it stole away his breath. Yet she couldn't be trusted in the relationship department any more than he could.

So lust it was. They deserved each other.

Still ruminating on that first meeting, he pulled into the local McDonald's drive-thru and ordered two large coffees and two sausage biscuits.

"I don't want one of those." She eyed him suspiciously while they waited for their order.

"Didn't order you one."

"Just so you know, that's not a real egg. And the meat? Mystery."

"This early in the morning, who cares?"

"It's almost nine-thirty. And a beautiful morning it is."

The tree-covered mountains, freshly washed by last night's storm, leaves filling out overnight to dress the bare branches in multi-shades of green, the grass a matching hue, flowers blooming as if by magic. She rolled down her window and took a deep breath, glanced at him. He had his eyes closed, head leaned back.

Dammit, if this thing messed him up she was going to be doubly pissed at the guy upstairs. Made her so frigging mad when the good guys had to pay so much more than the bad ones. And Dal was a good guy. Besides, she liked that they had the kind of rapport where one played devil's advocate just to help them both think better. Wasn't sure what she'd do without him if it came to that.

The boy inside reached both coffees through and Jess touched Dal's shoulder. He jumped, glanced at her, then accepted the two cups, passed her one, put the other in the console, and took the sack. Placing it between his legs, he pulled away from the window a few feet, stopped and opened his coffee. Sipping cautiously to check the heat, he tossed a pill in his mouth and swallowed twice, placed the cup back in the console.

"We've got plenty of time. Why don't you park there and enjoy your breakfast?"

Without replying, he whipped the car into a slot and opened the sack. Snuck a peek at her. "Sure you don't want one of these?" He waved a stuffed biscuit at her.

She shook her head. "I'm good." Not like him to be so agreeable to her suggestions. He appeared simply too beat to argue. That worried her.

"Reilly is in the import/export business," she ventured after he inhaled one sausage biscuit and dug the other one out.

"Yeah, so?"

"He'd have a lot of contacts. Collectors, sellers, prices." She watched him closely, waiting for his reaction.

"And?"

"When did he buy that property?"

"I can't remember. Did you ever tell me?"

Dammit, she was leading him by the hand through this, and he still wasn't getting it. Maybe if she had something hanging over her head like he did, she wouldn't be thinking straight either.

"No, but it's not like you not to want to know."

"Just stop playing games. I'm not in the mood. When did he buy the property?"

"Actually, late in 1979. Around November, if I remember. I've got it in my notes."

"Okay. So the following summer there's a rash of robberies of collectible items in the area. And he marries Delia Miller." He took a ravenous bite of the breakfast biscuit.

"Could it be that easy?"

"Maybe so. It's only a tiny bit of the puzzle, though. If it's all connected, the diamond heist, the murder, then whoever knows the location of the stash is probably who killed our John Doe."

"But the murder isn't your case. And why kill after all the years of being so careful not to? Or….” She paused, peered at him over the rim of her cup. “Those two had nothing to do with the robberies, did they?”

“Don’t think so. Too young. While we’re talking to these people, I want to take another look at the crime scene.” He chewed the last bite of his breakfast, keyed the ignition, and drove out of the lot heading north toward Dogtown Road.

She clamped her lips together and said nothing. It would only make him mad if she reminded him that he wasn’t supposed to be in the field, and it sure wouldn’t stop him doing it. Best if she went along in case he did something dumb and got hurt. At least she’d be there to pick him up. If she dared hint at that, the inside of the SUV would probably fill with smoke from his venting.

She tied her hair back with a scarf and left the window down. The day was so perfect, warm air tinged with the smell of last night’s rain. Damp grass, wet soil, the fragrance of lilacs bursting into bloom on bushes in every yard and in pastures where once a home place stood. Along the banks of Cedar Creek, sycamore trees worshipped the morning with great gnarly branches. Their white and tan bark like scales on the twisted limbs reached toward the sky like arms paying homage.

She pointed out the Sims property. “Turn left at the next mailbox, that’ll be the Durning place.”

When the car came to a stop in front of the neat rock house, he squinted through the windshield. “Why don’t you go to the door? If you need me, just wave. I’ll wait out here.”

For a moment, she studied him. But he didn’t look at her, just stared out the window like he was off somewhere else.

Dragging her bag from the back seat, she strolled up to the porch and knocked on the wooden screen. The big door stood open to the warm day.

A dumpling of a woman answered. Sparkling blue eyes took Jessie's measure with a curious gleam. She introduced herself. The flush that bloomed on the woman's cheeks told Jess they had located their caller, and she waved at Dal.

In silence, they waited while he hobbled toward the door, tall and official looking in his uniform. The ends of the crutches sank into the rain-soaked yard.

"How did you find me?" Dumpling woman subconsciously fingered her short gray hair, tossed a bit by a soft breeze, nervously taking in Dal's sidearm. "Am I in trouble? I'm not sure I want to talk to you. I told you I didn't want my name in the paper."

"No trouble at all," Jess replied. "And it's not necessary to use your name. But it would sure help us if you could give me the information. I could print it without giving a name, just a local resident. We need your permission to tell what you have to say."

Dal reached the porch, navigated the steps, and smiled down at her. Nodded. "Good morning, ma'am. I'm Deputy Dallas Starr."

"Nita. You may call me Nita." She dimpled and pushed the screen open.

How he managed to do that was beyond Jess. He turned that thousand watt smile on, and women melted around him like butter in the sun. And that he could do so even when in the foulest of moods was doubly amazing.

"Come on in here," Nita said. "Would you like coffee or some iced tea? My goodness, son. Did you break your leg?"

"No, ma'am, it's just a bad sprain."

"Well, you find the most comfortable chair, and I'll bring you something to drink. Did you say coffee? Or iced tea?"

"Coffee's fine, ma'am."

In light of the handsome Cherokee deputy, Jess turned invisible. She slipped quietly into a chair, leaving the larger one for him, and pulled out her recorder, pad, and pen. Let him lead this since he'd been such an instant hit with Nita.

He took the requested cup of coffee and some cookies from a plate Nita produced. Jess declined either, caught his eye, and nodded.

He held up a cookie. "These are delicious. What kind are they?"

She grinned. "I call it trail mix. They have everything I can find in the kitchen dumped in them."

He sipped from the china cup and finished one off, then holding another turned to Nita. "I understand that you've noticed some strange goings on across the way. Would you mind sharing that with us? And could Jess tape your story? Of course, she won't use your name."

Nita lowered herself onto the couch, a round table between her and the two chairs in which Jess and Dal sat. "Is it to do with the killing?"

"Well, we're not real sure yet. But if you've seen activity on the SE-FOR property, now that would be trespassing."

Glancing around as if someone might be eavesdropping, she said, "Well, yes I did." Plump fingers smoothed the lavender print dress over her knees. "The latest was after they found that dead body back yonder." She pointed vaguely out the window, then gestured toward Jess. "And after her story was in the paper about the diamonds."

"Nita, that could be really important to the case we're working on." He leaned forward, speaking more intimately. "And it would help us a lot if you could repeat your story."

A quick glance darted toward Jess. "How come she's taking notes and you're not?" She squinted her eyes in his direction.

"Sometimes we work together investigating something like this. It saves time if she just shares her notes with me later on. And to tell you the truth, I can't even read my own handwriting once it gets cold. It's sort of embarrassing, but there it is." His smile honored her.

"Well, that's very strange, but if you say so. I tell you, some folks do the strangest and dumbest things. Imagine waiting till after dark to stumble around that old place. And everyone knows it's radioactive over there. Wonder it don't glow. For the past few nights starting last Wednesday, I believe it was, there's been people inside the fence over yonder with flashlights. Darting around here and there, sometimes for several hours." She squirmed and blushed before continuing.

"You understand, I wasn't spying or anything, just walked by my windows and noticed the activity. I mentioned it to my husband and son, but they didn't think it was any of our business. Let folk do stupid things, is what my husband told me. My son Jeffrey wanted to go over there and see what was up, but Samuel, that's my husband, said no sirree bob. Wasn't having him shrivel up his privates just 'cause he was snoopy." Another glance at Dal and she flushed to the roots of her white hair.

Jess covered her mouth and feigned a cough to cover laughter.

Amusement lit Dal's eyes, but he made an effort to remain sober. "Nita, you mentioned something to my—uh—partner here about pickup trucks. When would that have been?"

"Oh, gracious, several years ago. Time flies when one grows older. Could a been five or ten years, I expect. Come in on a regular basis. Them kind with the covers over the bed so's you can't see what's in 'em? But I could see where they went with the stuff."

"Where was that?" Jess leaned forward, and Dal threw her a glowering look.

"Why, inside that SEFOR place." She glanced around, eyes darting here and there as if to make sure no one else could hear her. "But they ain't been around in a good long while. Years and years."

"I wonder. Would you mind coming out in the yard and pointing out the places where you saw the trucks?"

Nita peered from Jess to Dal, then back to Jess. "Oh, goodness no, I couldn't do that. Someone might drive by and see, then everyone would know I told you."

It obviously hadn't occurred to her that Dal's SUV, parked out front, with Grace County Deputy Sheriff on the doors, would pretty well tell that story.

"Well, then, maybe you could just stand here at your window and show us. Could you do that, Nita?"

Good God, he flashed his dimples with that smile. She wanted to smack him, but Nita agreed, so she held off on that.

While dumpling woman showed him the general location of the trucks' route in and out, Jess drew a quick diagram that might help, though she doubted it. Even when and if they got permission to go on the property, it would be difficult to locate the same areas. They'd probably have to search the entire property, and then might not turn up anything, anyway.

"And these lights. That's only been recently. Never before?"

"First I noticed them. Course, I do go to bed." Her plump cheeks dimpled toward Dal.

Holy crap. Jess glanced at Dal, but he seemed unaffected by the outward flirting.

"Did you see any vehicles parked alongside the road?" he asked.

"Well, now, it was pretty dark for that, and I sure didn't see head-lights come up."

He thanked her and accepted a plastic baggie filled with cookies, thanking her again as he thumped out the door behind Jess.

"You're shameless," she told him on the way to the car.

He held up the bag of cookies. "And look what I got for it, plus your story. I'll share if you be good."

"Not a story yet, but I'll take a cookie."

He handed her the bag before going around and hoisting himself into the SUV. He pulled out, drove a few hundred yards and off the road onto the Reilly property, following churned up tracks into the woods to nose in close to the yellow and black crime scene tape.

Without voicing her concerns, since it would do no good whatsoever, Jess climbed out and followed him, raising the tape so he could duck under with an awkward hop that made her catch her breath. Like the Durning's yard, the ground was soft from last night's storm, and he cursed, handed her the crutch from under his right arm and hopped along, using the other one to keep one foot from touching down.

"Use my shoulder if you'd like," she said.

"I'm okay. Just keep back."

But he wasn't okay. Dal knew it the moment he stepped on the spot where the body was found. If Jess had listened to him, he'd have sprawled out flat on his face. As it was, she stepped under his shoulder, and supported his weight the moment he took that last step.

Trouble was, she stepped into his mind along with the killer and his victim, just like he'd known she would. The darkness, the emotions of terror and crazed violence engulfed him, splashed through her and she tensed, made a funny noise down in her throat. To her credit, she held steady under the assault of words.

"Damn you, Jasper, I done tole you we leave 'em alone for now."

A pair of hands wrap around his throat, Jasper croaks. Can say nothing, but his brain begs. "I need—need...."

The hands tighten, Jasper's fear ramps up till the air flames. Heels digging clods of dirt, he falls to the ground.

A rock. Grasped by the other one.

Dal shuddered, guessed what was coming, and tried to claw his way out of the cage of darkness. The sound a rock makes when it crushes a skull is heart-stopping. Gut wrenching.

He couldn't breathe. Sensed the same reaction from Jess. He fell to his knees, pawed at his throat, clasped Jessie's shoulder so hard she went down with him.

The pain sent red hot tendrils of fire up his spine and out the top of his head, and blackness closed in.

He awoke with Jessie kneeling beside him saying his name. He grabbed her by the shoulders. "Pocket. Pills." All he could spit out.

"Yes, okay." She dug in his pants, came up with the prescription bottle and produced a bottle of water, God only knew from where.

He couldn't think, just took the pill she shoved between his lips and drank from the bottle that followed. She collapsed beside him and nestled his head against her. Sirens echoed from the surrounding mountains. He blinked his eyes, but still couldn't see through the dark haze.

"What'd you do?"

"Ssh, it's okay. Just stay still. Don't move."

"Dammit, Jess."

"Yeah, I know. I know."

Despite his anger, her hand felt good cradling his head, her lips soft against his cheek. Something wet falling there, too.

The next time he opened his eyes, he was lying in a hospital bed, an IV in one arm, and Jess sitting next to him, holding his hand.

"What'd you do?"

"I could ask, why did you do that?"

He struggled to move, erupting a pain he had thought long forgotten.

"The button, there." She rose and put his finger on a red button. "Morphine," she whispered. "Oh, God, Dal." Her tears splashed the skin on the back of his hand.

He came down hard against the pain, couldn't talk.

"I'll call a nurse. They want the name of your doctor in St. Louis, to make sure they do the right thing here."

"I don't want them doing anything. I want up and out of this god-damned bed. I'll not stay here."

She sprawled across his chest, stopping his thrashing. "Everything's going to be okay. Just quit fighting."

The morphine must've kicked in, 'cause he felt this absolute bliss flow through him. "You're so beautiful, Jess. So beautiful."

"I know. So are you."

The nurse responded to her summons. "I'll get the doctor. He's just down the hall. He'll be here in a few minutes."

Dal waved a hand at her, tried to tell her to tell the ugly bastard to go fuck himself, but didn't get the words out. Might've been a good thing too, since the guy who came in was a giant. Still, he could probably take him, since he was a doctor and soft.

He stuck out a huge hand. "I'm Doctor Magoddy, and spare me the wise cracks. Feeling frisky, Mr. Starr? How's your pain?"

"My pain is alive and kicking, thank you."

"Could you give me your doctor's name, please? Miss West tells me he's in St. Louis."

"All I need is to stay off it for a while. It'll be okay."

"Is that what you were doing yesterday? Staying off it?"

"I slipped, didn't mean to fall on the… yesterday?" He drifted into a pretty blue misty cloud in which the doctor's words were garbled and his own nonexistent. "Tell him, Jess."

Though sure he'd said something, no one paid him any attention at all. He tried to shout, but no sound came.

Sweet-voiced nurses moved in and out of his room, hovered over him, peered down at him, took his blood pressure, stuck needles in his arm, patted him and called him sweetie, but all he knew was where the red button was, and he kept it pushed as much as was allowed. He knew the rules. After a while, the magic juice would all be used up, and nothing would happen, even if he clubbed the damned thing with a water pitcher, which he'd tried once during that other time they'd tossed him in a bed and wouldn't let him up.

Jess returned. He wasn't sure if a night or day had passed.

She bent over and kissed him on the forehead.

"Forehead kisses are for kids and old people. Give me a good one, right here." He touched his mouth. "And then take me the hell out of here."

She smiled and did, and he liked it just fine. "Mmm, that was good."

"You're drunk, Dal."

"Better than that, I'm high. Did you not hear me? I want out of this damn place."

With a forced smile, she gathered his hand and sat in the chair next to the bed. "Soon, if you behave yourself. Stop fighting."

"Listen." He clutched her fingers tight in his. "I thought Crow, it meant he was seeing the birds. They were roosting in that big tree just above, you know, where we found the body. But I think he's saying someone's name. Would you check on your list? Isn't there a Crowe there?"

She lay two fingers over his lips. "Sweetheart, you need to rest. We've already talked about this. Stop worrying about the case. Mac will be in to see you later tonight. Sorry I didn't make it yesterday. We didn't finish getting the paper out till about one o'clock this morning. You know how Mondays are."

"I don't even know what day it is. I'll just bet Mac's pissed, isn't he? Yep, he's pissed. Don't forget about Crowe. Sweetheart?"

"I won't, and yep, he is indeed pissed. Mostly because you hurt yourself and he feels it was on his watch. Even though he put you on desk duty and warned you not to go out loping around like a maniac. Your own fault. Sorry about the 'sweetheart.' It slipped out. Won't happen again."

"S'okay. Sort of liked it. I hope I still have a job." He forgot what he was going to say and closed his eyes, settled in to fight the pain by going with it, riding the waves and taking deep breaths.

When he awoke, Jess was gone and Mac sat in the chair, Stetson in both hands resting on his lap, a scowl wrinkling skin between his pale eyes. "Hey, boy. Good to see you awake."

"Mac, I'm sorry. Guess you're pissed."

"Oh, I'm that. Ought to smack you upside the head, but that can wait. I'm worried about as much as pissed. These good folks want to help you but say you won't give them your doctor's name. Tell me. That is, if you want to get out of that bed and have your job back."

Head clearer than it had been all day, probably because he'd used up his quantity of morphine and was shooting blanks, he said, "Mac, I reckon I fucked up big time. Probably won't do any good at all to call my doctor or any other. I felt it when I fell, a damned shred from one of the bullets that son of a bitch shot into me. Guess he's accomplished what he set out to do. Kill me."

"They don't think so, but they need some info from your doctor."

Dal closed his eyes and took a deep breath. Could it be he'd dodged this bullet one more time? "Swinton. His name's Swinton. He's at Mercy Hospital."

"Good boy. I'll pass that along."

"If I didn't mess up, why can't I move?"

"'Cause they've got you tied down so you can't even wiggle so much as your big toe until they hear from your doctor. The x-rays, CAT scans, and MRI, none show anything there. Jess told them or they wouldn't have known where to look or what they were looking for. They want to make sure, compare notes with your doc up there. Glad you share with someone, son."

Dal rolled his head back and forth, not sure he ought to hope yet. Wait till they got his results from Swinton. Too early to celebrate. Wonder when he told Jess. He couldn't for the life of him remember. Fists doubled, he beat the mattress. How could he have been so stupid?

10

CHAPTER

Eager to get started on a search of the breeder plant, Jess called Kathy Spacey, who picked up the phone on the third ring.

"We just received permission to search the old SEFOR plant property. You think you and Dave could lend a hand looking for something?"

"Good afternoon to you too, Jessie. And how have you been?"

"Sorry about that. I'm fine. How are you? Haven't seen you in a while."

"I know, you know how spring is. Getting all these kids finished up and out of here. What you got going on?"

"Oh, it's just if you have the time. Let's see, this is Wednesday. Maybe we could do it Sunday morning, then go to your place for some of Dave's fabulous barbecue. I'll bet Tink would help."

Kathy laughed. "Just like you to manage to get an invite to eat for you and your friend. When are you going to learn how to cook, girl?"

"Why should I when you and Dave are so good at it?"

"Ha-ha. So tell me about this project. Is it murder, a story, a cold case, or all three? I've been hearing all sorts of rumors, some mild and

some pretty wild. And is this search legal? I know how you push bound-
aries. You got *permission?*"

"Guess number four is probably right. And it is legal, though a bit
iffy on how legal."

"I knew it. You amaze me."

Jess laughed. "How do you feel about digging around in that old
nuclear plant?"

"Depends on where we dig and if we're going to get shot. Don't feel
at all good about going into the reactor, but then you'd be too smart to
do that, wouldn't you?"

Not feeling at all smart after allowing Dal to get hurt, Jess sighed.
"Some buildings back there. I thought we could take a look around
them. Might be some vents, ducts, nooks, and crannies where something
would be safe all these years."

"Sounds interesting. Sunday would be okay with me, though I'm
not so sure we can help you much," Kathy said. "Gives us a few days
to plan it. Don't think the chief cook and barbecue man has anything
on for the weekend."

Jess let out an explosive laugh. "Like he'd do anything without you."

"Okay, you're right, but he might have arranged something for us he
hasn't mentioned. Let me talk to him and get back to you later today. Is
Dal in on this hunt?"

"Kathy, Dal is in the hospital, and it might be bad."

There was no sound from the other end of the call for a long beat.
"Dear God. What happened?"

Even though they didn't get to see each other much, Kathy had a soft
spot for Dal since they'd clashed at their first crime scene, then made up.

"It's a long story. Let's just say the past may have come back to slap him down once more. I'm sorry I didn't let you know sooner. Just so much going on."

"Sure, I understand. If there's anything I can do, let me know."

"We'll just have to wait till his medical records come from his doctor in St. Louis, then we'll know more. Right now, they've got him strapped down, and he could use visitors if you guys want to drop in and see him. He's here in Cedarton."

"We'll go by and pay him a visit this evening. Is this thing you want us to help with related to one of his cases?"

"Yeah, in a way. We were out there at the crime scene when he got hurt. If we could get this search out of the way, I think it would make him feel a lot better. The thing is, don't mention this to him. He'll plot an escape to go with us and that could be really, really bad. Okay?"

"You got it. Whatever. For Dal, the answer is yes."

"Oh, good. Call me tonight. We'll make a plan."

The Spaceys were forensic anthropologists and archeologists. They taught at the CJC, and often helped the Grace County Sheriff's Department with official investigations. They'd been the ones who helped identify the skeletal remains in the stolen skull case the previous fall.

When Jess first became involved with the couple, she had learned the difference between anthropology—the science of the origin, culture, and development of human beings and archeology—the systematic recovery and detailed scientific study of material evidence of human life and culture in past ages.

When the term *forensics* is added to the mix, then it involves the use of findings in legal proceedings or public debate. Which meant, more or less, they could legally prove what their findings meant. With a wry grin, Kathy had explained that this was a simplification of what they did. Jess accepted that without question. Probably wouldn't understand any further explanation anyway.

The plan for the search was simple. If there were safe, dry, undetectable hidey holes for the diamonds inside the building, the Spaceys with their trained eyes could perhaps point them out much quicker than turning loose a bunch of people to fumble around and get nowhere.

This search Jess planned was without the sanction of Mac and his deputies as well as Dal Starr. If she found something, she would have a terrific story, and she could then point Mac and his deputies to the spot. Disturbing the stuff would not be a good idea, and they could be in a world of hurt. But if the Spaceys could narrow down the best areas for a later search, that would be fine with her, too. She had no expectations of finding the diamonds on this run, but wouldn't it be cool if she did?

That evening, the couple didn't call but came straight to Jessie's from visiting Dal at the hospital. Said he was still fighting some pain, but roaring to get up and out of there and real happy to see them.

"It was hard to keep the planned search from him, but we managed," Kathy said.

Sitting with them in her living room, Jess gave them a quick rundown on what was going on and discussed the pros and cons of poking around the old SEFOR plant.

"If we find something and disturb it, we could all be charged." She stared first at Kathy, then Dave. "What the charges would be I'm not sure, but I know it's illegal to knowingly nose around in a stash of stolen items, most especially when they're evidence in a case under investigation. At this point, that is iffy. You guys still want in?"

The ever-silent Dave nodded and tented his fingers under his chin. Kathy spoke for them both. "Hey, we know what we're doing and how to preserve what could become part of a criminal investigation, if not the actual crime scene."

"I think to stay out of trouble, all we need to do is find what we're looking for, leave it be, and go tell Mac. Isn't that right?" Jess eyed Kathy, then Dave.

"Technically." Dave glanced at his wife.

She finished for him. "If we disturb the area around where evidence might be found by a forensics team, we're not so innocent. If Dal were with us, he'd know how far we could go without messing up evidence."

"Well, he's not, and he's not going to be. If he doesn't stay in that bed until these doctors finish their diagnosis, he could be back in a wheelchair, this time for the rest of his life. So he *cannot* find out about this. You guys agree? 'Cause I'm not doing it if we can't keep it a secret from him." She swallowed and averted her gaze to hide a sheen of tears.

Kathy eyed her silently for a long time. "Wow, you really got it bad for him, don't you?"

Before she could deny it, tears poured down her cheeks.

Kathy moved to her side, put her arms around her. "Aw, honey. He's going to be okay." She smiled and wiped at Jessie's tears. "I remember a time I had to beg you to give him a chance."

"Yeah, I remember that, too. If he's not okay, I'm gonna kill him. How could he do something so dangerous? He doesn't even know how I feel, 'cause I've never told him. He would run so fast he'd leave only a blue streak if he knew. And you'd better not tell him, either."

Kathy smoothed hair away from Jessie's face. "But I thought you two were an item. He spends the night here a lot, I know he does. Don't tell me he sleeps on the couch with those long legs of his, not to mention that sexy physique."

Jess made an effort to dry her cheeks with a swipe of her fingertips. "Of course we sleep together. He jokes that he's in lust with me. We can't keep our hands off each other, but he claims it's just chemistry. That real love doesn't exist. That it's all a myth. His wife's betrayal and death cut big holes in his heart, and he's never healed. Plus, he despises reporters. It's a wonder he comes anywhere near me. No romance, no sirree, just pure sex. As for me, I don't deserve to find someone to love, so what the hey?"

Dave rose and walked into the kitchen, rattled about with the coffee pot and some cups.

"I'm sorry. I shouldn't have said that. It's not the time for a pity party."

"Oh, don't worry. Dave won't say anything. He just figures we need some girl talk, and I think he's right. You're way too hard on yourself. Whatever you've done is in the past, and you ought to work on today and your future. Now listen, this is what you do."

Jess leaned forward expecting advice about her love life. No such luck. Kathy was all business.

"We need a couple of young bodies to help us out. Heavy stuff may have to be moved around. It has to be someone who won't squeal to Mac or any of their friends who could carry this back to him. Tinker is a good bet, but who else?"

"Burt Sample. He's a deputy but he's young enough to be a daredevil, and him and Dal are close 'cause of something Dal did for him when he first came into the department. I never found out what it was, but Burt feels like he owes Dal. Besides, him and Tink are getting along well. And it would be good to have a deputy with us to make suggestions. Course he's green." She chewed at her thumbnail. "Yes, I think Burt would be good, since technically Tink isn't allowed to function in that capacity.

Mac is so stubborn about that. I'll feel Burt out casually. If he balks at all, I'll not tell him more."

Dave meandered back into the room with a tray holding three mugs of steaming coffee. "I looked for cookies or something, but all I found were Honey Buns."

Again, tears poured silently down her cheeks.

"What is it?" Kathy passed her a mug.

"Crap." Jess angrily wiped her face once again. "I can't remember when I've cried so much." But she had. Once, a long time ago. That time it was because of a man, too. A man she'd betrayed and destroyed with her mad desire to write a big career-making story. "Forget it. I'm okay. Let's get it planned out. You're both sure about this? We get caught, we could be in a shitload of trouble."

Jess eyed them both. "We're in. We'll plead stupidity if we get caught. Besides, we're just going for a Sunday morning stroll, aren't we?" Kathy said.

Yeah, a stroll inside a building we've broken into. She kept that thought to herself and joined their nervous chuckles.

After the couple left, she stripped and stepped into the shower. She had just soaped up good when the phone rang. Ordinarily she would've let it ring, but with Dal in the hospital, she didn't dare. So she wrapped up in a towel and ran to answer it.

For a moment, there was only dead air. She almost hung up before the voice grated, "Bitch, this is your last warning. Stay away from this. You and that screwy deputy. Done tole you don't write no more stories, don't poke your nosy nose into it, or you'll get the same as John Doe. And quit running his pitcher in the paper. You hear?"

"Hey, hey, you dumb, stupid, illiterate…." She shut up because there was no one on the other end.

Furious, she threw the phone on the couch.

The freaking idiot. That was exactly the wrong thing to do. Now they'd gone and pissed her off big time. Fuming, she stomped back into the bathroom where she'd left the shower running and stepped under to wash away the soap and shampoo.

That did it. She was getting a gun. Come after her again, she'd shoot their asses. Her stop chasing this story?

Not in this lifetime.

She went to the newspaper office early Thursday morning to ensure she had a story about the diamond heist ready to go in the next issue. Whoever this prick was, he was in for a big surprise if he thought he could scare her into submission. She left the story open-ended so she could finish it after the planned Sunday hunt at SEFOR if they found anything. If not, she'd wind it up with unanswered questions. Readers might still come forward with information. No one had called to identify the photo they'd run of Jasper no-last-name. When she had her story pretty well drafted, she leaned back, picked up the phone, and called the sheriff's office.

Tinker was on duty, and she made a date with her to meet for supper somewhere quiet where she could talk her into joining the hunt for treasure. With Dal in the hospital, she and Tink had cancelled their weekly Wednesday night movie date. She asked her to invite Burt Sample to join them for supper.

"Burt? Whatever for? I thought you were hung on Dallas."

"He's not for me, Tink. This is something else entirely. And don't make a big deal out of it. Just quietly ask him. If he refuses, tell him it's for Dal, would you? He'll come then. How about Artego's? Six o'clock?"

"Afterward, let's ditch the kid and go back to my place for a movie.

My turn. We haven't done that in a while. Seems like you're always busy lately looking after Deputy Dal. How is he doing, by the way? I was sure sorry to hear about his accident."

"Yeah, me too. Me too. I was with him, you know. Scared me half out of my wits. How he does what he does without going crazy is beyond me. But when he gets hurt doing it, well, then I want to beg him to stop."

"You mean he was in one of his trances? I hadn't heard that. Geez, I wish I could see that."

"No, you don't. You don't at all."

Yelling from the background on Tink's end put a stop to their conversation. "Gotta go kick some ass, Jess. See you at Artego's. Six. Right?"

Tink hung up before Jess could say anything else. She grabbed her pack and headed to the Red Bird for a hamburger and French fries, then she was going to the hospital to see Dal and find out what was up there.

When she arrived, his bed was empty and she grabbed the door frame to steady her nerves. He could be taking tests, he could be.... She stopped before her vivid imagination had her climbing the wall. Out in the hallway, she looked one way then the other. No one. The nurses' station seemed to be a gathering place and she headed there.

"Anyone seen Dallas Starr?" She aimed the question at a group of nurses having a talk fest.

Several sets of eyes turned toward her. One of the bunch spoke up. "You mean the tall, dark, and handsome one?"

"That's him."

"He checked out this morning."

"He what? He was tied down flat on his back with orders not to move till they heard from his doctor."

The nurse shrugged. "Guess he decided not to wait. He signed an AMA and lit out."

"Holy crap. Do you know, was he walking?"

"Soon as they wheeled him out the door. Got up and walked away." The pretty nurse pointed down the hall.

"With crutches?"

"Didn't see any. Limping, that's all."

"Dammit. Thanks." Jess flew down the hallway to the exit, stumbled around trying to remember where she'd parked his patrol unit after they brought him to the hospital. It wasn't there, so he'd driven off. At least he wasn't wandering around on foot. She found her Jeep and, upset as she was, managed to climb in, stab the key into the ignition, and take off. Where would he go? Why had he taken off like that? Didn't he give a damn about his own self?

And the last question. Was she his protector?

She cruised by the sheriff's office and though Dal's car wasn't there, she stopped anyway. Inside, Tinker's desk was empty, and she could hear a good battle going on back toward the cells. Mac's office was empty, too. What the hell?

Outside, a deputy hurried to his vehicle, got in, turned the lights and siren on, and took off with a screech of tires. She leaped in the Jeep and tore out of there behind him. If something had happened and Dal got wind of it, he'd be there. If not, Mac would be, and maybe he'd know something about Dal's whereabouts. God, suppose something had happened to Dal?

The deputy headed north, made a sliding turn on Dogtown Road. Something else had happened out that way, and she'd bet her last nickel it had happened around the SEFOR plant. Dal would never go there.

Sure enough, several deputy's vehicles, including Mac's, were nosed into the woods just past the plant's high chain link fence. Looked like a story here. Even though she wanted to find Dal, she parked alongside the road and hot-footed it toward the scene. Les Howard was stringing crime scene tape around small trees. Before she could reach Mac, Doc Cramer rolled up in his black van.

Another body sprawled less than five-hundred yards from where they'd found the first one. The body count for the year, of humans at least, had gone from zero to two in four days. The body meant Dal was around here somewhere. Why else would he have left the hospital? Mac would have a cow. Come to think of it, she was about to give birth to something herself. Maybe a raging bull. Instead of approaching Mac, she circled through the gathering of deputies and a few curious neighbors until she spied Dal's SUV hidden under some trees a good distance away.

The coward. Dammit, what was he thinking?

Running, the pack slapping against her shoulder, she reached his empty vehicle, leaned against it a minute to catch her breath. Where was he?

"Looking for me?"

She whirled to see Dal coming around the rear bumper. "You're damn right, I am. What are you doing out here? Why did you leave the hospital?" Fists clenched, she hammered on the car because she didn't want to hit him.

Wrong. Because she *wanted* to hit him.

"Take it easy, Jess. I'm okay. Really." He touched her arm, and she whirled to face him.

"How dare you do this to yourself?" Tears filled her eyes, and she blinked them away.

He pulled her against his chest, tucked her head into the curve of his shoulder. "Babe, I'm fine. Everything is fine. Give me a chance to explain. Come on, settle down before you hurt me." He chuckled.

"It's not funny." The words muttered into his shirt.

"Get in the car." He swung open the passenger side door. "Come on, get in."

"Why should I? Where are you going?" Even though she objected, she climbed up into the seat and he shut the door, went around the hood, and folded his large frame into the driver's side.

"Not going anywhere right now. Just cool off and let me explain. Not that it's any of your business." His eyes glinted sparks at her.

"Where do you come off being the one who's angry? It is my business, damn you. You scared me to death. I go to the hospital, your bed is empty. Terrified of what might have happened, I finally find a nurse who tells me you signed out against medical advice. Why would you do that? Why would you take a chance on being—?"

He spread his fingers over her mouth. "Okay, okay, Miss Nosy. All the tests showed the damned thing simply disappeared. They can't find it on any of the scans they ran. Doc Swinton took a look, too. They sent them to him by email. He said he can't explain it, but he has seen it happen. It may have burrowed into a muscle, or any number of other things. But the main thing is, it's no longer near my spinal cord. They were going to spend a whole day passing papers back and forth, releases and shit like that, and I couldn't wait. Not when I heard they'd found another body. And before you say anything about my damned leg, those crutches were irritating as hell. I can limp and hop better than that. Okay, go." He shut up, pointed at her, crossed his arms in self-defense, and pinned her with a dark stare.

Without saying a word, though there were a few she would gladly have spouted, she shot him a dark look, fumbled for the door handle, piled out, and stomped away, her only words muttered curses.

None of her business. How dare he say that? Acting like she didn't matter, like they meant nothing to each other.

Well, maybe he was right. Maybe she was wasting her time caring a whit about him. The big lunkhead. By the time she reached the crime scene, she had the fury tamped down to a simmer and pulled out her camera. That would teach her to fall for a tougher-than-nails lawman. Well, no more. Absolutely no more.

Mac glanced up and saw her, gestured for her to duck under the tape. "Glad you showed up. It seems you're the only camera here. Would you go ahead and take the shots for me? Usual rules."

"I know the damned rules. Don't worry about that." Voice harsh to dump the remainder of her anger at poor Mac's feet.

Wisely, he cast her one glance, then moved away.

Carefully, she stepped to where Doc Cramer was examining the body and began the series of indicated close-ups required. After a long while, he and two deputies zipped the body into a black bag and took it to the van. It would join Jasper in Little Rock for an autopsy. Deputies continued to scour the area, but the only footprints were scrubbed out.

"Looks like there was a real fight here," Mac said. "Damn shame Dal ain't here, he could figure out what happened."

"Oh, he's here all right. Hunkering over there under the trees like the skunk he is. He left the hospital this morning against medical advice. Says it's because of the time they were taking releasing him. Claims he's been cleared by all the doctors. He signed the AMA paper so he could leave when he heard about the body being found. Guess he's too cowardly to come on over. You have my permission to go shoot him."

He raised an eyebrow at her. "Cool down. And he damn well better not crawl out of that truck and show up here at the scene. If I let him back in the field before they actually release him, my ass is grass." He glanced down at the bloodied ground. "Looks like we've got ourselves yet another unidentified vic."

"Dammit, I'm so mad, I could smack him right upside the head. Said it wasn't any of my business. What's wrong with him, anyway? We all care about him, and he goes and does something like this, then says it's none of my business. I swear." She threw her arms around his neck and bawled into his shoulder, him patting her on the back and saying nothing.

After a while, she became conscious of several deputies walking a wide circle around her and Mac and trying not to stare. "I need to… you're going to send a release on this to the paper? I think I'm going on back. Sorry. Thanks for lending me a shoulder to cry on. I hate bawl babies."

"Don't blame him so much, girl. He's a fine man, just once a man's been through hell and back, he don't know who to trust besides himself."

"I know that, but I thought we… I thought he and I had something… something he could trust in."

"It don't come easy for a man like him to trust love, most especially when he's been betrayed once."

"Well, bullshit. It's time he got over her."

Mac gazed at her with rheumy eyes. "You over that feller out west yet? You never think of what happened, what you might've done different, how it might be best if you didn't let that happen again? You ought to give Dal another chance. He loves you, he just can't admit to it yet."

"Well, when he can, he knows where I live."

"Aw, gal." Mac shook his head. "Gotta get busy. You take care of yourself now, you hear?"

She nodded and tramped back to the Jeep, tossed her pack into the seat. She deliberately hadn't told him about the earlier telephone threat. He'd put her under guard, and the Sunday morning hunt wouldn't take place. Knees shaking so badly she couldn't stand, she slid to the ground. Sat there for a long time thinking about what Mac had said about Dal before she rose, climbed in, and drove home. In no mood to write the story, she would wait till tomorrow. By then Mac should have a release for her.

Time to get her mind off her own feelings. What in the world was going on that out of the blue two people were dead and a bunch of others were involved in a treasure hunt that could very well get someone else killed? Either this latest victim came too close to finding the stash, or he knew something. The first killing had been more of an accident than a planned murder. Two men getting in a fight and one killing the other wasn't the same as a deliberate murder, plotted and carried out. Which was this latest?

All the way home, she worked at the knots tying the two murders and the diamond heist together. And all going on with Dal as well. Getting nowhere, she parked, went inside, and dropped down on the couch, her mind awhirl with confusion.

Hard to tell how long she'd been sitting there when she came back to the present. What time was it? Five-thirty, and she was supposed to meet Tinker at Artego's at six. Crap. She'd better get her ass in gear.

In the bathroom, she brushed her teeth, changed from her tee shirt to a frilly blouse, combed her hair, tied it back with a lemon yellow scarf, and stuck her feet into high heeled sandals. The jeans would be okay. Removing a billfold and keys from the backpack, she stuck them in her pocket and left, remembering to lock up and turn on the porch light.

When she rushed into Artego's, Tinker and Burt were already at a table in the back. She had no more than slid into the booth, trapping Burt between them, when a margarita arrived.

"Thanks. Bring me another one in about five minutes."

The sexy, dark-haired waiter grinned and nodded.

Neither of her companions spoke until she sucked down almost half the drink and leaned back with a satisfied sigh.

"Hard day?" Tink asked.

"Don't even ask. Glad you could come, Burt."

He blushed. "Not sure why. Tinker here said you needed help with something for Dal. He's been good to me, helped me get used to the weird hours and the crazy stuff that comes with this job. So I came. But I gotta tell you, I can't do anything illegal or immoral."

Tinker burst out laughing. Jess took another long drink. He looked so serious, she finally began to laugh despite herself. Dal was right about this kid. He was straight as they come and still wet behind the ears. On top of that, he blushed every time Tink looked at him.

"Yeah, you wouldn't ask us to break the law would you?" Tink finished off her margarita and held up the glass.

Burt looked from one to the other then shrugged and downed all of his *cerveza*. "Ah, well, hell." He set down the empty bottle.

Into their second round of drinks, Jess laid out what was up and asked if the two would lend their bodies to helping the Spaceys search the SEFOR buildings.

"They can point out the most likely spots and with four of us there, we ought to be able to cover the whole place before noon. Mac has permission to do a search." She left out that the warrant was for the property only. They had no right to break into the buildings.

"Only one problem with that," Burt said. "We ain't Mac."

"Technicality. A mere technicality. And you do need to say yes because Dave Spacey cooks up the best barbecue you ever tasted, and Kathy is a whiz with the trimmings." Tink touched his wrist and he jerked so his drink splashed into his lap.

Poor boy. He had it bad.

To reinforce Tink's statement, Jess said, "She's right. We thought about ten a.m., when most everyone is in church. There've been treasure hunters on the land, but only at night so far. You wear your uniform, that way if we do meet up with any you can run them off."

By then, he'd consumed four bottles of Mexican beer, and so he grinned, shrugged, and said, "Why the hell not? I haven't been having much fun looking for stray dogs. Even pulled a cat out of a tree the other day. All along I thought that was an urban myth."

All three of them exploded in laughter. Before they finished their meals, Tinker glanced at the young deputy. "Say, do you like movies?"

After they ate, he went to Tinker's with them. When Jess left around eleven, he was still there. Tink winked at her and grinned. In the Jeep, Jess checked the glove compartment for a flashlight, checked it to make sure the batteries were up, then headed north toward Dogtown Road and the crime scenes where she'd bet her bottom dollar she'd find Dal.

Her anger at him had cooled, replaced by a firm resolve to keep him at arm's length. Controlling her feelings while continuing to work with him could become impossible. There was little choice but to shut him out of her life. Refuse to react to her desires. Or his. The job was too important to her to quit, and she would not leave Cedarton. She had run once because of her inability to deal with a man and would not do it again.

None of her business, indeed. If that's how he felt, then he would become none of her business.

So what the devil was she doing chasing around in the middle of the night hoping to find him? Actually, she needed to check out the crime scenes when no one was around. Yeah, sure, she'd keep telling herself that.

At the first crime scene, she cut her lights and pulled slowly off the road into the trees. The moon had not risen. A glow from low hanging clouds cast deep shadows under the trees.

Using the natural light to find her way, she crept under the crime scene tape that swayed gently in a night breeze. Underfoot a limb cracked, and she paused. All manner of night critters sang, their croaks and chirrups filling the air with a constant buzzing. The frantic screaming of a screech owl startled her, then she laughed at her own silliness.

What she would find out here, she didn't know. But someone she probably saw often had killed a man viciously with a rock. The realization sent a chill through her, as if a monster walked behind her set to grab her by the neck. How must Dal feel when those evil spirits he called *anasgi`na* literally attacked his mind? How in God's name could he handle it? No wonder he left the crowded Dallas area for the peaceful surroundings of Cedarton. And why was she continuing to think of him when she'd just vowed to forget him?

Shrubbery whispered and she froze. Okay, that was it. She snatched the flashlight and turned it on. If anyone was around ready to pounce on her, she'd give them a target. Maybe yell 'Come and get me!' into the darkness. But that might be a bit much, so she settled for spreading the beam around, letting it crawl over the body's final resting place.

While she walked the scene, looking for she knew not what, a waning moon peeked over the mountains to the east, sprinkling pinpoints of light through the leaves and onto the ground around her. Something glimmered, and she brushed away dried leaves to pick it up. A wrapper from a piece of candy. She shone her light on it. Hershey's Mini Bar, Dark Chocolate. Why did that remind her of something?

Not good for evidence, but interesting all the same. Too many people had been messing about here since the deputies searched the crime scene. Anyone could have dropped it. Yet she couldn't shake the feeling that it might be important. So she stuffed it into her pocket. Now she had done something illegal. Picked up what could be evidence from a marked crime scene.

To hell with it. Just to hell with everything. She sat down on a boulder. Dry eyed, she buried her face in her hands. She was damned sick and tired of feeling this way. Especially over a man who obviously was not worth it. A man who claimed he was none of her business.

11

CHAPTER

After fleeing the hospital, Dal left the bustle of the latest crime scene before Jess could tell everyone he was there. He drove east toward Harrison, checking names on mailboxes as he went. The list Jess had given him was back at the trailer. He was looking for a specific one, and when he rounded one of the S curves that climbed the mountain, he spotted what he was looking for. The address of Julie Crowe from Jessie's list, the number on the first of two boxes on the right hand side of the road. The second box read Wells.

He sat there a while, peering up the driveway on the left, then the one on the right. Both boxes were on one side of the road for mail delivery. Their deceased robber and this Crowe woman had not originally lived across the road from each other, and Wells was a pretty common name. Wells lived in Hot Springs, but had moved up here a long time ago.

He chose the right turn and parked near a small bungalow with a sloping roof over a front porch that ran its width. A typical Ozark structure that looked as if it had been built more than fifty years ago.

A small fit woman in sweats with graying hair and sharp blue eyes answered his knock. Though he was out of uniform, he was sure she'd watched him pull up in the county car and knew he was a deputy.

He introduced himself as such, and her eyes grew sharper, regarded him closer. "What do you want?"

"I'd like to talk to you about your husband, ma'am."

"He's dead."

"You are the wife of Mathon Wells?"

"His widow. And I repeat, he's dead. I got nothing to say about him."

"Mom, who is that?" A lanky man about Dal's height came in from another room.

"It's the law, Lennie. Come to talk about your dad."

Before the man could reply, Dal's ears perked. Lennie Wells. He listened carefully when the man spoke.

"What about?"

That voice. He was neither of the two at the first killing. With difficulty, Dal put on his best manners and smile. "I just have a few questions, if y'all don't mind."

The woman deferred to her son, who drew himself up and glared at Dal. "Well, 'fraid we do mind. Got nothing to say to the law. All that went away when he was killed, 'n we ain't done nothin'."

"Did he leave anything, like letters, the like?" He reached in his pocket, drew out the sketch of the victim, and handed it to Sara.

Her eyes widened for an instant, but she gave it back without comment.

"You mean a map that shows what he did with…?" The man broke off, anger diffusing his thick-set features into an ugly mask. He glanced at the photo Dal held out then went on with his rant as if he hadn't seen it. "Hell no. You ain't the first to ask that, but we hoped people had finally forgot. It's been years since anyone has said anythin'. Till that dad-blamed reporter wrote that story in the paper. Now it's goin' to start all over again. You can git on out of here and tell that gal to stop writin' about what's dead and buried."

The voice grated on his nerves. Dal nodded as politely as he could. "So neither of you know this man?"

"Never seen him. Now git." Sara bustled from the room, leaving Lennie to kick him out.

Dal tucked the sketch away and left before Lennie could try to do just that. Clearly the woman was lying. She'd recognized the dead man as Jasper, but that's all he got. He could commiserate with the Wells family, though. Reporters were a pain in the butt. Bringing up stuff that wasn't anyone's business. But Lennie was involved in this mess up to his ears, had definitely been at the second crime scene. Sure as hell both recognized the man in the sketch, and he might've killed the second victim. If so, he wouldn't get away with it.

Both the woman and her son peered out through the window when he pulled away. Crossing the road, he followed a longer lane till he reached a trailer not much bigger than his. The home of Julie Crowe. Prepared for the same reaction to his questions, he was surprised when the attractive woman, also in sweats, politely asked him to come in and sit down. What was with the sweats?

"I'm looking into a death over by SEFOR, ma'am, and your name has cropped up as maybe knowing the victim. We haven't been able to identify him as yet. I was hoping you could help me."

She nodded, sat down across from him, and studied him with chocolate brown eyes. "I'd be glad to help if I could, but I don't know anyone who has died."

"Well, ma'am, you wouldn't know about that yet because we haven't identified him, so no one has been notified. I have a picture if you wouldn't mind looking at it. I apologize, because it's a drawing made after he was killed. Is that agreeable?"

She raised her shoulders and glanced away. "I guess."

He handed over the sketch and she looked closely at it. "My goodness."

Without saying more, she shouted over her shoulder. "Merle, come in here a minute, son, could you?"

A tall, rather muscular teen-aged boy lumbered into the room. "What, Ma? I'm playing D&D." He cast a quick look in Dal's direction out of wide set blue eyes. The very same eyes Dal had seen only a while ago in the features of Sara and Lennie Wells.

He'd discovered something really important here, but he waited in silence, watched to see their reaction.

"Just come look at this picture. Ain't this… ?"

The kid grabbed the picture out of her hands. "Is this the guy that was killed the other day down by SEFOR?"

"That's him. Do you know him?"

His mom nodded. "Go on, tell him."

"I'm not sure."

"Yes, you are, and so am I. That's Jasper Long, and you well know it. He's a cousin to Lennie Wells."

"Aw, Ma."

"Reckon y'all don't take the paper, or you would've seen his picture and come forward, wouldn't you?"

Mother and son glared daggers through him, but neither replied.

And Dal wanted to snap his fingers and yell Eureka, but he simply sat there, watching the exchange and pondering on those blue eyes. This boy's mother's eyes were brown, but he'd bet his bottom dollar his pa's were that same blue. The blue of Lennie Wells. What this might mean to the case he hadn't worked out yet. But he would.

"Well, tell him," Julie ordered.

The boy nodded, his look sullen, and handed back the picture. "Who killed him?"

"We're not sure yet, but we will find out." He turned his attention back to Julie. "Does this Long boy have any kin around here? I mean a Mom or Dad?"

"No, he just sort of lives with whoever will put up with him. Spends a lot of time with Sara and Lennie Wells."

Dal nodded. This entire family had been quite clever in evading his questions, and they hadn't come forward after the picture was published Wednesday in *The Observer*. Wonder why. He made no mention of the second body, and they didn't either.

He wished he had Jess to bounce this off. She was so good at connecting the dots. Dammit, he hated what had happened, but they were getting too damned close for comfort. This time he'd do his best to keep his distance, not be wooed by her charms, the way her nose crinkled when she laughed, how her skin felt… time to stop before he went running right straight back to her.

"Thank you both. I appreciate your information. I'll likely not need you to come identify the victim."

He stood, the damned leg refusing to work for a minute. He supposed he ought to be using those crutches, like Doc Swinton said, but they were so awkward. Eventually he'd walk this out if he kept at it.

Both stared at him until he turned and left. On the way back, he idly glanced at a few mailboxes and noticed one with Marcy on it. That was the guy who found the blue Falcon in the woods. No one had actually talked to him yet. He appeared to be missing or dodging being questioned.

He slowed and turned onto the road that petered out after about a quarter of a mile with still no sign of a house. It narrowed to a track with grass growing thick in the center. After another half mile of winding deeper and deeper into the trees, it became a mere trail with weeds growing high in the center. He might as well back out before he ran plum out of road. Guy must've moved somewhere else and didn't take down his box. Just as he glanced behind and shifted into reverse, he caught sight of sunlight glinting off glass off in the woods. He parked and climbed out, leaned forward a bit. Hidden deep in the trees sprawled a new-looking log cabin. One of those fancy kits with perfect logs all notched to fit.

Hmmm. Interesting and expensive for this neck of the woods. Someone must've bought the land from Marcy and built a new home. Odd they hadn't improved the road, but maybe that was their next project. In a hurry to get some supper at the Red Bird, he backed out till he found a place wide enough to turn around and returned to the county road.

Later that night after everyone had cleared away from the new crime scene, he would spend some time there, see if he could connect with the victim and the perp. Learn more about them. Right now, he headed for town. Likely there would be plenty of talk at the Red Bird about the most recent death. The entire county usually didn't average more than five or six killings a year, and they were mostly by people from away or a fight that just got out of hand. Now here they had two right together, and it was beginning to look like both were connected to a thirty-four-year-old burglary spree over in Harrison. Still, that was going to be damned hard to prove if he didn't turn up something.

Tomorrow he'd get back to the hospital, pick up all his release papers, and see if he could talk Mac into putting him back on full-time duty so he could get to work on this. No reason now for him to be laid up a month with nothing more than a sore leg. No sense in it at all. He'd dodged the bullet again. He smiled at the pun.

The usual men were at the busy little cafe, because this was the place to pick up the latest gossip. Some actually came there only to eat, most came to catch up on whatever was going on in town.

When Dal sidled into a chair nearest the front door, Norma saw him and brought over a cup of black coffee. He smiled at her, and she grinned right back. "I'll have the usual."

Banjo and Fudge sat at a nearby table, and both greeted him. "Heard you been laid up. Hope you're feeling perky by now," Fudge said.

"Yep, I'm fine, thanks. You boys okay?"

A man of few words, Banjo nodded and Fudge spoke for them both. "Thought we'd catch up on the latest gossip."

"Catch me up. I've been out of the loop."

"Aw, Deppity, now you know better than to think we know more than you do."

"Hell, I been strapped to a bed in the hospital. What's the word?"

"That first feller was killed? Someone said they thought they might know who he was."

Dal sipped at his coffee. So the news had gotten around about the second body. He studied Fudge over the rim of his cup. "That right?"

"Might'a been that Long boy what lives with Sara and Lennie Wells. Say, you don't reckon that's connected to that jewel robbery ole Mathon pulled over in Harrison all them years ago?"

"Is that what people are saying? If so, sure wished they'd a said it to me. Would have saved me a lot of work."

Fudge and Banjo guffawed. "Well, they never did find them diamonds, now did they?" This from Banjo, who poked his friend with his elbow. "Reckon who that second one 'ud be?"

Dal shrugged, stared into his coffee.

"I don't know nothing about no diamonds," Fudge said, as if Banjo had not brought up the newest dead man.

"Just yanking your chain," Banjo said.

"Anyone know Julie Crowe?" Dal glanced around.

"Sure. A nice lady." Fudge hurried to reply before Banjo could add his laconic remarks.

"Is she a widow?"

"Miss Julie, she's never been married. Some say the milkman stayed over one night is where Merle come from. Others know the truth, but they ain't talking. Stuff like that don't matter much anymore, except sometimes."

Dal glanced at Fudge. "He looks like Lennie Wells, don't he?"

"They were courting at one time. It's been thought on. Shit happens, no one knows why they didn't marry."

"What do you know about Mathon and Sara Wells?" Dal shifted to get more comfortable in the hard wooden chair.

"Mathon, he come here back when SEFOR was up and running. Worked there along at the last fore it closed down. Reckon some others what wasn't skeered a their hair falling out was, too. Wasn't him, Wesley, his sister Delia, and Sara great friends years ago?" Fudge shot the question at his silent friend, who nodded.

"Yep, till Delia, she married John Reilly and they moved off up to Kansas City."

There it was. The connection between Reilly and Delia Miller. Might as well see what else these fellows knew. "I was off out in the woods today. Sort of got lost and come upon this mighty fancy log cabin. Surprised to find something that huge buried in the woods like that, at the end of a road looked like it wasn't fit for a four wheeler."

"That'd be the Marcy place," Fudge said. "Hear tell his wife come into some money some years back, or that's what was told around at the time it happened. He went and bought that young'un of his a new Corvette for graduation last year so they ain't spent ever' dime yet."

"Lucky man. Too bad we can't all marry money. Wouldn't have to work no more," Theron said, digging in his overalls to pull out a wad of bills from which he peeled a few and laid them on the table. "Well, I gotta git. Want to plow my 'mater field. Won't be long fore it'll be time to plant. We sure could use some more rain." He raised a hand and waved.

"Who'd Marcy marry anyway? A Tyson or a Walton?" Dal asked.

Laughter went around the emptying tables. "Nah. No such thing." Fudge snorted. "Little ole gal from over to Fayetteville. Think her name was Somerset. No one knew her, though. Still don't. They keep pretty much to their selves."

"When did that happen?"

"Shoot, who 'members dates like that? A long while ago." Banjo finally got a few words in, and Fudge just shook his head.

Norma brought Dal's burger and fries, and he dug in. No more was said, and the diner cleared out except for a couple of guys in the other room shooting pool, the balls cracking the silence. He finished, left Norma the usual tip, waved at her, and edged out the door. It was almost full dark, and he decided to go on home till later in case a few guys were still hanging around the crime scene. He had plenty of time.

At the trailer, he kicked off his boots and collapsed across the bed. His back hurt, but not like before. Just felt like aching muscles. The leg was another story, but he'd put up with that since coming here. He fell asleep thinking about Fred Marcy and his heiress wife name of Somerset. Have to check that out.

When he turned over sometime later, a bright moon shone through the window into his face. He raised a wrist, checked his watch. Ten-thirty. He crawled off the bed, rubbing at his stubbled jaw. Being in the hospital had wreaked havoc with his schedule. He'd need to shave first thing in the morning before talking to Mac, but for now, he'd go on out to the site, see what he could learn when no one else was there to interrupt. If he ended up writhing around on the ground, so be it. At least he wouldn't have to explain it to anyone. Most all the deputies who'd seen him work—with the exception of Mac, Burt, and Les—were half scared to death of him, thought he was crazy. Then there was Jess, who understood him better than anyone else. He missed her already. Dammit, keep her out of this.

He parked the SUV deep in the woods so no one would see it and get curious, then using a small flashlight made his way to the latest crime scene. Peepers filled the night with song, an owl called and received a reply, called again. The wind had laid and the night air smelled of damp earth and last year's fallen leaves. His regrets for upsetting Jess the last time he'd seen her echoed louder than his footsteps in the dry leaves. Now she'd stay away from him. But could he leave her be?

He lifted the crime scene tape and stepped onto the spot where the second body had lain. Knelt on one knee and spread his hands on the damp ground.

Caromed back to the killing. Darkness, clouds over the moon as if to keep the vicious action hidden. Sweating, shouted curses. He shuddered, sweat poured over his face. Hatred of the purest kind filled him.

"No excuse for you raping her. I thought I raised you better. You ain't no better than your Pa."

A woman. My God, a woman. He knows the voice. Sara Wells.

Evil laughter. "She was asking me for it all along." Lennie. "Who'd know she'd get knocked up?"

"Keep the kid out of this. You showed him the map, didn't you?" Another man, a soft voice.

"My kid? Hell, yeah. He deserves to know." Yep, definitely Lennie. But what was this about a map?

The woman sees someone coming, shouts and tears into the woods making an awful clatter.

"The hell's the matter with her? We can split it between you and me. She's your Ma, he's your kid. You can take care of the both of them." The one with the more cultured voice hasn't heard what the woman has, and he continues speaking. "That'll have to satisfy you." The speaker must hold something over Lennie, for he doesn't object to the offer.

Senses alert, fear slams through Lennie and he shouts, "We got to get the hell out of here." Takes off in much the way the woman has, leaving the lone man there to face the terror. The murdered man.

"I thought you were… What are you doing? I did what you said." A terrified shout, pain, more pain, agonizing. Blood everywhere. Terror so intense Dal cannot make out the killer who never utters a word. Darkness, then nothing. A heart no longer beats, the blood slows down. Stops.

Someone shook him by the shoulder, jerked him away from the killing ground. He grabbed the arm, yanked hard.

"It's me. Jess. Turn me loose, okay? Are you all right? Come on, snap out of it."

He let her go, remained on his hands and knees a moment, shaking away the images, the sounds of violence and death. "Goddammit, Jess. What the hell? I was working the scene."

He staggered to his feet, leaning against her. One hand grappling, touching her. Dammit. Breathing hard, she wrapped an arm around his waist.

"Shit, I almost had him." He put both hands on her shoulders, tried to push her away.

"Just hold it a minute. I don't want you going flat on your face. You okay now?"

Her mouth so close to his, sweet breath on his cheek. He only had to lean down a little and cover those luscious lips with his. So he did, and it shot through him like he'd touched a live wire. His body shuddered with a dark desire. Damned if he didn't forget all about why he'd come out here. Only her. Her and the night and the contemptible beast that drove him.

Her mouth opened to his and she moaned, then pushed at his chest. "Stop it. I won't do this with you again. It hurts too much. You let me go. Now. I'm sorry I bothered. Stop it. Should have just left you laying there in the dark. Damn you, damn you." Her voice softened.

Lifting both hands away from her, he held them open and backed away. "You're right. I'm sorry." He staggered and leaned against a nearby tree.

"Dal?" Her voice soft, afraid. "I can't… dammit, why do we do this to each other?"

Crooking his arm against the rough tree bark, he leaned his forehead there and took several deep breaths. She touched his back, her hand firm against his sweaty shirt.

"I won't leave you here like this. Damn you, Dal Starr. Damn you to hell and back."

"Been there, done that."

"Oh, yeah, I know, and for that I'm supposed to forgive you anything. Everything?"

"No. Hell no. You should run the other way as fast as you can."

She leaned her cheek against his back. "I'm trying, but I can't. I can't."

He turned, let the tree prop him from behind and grasped her arms, pulled her so close he tasted her warm flesh, smelled something akin to fear. "Then we have to figure out something. Something we can live with. 'Cause it doesn't look like we can stay away from each other. Just don't love me. Don't ask me to love you."

Within the cloak of night, unable to make out her features, he released the tight grip and curled his arms around her. "Dear God, Jessie." Whispered close to her moist skin. "I don't know what to do."

She exhaled a ragged breath against his neck. Ripped at the buttons on his shirt, went to work on his belt buckle, and dragged down the zipper. "If you can't love me, Dal, then fuck me like you do."

"God help us both." He tore her blouse and bra off in one swift motion.

Kicking out of her jeans, she leaned into him, breasts soft and warm, stomach and thighs muscled. Rippling. Teasing him into full arousal.

A wilding possessed him, terrifying in its feral desire. He would howl at the moon if he could find a voice. He cupped her buttocks with both hands and lifted her. Legs coiled around his waist, she took him deep inside, sucking the very breath from his soul, freezing his mind. He sank to the ground, her on top. Locked together as one. Animals in rut.

Shame passed briefly through his mind before he took her breast in his mouth, moving rhythmically with her, gently then harder and harder. He could no longer take a full breath, or see or hear. All he could be was a man locked to a woman, both appeasing their passion. He came with a burst of fury. Fury at himself. At her. At a world filled with evil that would not leave him in peace. He held her, both gasping air into their lungs, until at last they relaxed in the refuge of each other's arms. Silent darkness settled, the moon hiding behind a drift of clouds as if ashamed to watch.

She lay stretched out over him for a long while, until the moon came into view above the thick canopy of trees, cold light they could not feel. The peepers having gone silent, tuned up again.

"You okay laying here on the ground?" Her words hot and soft against his throat.

"As long as you're okay laying on me."

"Why would I not be?" She snuggled against him.

Lost again. He could not fathom being without her, even as he warned himself of such foolishness.

He followed her home. Where else would he go? Parked. Watched her climb from her Jeep and turn toward him, the light from above casting shadows that made of her someone he did not know. Fists doubled, he pounded the steering wheel, turned off the key, got out, and trailed behind her to the house. Lagging, trying to make himself get back in his car and go home where he belonged. He did not see, only heard her open the door. A split second when he knew. A gunshot. Too goddamned late, he knew. All the things he should have done slamming through his mind. She cried out. The world tilted, he roared a protest. His feet flew over the ground getting to her.

Weapon in hand. On the porch. Follow protocol. No, get to her. To hell with everything else. Stupid reigned supreme, and he burst into the room. If the shooter was still in the house, he was dead. Moaning, low and indistinct. She lay so close, his toes bumped her. Sprawled on the floor, a pool of blood widening around her head. Feet pounded. The back door slammed.

Grandfather's warning echoed in his ears. "She treads close to the edge, my grandson. If you don't catch her, she will fall." And when he'd asked what he meant, the old man said softly, "You will know when it's time." Dear God, had that time come? Was it too late to catch her?

Adrenalin kicked in, blinding him. Turning him deaf. In the profound silence, he dropped to his knees, pain blocked, and blackness choking him. With one trembling hand, he touched her shoulder, terrified to turn her over. So much blood.

Dear God. *Jessie!* His throat filled and he swallowed hard. Do something. Do it now.

The hand that had held his gun held a phone. How? He dialed 9-1-1, yelled he needed an ambulance, threw the phone down and sprawled on his butt, legs splayed. Turned her over. Dragged her limp body into his lap. Hot blood soaked his shirt. Bleeding meant living. Living. Alive.

He couldn't see. Or hear. Or breathe. Or move. Held her cause that was all he could do.

A head wound. For God's sake. He pulled her tight to his chest and began to rock her, saying her name over and over. Shaking, my God. Shaking so hard his teeth chattered. Fear and remorse and anger swarmed over him.

"Don't you die on me. Don't you dare die on me. I'm right here, darlin', right here." Fury, rage. A roar like only an animal could manage. "You bastard, I'll get you, you son of a bitch." His aching throat closed over the words, choked off his breath.

She moaned. Moaned? Bullet to the head and she moaned?

"Jessie?"

"What happened? My head hurts." Indistinct, but spoken.

"Jessie?" Dumb ass. Do something, say something besides her name.

Look at the wound. Gently, he lowered her to the floor, pulled his shirt off and mopped the blood from her face and out of her eyes. Eyes that were open, looking at him.

"Dal, don't go away." She went limp. Passed out. Not dead, surely not that.

Frantic, he grabbed an afghan off the couch, covered her, picked up a pillow and lay her head on it. Touched her chest that moved up and down. Once more wiped away the blood. The track the bullet had taken continued to bleed. The bastard had creased her. Cut a path across her forehead and temple deep enough to bleed like a son of a bitch, maybe gave her a concussion, but she was alive.

Once more, he took her into his arms and held her close, her blood sticky on his skin. EMTs burst through the front door and took her away from him. He hadn't even heard the sirens. Hands, face, clothing, slick with her blood, the coppery smell permeating the room. He slumped, propped himself up with both arms, and watched while they hooked her up, put her on a stretcher, and hauled her off.

One of the young men bent over him. "Sir, are you hurt?"

"Who, me? No, no it's all her blood."

"You want to ride in the ambulance?"

"No, I'll follow. I want to have my ride." When he tried to get up, he couldn't.

"Sir, are you sure you aren't hurt?"

"I'm not, but could you give me a hand?"

The EMT helped him clamber to his feet. "I'll be okay in just a minute or two."

"Say, aren't you Dallas Starr, the crime scene investigator with the sheriff's office?"

"That's me."

"Good to meet you. She'll be okay. Lucky young lady."

"Yeah, lucky." Shaking so hard he could barely navigate, Dal thanked him and staggered out beside him. He remembered to lock and close the door. Like it had made any difference earlier. His heartbeat slowed down some so he could think rationally, and he fished out his cell and called Mac to assure him she was alive. He would've heard, been half out of his mind.

"I heard the dispatch," Mac said. "I'm on my way out there now. What happened this time? Is Jessie all right?"

"She was creased in the head by a bullet. It was meant to kill her, Mac. Goddamn, who would do a thing like that?"

"Where are you?" In the background, a siren wound down.

"I'm on my way to follow the ambulance."

"I assume the perp got away?"

"Hell yes, he got away. It was Jessie laying there in all that blood. I wasn't gonna chase the bastard, leave her, and he knew it, too. Went out the back door after I got in the house."

"Calm down, Dallas. You sound high as a kite."

"I am. Mac, if I could've laid hands on him, I'd have beaten him to death, right there in her house."

He slid into his car, slammed the door, and keyed the ignition. Took several deep breaths. Only then registered the burning pain in his leg. Ignored it. "I'm going to the hospital now, Mac. The house is locked."

"That's okay, we'll get in and see if we can find some evidence. Probably won't be any, though."

"Gotta go." Dal disconnected, tossed the phone in the console, and dug ruts turning around and heading out. The SUV rocked over ninety on the two-lane, caught the ambulance after about a mile. The siren screamed. He had to settle down before he got to the hospital or he'd kick down some doors. The anger that raged in him was unlike any he'd known since he found Leann dead with a needle hanging out of her arm.

He'd worked hard to keep from caring for this woman, to keep from loving her, 'cause love led to all kinds of weird behavior, to unbelievable suffering. Like this very moment. Sometimes the heart rares up like some sort of monster, and there isn't much a fellow can do about it. Sounded like a country song. Emotions ran rampant. All he cared about was getting there and holding her, making sure she was safe. And catching the son of a bitch who did this. Sara's voice at the murder scene. Behind this whole mess? Yet he hadn't felt her in Jessie's house. All things considered, he might not have been reading things correctly.

At times, he wanted to bump the ambulance, but he held back, parked directly beside it at the emergency entrance, and leaped from the car, grabbing hold of the swinging door to support himself. The EMTs rolled her out of the back of the vehicle. Smears of black crusted blood reflected on her hair in the falsely lit night.

"Hey, you can't leave your car there, deputy," one of the men shouted.

Another went over to the guy, talked to him, then came running to Dal. "Give me the keys, I'll take care of it, Deputy Starr."

It was the EMT who stayed with him after they took Jess out of the house. He dug the keys from his pocket, handed them over. "What's your name, buddy?"

"Mike Henley, sir. I'll leave your keys at the sign-in desk inside."

"Thanks, Mike." He pounded him on the shoulder, then followed Jessie into emergency.

All he could see was an oxygen mask over her face and her bare, blood-soaked feet sticking out from the blanket they'd covered her with. Throat stinging, he dropped into a chair in the waiting room, elbows on his knees, hands over his face. The tears came, surprising him with their intensity. Grown men who carry guns don't cry. That didn't help him stop.

Much later, someone laid a hand on his shoulder. He glanced up to see a nurse with a concerned expression on her face. "Deputy Starr, if you want to see her now, she's asking for you. Follow me."

"How is she?"

"She's doing just fine. Here." She pulled a curtain open enough to let him in the small enclosed cubicle. "We'll take her to a room shortly. Doctor wants to keep her overnight."

He went to her side, captured her hand that was free of needles and held it to his lips, studied her face. They had those oxygen tubes up her nose and a bandage swathed her head, but her blue eyes were open. Puzzled. Frightened.

"Dal?" She sounded sleepy and scared.

"It's me, honey. You'll be okay. I have it on good authority." Dammit, the tears were flowing again, wetting her hand. Better than kicking walls or shooting someone, which ran a close second.

"If you hadn't been there…."

"Shh. I was there, and everything is fine. You get some sleep, and I'll be here when you wake up."

"We have to stop meeting this way." The words slurred away, but he understood them and smiled, bent down and kissed her cheek. Only a few days ago he was the one lying in the hospital bed, her beside him, crying and holding his hand. Nice feeling, holding hands. When you loved someone. Dammit to hell. Better if it didn't have to be done near a hospital bed, though.

When they took her away, he shoved outside, that familiar dark vengeance growing in his chest like a tumor that couldn't be stopped. Working on the streets of Dallas, seeing so much death and the destruction of so many lives caused by drugs, a beast had settled in his soul. A beast he'd thought gone, yet he found it waiting this night. Wished he could not be a cop for one night, hunt the SOB down and blow his ass away. Someone took a gun to the woman he cared for and they would pay, maybe more than what the law allowed.

The phone vibrated in his pocket and he was surprised that he'd thought to grab it from the console when he bailed from the unit. He fumbled it out and punched the button.

"Starr here."

"Mac. How is she?"

"Okay. Knew me."

"Thank God. We haven't found a thing. Taking fingerprints now and will try to eliminate those that should be here, maybe by morning. See what we've got left. Perp probably too smart to leave any."

"Don't forget the back door. That's how he got out. If he took off his glove to fire the gun, then he just might've touched the door with that hand. It happens."

"I know. We'll do everything we can." Pause, like he was fearful of what came next. Then he asked it. "Absolutely sure she's gonna make it?

"Yep. Son of a bitch missed by a hair. She's scared. Resting."

"You sound—"

"You're damned right I do."

"Take a deep breath. Stay with her, we'll handle this. I let Tink and Parker know what happened. Told 'em they couldn't do nothing now, to come by in the morning. But listen, we don't need a damned wild Indian out there on the warpath. I'll get back to you soon as I can."

"Thanks, Mac."

"S'okay. I love her too, you know."

"Yep, I do." He disconnected, dropped the phone in his pocket, and slapped open the doors with the flat of both hands. Twice now he'd admitted to loving her.

A nurse directed him to the waiting area nearest Jessie's room, where he slumped into a chair. She leaned down, touched his arm. "She'll sleep till morning. Maybe you ought to go home, get cleaned up, and get some sleep yourself. You look beat."

"What time is it?" He rubbed his eyes with his fingertips.

Down the hall, an alarm of some sort sounded and a Code Blue echoed through the dim corridors. His eyes flew open and he started up, heart hammering at his temples till his head wanted to burst.

"Relax, it's another patient. Have to go." The nurse scurried away, doing her job.

Someone dying this night. It took him a few minutes to settle down. It had to be late. He finally found a clock on a wall across the hall behind the nurses' station. Two-fifteen. He could go home and catch a few hours sleep before the hospital came to life and they woke her. Exhausted as he was, he couldn't make himself get up and leave her here. No one else was in the waiting room, and the hospital was quiet. He lay down on a couch-like affair, dangled his legs off the end, and covered both eyes with one arm.

An old familiar nightmare crept inside his brain, the terror so real he walked in that dark alley once again. Heard the gunfire, this time the bullets found Jessie. Paralyzed by a deep sleep, he couldn't escape. Not the pain, the anger, the fear. So intense it ground through him as if he'd been laid out by a steam roller. Just like it had been that night. Except not him but Jess in pools of blood.

He awoke sweating, arms wind-milling, and sat up, scrubbing at his face, not sure where he was for a moment or two. Jess. Jessie.

Pink-tinged daylight bled in through an outside door across the way, and he searched for the clock. A little after six. He crept down the hallway to her room. He had to see her. Now, this minute, make sure she was still okay. Make sure her recovery was real, hadn't been a dream.

With the tips of his fingers he eased the door open just enough to get a glimpse of her in the bed. With one more glance over his shoulder, as if anyone coming could stop him, he moved in and pushed the door closed behind him. A chair sat not far from her bed and he moved it over, dropped down in it, and found her hand, held it gently. She grabbed on and squeezed.

"Hi." His voice was hoarse, as if he'd been screaming for an eternity.

"Hi." A near whisper.

Throat burning, he lay his head on the mattress next to her, and she fisted up a handful of his hair. Why the hell did it hurt so much to love? Closing his eyes, he let out a thankful breath and drifted off to sleep, her fingers massaging his head.

A nurse awoke him. "You shouldn't be in here."

"Why not? I'm not hurting anything. Just being with her."

"Well, you can't be with her right now. Rounds coming, you'll be in the way. Besides, you need to get out of those bloody clothes. Go home, clean up, and you can come back and be with her." To her credit, she softened the instructions and gave him a kind smile.

He glanced down, surprised to find that he was covered in her dried blood, wearing the shirt he'd cleaned her up with. Didn't remember putting it back on. Probably even blood on his face. "Shit, I'm sorry. I didn't… didn't think about it."

"I know," the nurse said, taking his arm. "Come on."

Before she could pull him away, he bent down and kissed Jess on the cheek. "Love you," he said. That made three.

Out in the hallway, he stopped for a moment, glanced back at the room in which she lay. Had he really told her that? If she was awake, she'd always remember it, hold him to it.

Tink and Parker waited outside her room and he reassured them that Jess was okay.

"Is that her blood all over you?" Tink's eyes widened with fright.

He nodded. "Head wound. Bled a lot. They say she really is going to be okay. I guess you could wait around to see her if you want. I'll be back soon as I get cleaned up. I've got something to do first, though."

"You aren't staying?" Parker shot him an accusing look.

"I'll be back. You tell her. I'll be back." He picked up his keys at the check-in desk, tromped out to the parking lot, found his unit backed into a slot by the thoughtful Mike Henley, EMT, former special ops trying to make up for the death and destruction of war. Memories so vivid in his mind and soul, Dal had experienced them with only a touch.

He drove home where he stood under a hot shower until the water cooled, her blood swirling around his feet and floating away down the drain.

Dressed in his uniform, he strapped on his weapon and headed for work. Soon as he found out what Mac had learned at Jessie's, he'd return to the hospital to her, because he could do no less.

A killer walked loose, and he was after Jess or the both of them because they were too damned stubborn to back off. He would not leave her alone, exposed to that kind of danger. Yet it could be possible he himself posed even more of a threat to her.

12
CHAPTER

Jess eased her eyes open, so as not to activate the steady hammering in her head. Maybe if she held her breath it would go away. Dal had been right there, in that chair, when he told her he loved her. But for the life of her, she couldn't remember anything before that. What happened to put her in this bed with him holding her hand? And her head, oh, God, her poor head.

Parker's familiar face drifted into view. He took her hand, kissed it. Said nothing. Tink crowded close, tears wetting her cheeks.

"How are you, sweetie?" Whispered like she might know Jess couldn't stand noise.

At the foot of the bed, a third face, that of someone who didn't know about keeping his stupid mouth shut. "How are you feeling this morning?" The voice shook the walls and rattled the windows.

"Please be quiet." She covered her ears. "What happened?"

The speaker held a clipboard. A doctor, perhaps, but he looked about twelve years old. Had she fallen down the rabbit hole?

His mouth moved, the words coming slowly, like when a movie gets messed up and the sound doesn't match the lips. "You don't remember?"

"I'd shake my head, but better not. No, I don't remember anything till Dal holding my hand." She kept a firm grip on Parker's fingers, wished the stranger would leave her be.

"What's the last thing you remember?"

Concentrate. You know your name, you know Dal loves you. Tell this fool something so he'll go away. "When?"

"Just the last thing you can think of."

A man... oh, God... he has a gun. Nope, nothing else. "There was a man with a—um, the world exploded but that's all. Did I get shot?"

"And before that, anything else?"

"Dal and I." She covered her mouth, closed her eyes and there they were, making love in the woods in the moonlight. But he didn't shoot her, she shot him. Confusion.

"Yes?" The silly idiot just kept staring at her with that goofy I-really-don't-give-a-damn expression.

"Why don't you come back when she's feeling better?" Parker's voice, firm, insistent.

The young doctor continued to watch Jess, ignoring Parker.

"That's all I can remember. Where is he? Dal, I mean. Not the man with the gun."

"He is right here," came the familiar lyrical voice, then his hand sought out hers on the opposite side of the bed. "Sorry, I had to go by the sheriff's office to see if they'd found anything last night at your place." He acknowledged Tink and Parker with a nod.

"I can't remember what happened to me." She dare not move her head, it hurt so bad.

Dal glanced at the doctor, but she didn't. She just kept staring at him. "He didn't tell me. Dal, you tell me. Please."

Clasping her hand tightly in both his, he sat in the chair and leaned close. "Someone took a shot at you, creased your head." He took a deep breath, and she saw in his eyes a flash of raw fury before the tenderness returned. When he tried to say more, his voice caught and failed. He ran one finger along her cheek. Whispered. "I thought you were dead."

"As soon as the headache lessens, we'll release you," the doctor said. "You may have residual headaches for a few days. If they persist, see your physician. Otherwise, you'll be just fine. You were a mighty lucky girl." He was gone like he'd come, on silent feet.

"I suppose if you look at it one way," Parker mused. He leaned down, touched her forehead with his lips. "Get some rest, and we'll see you later."

Tink touched cheek to her cheek. "I love you. See you soon."

"A mighty lucky girl," Dal repeated, the anger lingering long after the door closed behind Parker and Tink.

"I got shot in the head. Sorry, I don't feel very lucky. What's going on?"

"Not now, honey. Relax, rest, get rid of that headache, then we can discuss it. I'll tell you everything."

"What if I want to know now?" She turned to look at him, and the world tilted. "Oh, God," she moaned.

"Should I call someone? Are you all right?"

If everyone would only whisper instead of roaring. She tried it with her next question. "Of course I'm not all right. Do I have a bullet in my head?"

He leaned closer, whispered his answer. "No, your skull is too hard and the bullet just ran around the outside edge."

"Funny."

"But true."

He barely touched her cheek again. "I was so scared."

Did she dare ask him if he still loved her, or had that only been a reflex of his fear? Instead she asked, "Where's Mac?"

"He was with you last night for a while. Now he's out there chasing the ones responsible for this."

For now, she'd keep quiet about having heard Dal say he loved her. He probably thought she had been asleep. His eyes batted. Crawling around in her mind again. "Sorry, I didn't mean to... As soon as they release you, I'll take you home." He kissed the back of her hand. "You'll be okay. But you need to lie still. Rest."

"Oh, you mean I shouldn't just check myself out and go running off to do God knows what?"

"Ouch. I see your wry sense of humor hasn't deserted you. Don't you know men do things like that 'cause we're stupid? Women are smarter than men, they let us take care of them."

The next time she awoke, an aide was standing beside the bed with a tray. He moved the rolling table across her lap, set it there. "Can I raise the bed for you?"

"Very carefully, please."

He did, and she caught a glimpse of dinner. A cup of broth, a container of juice of some kind, and green Jell-o. "Oh, dear, I thought green Jell-o was a joke." She poked at it with her spoon and it wiggled.

"Maybe I'll just drink the broth and juice." And ask Dal to bring some ice cream for dessert. Eating anything green that wiggled was out of the question. "Did you see a tall, good-looking Cherokee hanging around anywhere?" Immediately she wished she could bury her head in a pillow.

"No, ma'am." The aide looked as if he expected an Indian massacre.

"Oh, don't worry. He's harmless."

The aide left, and she picked up the cup, sipped at the hot broth. Her stomach wanted that badly, and much more. She pawed around on the bed for the phone that should be there, found it, and dialed Dal's cell.

He replied after only one ring. "Hey, you okay?"

"Hey, yes. Know what I want?"

"A good looking bed partner?"

"Already have that, thank you. I want a strawberry milkshake from Sonic. A big one." She paused for effect. "They gave me green Jell-o."

A longer pause, then he laughed, and it sounded so good she almost cried. "I'll be there in fifteen."

"Dal?"

"Yes?"

"Don't forget the milkshake."

"I surely won't. Your wish is my command."

"About that bed partner."

"Uh-huh."

"May have to put a hold on that till this frigging headache goes away."

Again he laughed. "See ya."

"See ya. Love ya." She only said that because he had already hung up.

She watched the clock till he arrived, and it was only ten minutes. The gigantic cup he held must've contained a quart of milk and the same amount of ice cream with a huge mound of whipped cream nesting a bright red cherry. He set a tote bag on the floor beside the bed, placed the milkshake on the table, glanced at the green Jell-o, and made a yucky sound in his throat.

"I never knew anyone ate green Jell-o." She pushed it into one corner of the tray.

"They don't. They just play with it. Look how it jiggles when I stick it with a fork." Again he laughed, his lingering fear slurring the pleasant sound.

She flipped the top off the milkshake, and he produced two straws and two spoons.

"Thought you might share with me, since I missed my dinner. You look better. How's the head?"

"Better. I can go home soon as they get the releases and stuff finished."

"Good. I'll just stay right here and take you."

She studied his regal features for a long moment. "Thank you, Dal."

He looked up. "You're welcome. For what?"

"For being you, I guess. I don't know. It's like I can always count on you, even when you're angry with me." She glanced down, changed the subject. "I get the cherry."

He took her spoon, fished up the cherry and offered it to her. Silently, he ate ice cream for a while, concentrating on each bite and not looking at her. "Jess, I thought they'd killed you." His eyes filled, and he turned away.

She wanted to touch him, to kiss him, to tell him she loved him. She did none of those things, just let him get over the emotional moment without embarrassing him.

Halfway through the gigantic milkshake, she put down her spoon. "When are you going to tell me what happened? What you guys are doing about it? Why it happened?"

"I thought maybe after you felt a bit better."

"I'll feel better when I know what's going on. Why you think someone took a shot at me? When I'm home in my own bed and you're there with me, for Christ's sake."

He grinned wickedly. "Don't you think we ought to ask Doogie

Howser out there if it's all right for us to sleep together so soon after your injury?"

"I thought perhaps I'd ask you how you feel about sleeping with me because you care, not because you need a little nooky."

"Jessie. I distinctly remember us sleeping together, a week or so ago, and there was no nooky involved at all."

"That was because I care." She was able to laugh gently without causing an explosion in her head. Didn't ask him if he cared. He finished the milkshake without comment.

A nurse hustled in. "We've about got everything signed for your release, Miss West. If you'd care to get dressed someone will be in with a wheelchair in a few minutes."

"Dressed? Where are my clothes?" She glanced at Dal and he looked back at her.

"Well, shit." He raised his shoulders in a shrug. "Never occurred to me you couldn't go home naked."

The nurse frowned at him. He smiled, and she spread a palm over her chest and blushed. Even nurses melted when he used that weapon. He picked up the tote bag and swung it.

"It just so happens I have in this bag a pair of jeans and a tee shirt and two matching sneakers. One for each foot. Oh, and underwear. Hope you don't mind my going through your unmentionables."

"Not at all," Jess said, and they both chuckled while the nurse exited the room without a word.

Safely tucked into his car, Jess relaxed. He drove carefully, taking corners so slow a car behind him blew past, the driver shaking his fist.

"Hey. Watch it, buddy. I'm the law, and I'm armed." He glanced at her and grinned. "You okay?"

"I'm fine. It's just a shot in the head. Why wouldn't I be?"

"Oh, yeah. Now you can joke about it."

She remained quiet, preferring to study his profile, his casual control of the car. When he parked in front of her house, he turned off the ignition. "Stay put. I'm coming around for you."

And he did, swinging open the door and gathering her close against his chest. She looped her arms around his neck and kissed him under the jaw, inhaling his scent that was more man than cologne or after shave. His limp made her conscious of what had so recently happened to him.

"You should let me walk. I don't need to be carried."

"Yes, you do. Hush."

The door was locked. "Shit. You keep a key outside anywhere?"

"Where's my key? My backpack?"

"Inside. Dumb me, going off and forgetting something of such importance." He grinned. "Want me to break in?"

"No. Around back. You know where the spare key is."

"Oh, I'd forgotten that. I'm gonna put you down here in the swing, go and unlock the house. That okay with you?"

"That's very okay with me."

He settled her into the swing and disappeared around the corner. Pretty soon he returned. "It's not there. You sure you put it back last time you used it?"

"Very sure."

He gazed at her for a long moment. "Who else knows where you keep the key?"

"Well, there's Tinker, Kathy Spacey and…." She shrugged.

"Think. The guy who shot you came in the back door. The key opens both doors, doesn't it?"

"Yes, but I can't think who else…." She didn't have the strength to think about it right now. "Can you break in? I need to lie down."

"Damn right I can. The destructive way or the kinder, gentler way?"

"Don't break my door."

He dug in his pocket, pulled out a small black case, took some instruments out of it, and picked the lock. Took her once more into his arms and carried her through to her bedroom where he laid her on the bed.

While he was bent over, she cupped his cheek in her palm. Said nothing. Their eyes met and held, his so deep a green they looked black till the sunlight slashing through the window caught them.

He cleared his throat and moved to take her shoes off. "Want your clothes off? I'm really good at that."

"I know you are, honey. Maybe just the jeans."

He nodded and spent a lot of time easing them down over her behind and peeling them off her legs, all the while checking to make sure he wasn't hurting her. She didn't complain, so he ran a long finger under the top of her panties and carefully adjusted them, creating a buzz where he touched her skin.

"All fixed." Another of those smiles that made her feel like the sun had come out on a rainy day and touched her with its warmth.

"We need to talk about what happened here. What you've found out."

"We will, but not now. Now you go to sleep. I'll be here. If you need anything, holler. I'm taking the couch."

"You can sleep in here."

He touched her lips with two fingers. "No, I'm putting myself between them and you, whoever 'them' might happen to be."

"Make yourself at home, then. Watch a movie, make some coffee. Sorry there's nothing much to eat."

"Oh, that ice cream will do me till morning no problem. I presume you have Honey Bun, though?."

She smiled lazily, drifting nearer to sleep. "Yes, I do." And closed her eyes to the darkness.

Dal made a tour of the house, checking windows and doors, started a pot of coffee, then settled down to watch Dexter, a man who did what he sometimes fantasized about doing to child abusers and drug dealers. Cut them up in little pieces, put them in black trash bags, and dropped them in the ocean. By the time it grew dark, he had checked on Jess several times, gone through the pot of coffee, and turned off the television to enjoy the silence. Mac called about then, and they discussed the lack of any evidence found at Jessie's and the missing key.

"You know, I think I'll go through these files from Detective Morris again," Dal said."Maybe we missed something. There's got to be something here we can link to these two killings and this attempt on Jessie's life. Whoever it was used the key out back to get in, so they know someone who knows where she kept it."

"You staying the night, I presume."

"You're damned right. And you know something, Mac? I hope that son of a bitch comes back and gives me an excuse to blow him away."

"Take 'er easy, Dal."

"Oh, I will. Don't you worry none, Mac. I'll do it real easy. See you tomorrow sometime."

Jessie's landline rang a few minutes later. It was Tinker, and he gave her an update. She offered to let Parker know Jess was home, as well as the Spaceys.

"Thanks, Tink. I appreciate it, and I know Jess will, too."

"You gonna take good care of her, Deputy Dal?"

"You bet I am."

An hour or so later, well into another pot of coffee, he ran across an interesting note in the old files. A Delia Reilly had been interviewed after one of the burglaries that summer thirty years ago. Her brother, Wesley Miller, was a person of interest in the case, but they never pinned it on him. Now he could definitely link Delia Miller to John Reilly Imports and to the diamond heist. He'd heard it at the Red Bird. She married John Reilly and went off to Kansas City with him. Still not sure how that connected to the robberies. She and her hubby might be involved, considering Reilly's connections. But it was Sara's gruff voice he'd heard during that last crime scene replay.

Too many variables yet, so he finally tossed down the last file, placed his .45 on the floor within easy reach, and stretched out on the couch, one hand hanging near the gun's grip, feet propped on the arm. When he was younger, he could go for forty-eight hours or more without sleep, but after barely any sleep the previous night, he drifted off.

The rising sun slanted through the kitchen window into the living room, touching his face. He jerked awake, sat and rubbed his eyes, then picked up the weapon. He went to the bedroom to find Jess still sleeping and hit the bathroom before starting some coffee. Rummaging through the cabinets, he found her stash of Honey Buns, took out two packages, and went back to her room.

There he sat on the floor next to her and leaned his head against the mattress. Her fingers ran through his hair. "Good morning, Sleepy. How's your head?"

"Mmm, hurts inside and out."

"Coffee's making. Want some?"

"Yeah. Bathroom first."

He rose and supported her the few steps, parked outside the door till she finished, then took her back to bed.

"Thank you. Did you get any sleep last night?"

"A little. Stay here, I'll bring coffee and Honey Buns."

"Mmm, I can smell it."

"Yeah. I thought about making pancakes, but…." He shrugged and grinned when she made a face at him.

When he returned with a tray, she had moved over in the bed so he could sit beside her.

Peering through the steam from her mug, she asked, "Have any idea who did this and why?"

"Not yet." He unwrapped the Honey Buns, folded a napkin around the lower half of one, and handed it to her. "Thought about plates and forks, but let's face it, I'm just an uncivilized Indian."

"Definitely, but stay that way, would you?" She took a big bite and closed her eyes to chew. "What is today?"

"Kidding?"

"No, confused. I can't remember when this happened and how long I was in the hospital."

"Let's see, it happened Thursday night and today is Saturday. Why?"

"Have you talked to Tinker?"

"Yep. She might come over today. Wants me to call and let her know if you're up to company."

"And Dave and Kathy?"

He glanced at her with a curious frown. "Sure, she called them. What's up?"

"Just wanted to see them, that's all."

He nodded but continued to study her for a while. "We finish our coffee and you want me to, I'll call them so they can come over and visit with you." He resisted poking around in her head, though he sensed something secretive.

"Yes, I'd like that."

"Just one thing," he said when they'd finished and he stood to take the tray to the kitchen. "You'd probably better put on some britches before they get here."

She poked her tongue out, then grinned. "While they're here, would you mind running to the office and picking up my laptop? I left it there, and I'd like to do some work later. I have a story to write for tomorrow."

"Sure, okay, if you feel up to it."

"I do." And she needed him gone so they could discuss the plan to search SEFOR Sunday morning. If Dal found out, he'd pitch a fit. He was a stickler about the law handling everything. A tampering charge wouldn't go over too well for any of them. Tinker and Burt could lose their jobs if they were caught. With what had happened to her, it was best if they cancel their plans and let Dal handle it however he saw fit, long as he followed Mac's rules about him being on the disabled list.

"I'll run that errand as soon as Tinker gets here, then I'm going by the sheriff's office to talk to Mac. Got the keys to the newspaper office?"

"In my bag, but you may not be able to find them so you can bring it in here if you need to."

He carried the bulky backpack to her and set it on the bed. While she dug around for the office keys, he asked, "Did you think of anyone else who might have known where you kept the spare key to this place?"

"I told you, Tink and Kathy. Oh, and Parker knows. And Mac." Still digging in the bag, she thought for a minute. "That's all, far as I— Wait, I think I told the guy who came to fix my Wi-Fi when I wasn't here."

"Do you remember his name?"

She paused, one hand filled with Kleenex, a couple of pens, and something he couldn't identify. "Nope, but the paperwork is in my desk somewhere. I'll see if I can find it."

"No hurry. I don't want you doing too much. I'm responsible for you."

She laughed. "How do you figure that?"

"Hey, I saved your life, didn't I? Doesn't that make me responsible?" He turned away fast so she wouldn't see his expression, but she did, and it was far more serious than his teasing tone.

"Could I ask you something?" She fisted up the keys from the detritus in the bottom of the backpack.

How come women always carried so damn much junk around all the time? "Sure. Anything."

"Why is it okay for you to take care of me and see to my needs and you don't want me to do the same for you? What is with that?"

He studied her as if he was seriously thinking about it, then said, "Don't be silly. A big old lunkhead like me doesn't need looking after. Now you, on the other hand, being a helpless woman, need all the care I can give."

She made a face. He leaned down and gave her a quick kiss.

Tinker busted in without knocking, Burt Sample in tow. Dal raised an eyebrow in Jessie's direction, greeted his deputy friend, grinned owlishly at Tinker and left. "Be back in a while. Watch her, would you, Tink?"

Jess made herself comfortable on the bed while the couple settled on the floor nearby. Tinker studied her closely. "Wow, I never knew anyone who was shot in the head before. Does it hurt?"

"Only when I move or laugh or eat. That pretty much covers it. Seriously, it's much better today. Hurt like a son of a gun yesterday."

"Sure put an end to our plans for tomorrow morning, huh?"

"Might be a good thing. I'd hate if you guys ended up being charged with tampering with evidence. I was so upset over Dal being laid up I couldn't think straight. Since he's convinced he's back to his old self, it's probably best if we let him organize the search, when and if he decides the loot might be hidden at SEFOR. I think he's going to need a lot more evidence, even though Mac did get permission to search, just in case."

"Too bad. I was looking forward to it. Sort of an exciting idea."

"Yeah, but I was crazy to ask you and Burt to take part. You could lose your jobs. I apologize. I'm glad I had time to think, even though getting this," she pointed toward her bandaged head, "wasn't exactly what I had in mind."

Tinker grinned and patted her hand.

"Say, did you know Julie Crowe?" Jess asked. "She's about your age."

"Julie? Sure did. We were best friends through high school. That is, till she got pregnant. We had a dreadful row. I told her the father ought to have to take responsibility, and she told me to mind my own business. She never did tell me his name. 'Course, when that kid started turning into a grown person, everyone in town knew immediately who the daddy was. That no-account Lennie Wells, who never himself owned up to it. Stupid bastard. Hmm, I hadn't thought of Julie in ages. Always felt bad about not supporting her when she needed a friend."

Jess went on to explain to Tinker why she'd asked about Julie Crowe, and they visited some more about the murders and how people in town were taking the crime wave. It was close to noon when someone rattled the front door and Burt went to open it.

"Hey, anyone home?" Kathy and Dave came in carrying two baskets, a most heavenly smell of barbecue accompanying them. "We decided the search was probably off, and since you couldn't come to us, we'd bring the barbecue to you. Just because our search was cancelled doesn't mean we can't have a barbecue."

Kathy took out a tablecloth, spread it on the floor near Jessie's bed, and unpacked the baskets. Barbecued ribs in Dave's homemade sauce, potato salad like only Kathy could make, fresh rolls still steaming hot, a tossed salad to which she added dressing before heaping it into five bowls.

"And *voila*," she said, sweeping the top off a cake keeper to reveal her special chocolate cake.

Tinker ogled it. "I'll have a piece of that first, that way if I get too full I will have enjoyed my dessert."

Everyone laughed, and Dave piled food in plates and passed them around. Gathered companionably on the floor, with Jessie propped up on pillows in the bed, they discussed all manner of things. Never once did they mention Jess being shot, like they were all a bit afraid to dwell on the possibilities.

"And so what about our plans that went awry? Will you reschedule?" Kathy asked.

"No, it was foolish of me. I wasn't thinking. That's off. Thanks anyway. I'm gonna let Dal take care of it, now he's back on his feet."

"How's he doing?"

"He seems to be fine. Other than they can't find the sliver of the bullet. Not talking about it yet, though. He's been cleared by all his doctors. 'Course, he leaves out that he was supposed to stay off that leg for a month so the ligaments can heal."

"Big tough guy," Tink said. "When he was leaving, he asked me and Burt to hang around till he comes back."

"Yeah, he's worried about me, that's all."

"With good reason, I'd say." A lot of words for Dave. He usually watched his talkative wife, whom he clearly adored, and nodded once in a while to show he agreed with something she'd said.

That's as close as they came to bringing up her being shot, like they were all afraid to speak of it. Didn't bother her. She sure didn't want to talk about it.

After Dave and Kathy fixed Dal a plate, gathered the remnants of their barbecue and left, Jess asked Tinker if she'd bring her the paid bill file from her desk. "It's in the bottom right hand deep drawer, a bright yellow folder that says PD on it."

While she was gone, Jess asked Burt what he thought of Tinker.

"She a wild chick, but I really enjoy her company. I like tough, smart women who aren't afraid to enjoy living."

Jess laughed with appreciation. "Just wait till you get her in the dark, you'll see she's not so tough."

"No kidding? She's actually afraid of the dark?"

"Worse than afraid. It's a phobia, so seriously, don't tease her. She's sensitive about it. And never leave her alone in a dark room, dark car, nothing like that. Then you'll see the real meaning of wild."

"I would never take advantage of her fear like that. We're getting along pretty good for having just met. I'd like to see where this could go."

"I'm pleased. She needs someone stable in her life. You are stable, aren't you?" Tinker's personality appeared to be rubbing off on him. No telling what the two had been up to that made him suddenly so outgoing, but Tinker had that effect on people. She brought out their inner self, was the way she often put it.

He grinned, his youthful features lighting up. "Most of the time. I have my weird moments."

"Oh, she loves weird. Has she introduced you to her Ouija board yet?"

"No, but I look forward to that." Again he laughed, and she saw why Tink was attracted to him. His hazel eyes came alive, laugh lines outlined his lips and accented his flushed cheeks. A pleasant face. Nice skin and hair, too. Best of all, likeable.

Tinker returned with the folder. "You guys telling jokes in here?"

"Nope, talking about you," Burt said. Grinning at him, she handed Jess the folder and sank down on the floor, patting his knee. "Whatcha looking for?"

"The paperwork for some repairs I had done a while back on the Wi-Fi. Dal wants to know who did the work."

Tinker and Burt chatted in low voices while she paged through until she found the receipt. "Can you read this signature?" She handed the paper to Tinker.

"Looks like a double N in the middle but the rest is just a scribble. Do you remember what he looked like?"

"I never saw him. We talked on the phone, and he wanted to come out on a Monday. It never occurred to me to worry about it. Shoot, we let service people in all the time, so I told him where the key was. He acted reluctant at first to be here when I wasn't home. Dammit, I'm the one who urged him to come on. I missed my Wi-Fi, wanted it back."

"Dal thinks this guy may have told someone about the key, or he might be the one who lifted it, came in, and shot at me." She shivered. "I'm afraid he was trying to kill me and was a bad shot."

"Or a very good shot, depending on his intent." Burt studied the signature closely. "Do you have a magnifying glass?"

She told Tink where it was and she came back soon with it. Burt again pored over the signature. "I see two Ls here at the end. I'm sure of it. The others are so scrawled. Damn, when did people quit learning how to write cursive?"

Tink scrubbed at his cropped mahogany hair. "Well, listen to you."

He grinned. He did that a lot, maybe knew it improved his looks a hundred percent. Maybe not. He appeared totally self-effacing. "Hey, at least I can sign my name so you can read it."

She hit him with a pillow, and he wrestled it away from her. Tickled her, and she giggled. Jess hadn't seen her friend this happy in a while. Maybe this would work out for her. At least they were having some fun.

A car door slammed outside, and Burt peeked out the front room window. "It's Dallas. I think it's time we let Jessie rest. Hey, want to go down to the swimming hole? I need to work off that superb dinner."

"Love to." Tink gave Jessie a kiss, Burt held up a hand, then grabbed Tink's. "Bye. I don't have my swimsuit with me."

"Who cares?" And they went out of hearing.

Head pounding from all the excitement, Jess scooted down in the bed and closed her eyes. Dal would come in, sit on the bed, hold her hand, and look at her the way he had of looking, so intently, so deeply. It no longer bothered her that he could tell what she was thinking. He was good to stay out of personal stuff. Could she actually be starting to trust him? Well, maybe not yet. She hadn't told him reading her mind was okay.

The front screen eased shut and she waited. When he didn't come right away, she peered toward the door. Maybe he was standing there looking at her. But he wasn't.

"Dal?"

No reply. Burt had said it was him, but what if someone had snuck in while they were visiting out there? She moved to the far side of the bed, eased to the floor. Terror slammed through her like a jag of lightning.

13
CHAPTER

"Jessie, where the hell are you?" Dal's voice. Definitely.

Hunkered in the shadows in the corner, head pounding with every thud of her heart, the fear faded, but she couldn't move.

"Jess." He stood at the foot of the bed frowning down at her. "What are you doing? What happened? You okay?"

She hunched forward, tried to stop the shaking, but couldn't. Though her mouth worked, no words would come out.

Big hands under her arms easily lifted her to the soft mattress. He sat down and took her in his lap as if she were a child.

"You're okay. I'm sorry I frightened you. I was taking a look around back to see if I could find something we might get prints from. Where you kept the extra key. Ssh, be quiet now. You're safe."

She was whimpering, for God's sake. Whimpering like a child. But she couldn't stop. Someone had tried to kill her. Not just scare her, but kill her, and they would try again. The realization at last grabbed hold and terrified her. Brought back dreadful memories she'd thought conquered since fleeing the same threat over a year ago. How long Dal held her she didn't know, but it might never be long enough. His chest was big and warm, his arms reassuring and gentle.

"All right, Jess. Can you tell me what happened? Everyone was here. I wouldn't let anyone come in here and hurt you."

"Dal," was all she could say.

He sat there with her in his arms, soothing her and making no more demands. Finally she stopped being afraid and began to feel like a dumb ass. Told him so in a quivery voice. He chuckled, the sound rumbling deep in his chest.

"Well, honey, you're not a dumb ass. Not really."

"Not really? What do you mean by that?" Even though she was feeling much better, she didn't want to leave his lap. This was something he'd never done, held her without trying to make out, and she liked it a lot. It gave her a feeling of deep intimacy. What did that say about her?

He didn't answer her question. "How's your head?"

"It hurts."

"I'm not surprised. Do you want to sleep?"

"No, I want to get out of this bed and sit in the living room like a normal human being. Did you get my laptop?"

"'Course. I always fulfill your every need." Without asking, he rose with her in his arms and carried her to the couch where he deposited her with great care, fetched the laptop, opened it on the coffee table in front of her, and kissed her on the forehead.

"I have the best nurse in the world." Her eyes glimmered, and a single tear rolled down her cheek

Dal turned so he wasn't looking at her. He had to get away from her and fast. This was getting out of hand. Out of her reach in the kitchen, which was divided from the living room by a waist high bar, he began unpacking grocery sacks and stuffing things in her refrigerator. If only he could not look at her.

"Hope the thing doesn't stop running from the shock of having actual food in it." His laugh sounded forced.

"You have room to talk. But thanks for shopping for me."

"Well, I figured you'd be here a few days, so you might need to eat occasionally. Besides, turn about… and all that."

"Oh, that reminds me, Kathy left you a plate in the fridge. They brought their barbecue here to me."

"This, covered with aluminum foil?" At last, he sounded in control again.

"If you want, you can heat the ribs in the oven or microwave, everything else should be good."

She continued tapping away at the computer keys, while they talked. He finished putting away the groceries, not asking where anything went. Aluminum covered plate in hand, he went to the microwave, removed the foil, found a paper plate to put the ribs on, and nuked them. When they were hot, he pulled a beer from the fridge and brought everything to the table.

"By the way," she said, not stopping her work. "Burt deciphered some of the signature on my Wi-Fi repair receipt. The guy I let use the key to get in?"

"Where is it?"

She told him, and he studied the receipt for a while. "Lennie Wells," he pronounced at last, licking sauce off his fingertips. "Damn, that Dave can cook."

"How'd you do that? Oh, crap. That's Mathon Wells' son." She stopped working to stare at him.

"And of course you remember where Daddy once worked, our diamond robber guy?"

"Wait a minute? SEFOR? I'd forgotten." She stared at him, and again he nodded. "I'll be damned."

"Indeed. I met Lennie the other day. Him and his mother. She's a hard case, and he's no better. And they were both at the second crime scene. Then I went across the road and talked to Julie Crowe. Her son's name is Merle, and Lennie Wells is his father."

"Holy crap. Well, I'll be darned."

"Can't prove yet that it means anything to our case, but I found it interesting. By the way, the kid knows, and so does his father, but Julie never told either of them. Hell, far as I can tell, everyone in town knows. She's about as dumb as a bucket of rocks. Go figure, living right across the road from each other and both of 'em clueless. Mom thinks he doesn't know, he knows and thinks she knows he knows. Have to wonder who told him."

"You been reading minds again?"

He cocked his head and gave her his smartass grin.

"Dal, seriously."

"Hey, that's why Mac hired me, and you damn well know it. Mac needed someone who could be worth two deputies and he got me, beat up and burned out as I am. The lifestyle suits me, I like the people. And I'm really careful, Jess. You know I am. Hell, I could clean up if I wanted to. When I meet the person who knows where the loot is hidden, I'll know where it is, too. So far no luck there, but I've got an idea. Tell me, do you remember hearing the name Delia?"

She stared out the back window across the creek and into the woods. "It's familiar. Let me think on it. Why, who is she?"

"Hey, you've got your computer. Let's find out for sure. According to the good ole boys at the Red Bird, she's married to John Reilly. And guess what? She's Wesley Miller's sister. According to Harrison PD's records, she was questioned about the rash of burglaries during that summer."

"Well, I'll be damned this time. Darned isn't strong enough." She typed the name in Google to begin her search. After about ten minutes of clicking here and clicking there, she accessed what she wanted. A marriage license for John Reilly and Delia Miller issued in 1980. "Here it is, Dal. You're right, if it's the same Delia Miller."

"No such thing as that kind of coincidence. Not in a murder investigation. They haven't identified the latest body, but whoever it is, I'm certain that Lennie and Sara were with him. They used the typical expletives in place of names. Argued about the loot. This murder was premeditated while the first was spur of the moment anger and not meant to kill the victim. I'm fairly sure neither of them killed the unknown vic. On top of that, the victim didn't see the perp, so neither did I. But I know something about him. Lennie saw him, but didn't appear to know him. Turn on your recorder so we can get this down while it's fresh in my mind. Some of it's confusing as hell."

When she did, he gave her a step by step recital of the murder scene.

"'No excuse for you raping her. I thought I raised you better. You ain't no better than your Pa,' a woman says. I figure that's Sara. They're talking about Julie Crowe, 'cause then a man says, 'She was asking me for it all along. He's my kid.' That would be Lennie referring to Julie and Merle. So he does know, even though Julie didn't tell him.

"But another man, softer of voice, says, 'Keep him out of this. You showed him the map, didn't you?' And then Lennie says, 'My kid? Hell, yeah. He deserves to know.' The woman starts yelling, runs off, and the other man hollers, 'The hell's the matter with her? We can split it between you and me. She's your Ma, he's your kid. You can take care of the both of them.'

"Then Lennie shouts, 'We gotta get the hell outta here,' and he leaves. Someone comes up, and our unknown vic yells, 'I thought you were…. What are you doing? I did everything you said.' Disbelief. A terrified shout, pain, more pain, agonizing. Blood. Then there's a lot of terror, pain, more pain, then blood everywhere. Remorse from the killer, like he's sorry, then I space out."

Jess had opened a new document and took notes as well as recorded his words. Aware she couldn't use what he was telling her in her story, she still wanted to get it all down. Once everything was said and done, the case solved, she'd have a much better in-depth article with what she learned from him.

"The map? He must mean Mathon passed a map on to his son Lennie showing where he hid the diamonds, and Lennie then showed it to Merle."

Dal moved behind her, looked over her shoulder. "Hope you have a really good password. I'd hate for any of that to get out."

"Oh, yeah. I do. This baby is filled with stuff I can't share or don't want to share."

He leaned on the back of the couch. "How do you keep it straight? What you can use when you write a story? Looks like you might slip up once in a while and use something you shouldn't."

She pointed to the initials OTR in the little red balloon next to the paragraphs of notes she'd just taken. "I use the track changes in Word to tell me which is off the record."

"And no one can get in to these files?"

"Of course not. First they'd have to have my computer, then they'd have to figure out my password, and honey, it ain't my birthdate or favorite pet. The secret is to use a combination of fourteen letters, numerals, and symbols. By the time they broke that, the story would be long gone and so old, no one would care anyway."

"And you don't write it down anywhere? You surely can't remember such a password."

"Of course I have to write it down. I have a little black book with all my passwords, and believe me, no one can find it but me." She glanced up, studied his expression. "You can trust me, you know." At least she hoped the hell he could. Sometimes she doubted she could trust herself.

He scowled, looked away. He didn't trust her, that was easy to see, but she could do nothing about it but keep working to earn that trust. Maybe for the both of them.

According to him, reporters weren't supposed to be let so deep inside open cases, and it had taken him ages to realize he had no choice in the matter because Mac trusted her. However, because of his history with the press in Dallas, Dal did not. Mac had used her knowledge in photography to get the best photos until he hired Dal, and still had her take crime scene photos when Dal was working on something else. So she was in on a lot of stuff she wasn't able to use until the case was solved. And not once had she betrayed that trust. She knew he secretly believed one day she would, when a story so big came along it could rebuild her ruined career.

Frankly, sometimes she worried about that herself.

So he watched her closely and she put up with it, understanding the reason. But occasionally she grew impatient with his doubt.

Her head began to hurt again, but she struggled to finish the story she'd started before she was shot. That of the latest murder. She leaned against the back of the couch and closed her eyes.

"Why don't you go lay down?" He massaged her shoulders, and she moaned in pleasure.

"I want to send this to Parker, and I need to go through the photos I took for the best one."

"Why not send him all the pictures and let him pick?"

"Help me choose some. I've got too many to forward all of them. My DSL isn't fast enough for that."

So he nestled in beside her on the couch and watched as she clicked through her photos of the crime scene. "You're one hell of a photographer." He pointed out a few. "How about those?"

"Good. Now we need one showing the guys working the scene, 'cause that's what Parker will want. He says, over and over, 'People, Jessie. Give me people.'"

Dal chuckled. "Well, there's a good one of Mac giving orders. Make him feel really good to see that in the paper."

She zipped the photos, attached the file to her article, and clicked send, her head throbbing so hard she couldn't see.

"I need to go lay down, now. Would you help?"

"No problem."

She'd meant take her arm and guide her, but he picked her up and carried her to the bed. She nestled against him, the world whirling around her, but him steady as a rock, keeping her from flying off into space. She was barely conscious of him peeling her out of her jeans once more and tucking her under a sheet. His lips against her temple soothed her into sleep.

What in the world had she ever done without this man? Her last thought right on top of that one…. What would she do with him?

Dal sat on the edge of the bed for a long while and watched Jess sleep, once again fighting the increased attraction gripping him since he sat in her blood and rocked her in his arms, begging her not to die.

Surprise, you asshole. You actually felt something important. You're not dead after all.

He rubbed a knuckle gently over her cheek. What in the hell? He couldn't name the emotion, let alone deal with it. Something had to give. It gripped his heart like a vise, would not let go. Ignore it, that's what. Lock it away in the dark recesses of his mind. Do not be foolish enough to give her your soul. No one will ever get that again. Pure love is not complete without the soul. And his was not available. Keep things like they were. It suited both of them just fine. Or so he liked to tell himself.

With a sigh, he arose and crept from the room, leaving the door ajar.

In the living room, he took off his uniform shirt, utility belt, and gun and hung them over a kitchen chair. Kicking off his boots, he moved sock-footed to her desk where he searched, leaving everything neat as a pin. Couldn't find the password written down anywhere. Spent some time going through drawers in the kitchen and living room, then tackled her backpack. Could be at the newspaper office or in her bedroom, but those were out of the question at the moment. With a sigh, he made himself comfortable on the couch.

It was time to check clues. Solve the crime. Wade through these files again. This new murder was deliberate. The first one an accident because one wanted to get the buried stash, the other didn't. Suppose the second one involved the same argument, but was far from an accident?

Much later, he raised his head, surprised to see it had grown dark while he searched the records from Harrison PD. She was awake. Her fear that she might be alone drifted over him like a cloak. He tossed the files down and rose. She stood in the hallway, one hand on the wall as if steadying herself. Appearing dazed, she wore only the thong panties and a tee shirt.

He held out a hand and went to her, slipped an arm about her bare waist, like touching a live wire that gripped him and wouldn't let go.

"You shouldn't be up wandering around."

"I'm hungry, and it was so quiet I was afraid you'd left."

"I'm not going anywhere till we catch this bastard. You know that."

"I guess. What did you buy to eat?"

"I'll get your jeans or a robe or something." Had to get his eyes and his hands and his mind off her bare flesh.

"A robe's okay." She waited while he took one off the back of the bathroom door and brought it to her, helped her into it with a sigh of relief that she was covered up.

"Come on, let's see what I bought." He wasn't about to pick her up again, not after his earlier reactions to her curled against his chest. Instead, he slid his hand down her arm, twined her fingers in his and led her into the kitchen. "Sit. I shall demonstrate."

Throwing open the fridge he made a show of pointing out everything. "Here's tiny little cups of yogurt, apples, oranges, salad greens, tomatoes, cucumbers, celery, eggs and bacon, cheese, milk, orange juice. Then there's sliced ham and turkey and mayo to put on the bread. Anything my lady desires." Aware he was babbling, he closed that door, swung the freezer section open, and managed to wind down. "Let's not forget ice cream, frozen strawberries and blueberries."

"You spent a fortune on food. We'll never eat all that."

"You haven't looked in the cabinets yet, but that can wait. There's something special I know anyone with a head injury absolutely has to have." He smiled and swept a gold bag off the cabinet. "I know these aren't the most expensive, but the best Harp's had to offer. Dove dark chocolates for your most decadent taste buds."

"I want those right now." She snatched the bag. "I haven't had chocolate in a week or more. Since the last time Tink and I had our movie night at her house."

"Pretty swift move for someone shot so recently."

"Thank you, kind sir. You are a most thoughtful and beautiful man." She unwrapped one and popped it in her mouth. Closed her eyes and savored the flavor. There was something sexy about a woman enjoying chocolate, but he kept up the banter.

"Now wait a minute. Men are not beautiful. We are indeed kind and thoughtful, also handsome and strong." He crooked an arm, flexed his muscles, "but not beautiful."

She opened her eyes, looked him up and down real slow. "That's what you think. Have a chocolate, you deserve one." She unwrapped the small bar and stuck it between his lips.

Standing there in his tee shirt, khaki pants, and white socks, with a day's growth on his cheeks, short black hair in tufts from running his fingers through it, and still she saw him as beautiful. The chocolate melted in his mouth, a sensual pleasure while so close to her. He shook off the way she made him feel. Sometimes her thoughts dug around inside him, prying away at feelings he didn't want to possess.

"Well, what can I fix you to eat?" He put his hand on the refrigerator.

"Cooking is out, so let's be practical. I'll take a ham sandwich with cheese and lettuce and tomato, and an apple with… did you buy peanut butter?"

"Sure did. No human can exist for long without peanut butter."

"Okay, an apple and peanut butter for dessert. And maybe another of those chocolates. Ice cream for a snack before bedtime."

"Lord God, woman. Guess you meant it about being hungry." He set out all the fixings and joined her at the bar where they put together fat sandwiches.

"Wait, what to drink?" Her eyes searched his face.

"Ah, I'm having a beer," he said. "But you'd better stick to something non-alcoholic while you're still taking pills. Like milk or orange juice."

She wrinkled her nose at him, and he squirmed. That was one of her expressions he especially liked. "I'll take milk, then. Let's eat on the sofa. More comfortable than these old straight-backed stools."

"Long as you don't mind. You go sit. I'll pile it all on a tray."

Once they were seated and the food arranged, he twisted the cap off a bottle of beer and took a sip. "I been thinking about that first murder." He glanced at her. "Do you mind if we discuss the case? I could use your brain." Plus, he couldn't take much more of the thoughts zipping through his mind straight to his groin.

"Can I turn on my recorder?"

"Sure. Usual rules apply."

"In my bag."

He put his sandwich on a square of paper towel, hobbled to fetch her bag from the far corner of the living room. They got the recorder going, then began to eat and work.

"At first I thought it was the first guy who wanted to recover the diamonds," he said. "But looking back on it now, I'm thinking it was the other way around." He took a big bite, chewed and swallowed before going on. "So, that means the killer was going after the stash and the guy he hit over the head wanted to leave it put. I think the killer knows in what building the loot is hid, 'cause that's all I got. He's the one with the map, is a good guess. Which we've decided is Merle. Yet, I don't think Merle killed anyone. He's a relative of our vic, Jasper Long, 'cause he thought of him as 'cuz.' But the killer, he's not too familiar with his cuz. Otherwise, I'd have had names. He's big, a lot bigger than Long."

She held up a finger, indicating she wanted to say something as soon as she swallowed, so he took a big bite and gave her a turn.

"Well, Lennie Wells is the most likely to know the location since his father was one of the thieves. He might've told him, or left a map."

"We know Lennie was at the second murder scene, but probably didn't commit the murder. They were talking about Merle and Julie, but neither of them were there. Wait a minute, who told Lennie Merle was his kid? At the second scene, he clearly says, when the other man accuses him of showing the kid the map, 'He's my kid, he deserves to know.' We know Julie said she didn't tell him. The woman on the scene, I swear was Sara Wells. I'm also sure this Delia Reilly and hubby John are involved in some way."

Daintily, she fingered the last bite of sandwich into her mouth, wiped her lips with the paper towel, and tilted her head. "Crap. I told you John was involved. But I thought the Reillys lived in Kansas City. They have a son and a daughter. Maybe there's the other man."

"Yeah, you definitely nailed it about Reilly. We can't prove it yet, but we're going to look into his possible involvement from the get-go. And it's possible his son Rand is involved. I don't know how, yet. Wife Delia lived over in Harrison back in the seventies. Don't know yet how or when she got tangled up with Reilly, but they were married before the robbery. She was questioned during the robberies that summer. Want me to peel your apple?"

"Yes, and make quarters out of it and take out the core so I can smear peanut butter on them."

He flicked his fingers at his forehead in a sloppy salute. "Yes, ma'am. Can I do anything else for you, like chew them?"

She laughed. "We'll discuss that later."

Yep, the way he was feeling they probably would, if he didn't come up with an excuse. "Do you recall hearing Delia's name mentioned by someone we interviewed? I'm sure it came up, I just can't think with who."

While he quartered, peeled, and cored her apple, Jess wrinkled her forehead in thought. She couldn't come up with anything.

"I know there's a woman involved in this. I got it strong at both crime scenes, though I don't think she was actually at the first one. I'm reasonably sure it's Sara, but at this point, I'm not ruling out any of this bunch. Could be a real family enterprise."

She was busy applying peanut butter to a wedge of apple, so he went on. "For women, we've got Delia, Julie Crowe, and Sara Wells, a real ball buster. Besides Lennie and Merle and John Reilly, though, who else? Jasper is dead and someone else we haven't identified is dead. Just how the hell many were involved in this deal? Merle is too young to have been in on it thirty-four years ago, and so are Lennie and Julie, for that matter."

"This is getting more and more complicated. The woman accuses Lennie of raping Julie, just without naming names. But that doesn't mean it's true. I thought at first they were close. And neither of them has ever married, though that doesn't let out a relationship."

"This is making my head hurt," Jess said. "How about some of that ice cream and strawberries? Then I'm going to bed. It's almost eleven and I'm beat. You look tired, too."

He was already on his way to the freezer when she finished. He fetched two bowls, a couple of spoons and the carton of ice cream. "I'll go back for the strawberries."

She waved a hand at him. "Let them go for tonight. I just want a few bites of ice cream, then I'd like to take a shower, if I could get a little help."

There it was. The invitation, cloaked in a plea for help so he wouldn't say no. And of course, he didn't.

Jess awoke sometime in the night to find Dal spooned around her backside. She wiggled against him and smiled at his instant reaction, though he slept on. Sex in the shower had been slow and easy. His idea, because he was afraid she might bump her head if they got wild. It had been nice. This was nice, waking up feeling warm and safe against him.

End of that. Such ideas led to the wrong conclusion. She stared through the window at the star spangled sky, an occasional meteorite slashing open the darkness for a millisecond. Not time enough to make a wish before it disappeared.

Dal's hand lay across her hip, and he moaned in his sleep. Moved to spread his fingers across her breast. Under his touch, she drifted off. The next time she opened her eyes he was gone, and the sunlight through the window formed warm puddles over her legs. For someone having been shot in the head, she felt pretty good. She eased to the edge of the bed, sat up, pulled on the robe discarded last night, and padded barefoot into the living room.

He sat on the couch, papers spread out on the table and a steaming mug of coffee in one fist.

"How long have you been up?" She headed for the kitchen and a mug for herself.

"Hey, how's the head?"

"Good."

"Yeah? In that case, decipher this for me, please." He handed her the chart she'd worked up a few days earlier. "What in the world is a Gocbel?"

"No. Goebel. It's a figurine. Some people collect them. Sort of like a Hummel figurine."

"Oh, that helps a lot. Never heard of that, either."

"Well, you need to. There's one called 'On Our Way.' With the box, it's worth $939.95. And it seems one of our burglarized families had an entire wall of glass shelves filled with these expensive little buggers. Only the most expensive ones were taken."

He cocked his head and watched her drink for a moment. "Glass thingies? That break really easy? I can't see anyone trying to steal something like that. How would they get away without breaking them?"

"Okay, I've got a theory. After reading the lists of stolen items till I'm cross eyed. A lot of coin collections with specific high dollar coins, stamp collections the same, and jewelry with large emeralds, diamonds, rubies that could be removed from their settings. All easy to ship unbreakable stuff. It almost looks like someone was ordering specific items and the thief or thieves were filling the orders, then taking something for themselves, which explains gaudy belt buckles and insignificant trophies. Maybe someone took a shine to the Goebels."

"And that brings up a good question. How would they know who collected what and what they would buy? There's surely not a Collector's Club Anonymous in Harrison where people gather and get up and confess whatever their weakness is and what they are looking for."

"I can't figure everything out. But I think when it was diamonds someone ordered, they pulled the Hamilton job. The guys go to prison before they can deliver." She snapped her fingers.

"And die there," he finished. "What about the demand? If you ordered something, you wouldn't wait over thirty years to start looking for it. No, you'd cut your losses." He pinched his temples.

"You okay? A headache?"

"Nah, just thinking. No, they wouldn't wait over thirty years. Okay, how about this? They were set up to deliver the diamonds to Reilly on time, then they got caught and couldn't or wouldn't get word to him where they'd put them. Saving them for when they got out. Maybe afraid he wouldn't pay them their share in a few years. So it fell through, but everything else prior to that continued on schedule. Stolen, delivered to Reilly, and in turn delivered to the collectors. Everyone went on about their business. He hired more thieves and forgot all about the diamond deal. Maybe even paid the guys visits, but being unable to trust anyone, they decided not to tell. To make Reilly wait till they were released so they'd get their share. Then they're killed in that riot. What can anyone do then? Disappointing but… oh, well."

"Then some thirty-odd years later here's an article in the newspaper about the special Vandergriff necklace containing almost a million dollars worth of diamonds still missing. And wham, we've got ourselves a treasure hunt. Only someone knows where those babies are hidden. But if that were so, why leave them there?" She glanced up from her notes.

He met her gaze. "Maybe, just maybe, that someone only found out where they were hidden recently. Found something left behind. A note, a map, something left by the guys who took the stones to begin with. Just in case. So who would they leave the note or map with?"

She grinned. "Someone they trusted. A son or grandson. For sure a family member."

"A widow or lover," he finished.

She poured another mug, held up the pot. He nodded, let her bring it and pour him some. "A son, brother, sister, widow, or lover. Simple." She returned the pot to the kitchen and came back to sit beside him. "I think we ought to concentrate on the diamonds and not let those other thefts cloud the issue. I imagine they're all gone by now."

"I agree. What's not so simple about this case is why a murder? After all this time. Who's killing who and why?"

"One thing's for sure. This is going to be harder to solve than our stolen skull murder case." She studied him for a while, noted the circles under his eyes, the permanent crease between his brows that denoted pain. She had to let go her worries. He was, after all, a grown man. And that's precisely what worried her.

"It's Sunday, and you look like you're pretty chipper," he said. "Why don't we just go on over to SEFOR and walk around. Nothing like taking shovels or anything. It's a beautiful day for a stroll through the woods."

She was up for it. What she'd had in mind originally for Sunday morning, except now it would be more or less sanctioned. "But what about your family jewels? Not afraid they'll shrivel up and die on you?"

"You had to bring that up, didn't you? I don't believe the college would own something so dangerous without posting more than just no trespassing signs. They could get sued. That radioactive business is probably just a crock of bullshit. They might even have started the rumor themselves to keep people from trespassing and vandalizing the place. I'm more and more curious about what's there."

"Let's call Mac first. He got permission. If they were worried about it, they'd have warned him."

"You call him. He'll let you do anything you want."

She was already punching Mac's number, grinning at him. "Poor baby," she said and listened to Mac's phone ring. Voicemail picked up and she punched off. "Not home or not wanting to be bothered on a Sunday. Odd though. He claims to be on duty twenty-four seven. Oh, well, let's just take some water and a snack and go for a walk."

Dal agreed. She grabbed some granola bars, a couple of apples, and two bottles of water. Before she could toss them in her heavy back pack, he rescued a plastic bag from the cabinet and packed them inside. "Here, that thing weighs a ton. At least let me carry the food."

"Yeah, you just want to have some goodies near at hand," she said but let him do his manly thing.

When he strapped on his .45, she raised an eyebrow.

"Snakes." He shrugged, wary of taking her unarmed where two killings had been committed.

So the SUV wouldn't be visible from the road, he nudged it deep into the trees near the SEFOR chain-link fence. No sense in stirring up those who were already conducting night time searches.

"Let's walk the perimeter to the back of the property before we break through. Maybe we can find an easier way in than climbing that fence." She had a good reason for suggesting the tactic. Considering recent events, neither of them was in any shape to climb the eight-foot-high fence, but he'd never admit it.

He led the way, following animal trails that made for easier going through the underbrush. "Good idea. We can sort of reconnoiter the place in case there's already someone in there prowling around."

"You're the law. Can't you run them off?" She trailed along behind. Running shoes weren't exactly made for tearing through ground-hugging ivy and brambles like the boots he wore.

They walked for several minutes in silence before they came to the corner of the fence and started along the back stretch, well out of sight of the road. The woods were quiet except for the rustle of small critters along the leaf strewn ground and the trilling of birds. Though trees had greened some in the past few days, sunlight poured between the tree branches, and she was soon sweating through her tee shirt. A deep wet vee darkened the back of his as well.

Up ahead along one side of a tall metal post, the fence had been cut away. He stopped and fingered the opening, pulled it back. "Here's where they've been coming and going. You first, then hold it for me."

She bent down, hugged the pole and slid through, then widened the opening for him. They were at the back of the largest of the low-slung buildings.

"Did you see any signs except No Trespassing?" she whispered and straightened her tee shirt.

"You mean any of those yellow and black radioactive warnings? Nope. But the way kids love to steal signs and hang them in their rooms, that doesn't mean a lot. And why are you whispering?"

"I don't know. It just seems appropriate. Can we go inside?"

"No, definitely not." He pointed to a chained and padlocked door on the back wall, remained at a distance when she tramped over to finger the lock. Glanced at him.

"You could pick this easy."

"Nuh-uh. Permission to search the grounds means just that. Grounds only. We can't go inside without a warrant. The people at the college insisted."

"Makes you wonder what they're hiding, doesn't it?"

"Not particularly. I know what's in there, and I'm not interested in poking about."

She gave in, and they strolled around the cluster of buildings. Nearby a huge round structure rose high into the sky. When she looked toward the top, she grew dizzy and grabbed at him.

"You okay?"

She nodded. "The stones could be anywhere, but why risk putting them out here on the grounds? Too much chance it'll be dozed over at some point."

"Well, we're not going inside that thing even if we could find a way."

He led her in ever widening circles seeing nothing but weeds and saplings and occasional holes where someone had dug in the ground. Finally, they reached the enclosing fence.

"Well, I don't see anything that could possibly offer a secure hidey hole," he said. "Besides, you're right. Only a fool would bury something like that in the ground. This is useless. Time to regroup."

"Let's get out of here, find a shady spot, and have our snack and some water. Think about this some more."

14

CHAPTER

In the woods outside the high fence, Jess spotted a grouping of large rocks dappled in shade. A comfortable place to sit out of the sun. Dal boosted her up, then settled beside her, handed her a bottle of water and opened one for himself. Around them birds sang and squirrels chattered. A crow scolded, a strange rattling sound down in its throat.

"Nice and peaceful." He passed her an apple, bit into one himself.

"Thanks. It is nice here, isn't it? Couldn't you... I mean, if there had been a lot of passionate stuff going on around here, couldn't you tune in, or whatever it is you do?"

"I'm not like the dial on a radio. I would go out of my mind if everything that went on invaded my brain. Happily, it just doesn't work that way. Listen. Do you hear that squirrel? They make that sound down in their throat when something they don't like is too close to them. He feels threatened and it's a warning. There's probably a cat or coon strolling through his turf."

"Oh, yeah? Just how many of these informative little tidbits do you have? Is it an Indian thing or what?"

"We do happen to know a lot about animals. Our myths are filled with their stories. But you were saying?"

"Uh... yes. We've discussed the second murder, but not much about the first. You definitely know Jasper Long had a fight with the unknown killer over recovering the diamonds. Right?"

He nodded, chewed thoughtfully.

"So are we presuming the same person killed both Jasper and our unknown victim?"

"Not at all. Where are you going with this?"

She pulled out her recorder and located his recount of the first murder scene.

"Two of them, both alive when they got here. Angry, viciously so, fought. Look for a rock, baseball-sized, with blood on it. I think he threw it so you'll have to scour the perimeter. Something I'd usually do, but can't right now." Pause. "They didn't know each other really well, yet something tells me they're closely connected. One is angry at the other, but I can't quite tell why. A secret, a discovery, a disagreement."

"There," she said. "You say they didn't know each other really well. So our killer is someone who hasn't been around when the vic was growing up, yet they're closely connected. Related, yet strangers. Mmm. We might need to rethink this."

Dal regarded her for a minute. "Other way around. You've got it backwards. It's the vic who wasn't around a lot when the killer was growing up. Well, there's Lennie and Merle, father and son. Even though we're pretty sure they know it, have they ever faced each other and spoken of the relationship? Does Sara know Merle is her grandson?

That's another possibility, since a woman is involved. And Merle *does* happen to be a Crowe."

"But you also said that, though you thought a woman was involved, you didn't think she was present at the first murder scene. It's been my experience that women family members usually know a lot more than they let on. And I'd be willing to bet Sara knew Merle was her grandson. She may never have spoken of it, but she knew." She eyed the apple she hadn't yet tasted.

"I'm really thinking Merle is the only one related to our vic who might not know he was, since the vic is Lennie's cousin. And according to Sam, Jasper was away a lot of the time. I've got a pocket knife, if you want me to peel that for you."

She handed him the apple. "Yes, please. I don't like the skin. That boy is only fifteen, sixteen years old. You saying he's our killer?"

"I'm saying he could've killed Jasper out of anger. He's much the larger of the two. They fought and without intending to, he got too rough. Kids don't understand how fragile the human body can be. And further, I don't think he planned and carried out the second murder."

"Okay, could be. So where does that leave us? We still have a stranger in the mix. Who the heck is our second victim?"

He pursed his mouth and continued creating one continuous curl from the peel. "Could be John Reilly. He's the only one in the mix educated as to how to fence all these items, or how to find people ready to pay good money for specific items like they were stealing. I'm going to contact his place of business and see if he's missing."

She trailed him around through the surrounding woods until they wound up down at the creek. Neither spotted any further possibilities. Nothing that came close to offering a secure place to stash diamonds.

He tossed a rock into the roiling water. "I think we've just about exhausted any possibility except inside one of those buildings. Only a blithering idiot would hide them in the reactor itself. Let's head back."

"From what little I've learned, both of those guys who stole the diamonds qualify as idiots."

"Yes, but they're men terrified of losing their male prowess, and those kinds of guys are quick to believe the tales about radiation. They're the hired help."

She grinned up at him. "Like you?"

"Yeah, I guess like me. Testosterone makes us half-crazy sometimes."

Her laughter soon brought his own.

She followed him up the incline to where he'd parked. He was cursing before she saw why. The passenger side window of his SUV was broken, the glove compartment stood open, contents scattered on the floor and in the slashed seat. On the windshield was spray painted, *Butt Out Pig.*

"Pig? Haven't heard that in a while," she said.

"Gives us an idea of his age, huh?"

"Yeah, an old hippy. Mac's gonna be pissed about this."

Dal slammed a fist on the hood. "Not near as pissed as I am." He opened the car door and picked up the tattered papers. "Sure glad I didn't leave my weapon locked up in here. Pissed would be mild then."

She eyed the police radio, GPS, and CD player. "Why didn't they take those?"

"Not sure. Why? Does it matter?"

"Sure, it goes to motive." She grinned, obviously proud of herself for figuring that out.

He stared off over the top of the vehicle for a moment. "Okay, you're right. Whoever did this did it purely to get us to butt out, not so they could steal something. That means they're involved in some facet of the diamond heist, almost surely."

"Fingerprints."

"Let's hope," he said. "Come on." He grabbed an ice scraper from the side pocket and cleaned bits of glass off the seats, popped open the glove compartment and took out two pairs of latex gloves.

"Put these on. Maybe we can find some good prints inside."

The Ford kicked up a thick cloud of dust as he backed out of the woods.

"Uh, take it easy."

Chagrined, he glanced at her. "Sorry, I wasn't thinking. Your head hurt?"

"Not yet."

With a bit more care, he drove into town and parked at the county jail. She slid out, closed her door, and followed him inside where he commandeered a fingerprint kit from the intake room, took it out to the vehicle, and went to work.

"Can I help?"

"If you don't mind, go inside and tell whoever's on the desk I need a form to report this damage, would you? And I would be mighty grateful if you could fill it out for me. I hate paperwork. I find who did this, that's why I'll box his ears, for all the paperwork I'll... you'll do, plus having to use one of the spare cars till mine is fixed."

While he finished going over both the interior and exterior for prints, she sat down at a desk in the office, peeled off the gloves, and filled out the forms, then she laid them aside for him to sign.

Sam Watson came sauntering through. "Saw you here, Jess. Sorry to hear about you getting shot. A lot of that going around. You sure were lucky there." He glanced at the bandage that had taken the place of the wrappings around her head, then peered out the window at the SUV. "You weren't in an accident, were you?"

"Nope. Someone smashed the window. Dal's outside fuming. Going to take names and kick ass."

Sam chuckled. "Boy's good at that." He stood there watching her for a moment, then asked, "He okay?"

She sighed. "Wish I knew. He seems to be, but I don't know. You know how he can be. Keeps everything locked up tight inside."

The older man laughed. "You keep an eye on him, would you?"

"You bet I will, what he'll allow at any rate."

"Well, I'm gonna go outside and visit with him while he finishes up. You take care, would you?"

"Sure will. You do the same."

He raised a hand and went out the door.

The two men talked while Dal finished printing the car. She perched on the corner of an empty desk and watched them for a while, then went on out, retrieved her backpack from the car and took out a snack bar. She sat on the rock wall alongside the parking area and admired Dal's movements, graceful even while he favored the injured leg. His body language, the care he took obtaining prints off the car's surface, were something to watch. She continued to sit there, enjoying the view and wondering if she'd ever get up the nerve to tell him how she really felt.

He was unusually quiet all the way to her place in the rattling unmarked vehicle he would drive till his was repaired. The inside smelled like something she didn't care to consider. When they arrived at the cabin, he went in first, then signaled for her. By the time she got inside, he was gathering up the files they'd worked on together and putting them back in the bank box.

"I'm taking these in to let Mac take a look at them, get some input from him."

"I'll see you later then?" She was a bit worried about being alone, but she was more worried about his reasons for leaving. What had changed his mind about remaining there till they caught whoever was threatening her?

"I have to get back in the office in the morning, so I'm having a deputy put on you this evening. All the same, you be careful. Lock up and be careful."

With those words, he was gone. Without even a kiss. Looking back on the day, she couldn't find a reason for his withdrawal, but he was a strange guy. He ran hot and cold, so she'd just wait for the temperature to change. Their relationship had always been this way, and she told herself it was fine with her since she didn't want anything permanent, either. But she always missed him when he took off, like he was doing now.

The following week went by peacefully compared to the previous few. Monday Jess worked at the paper and her story about the second murder made the front page. Not really much information. For the most part, Mac's release with nothing added. With an ID on the first body, the artist from CJC had done a sketch of the second victim and it ran with the front page article. That finished, Jess wrote one on SEFOR for the following week, and mentioned nothing about the diamonds, because Parker told her he didn't much like her getting shot so she should lay off and see what happened with the threats. She remarked that she didn't much like laying off. It sent a message that violence could stop the telling of truth. He only glared in silence.

She didn't see Dal, either, which put her in a sour mood, so she spent Tuesday cleaning the cabin then eating some of the chocolate he'd brought and going to bed with a good book. Tink cancelled their usual Wednesday movie night because she was keeping steady company with Burt Sample. She secretly confided that she was falling in love and hoped it worked out. Mac put a deputy on Jess twenty-four seven for the week, but all remained quiet. So quiet she was lonely and bored.

Wednesday morning, she peeled the bandage off her head and examined the reddish purple slash. It would fade some with the healing and meanwhile the right hairdo would cover it. A bit of experimenting and it didn't show at all. Satisfied, she left and drove to H. C. Hammer's gun shop south of town where she bought herself a .38 revolver with a short barrel, small enough to conceal in her bag or on her person. Then she went online to apply for a permit to carry a concealed weapon. She would have to take a course from a licensed instructor, and it could be up to four months before the permit came through. She could be shot dead by then. Digging some more, she found to her surprise and delight that Grace County had enacted an open carry law. If she wanted to, she could hang the damned thing on her waist in a holster just like in the old West. But not until she took the course and got her permit. Not ready to go that far, she decided to keep the weapon on hand at home. Nothing said she couldn't do that. Hell, maybe she'd lay it out on the car seat. Would that be considered open carry? It sure wasn't concealed, was it? For now, she wouldn't mention it to Dal, which was simple, for he hadn't been in touch since he quietly moved out. Was this a silent message to her to back off? With him, it was hard to say.

On Thursday, her usual day to compose articles for the following week's edition, she finished the SEFOR story. Sitting at the computer feeling sorry for herself and her suffering love life, she held down the letter x and watched it race across the screen. Someone rapped on the outside door. A little skittish, she peeked out the window and was surprised to see Julie Crowe.

"We're not open today," she called, not anxious to be alone with the woman.

"Miss West, I'd like to talk to you."

"What about?" Seeing as how Julie was involved up to her ears in this whole mess of stolen diamonds and two dead bodies, she wasn't about to let her in.

"It's important. I may know something about those two murders."

Curiosity got the better of Jess, and she ran to her desk, grabbed her tiny recorder, and set it on voice activation before dropping it in her shirt pocket. Outside she pulled the door firmly shut behind her and invited Julie to sit with her on the bench in front of the office. They were in clear view of several burly firemen washing the fire truck at the station across the way. She should be safe.

Once they were settled, she studied her visitor and waited.

Julie fiddled with the fringe on her leather purse, obviously not sure where to begin.

"Why don't you just tell me what you know, outright."

With a nod and a frown, Julie launched her tale. "I think maybe Lennie had something to do with the killings." She refused to meet Jessie's gaze.

Heart kicking at her chest, Jess asked, "What in the world makes you think that?"

"'Cause he came to the house the other night acting really strange. It was the night after they found the first body. He wanted to talk to Merle, but I wouldn't let him."

Jess stared at her. "Did you tell Merle Lennie is his Daddy?"

A look of surprise on her face, Julie half rose, then fell back. "How in thunder would you know that? And no, I did not tell him. Would you just please tell me who told you?"

"No one had to tell us. Deputy Starr visited with Lennie and his mom, then came straight to your place where he laid eyes on Merle. Only a blind man wouldn't see the resemblance. Lennie and his mom and Merle all have eyes the same unusual shade of blue. Hadn't anyone else ever noticed?"

Julie's mouth hung open for almost a minute and Jess didn't say a word. How dumb could this woman be not to notice that herself, and realize Lennie and Sara could put it together even if no one else could.

"Are you sure Merle doesn't know?"

Julie stuttered, nodded her head.

"But that's not what you came to talk to me about, is it?" Jess asked. "You came to lay the blame on Lennie for something Merle might have done, didn't you?"

"That's not true. Why would you say that? Merle's only fifteen years old, and is not a killer. You reporters always making something up. Merle never done nothing to nobody. He's just a boy. If anyone killed Jasper, it was Lennie."

The woman's accusation made her squirm, but she forged on. "And you know that how?"

The nervous woman put more space between herself and Jessie. "Never you mind how. I'm just telling you so you can tell that deputy to go arrest Lennie and quit coming around our place. Now Merle is asking all sorts of questions."

"Oh? Like what?"

"Like is he going to jail?"

"Why in the world would he wonder about that if he's innocent?"

"Listen, I didn't come to answer your questions so you could write a lying story about me and mine. I came to ask you to stop bothering my boy. He ain't done nothing wrong but be the son of a man like Lennie, and that's on me. Further, I don't want him knowing who his daddy is. I told Lennie the same thing."

"So Lennie knows he's Merle's daddy, but Merle doesn't know? And you didn't tell Lennie, but he knows? Wonder who did tell him? I find this all hard to believe. But I'll pass your message on to Deputy Starr. I'm sure he'll be interested in what you had to say here today."

Julie leaped to her feet. "I knew I shouldn't'a come. Didn't want to, but he.... Never mind. If you write anything about me or Merle I'll... I'll sue you and the newspaper." With that declaration, she stomped off, climbed in a decrepit red pickup parked on the street, and drove away.

For several minutes, Jess remained on the bench staring after the disappearing truck. What in the world had that truly been about? She pulled the recorder out, set it to play back the conversation, and listened to the entire thing with a satisfied nod.

Back inside, she picked up the desk phone and called the sheriff's station. Tink answered.

"Tink, could you get a message to Dal?"

Silence for a moment. "Well, sure, hon, but why don't you just call him direct?"

"I can't."

"Can't? Why ever not?"

"Because he won't pick up for me."

"Oh, honey. Did you have a fight with our beautiful Deputy Dal? Not a wise move."

"No, that's not what happened. I don't know why. I've tried to call him a couple of times this week and it goes to voice mail. We... I... things got too personal for him I guess, and he's backed off. What else can I say? He is okay, isn't he?"

"Sure. Saw him this morning. His usual grumpy self. I thought he looked particularly annoyed when he came through, but he gets that way, and I've learned not to bother him about it."

"Well, this has happened before. I hope we'll work it out. Anyway, tell him I have a recording that he needs to listen to. If he doesn't want to see me, I can leave it with you and he can pick it up. Ask him what he wants me to do."

"Oh, honey, what have you done? If you taped someone's phone conversation without their knowledge you could be... well, it's against the law. Unless of course, you were the one talking to them. Then you're okay. One consent is all that's needed."

"I know. I recorded me talking to her. I did it because he can tell by what she says and how she says it what's really going on, and that might help run down this killer we've got whacking folks before someone else gets killed. Tell him it's pretty interesting."

"Who did you tape?"

"Julie Crowe. She came by the paper to talk to me. I had the recorder in my pocket. Tell Dal, would you?"

"Sure, hon. And you need to get things patched up with him. He's a keeper. Take it from me."

"Yeah, he is. If he'd just take the bait."

The remainder of that week, Dal studied the files from Harrison PD and went over the notes Jess had made for him. He tried to keep his mind off her refreshing face and desirable body but didn't have much luck. Daily he checked to make sure someone was keeping an eye on her.

As if he had to worry about that. Mac went so far as to okay overtime so a deputy could watch her place nights. Dal felt a bit guilty, but he had to get away from her. Things had already gone too far. And they'd been about to explode after the shooting. Hell, he actually thought about asking her to marry him, and that was definitely not okay.

Thursday he felt prickly and tried to concentrate on the second killing. So far, the body hadn't been identified. The fingerprints weren't in the system, so no record. Dental x-rays hadn't resulted in a hit with local dentists. There were no prints on his SUV other than his, Jessie's, and a few unidentifiable ones. They were stumped. A sketch of the unidentified vic was being run in the daily Harrison paper and *The Observer* in the hopes someone would recognize him. So far nothing. DNA wasn't yet available, and even when it was, there had to be someone to compare it to.

Damned hard to pinpoint a killer when they had no idea who the victim was. Hell, he could be anyone, but he was damned sure the two murders were connected, even though he had eliminated the possibility that the killer was the same. Anything was possible. When Tink buzzed him and gave him Jess's message, he didn't think twice, though he ought to have known better. He dialed her cell.

As soon as she answered in that soft, sweet voice, he was lost. Even though he'd vowed not to be.

"Jess." It was all he could say.

A pause, then, "Yes, Dal?"

Shit fire. "Where you at?"

"*The Observer.*"

"I'm coming over."

"Yes. Fine." She clicked off.

This time he'd made it four days without seeing her. Not a record. Last winter he'd managed six days and nights away from her, nights being the hardest. That time she showed up at his door, but he sure didn't turn her away. Theirs continued to be a volatile on-again, off-again relationship neither of them could manage to permanently end. Must be precisely what both of them wanted. Each time they came back together, it was with an explosion that rattled windows and a passion that ended with them even closer than before. It was as confusing as hell.

When she unlocked the door and let him in, neither said a word. Desire blazed through him. He took her in his arms, lifted her onto the counter that separated the entryway from the offices, and buried his face between her breasts. Good God, he plain didn't have good sense around this woman. She smelled heavenly, tasted even better.

To hell with it.

"Close the door, Dal."

He used his boot heel.

"Did you lock it?"

Reluctant to take his hands off her he fumbled with the knob while she kicked out of her jeans and took off her blouse. When he turned back, all she wore was a lacy bra and matching thong panties.

"You shouldn't stay gone so long." She unbuttoned his shirt.

He yanked off his loaded belt, draped it over the counter, lifted her so that she rested her fine behind there, and fastened her bare legs around his waist. No matter what happened, he would not tell her he loved her. A vow he'd made many times.

Much, much later, both dressed and sat together at her desk, a hum of satisfaction bouncing back and forth between them. Him listening to the tape, her holding his hand and watching him with those clear blue eyes. Might as well give it up, Starr. He smiled, and she twinkled. Holy shit. What was wrong with him anyway?

Once in a while, he would ask her to stop the tape, go back, play a phrase again, then comment on what he thought, so it took twice as long to listen as it had taken to tape the conversation.

"She deliberately tries to turn the blame away from Merle because she knows he was involved, otherwise why bother? Play the next part."

"That Lennie went to her house acting strange, wanting to talk to Merle, that has a ring of truth. I'm afraid Lennie knows Merle killed Jasper, but go on."

After a while, Dal stopped the tape. "All that stuff about who Daddy is and who knows. Think that's a crock of bull. She's lying to herself and everyone else. There's a touch of panic in her voice. She thought she'd kept this a secret, but if you know, how many others do? Maybe the killer? I think she knows who killed our second victim, and if she does, she also knows who the victim is. She could be in a great deal of danger."

"When I asked her if anyone had ever noticed the resemblance between Lennie and Merle, her mouth hung open and she stared at me. So I waited, but she never said anything. Listen."

'But, that's not what you came to talk to me about, is it?' Jess asked on the tape. 'You came to lay the blame on Lennie for something Merle might have done, didn't you?'

'That's not true. He's only fifteen years old and is not a killer. You reporters, always making something up. Merle never done nothing to nobody. He's just a boy. If anyone killed Jasper, it was Lennie.'

'And you know that how?' Jessie asking again.

'Never you mind how. I'm just telling you so you can tell that

deputy to quit coming around. Now Merle is asking me all sorts of questions.'

'Oh? Like what?'

'Like is he going to jail?'

He listened for a long beat. "When she says Merle wants to know if he's going to jail, I don't think that's what Merle is asking his mom. I'd bet he's asking her about the second murder, 'cause he knows he had nothing to do with it and he's scared shitless he'll be blamed. The kid knows the difference in what he did to Jasper and what was done to our John Doe. And he's trying to see if Mom blames him for both. Damn, I'd bet he thinks she knows he killed Jasper and who did the second one. She could put her son's life in danger, too. Play some more."

He listened to the rest of the tape. "Where she hesitates about not wanting to come to you? A mysterious 'he' sent her, told her what to find out, and probably told her to threaten to sue. You turned the tables and didn't tell her what she wanted to know. Damn, you did good." He put an arm around her shoulder and hugged her.

"Thanks. I wasn't sure. I don't see how you can tell what people mean when they say the opposite."

He laughed. "I really don't either, I just do. Most of the time. Not always, though."

"How is this going to help find the killer?"

"By itself it won't. It's just another step. Next is locating John and Delia Reilly. They are now persons of interest."

"Because of this?"

He nodded. "Sure. If we think about it, who involved has enough sense to know why Julie needed to ask you the questions she did? Certainly not Lennie or Sara or Julie. We have to bring in the Reillys for questioning. And Lennie, too."

"Did you find out if John Reilly is missing?"

"Haven't been able to reach him, and they won't say much on the other end of the phone. So it's possible."

"But why aren't you bringing in Julie and Sara and Merle?"

"Later, but not right now. We're pretty sure Merle and Jasper fought and Merle killed him in a fit of rage. When the forensics are in, we'll have proof. So that can stay on the back burner for now. What we really need to know is—first, is the second murder connected to the diamond theft?—second, who is the victim?—and third, why did he get killed? When we know the answers to those questions, we'll have our killer."

"But you have some idea who it is, don't you?"

"I will tell you this much. Our killer is not one of the idiots who are going around trying to scare us out of investigating the diamond heist. Two different MOs, different agendas. Someone has killed to keep a secret, they'll do it again. You need to be real careful. Do me a favor and make me a copy of that." He gestured toward the tiny recorder.

"On what? You got an MP3?" She knew he didn't, but it was fun to tease him about it.

"Sounds like a weapon of some kind."

"Okay, I'll put it on mine and you can borrow it. I suppose I'll have to teach you how to use it."

She made a funny face that wrinkled her nose, and he couldn't resist her any longer. "Busy tonight?"

"You make me so mad. I should say yes, I have a date. Or no, I don't want to see you anymore. But you'd know both were a lie." She hooked the recorder to her MP3 and made the copy.

He laughed. "So, what are you gonna say?"

"Damn you, Dal Starr. Okay, what did you have in mind?"

"You remember I was going to take you dancing and stood you up?"

She nodded.

"Wanta go tonight? Thursday won't be too crowded And we'll dance real slow. You can lean that pretty head against my shoulder. If you don't feel up to it, just say so and we'll go some other time."

"Well, knowing you and your slow dancing, I'm up to a couple of rounds. But you have to take me to dinner first. Not at Sonic, either. Some place where we can walk in, sit down and study the wine list, then the menu. Maybe enjoy an appetizer and a big thick steak. I can dress up in heels, the works."

"Oh, boy. Making me pay, huh? Okay, that's a deal. It's four-thirty. I'll pick you up in an hour. Need plenty of time to enjoy that meal, go dancing, and still get you home by midnight so we can both get up in the morning and go to work. How's that?"

And so, here he went again. Couldn't help it.

The idea of holding her in his arms and dancing some slow dances was way too tempting to resist.

"Sounds like you have it all worked out. And if you stand me up, I want you to understand I'm coming after you. I got me a gun."

"You what?" He sobered up quickly. "Why in hell? You'll shoot yourself with it, or someone will take it away from you and shoot you."

"I'd watch what I say. Considering who shot who recently."

She sure had him there. "Hope you know what you're doing, though. Seriously."

"I know how to handle a gun, just never felt the need till now. Grandpa taught me when I spent the summer with them the year I graduated college. Said living out in California, a gal ought to go armed. You surely aren't beginning to believe that silly story going around that I shot you?"

"I guess not. Did you carry one out in California?"

"No, never even bought one, but I didn't forget what he taught me."

"What'd you buy?"

"A .38 revolver."

"Okay. I'm taking you to the range to make sure you know what you're doing. Then we'll find you an instructor so you can get the permit."

"Thanks. And just for the record, it wouldn't have done you a bit of good to forbid me to carry it. I found out I can open carry it in Grace County. Doesn't even have to be concealed. As soon as I go through the requirements, I will, too. Gonna get me one of those fancy little bra holsters, keep that gun handy." Eyes flashing, she smiled.

Damned hard to resist her teasing and keep a straight face. He did his best. "May be legal to own it, but that doesn't mean it's a good idea. When did you do this?"

"This week. See what happens when you ignore me?"

A raised eyebrow was his only reply to that. "Does Mac know?"

"Heavens, no. He'd have a cow."

He laughed and hugged her again. "But you don't care, do you?"

"Not really."

"Lot of good it'll do me to say anymore. You'll do what you damned well please. But be careful. I'm outta here. See you in a while. And I'll let you show me how to work that thingamajiggy later tonight."

"Oh, yeah. I've got several thingamajiggies to show you. Right now, I'd better go get ready for my big date. I want to look pretty."

"You already do, pretty lady. And Jess?"

She gave him one of those looks that went straight to his groin. An expression filled with a little daring, a lot teasing, and the rest just plain sweet. "What?"

"Don't shoot your foot."

"Listen to who's talking."

It probably wasn't funny, but he went to his newly-repaired SUV chuckling like a fool because he was back where he wanted to be. In her good graces. He didn't have good sense. And he didn't give a damn. Time he faced the reality that he was a miserable prick without her. A prick who couldn't turn loose and be happy with her.

15
CHAPTER

All the way home, Jess sang along with Alan Jackson on the radio. Once again, she'd proved she was one easy chick. All that handsome deputy had to do was crook his little finger and she went running back. In his heart, he loved her. She knew that just like she knew the sun would rise in the morning. Trouble was, he wasn't about to admit it. Tonight, they'd go dancing, he'd spend the night with her, and tomorrow she'd go in to work in a much better mood. She already felt a whole lot better for having rolled around on the floor with him.

Good God. Wonder what Parker would do if he found out they'd made love on the floor between the layout tables? Easy to see he wasn't exactly thrilled about her relationship with the deputy. That was certainly a two-sided coin. Her boss tried to hold back his feelings for her, but once in a while they showed through. Though she loved him like a brother, it wasn't the same by a long shot as the way she felt about Dal. Probably too bad too, but it couldn't be helped.

As for her date tonight, all she had to do was tread carefully, ignore anything that tried to interfere, and be ready for him to show up or not. If he didn't, she'd go looking for him. He wasn't going to weasel out of it this time.

Showered, legs shaved, hair straightened, hanging down, then piled up, curled up, curled down. Finally, she left it that way, 'cause he liked it loose so he could twist his fingers through it. How good that felt, his fingertips rubbing her head while she leaned into him from her toes to her nose. At the closet, wrapped in a towel, she pawed through clothes till she found a broomstick skirt in blues, a sparkly top to match one of the blue shades, and kicky high heels to make her tall enough to rest her head in the curve of his shoulder.

Her reporter's mind recited a question and answer from some research she'd done for a past article. Why did they call them broomstick skirts? Because to launder them properly, they should be hand washed, then wound around a broomstick to dry so they'd keep their crinkled look. Amazing all the unimportant facts she had rattling around in her head.

In front of the mirror for a touch of blush and lip gloss, blue mascara on her pale lashes to darken them. Tiny blue stones in her pierced ears. Enough right there. Keep it simple. A small clutch with her keys and ID inside, just in case she got carded. It had happened once despite her nearly thirty years. But she always believed the bartender was being a smart ass or flirting with her.

"I'm gonna getchew," she sang and went to sit in the swing to wait for her date.

He drove up precisely at five-thirty, crawled out, and limped toward her looking like something out of a fantasy. Pale blue western suit, silver bolo, Stetson with its snakeskin band, and matching snakeskin boots. He stepped onto the porch, full-fledged dimpled smile turned on bright.

His scent drifted toward her like leather and a touch of wildness. She rose and let him fold her up against the solidity of his tall frame.

This indeed was a romance novel.

"You are beautiful," he whispered in her ear.

"So are you," she said.

He nibbled there a while. "Mmm, you smell like peach cobbler."

"Thanks, I think."

"Uh-huh. Sweet, gooey, and scrumptious. Well, then, let's go." He tucked her hand into the crook of his arm. "Gotta be real careful walking on those spikes. Just don't step on my toes when we get on the dance floor."

"I'll be careful. Wouldn't want to ruin those fancy boots. Did you kill that snake with your bare hands?"

"Mmm, and bit his head off."

"Somehow I don't doubt that a bit."

Laughing, he opened the car door and handed her inside. Walked around and yanked at the opposite door.

It swung wide, and at that moment, the driver's side rearview mirror exploded so close to his chest his jacket rippled. She screamed his name, but he'd already dropped behind the fender, gun in hand.

"Get down, Jess, dammit. Down."

Afraid he'd been hit, she forgot what a good target she made in the side window. When he yelled, she dived across the seat and tumbled out the open door to the ground next to him on her hands and knees.

"You hit?" He ran his hands over her.

"No, but you are." Fingers trembling she touched his face.

Blood droplets marred his cheeks, a gash on his forehead leaked a red-black thread into his eyebrow.

"Stay there." Pulling away from her exploring fingertips, he hunched down and darted for a nearby oak tree between the truck and the shooter. Racked his .45 and waited.

It was dusk, the time when it's hardest for the eyes to make out shadows from light, movement from stillness, the flash of a gun barrel from a flash of dying sunlight. She held her breath, listened till her ears ached. In her head counted one minute, then two. Just waiting gave her a headache. What if the guy was still there and knocked Dal out? Why was it taking him so long? When she could stand it no longer, she hollered for him., mouth so dry she could hardly make a sound

"Wait, honey. Wait," he rasped.

She sagged against the side of the truck, dizzy with relief. Another few minutes and he came scooting back. "He's gone. Son of a bitch. Ripped my new jacket. What about you? Stand up, let me see."

"I'm okay. Grass stains maybe. Look at me. Shaking like a leaf. Your face is bloody."

"Just nicks." He curled her up so close she could feel his thighs trembling. "My fault. Shit, when you didn't write a story this week, I figured they'd back off."

"Is it always this scary getting shot at?" A hard shudder passed through her and she hung on to him.

"Always. You're okay, babe. We're both okay. Hmm. Wonder if it was your little talk with Julie that caused it. Still want to go dancing?"

"N-n-no. Let's go inside. You?"

"I agree. Being fired at sort of kills the mood, doesn't it?"

She waited while he picked up his hat and shut the truck doors, let him support her across the yard and inside where he closed and locked the front door.

The sun hung low in the teal blue sky and shadows crept from nearby trees to darken the yard. It would be dark soon.

"Don't turn on any lights. There's enough light to see by. We don't want to give them a target in case they're still watching." Gun gripped in both hands pointed at the floor, he went through the kitchen and checked the sliding doors out onto the deck. He took a while coming back.

"No one in the house. Checked the closets, bathroom, shower, under the bed." He still held the gun, but he'd lowered the hammer. He laid it on the side table next to one end of the couch. "Come here, let me see you."

By the light coming through the window, he lifted her skirt to check her healing knees where she'd hit the sod-covered ground. Touched her temple gently, then let out a sigh of relief. "This keeps up, we're gonna have to hire some bodyguards."

She moved into the kitchen, ripped off several sheets of paper towels, wet them, and came back. Hands shaking, she caressed his cheek, traced around his chin and along the jaw line, checking for slivers of glass and wiping the blood from the gash. "I thought when you went down you'd been hit. For just a second my heart stopped. I swear it did. If anything ever happened to you, I'd kick some ass. Big time."

A nervous chuckle rumbled from down in his chest. He held her for a long moment, neither of them speaking. "Same here, babe. Funny, I thought I was coming to a peaceful little backwoods county to finish my days as a lawman. Now I'm not so sure. What the hell is going on anyway? Gotta be more than a handful of diamonds. What else could be important enough to kill a cop for?"

"But they haven't killed a cop. We don't know they've killed anyone."

He regarded her for a long moment. "Absolutely right. That head shot, though. Awful close."

They held on to each other for a few silent moments, then she wiggled away. "Would you mind if I changed clothes? These shoes are killing me."

"I'll come with you. Don't I have a pair of jeans in there somewhere? And a tee shirt?"

She took his hand led him down the hallway. "Yep, in here." In her bedroom, they stripped out of their clothes.. She put on a pair of sweats and he sat on the edge of the bed to slip into the jeans and tee shirt. They went barefoot back into the kitchen. She opened the well-stocked fridge and pulled out sandwich makings.

"Close that door. I don't think he's still out there, but no sense taking the chance he'd see the light Hey you know what they say about being shot at, don't you?" He piled ham and cheese on two slices of bread. Spreading mayonnaise on two more, he slapped them on top and handed her one.

She took a bite, held up a can of beer. He nodded, and she slipped out another for herself.

"That adrenalin surge after so much excitement makes for some wild-ass sex. It's near a necessity. Calms the body so you don't have a stroke or heart attack."

She laughed shakily. "Sounds reasonable to me. Let me finish this first. I'm starved. Then you owe me a dance before anything else. Let's turn on some slow music and dance, 'cause it looks like that's the only way we're ever going to get to."

Sandwich and beer finished, he stood, took her hands, wrapped them around his neck, and encircled her waist with both arms. Humming softly in her ear, he led her in a slow small circle, holding her so close she felt his heartbeat. Their bare feet made squeaky little sounds on the hardwood floor. He guided her body with a sensual caress, the graceful movements building a blazing fire within her. Made her want to crawl up inside him.

It would take a long time to put out these flames.

All she wanted, needed, or could think about was right there. Him holding her, humming in her ear, his breath warm against the sensitive spot on her neck. Everything would be perfect when they both stopped two-stepping around each other and admitted their feelings. Or would it? Possibly they weren't meant to be committed.

She was right. It took a long while to put out the flames.

At six o'clock the following morning, Dal slipped from beneath the cool blue sheets on her bed, admired her bare breasts for a brief moment, then slipped into his jeans, tee shirt, and boots and left silently out the front door. In the woods from where the lone shot had come, he trod in tight circles, angry gaze pinned to the leaf-strewn ground. The bastard almost hit him chest high. Could have killed him. The next bullet could well have been meant for Jess. He might just choke this SOB when he got his hands on him. The guy was either a very bad shot or Jess was right and he had no intention of killing them. Merely warning shots? It was beginning to look like that.

Not sure what he would find, he continued the search, determined to keep looking for a while. Whoever took that shot had to leave something of himself behind. Tracks on the ground, the wrapping off a cigarette pack, maybe even a butt with traces of saliva, discarded gum or a wrapper, or a casing from the shot. Had to have stood there for quite a while waiting for him to show up. Wanted them both, otherwise Jess visible in the cabin, or him arriving in the car, would've been his earlier target. The same guy who took a shot at her before? Hell, hard to tell anymore who was doing what where.

What was going on here? A million dollars was a lot of money to some people, but worth the risk of killing a lawman? Doubtful. Not here in the back woods where the tendency was to track down a cop killer and fill him full of lead. No questions asked, no quarter given. That reinforced their earlier theory that none of these attempts were intended to be kill shots, but rather were meant to frighten them away from continuing the investigation. Someone had a lot more to lose than the proceeds of one diamond theft. A set-up that was probably bringing in millions of dollars a year was at stake. And it was clear who was heading it up. All he needed to do was prove it.

Up ahead, the grass was tramped down behind a head-high tangle of wild roses in the edge of the trees beyond his SUV, parked where it was when the shot was fired. Careful not to step on anything of importance, he advanced an inch at a time, never taking his eyes off the ground. If the doer smoked, he left no butt behind. No spit if he chewed, nor gum, either. Careful as hell was what he was. If he'd used a semi-auto, which the distance would call for, he'd picked up his casing. The tromped ground matted in grass and weeds held no footprints.

A nearby oak tree made a hell of a good leaning post for a long wait, yet didn't show anything. Well, what did he expect? The son of a bitch would carve his initials in the bark? He turned to leave and something glinted in an early morning ray of sunlight. Caught in the thorny rose branches hidden until he turned back. What was that? He pulled it out. A wad of copper and brown paper. With two fingers, he held it by the edge. Hershey Dark Chocolate. The shooter was too careful to have left prints on it, but he took a plastic bag from his pocket and carefully inserted the candy wrapper inside. Just in case.

He headed back toward the cabin. Jess would crawl out of bed soon to get to work, and he wanted to be there to coax her back beneath the covers. Hold her sleep-warm body, kiss her fine lips, swollen with desire. His own desire grew just thinking about her. Inside the shower was running. He unbuttoned and unzipped his jeans on the way down the hall toward the bathroom.

An hour later he followed her out the front door, pulled it closed behind him, and tried the knob to make sure it was locked. He stood beside her until she started the Jeep, leaned in, kissed her, and stepped back, watching till she went out of sight before going to his SUV. He bent and picked up the shards of the mirror, sent an annoyed glance at what was left of it hanging from the door by a black cord. Mac was going to have a hissy fit. Another repair on the unit.

For one last moment he hesitated, gauged the line of fire. Hell, now he was sure this guy wasn't trying to kill either one of them. He was missing on purpose. He could easily have killed Dal last night. And the earlier shot at Jessie, though too close for comfort, could have killed her. But they didn't. Probably came a bit closer than the guy wanted. He was looking for a crack shot.

First on the list was to check with Mac, see if he'd ever gotten anything from NCIC on Lennie Wells and Jasper Long. Lennie was certainly close to the top of the list of persons of interest but he needed more. A lot more. And he was fairly certain Lennie hadn't killed the John Doe. He'd left the scene in a big hurry before the killing. But he was in on this up to his ugly snarl.

Favoring the aching leg, he climbed in his vehicle and headed out behind Jess toward town, the broken mirror swaying and smacking against the side window once in a while. He wanted to talk to Sam Watson some more, but wasn't sure if he'd be there today, it being Friday. If not, he was going to run him down. He might be at the Red Bird for breakfast. Everyone else would be. A good place to catch up on the talk around town. It never hurt to know what folks were thinking. Once in a while, they got it right. He watched Jess pull in and park at *The Observer*, then waited till she was inside before heading out again.

There were some questions that still needed answering. Who owned the blue Ford Falcon that was seen in the area around the time of the robbery and was later found by Fred Marcy, abandoned in the woods near SEFOR? Where precisely was it found? Had they thought to search it? Sam Watson could probably answer some of the questions. And he'd bet his bottom dollar the man knew something about Jasper Long.

When he arrived at the Red Bird, Fudge and Theron were already seated and greeted him, but Sam wasn't there. Dal sat at a table by himself so he'd have time to think or eavesdrop, whichever he preferred. The aroma of bacon frying hung in the warm, damp air.

Norma brought a cup of coffee and set it in front of him. "Want the usual, hon?" That had become the running joke between them since the first time he'd sat down in there during the dinner hour and saw the huge platters overflowing with hamburgers and French fries being delivered to tables for other diners who'd ordered the usual.

"You know what? I think I'll try some sausage gravy and biscuits. And plop me a couple of sunny-side-up eggs on top, if you would."

Sam strolled in as Norma left, and Dal motioned him to sit. The waitress pivoted and returned, magically holding another mug. Sam ordered, peered at Dal. "How you doing, son?"

"I'm fine, Sam. Was gonna come see you, but had this hole in my belly I needed to fill first. Glad you showed up. I have some questions for you, if you don't mind."

"Not at all." Sam poured sugar straight from the dispenser into the steaming brew and stirred, then took a sip, watching Dal over the rim of the mug.

"Did you know Jasper Long?"

"The man what was found dead over by SEFOR?"

"Um." Dal drank several gulps of the strong, black coffee. News certainly got around fast.

"He's been in these parts since he was a little kid. His mama took off with the preacher's son and just left him alone in the house. No one knows what become of his daddy. Sara heard about it and fetched him home with her. His mama was her sister, so she felt obliged. When he got older, he got to where he'd run off and no one would know where he was for months. Then he'd show back up again and Sara would take him in."

"So he would've known Mathon fairly well?"

"Sure, I reckon. What're you getting at?"

"I think he got killed 'cause he knew where the diamonds were and wanted to dig them up. Mathon must've left something, a clue, a note, and he found it. Probably couldn't keep his mouth shut. Maybe told Lennie. Odd how Sara didn't seem too broke up about him dying."

Sam nodded. "She's one hard woman. Can't imagine her loving anyone, even herself. Makes sense, Jasper getting killed that way, but what about that other body? Anyone figgered out who that is yet?"

"Nope, we ran his likeness in the paper again this week. If there's been a reply to that, I haven't heard."

"You know who he looks like?" Sam said, finishing his coffee and holding up the empty mug.

Norma appeared with their breakfast plates lined on one arm and a pot of coffee in the other hand. After she left, Dal stared at the platter filled with two huge biscuit halves covered in gravy lumpy with chunks of sausage, eggs with yellow yolks like two huge eyes.

"God almighty, reckon I can get around that?" He attacked it with vigor, glancing at Sam. "No, who does he look like?"

Sam poured syrup on his pancake stack and chuckled. "Good as it is, I'll just bet you don't have a bit of trouble getting around it. Now, where was I?" He stuffed a forkful of dripping pancake in his mouth.

"Who you thought the dead body looks like."

"Oh, yeah. Resembles that John Reilly, but I ain't seen him in a coon's age, and he ought to look older than that."

Dal punctured one of the eggs, and as the yellow flowed into the gravy, forked up a huge bite, chewed and swallowed. "I think it's time I called Kansas City and got those Reillys brought in for questioning. They're mixed up in this up to their ears. If the body is John Reilly, someone surely ought to have reported him missing by now. Do you know any of them?"

"Used to know Delia Miller real well. Purty woman, had lots of men panting after her when they come to Cedarton, but she'd already took up with John early on."

"What was he doing down here?"

"Far as I remember, he come here in '78, bought that there property over by SEFOR and everyone thought he was gonna build out there. Then he marries Delia and ups and moves to Kansas City. Next thing we know he's big in the import/export business. Say, you don't think he's involved in this diamond theft?"

"I think more than that. I think they've got something big going. It started over in Harrison in the summer of 1980 and ended here with the Vandergriff diamonds. I'd lay money on the same thing going on up in

Kansas City where pickings are bound to be more lucrative. And I think it's been going on for more than thirty years. The take must be enormous, and someone is getting worried we're going to uncover it. Trace it back. John may be the only one with enough sense and the connections to head this up. This leaving bodies strewn around isn't a good way to stay under the radar. I expect he isn't too happy about it. Someone took a shot at me last night over at Jessie's. This guy is probably missing us on purpose, at least I hope so. And if Reilly has anything to do with it, he's pretty pissed at this bunch of yahoos causing such an uproar. Might be he got himself killed over it.

"'Course, that first killing was more of a spat between cousins. We're dealing with a few people who are dumb as a bucket of rocks."

Sam played with the last bite of syrup-drenched pancake. "You ask me, if anyone's doing the killing it's that Lennie. Seen him near take someone's head off for looking at him crooked. And he's a hunter and a crack shot. Lennie and Merle. Father and son. From what I've seen, the two of 'em together don't have the sense to pour piss out of a boot."

Dal mopped a shred of biscuit through gravy and a yellow smear of yolk and stuffed it in his mouth. "Hell, does everyone in town but Merle know who his daddy is?"

"I reckon he knows, too. Who said he don't?"

"His mother implied that he didn't know."

"She ain't much smarter than her kid. Now the brains in that family is Sara. She's a mean old bird, smart as a whip. Too bad her kid didn't inherit her smarts stead of Mathon's ignorance. No one ever knew why she married him. 'Course, he was one good looking son of a buck when he was younger, but worthless as tits on a boar hog. Some women are intent on loving the bad boys."

"Is Sara from around here?"

Sam thought a minute. "Nope, by golly she isn't. Mathon brought her in here when he married and settled here, that'd be… oh, around the time of the diamond theft. Got her pregnant, and so she stayed when he was sent to McAlester."

Dal pushed the platter away. "Can't eat another bite. Been good talking to you. I need to get on over to the office and see if they found out who owned that old blue Falcon Fred Marcy found a few years back."

Sam munched on a strip of bacon. "You know, I think that old wreck is still right out there in the woods where Marcy found it. Sheriff never did bother to send anyone down to drag it out. Didn't think it had anything to do with the robbery, as I recall. You guys want to take a look at it?"

"Ah, maybe. All those years ago, it's probably not got anything to offer in the way of evidence." Dal gazed out the window at the wind whipping his battered side mirror. Sure strange that car hadn't been searched by the deputies.

"Maybe not, but you never know."

Dal tossed a few dollars on the table, rose, and went to pay at the cash register. "Still, maybe I ought to cover all my bases."

Sam stood behind him. "You follow me. I'll lead you to where it is."

Dal nodded. "I need to grab me some Duct tape and fasten that mirror down before it bangs back and breaks my window glass. Mac is going to be sore enough as it is."

Sam chuckled. "I'll wait."

"Hey, Deputy, when you gonna catch our killer?" Fudge hollered. "I'm anxious to see who it is."

"Me, too," Dal replied, and everyone laughed.

He dug a roll of Duct tape out of the back of the SUV and wrapped it round and round the mirror and frame.

Sam halted on his way to his truck. "Say, Starr. I just thought of something interesting. Did you know that Fred Marcy worked out at SEFOR right 'fore they closed it down?"

"Well, now that's right interesting, isn't it?" Pieces clicked together in Dal's mind. He was definitely on the right track.

"I'm thinking it is." Sam crawled in his pickup and led Dal out of town.

Jess had been in the office for a couple of hours when the phone call came in. It had been sort of quiet since nothing about the diamonds had run in this week's issue of the paper. The front page carried the sketch of the second murder victim. Wendy's friend was told not to come in, so Wendy answered the call.

"Jess, someone wants to talk to you. Real bad. She sounds hurt or sick or something."

Jess picked up the phone. "Yes, can I help you?"

"You still wanting to know about those diamonds? Didn't have nothing in the paper this week." A long, ragged sigh that sounded tearful. "Didn't find 'em, did you?"

"Who is this, please?"

"Rather not say. I know who killed those two fellers, too. I can tell you more if you—" There was noise at the other end, like something being thrown, then a muffled cry that sounded like the word bastard. The call was disconnected.

She hung up and dialed star sixty-nine. The phone rang on and on without voicemail. A local landline with no amenities. She might be able to run that down quickly.

"Wendy, did that caller say who she was?"

"Nope. And I'm not real sure I recognized her voice."

"Could it have been Julie Crowe?"

"I guess, but I couldn't swear to it."

Jess couldn't either, but something hinky was going on. Just hinky enough to tell Mac about it. He could send a deputy out there to check Julie's trailer, just in case. See if it looked like a fight had ensued. She made the call, told him what had happened, then went back to editing a long, handwritten missive from Mabel Simmons, their eighty-two year old columnist from Flat Rock.

When she didn't hear back from Mac, she called Dal's cell to see if he knew anything. He answered, sounded winded.

"Hey, what's up?" she asked.

"Ever get trapped in the front seat of a Falcon covered up in kudzu?" He grunted.

"Can't say I have. Need help, or is someone in there with you?"

"Get cute. Hell, no one but me would fit in here. I can handle it, though. What's up with you?"

"We got a strange call a while ago. Sounded like Julie Crowe. She offered to tell me who killed those two vics and hinted at knowing where the diamonds are. It sounded like someone might have grabbed her, and the call was disconnected. I called Mac and told him, but haven't heard a word. And nothing on the scanner. Normally, I'd be so nosy I'd already be on my way over there, but we're under the gun and I can't leave. Thought you might've heard something."

"Nope, nothing here. You sure it was Julie?"

"No, not completely. Star sixty-nine didn't answer."

"Interesting. Okay, thanks. I'll see if I can reach Mac. Did you try calling him back?"

"When I could hear your dulcet tones instead? No, but I can. Have fun playing with your Falcon, whatever that is."

"Ford Falcon. It's a car. Bye, see you."

He hung up before she could ask him where he found the car. Caught up in her own work, she hadn't realized what he was talking about for a while there. Where in the heck had he found that old car? Must've turned up in the woods ten or twelve years ago. On a hunch, she looked up Fred Marcy's number and gave him a call. His wife answered.

"This is Jessie West at *The Observer*. Do you remember when Fred found that old car they thought was involved in the diamond heist?"

"Mmm, why do you need to know? It was a long time ago, and I'm not sure I can remember."

"Oh, just wanted to include its sighting in my story. Could you have Fred give me a call when he comes in? Maybe he can remember."

"Uh… well, I don't know when he'll be back. You in a hurry?"

The woman sounded flustered, almost afraid.

"Well, sort of. I have a deadline."

"Well, okay, but I wouldn't count on his getting back to you today."

"Oh, is he out of town?" The man wasn't the type who went out of town, for any reason. He preferred the woods, didn't even come to Cedarton more than once a month to stock up on groceries and the like. Odd.

"No, no—not out of town. Just *out*. I'll tell him you called." She hung up—fast.

"Okay, thanks." Jess muttered the words into a dead phone, gazed out the window a minute or two and went back to editing. Didn't think about calling Mac back till she took a break to grab a cup of coffee and kick back to rest her eyes about half an hour later.

Before she drank the last drop, the scanner came to life. A call for fire engines at Julie's address. Fire trucks barreled out of the station across the way, sirens wailing.

"Parker?"

"Go," he said from his office.

Grabbing her backpack, she lit out. "Wendy, I haven't finished Miss Mabel's Flat Rock column," she said and shut the door behind her.

Leaping into the Jeep, she headed out after the screaming trucks. Chasing fire trucks was a lot more exciting than editing. Besides, it might provide pictures for the front page. But Julie's place? And where in thunder had Mac got to?

They headed north out of town and swung to the right on Dogtown Road. Off to the left, smoke boiled into the sky. She tried to see through the trees and almost ran up under the truck when it came to a skidding halt at the narrow road to Julie Crowe's place. The trailer was engulfed in flames. Angling the water truck onto the narrow road took some doing and the ladder truck barely got off the main road. Firemen bailed out like fleas off a hound, hauling hoses and yelling. Jess parked in the ditch, pawed her camera from her bag, leaped out, and took shots of the firemen at work, moving closer to frame each photo.

One of the men, temporarily taking a breather, told her that no one was in the house as far as they could tell.

"We like to not got close enough cause of Mac's vehicle. Thought he knew better than to block access like that."

Her heart skittered. "Mac…?" she began, but he ran off before she could ask him anything.

Staying out of the way, she ran along the far side of the trucks to Mac's SUV, nosed off the track at an angle. He was nowhere to be seen. She grabbed a passing fireman's sleeve. Asked if he'd seen Mac. He shook his head and kept moving. In a few minutes, the frantic urgency died away. The trailer was a total loss and there was no reason to waste more water on it, so they started dragging the hoses back onto the trucks.

Once again, she asked if anyone had seen Mac.

The chief approached. "Ain't seen him, but when you do you might tell him to keep his blamed vehicle out of the way of our trucks."

"You need to look around for him. He came out here on a call a long time before you guys left out. I'm worried he might've been inside. No one else was here? Who called in the fire?"

He shook his head, shrugged. "Check with 9-1-1."

All the while she questioned the fire chief, she dug around in her backpack till she laid hands on her phone, punched number one and waited for Dal to answer. It took him a couple of rings. Meanwhile the chief had shouted up a few of the men to scour the place. She heard the word "body" a couple of times.

Dal's voice cut through her apprehension. "Yeah, Jess. What's up?"

"Mac's missing. Oh, God." She fought breaking down.

"What? Missing how?"

"His unit's here at Julie Crowe's. Her trailer just burned to the ground. We can't find him, and there's no sign of her either. Dal, hurry."

"Shit. On my way, honey. Hang in there."

She dropped the phone, went to her knees to pick it up. Tears streamed down her cheeks, and she continued to kneel there, sobbing.

One of the guys came over. "Jessie, you okay?"

"Was he inside? Is there a body?"

He took her arm, helped her to her feet. "No, ma'am. No body in there. Nowhere. Now you quit your worrying. We'll find him." He sat her on the rear bumper of the water truck and ran off.

A few minutes later, a siren drew close fast. Dal's SUV slid to a halt at the turnoff, then nosed its way between bordering trees and the trucks until he couldn't pull forward any farther. He jumped out, spotted her and hurried to her side, lifted her to her feet and into his arms.

"Come on, honey. We'll find him. They didn't find a body?"

"N-n-no. But what happened to him? And what happened to Julie?"

"Any vehicles here at all?"

"Not when we all got here. Just Mac's."

"Let's go take a look at it. Okay? Or do you want to wait here?"

"No, I'll go with you."

The driver's side door of the sheriff's unit stood open, the shotgun locked in place, the radio spitting static, the mic and his Stetson tossed in the passenger seat.

16
CHAPTER

The stench of smoke from the razed mobile home filled the truck cab, choking Jess.

Dal gazed at the open door of Mac's unit. "Looks like he was going to make a call to dispatch, or already had, when he was interrupted. No keys. Had a habit of leaving his hat in the seat when he drove, but always put it on first thing before getting out. Leaving it here's not normal, neither is the mic just tossed aside that way."

He closed his eyes, laid a hand on the driver's seat. She waited, taking deep breaths to bring her emotions under control. The acrid odor of burnt plastic and wood and God knew what else flooded her nostrils.

Dal muttered something.

"What?"

"Something weird went on here. He wasn't frightened. More surprised, amazed, puzzled. Not sure which, but resembling that. A woman, must've been Julie, terrified. Why not Mac?"

He grabbed up the mic, asked dispatch if Mac had made a call in the past couple of hours. The answer was no. Dal ordered an APB, then shouted, "Anybody know what kind of car Julie drives?"

"Yeah, a 1996 Chevy pickup. Red, I think," a short stocky man Jess didn't recognize said.

Jess nodded. "It was red. The one she drove to *The Observer* the other day. Old, rattly thing with a banged up left rear fender."

Dal relayed the information to dispatch, added to approach with caution. "Anyone see Merle?"

No one had, but someone suggested he might still be at school. "Bus ought to be here in a bit. Someone should stay here to tell him what's going on."

Another of the firemen volunteered. "I just live down the road a piece, if someone could drop me there, I'll pick up my wife's truck. I can come back and wait for the boy."

Jess had to get back to the paper with her photos and write a story. By the time it was written, surely Mac would have been found, as well as Julie Crowe. She walked beside Dal to his car.

"Wonder why Lennie or Sara haven't shown up to see what's going on?"

He glanced toward their place across the road. "Good question. I'll just go over there and see what's up. Maybe they're not home."

"Could be. I'm going back to work. Please keep me posted, would you? I'm so worried about Mac."

"He's a tough old bird. He can take care of himself. He'll show up."

She nodded miserably, accepted his kiss on her cheek, and hiked out to the Jeep. The last thing she wanted was to go back to the office with Mac missing, but she didn't see any choice.

Back at the paper, it took more than five minutes to explain to everyone what had happened, then Jess got down to writing a story on the fire and transferring the photos from her camera. In less than thirty more minutes, she sent the story and photos to Parker's computer. He would have to add whatever he thought best about the local sheriff disappearing. She couldn't bear to do it. Still nothing from Dal, so she stepped into the editor's office.

"I'm going to see if I can find Dal or find out what's going on. Going over to the sheriff's office first. I didn't finish the story. Could you do it?"

Parker nodded, regarded her with soft brown eyes. "Get hold of yourself, Jessie. This could turn into a big story. If you don't think you can handle it, call me. You hear?"

She nodded. "What if Mac's dead?" She could barely get the words past her lips.

Parker rose, came from behind his desk, and wrapped his arms around her. "Don't even think that way. Go on over there, but don't forget to take notes or use that fancy little recorder you've got. Keep me posted."

"Okay. I can handle this." Her throat burned when she swallowed, but she patted him on the arm. "Thanks."

He nodded, and she left him standing there, gazing after her.

Dal sped up the drive to Sara and Lennie's place, leaving behind a cloud of dust. Lennie's old car was parked around back, but when he pounded on the door, no one answered. He twisted the knob, shoved it open a bit, and hollered. Still no reply, so he pulled the door shut and walked around the house.

Feet stuck out from beneath a disreputable car that had been driven onto two boards propped up by rocks. Dal kicked the bottom of one old work boot with his toe.

"Want to talk to you a minute."

"Busy."

"Get your butt out here, boy."

Lennie came scooting out, sat up, and glared at Dal. "What the hell? Cain't you see I'm workin here?" Grease smeared his forehead, and dirt clung to long greasy strands of hair.

"Didn't maybe notice your neighbor's place on fire?" Dal asked.

"Don't nose into my neighbor's business."

"Not even when it's the mother of your son?"

"That bitch. Just 'cause she can get one outta the oven don't mean she's a mother."

Dal reached down, caught Lennie behind his fancy belt buckle, and yanked him to his feet. "Same goes for you, then, when it comes to being a dad? Where's your mama?"

"In the house, I reckon."

"Nope. I near beat the door down and no one answered."

Lennie glared from beady eyes. "Well, then, she must not be in there. I don't keep track of her."

"Does she have a car?"

"What the hell business is that of yours?"

Dal grabbed the front of the dirty shirt and slammed Lennie hard against the door of the junk heap, rocking it on the uncertain planks. "You keep a decent mouth on you, or I'll run you in for sassing a deputy."

"Ain't no law agin that." A dirty paw dug into his pocket, brought out a piece of chocolate wrapped in brown and gold paper. Smirking, he unwrapped it and stuck it in his mouth, licking the tips of his filthy fingers.

"I just wrote one. Now, does your mama have a car?" Dal itched to arrest him, instead shook him so hard his head smacked the window glass. Dal's gaze slid down to the belt buckle. Sharpshooter award. Could it be his? Maybe, maybe not. Sam said he was a crack shot.

"Hell, yes, she's got a car, and if it's gone, why then I reckon she's gone. Sir." Lennie spit the last word, dodged Dal's clenched fist.

Rather than have another go at hitting him, Dal let him go. "She comes home, you tell her I want to talk to her. And I'll be back 'cause you've got some explaining to do yourself." Without waiting for a reply, he turned and walked back to the car, trying his best not to limp in front of that piece of shit. Too bad he couldn't cuff him on the spot, but a candy wrapper and a belt buckle weren't enough to make an arrest.

Driving away, he glanced in the rear view mirror. The broken, taped one. Shifted his eyes to stare at the one inside the car. Lennie stood spraddle-legged, shaking a fist and shouting something he couldn't hear. He and Sara were involved in this business up to their ears, but so far there was not enough evidence to prove it. It seemed a court of law didn't welcome Dal's unusual insights as real proof of anything. He had to use them to track down the evidence he needed to make an arrest or get a confession.

The radio crackled his name and he keyed the mic.

"That red truck? It's been found, but no one was around." Tink was handling dispatch and sometimes her reports were a bit too brief.

"Where?" Dal coaxed.

"Oh, yeah. Wes found it over toward Black Oak, just setting on the side of the road."

"Okay, thanks."

If Wes had the truck, Dal would not go chasing over there. The deputy knew what he was doing, and Mac and Julie were still missing. It was more important to find them and hopefully whoever had them so he'd have someone to question. Probably the one who set the fire. Sara was gone in her car, and he wouldn't put it past her to be the one they needed to pick up. And eventually her son as well.

He keyed the mic. "Tink?"

"Yes, deputy?"

"Can I get a description and tag number on Sara Wells' car, please?"

"Hold, Deputy."

Dal couldn't smother a wry grin. Someone must have walked into the room for Tink to be acting so formal. She came back on shortly with a description and tag number. Then asked, "Has anyone seen Mac yet?"

"Sorry, no."

"Would you check and see if Mac got anything in from NCIC on Jasper Long or Lennie Wells? Let me know if he did."

"Roger that," she said, and if things hadn't been so serious he would've busted out laughing. She'd been watching too much television again.

Damn, things were heating up. Kind of exciting, but scary at the same time. When something like this happened, word got around fast and someone could get shot easy, since most everyone in the county owned at least one gun, more than likely three or four. Open hunting season on killers wasn't unknown.

He got on the radio and asked for a call in and location from all deputies. He would cover some part of the county no one else was in. They had to find Mac and Julie, and he had a hunch when they found Sara and her car, they'd have them, though he'd bet she wasn't alone. Someone had to be helping her. Too bad Lennie was at home, but no matter, he was involved. Most definitely he'd done the shooting at Jess, then at the both of them.

Once the deputies had all checked in, he headed on out Dogtown road toward Harrison. A logical route to use to get away from Cedarton. With none of the deputies patrolling out that way, it was up to him. A couple of state highways led out of Grace County, both covered by Staties. The road to the top of Sugar Mountain headed into the Ozark National Forest where dozens of logging roads snaked off into the wilderness. The logical exit route if you knew where you were going. And no one was on it.

He picked up the mic one last time and gave Tink his itinerary, asked her if she'd learned anything from NCIC. She said no, and he floorboarded the Ford, fishtailing up a heavy cloud of dust. Mac might be able to handle himself, but against two or three armed thieves, the outcome could well be bad. These people had killed, they were just stupid enough to do it again. Julie had been used to lure an unsuspecting Mac into the car. It must have happened that way. Now he had to find them before Julie and Mac became a statistic.

Jess was unhappy by the time they wrapped things up at the paper as best they could for a Friday. Dal wasn't answering his cell. Tink only knew he was on his way into the Ozark wilderness of Sugar Mountain looking for Mac and Julie. There was no cell reception in that remote section, and even the police radios were iffy with no booster towers. He was on his own, and she didn't like that one bit. If something were to happen, it could take days to locate him, even from the air. She would rather be with him out there facing God knows what than imagine him alone.

True, even when he wasn't quite up to speed, he could take care of himself better than most. Yet when she cared for someone like she did him, she wanted to know he was close and safe. Same with Mac.

So where the hell were they?

Tink said the other deputies continued to scour all parts of the county in search of the missing sheriff and Julie with no luck. Nothing from the Staties, either.

By now it was assumed by everyone that Julie and Mac had been taken together and the trailer torched by the same people. Dal had probably figured out who, and with his innate talents had a better chance of finding them than anyone else.

Jess didn't want to go home. Parker didn't want her alone at the office. He offered to take her to his place, but his bachelor digs were not suitable for the comfort of female company. One of them would have to sleep on the floor… with the dog.

"I'll call Tink, see what she's doing. Maybe I'll go to her place for the night. I'll be safe over there. Besides, it looks like our bad guys are otherwise occupied."

Parker scratched his head of newly grown hair, mussing it attractively. "I wouldn't be so quick to suppose whoever took Mac works alone. The way this is looking, we've got a bunch of people engaged in breaking the law, and they've already left two bodies behind. Even if Merle did kill that Jasper boy by accident, it is directly connected."

"Well, Tink's apartment is over a carriage house and people live in the main house right close. We'll be just fine." She grinned at him. "Besides, she's armed."

"Little good that does her in the dark. Be careful just the same. Make sure no one follows you over there, and stay inside with the doors locked."

"Yes, Daddy," she said, and kissed his cheek.

He patted her arm. "I'll wait till you drive off, make sure you're okay."

She gathered her things and went out. "See you Monday. Hope this is all settled by then."

He followed her, locking the door behind them, and stood there waving till she couldn't see him anymore.

She swung by the sheriff's office to wait till Tinker got off work to follow her home. Sam sat behind the intake desk. "Hey, Sam. Where's Tink?"

He shrugged. "She got a call about half an hour ago, came running back and asked me if I could watch the desk, she had an emergency and had to leave. Didn't say where she was going."

"I hope nothing bad happened."

"She looked more excited than upset, so I reckon not."

Back out in the Jeep, Jess sat there a moment, then decided to go to Grandma's and eat some supper. If Tink still wasn't back by then, she'd just go on home, lock up good, go to bed with her gun, and read. She had, after all, bought the weapon to protect herself, and that's what she would do, by God.

She left the Jeep parked at the sheriff's office and walked across the square to Grandma's, where several families had already gathered to enjoy the scrumptious home cooked food, and most especially the pies still hot out of the gigantic ovens in the kitchen.

An hour later, she came out into the growing dusk carrying a piece of coconut cream pie she was too full to eat. It would make a good snack with a glass of milk later. The sun disappeared early behind the surrounding mountain peaks, and though the sky was a burnished bowl of silver, gold, and pink, shadows lay on the ground beneath shrubs and plantings in the center of the well-lit square.

Any other time she would not have thought anything about strolling in the downtown square at midnight, but now—at six-fifteen—her nerves sent tendrils of fear through her.

Who were all these people wreaking so much havoc in her peaceful hometown? Was it going to be even worse with the opening of the new highway between Tulsa and Branson? Some of these lawbreakers were from here, probably involved because they were easy to control. Or maybe they weren't even involved anymore and only wanted the hidden diamonds. If John Reilly was at the core of it all, he had moved his interests to Kansas

City. Possibly had no idea what was taking place here in Cedarton. No one here had any money or valuable possessions to speak of.

If Dal was right, the trouble had begun in Harrison, then spread to Cedarton when some of the crew moved here after Mathon and Wesley got arrested. Probably came to try to find the stashed diamonds, then just remained for lack of enough energy to do otherwise. Whatever Reilly was up to was going on up north in KC.

In the parking lot of the sheriff's office, she glanced around, saw no one lurking, climbed in the Jeep, and headed for Tink's, who might be home by now. If not, Jess was going home. There were no lights at the carriage house, and with Tink afraid of the dark there were always lights if she was there, even after she went to bed. No one followed Jess through town, so she started home.

The trip, considering all that was going on, reminded her of the night she took the same route to find a note from Caveman Jake that led her and Dal into a terrorizing solution to their first case together.

As then, the night was dark with no moon. Her headlights fingered through the inky blackness, pointed out the turnoff to her place. The thought of Mac and Julie being plucked away in broad daylight and the deliberate fire that destroyed Julie's trailer, almost made her turn around right there and drive back to town. But she kept going, growing more and more nervous till her chest quivered with anticipation.

The security light lit the front of the cabin where she had left the porch light and a lamp in the window burning. Her back itching with fear, she dragged her pack out, trotted to the porch, key in hand. She no more than stuck it in the door when she remembered that someone else had her other key. Someone who had been in her house to take a shot at her. A shot that had come within inches of killing her.

If this were a movie, she'd be saying over and over, 'Don't go in there. Don't open that door, dummy.' But it wasn't a movie, and she'd be damned if she'd allow fear to rule her life. She had chosen her career and it involved sometimes stepping on a lot of toes. People who might get angry enough to threaten her, come after her. She had to learn to live with it or go to work at Wal-Mart. It was as simple as that.

She turned the key, pushed the door slowly open and stuck her head in, looked around the dimly lit room. Next time she'd leave more lights on. The hallway stretched darkly toward the bedroom and bath. The kitchen lay in shadows. Creeping along, she began to snap on lights at every wall switch until the place was lit up like a twenty-four-hour casino. Despite the lights, her spine tingled with fear. She whirled, but no one was there. Before she ventured into the back part of the house, she slipped open the drawer of the lamp table, took out the .38 and checked the cylinder, even though she knew it was loaded. That was a stupid place to have left it. Slowly she toured the house, the gun in both hands in front of her, trigger finger lying flat, barrel pointed at the floor just like Grandpa had taught her. Don't want to startle shoot a friend.

After all the preparation, it was a bit of a letdown when no one jumped out for her to shoot at. What was wrong with her? Did she actually want to take a shot at someone? On thinking about it, she probably did, if it was the someone who had Mac, who might well kill him or harm Dal in the process.

Unfortunately, they were out of her reach, so she did as planned. Ate the pie with a glass of milk, showered, put on a nightshirt, and took a book and the .38 to bed with her. Sometime during the night, she awoke with a start, crept through the house carrying her powerful bed partner, peering from each window into the dark silence broken only by night songs of harmless creatures, then went back to bed to lie awake staring at the ceiling. What in the hell had awakened her in the middle of the night?

No missed calls on the phone. She called Dal, got only his voicemail, and hung up. Where was he? What was going on? Why didn't he call?

Dal followed the instinct passed to him by his grandfather and nothing more, and drove deeper and deeper into the rugged back country of the Ozark National Forest, heading unerringly where his mind led him. A narrow road wound deep into the pitch-black wilderness. No lights anywhere. Just him and the golden cones showing the way on the road ahead. Rounding a curve, the sweep of his headlights revealed a cabin squatting under an overhang in a gash cut into the bluff to his right. There, a flash of the image in his mind. Words of anger, the raw emotion of fear, pricked through his brain like fingers plucking guitar strings. Someone was in there. Someone furious and struggling. Without touching the brake, he drove on. At this angle, they could see him approach. They needed to see him go right on by.

Up ahead the road curved back upon itself after moving from under the rocky overhang. Once out of sight of the cabin, he cut the lights and turned off the engine. This was the first sign of life he'd experienced since leaving Dogtown Road and heading into the forest, tracking the lingering terror that floated like dust above the road. Motioning him forward into the unknown. No longer sure exactly where he was, going strictly on his instinct, he drove with determination. Someone was in trouble.

A few people lived up here, some who wanted only to be left alone, and the mental warning could be perfectly innocent. A family fight, maybe. Yet the fear mixed with raw fury. Too raw to be ignored. Usually loners lived at the end of barely visible trails deep in the woods. Rarely anywhere near the road.

Shotgun in one hand, he crept from the car. Sneaking up on someone keeping watch wouldn't be easy. Darkness clothed him like a heavy blanket. He couldn't see more than a foot in front of him. Each step could crack a branch, send pebbles tumbling through dry leaves. Grandfather would walk unerringly to that cabin in the dark, but Dal had grown up in Dallas, spending only a few summers in Oklahoma learning the old ways. His special sight would have to guide him, because he dare not turn on the flashlight. Hunching forward, he made his way back along the road till he reached a path. Trusting that it led to the cabin, he followed it and was soon in the cutback that hugged the ramshackle place.

At last, his eyes grew accustomed to the dark, and star shine revealed a vague outline of the slumping shed. No vehicles anywhere. This was not in his job description, and he'd almost rather be in a back alley in Dallas where he knew what to expect. The leg protested but held him steady. Doc Swinton would be very unhappy with him about now. He wasn't very happy with himself, coming off out here alone. But damn it, if Mac was in there, he had to get him out. And he could not do it on crutches. So they remained in the Ford where they'd been since he left the hospital.

Holding his breath, he approached the silent cabin, a buzz stirring in his brain like a fly caught in a spider web. He climbed onto the porch, feeling out each step so as not to go through rotten boards. Then he did all he could think of to do.

He stood beside the door, hammered and shouted, "Grace County Deputy Sheriff. Open up."

No reply, no reaction.

But an emotion so strong it nearly bowled him over.

Hell, he hadn't kicked down a door in a while. Probably better not do so now. Best try opening it first. Remaining to the side, he wiggled the knob, pushed, and the door swung open with a squeal that sent shivers down his spine. A vile odor floated out along with muffled noises. So dark inside it made outside look bright. Tendrils of caution turned to relief accompanied by a low broken grunting.

Too damn dark. If whoever was in here was going to shoot him, they'd have done it by now. He fingered the mag-light from his belt and snapped it on. The powerful beam swept over a filthy floor covered in rat droppings, wads of animal hair, a coating of dirt disturbed by recent comings and goings. Something small squeaked and scurried away. The beam swept over a figure hunched in the corner, half lying, half sitting. Not moving.

Oh, shit. A body. No. Moving. And furious. Heart drumming so loud the birds roosting in the trees could've heard, Dal crept toward the shadow. Knelt down and reached out a hand, not wanting to touch it, but knowing he had to. Just the palm of one hand. Easy. Warm. Alive, but maybe hurt bad.

"Mac? That you?" His voice sounded loud in the silence. Trembling like a rookie, he set the light down so the beam lit the wad of humanity.

Another grunt from the still form. Okay, conscious. And it was Mac.

Without warning, the figure began to buck and shake and shudder. The dust-laden beam revealed a Duct-taped figure trussed up into a ball, knees drawn up to his chin, arms wrapped under the butt. Telltale uniform and white hair.

"Good God, Mac. It *is* you. Hold still, let me see if I can get you out of there. Idiots must've used an entire roll of this stuff." When his fingers wouldn't loosen anything, he pulled out a pocket knife, opened it with fumbling fingers, and started cutting him free. "Stop struggling, dammit. I'm liable to cut off an ear or something worse. I can't hardly tell up from down here."

Identifying the bottom of the trussed bundle that was Mac, he hacked away at thick bindings of tape. Best to leave the face for last because he didn't want to listen to Mac berate him while he cut him free. Careful not to cut flesh, he finally loosened the last of the wrappings.

Sure enough, Mac let fly. "Thought I might stay here till I starved to death. Fools left me a bottle of water. How the hell was I supposed to drink it all trussed up like this?"

When Dal didn't reply, he ranted some more. "Took you long enough to find me. No cars went by till yours, then you drove right on by. What have you been doing all night? Where are the others?"

"We didn't exactly know where you went to. It wasn't like you dropped bread crumbs or anything. The others are searching the county in all directions. I came up here 'cause this was where I knew you'd be, and don't ask me to explain that, either."

Mac chuckled. "Far be it from me. But when you drove right on by, I figgered I was a goner. Could be no one would come up here for weeks."

Dal touched the old man's arm, more to reassure himself than anything else. "At first I couldn't tell how many were in here. I still get the sense of the others. Must've been one hell of a fight here, and not long ago. I kept getting that, so I came in careful. Went on by and walked back."

During the conversation, both men worked at removing the excess shreds of duct tape clinging to clothing and skin. "These guys watch too many movies. Trussed you up like a damned mummy." Dal finally allowed a laugh of relief at having found the sheriff alive and unharmed. "Where's Julie?"

"Ain't that danged funny. But you're right about the fight. Two men already had Julie when I drove up to her place. Sent her out to fetch me while they pointed a gun at her. I could see by the look on her face it was bad, but like a sap, I walked right into it. Then when we get here, they haul us both out of her truck, had thrown us in the back before setting the fire, then left it and transferred us to another one. Did you ever ride on your backside in the back of a pickup over blamed rocky roads? Like to beat me plumb to death."

"No, can't say as I have. Glad I haven't, come to think of it." Squatting, the leg was giving him hell. He pulled a long piece of tape off Mac's back and stood to stretch. "So where is Julie? That seems to be the worst of it. You can finish peeling yourself later. We need to get out of here. Let someone know."

Mac went on like Dal hadn't spoken. "Anyway, they get us up here and one hell of a fight breaks out between them. Julie gets in on it, yelling and screaming, calling them names. Threatening to tell everything. I was afraid for a minute they were gonna kill her, then me cause I was a witness. 'Bout that time, she ups and makes a run for it. Got away too, though I don't know how she can get back to town. They were so danged mad, they lit out in that same truck. They were still hollering at each other."

"Who were they?"

"That's the thing. They wore these masks and never took them off in front of me. I swear, Dal, it was like a danged movie, the way they talked and acted."

"Well, I think it's safe to say these old boys don't have good sense. Glad they were smart enough not to kill you, though. Did either of them mention the diamonds at all?"

"No, they seemed to think it was a big secret why they were doing all this. Oh, and one of 'em said, 'Neither of 'em won't like it if we kill him.'"

Dal considered the remark, then helped Mac to his feet. He continued to pick bits and pieces of Duct tape off his wrists and clothing. Grabbing up the shotgun and flashlight from the floor, Dal escorted the sheriff outside where the sky was lightening to the east.

"You call this in?" Mac asked, glancing around.

"Nope. Couldn't. Not a signal to be had up here. Haven't been in touch with anyone all night. Been wandering around on these back roads and haven't seen a soul. If anyone lives up here, they sure don't want to be found. You have any idea at all which direction those yahoos might have taken?"

"I listened to the rattles of that old truck, and I'd swear they headed back down the mountain, but they could've fooled me."

"Okay, let's get back to town and call the others in. Don't imagine we have a chance in hell of finding Julie. Hope she knows her way around. They've been out all night looking for you, 'cause I told 'em not to come back till someone found you. Actually, I hope to hell you know the way out of here, 'cause I sure don't."

"Well, that'll kill our overtime allotment for a while, won't it?" Mac halted, grabbed Dal's arm. "Thought you were confined to a desk. What the hell you doing, traipsing around up here?"

"Hell, Mac. Guess I could'a sent 'em all home at five and parked my useless butt in a chair. Maybe you'd a magically got loose from all that tape and hot-footed it back to town, all by your lonesome." Dal laughed, and Mac joined him while they hiked uphill to the SUV, Dal stumbling and catching at the old man's sleeve occasionally.

"You okay, boy?" Mac asked once they reached the unit.

"Fine, boss, just fine."

Jess couldn't get back to sleep after she heard the noise and checked everything. Getting no answer when she called Dal unnerved her even more, so she finally got up, dressed in jeans, tee shirt, and running shoes, poured some coffee into an insulated cup and left, locking up good. She slipped the gun in her pocket. To hell with the permit or the wait time. What she had in mind, she needed to go armed. She prayed she wouldn't have to shoot anyone, but by God she was just about mad enough to do so.

It was a couple of hours till dawn, and she wanted to do some serious searching. In the Jeep, she pulled her toolbox up into the passenger seat and went through it. Made sure she had everything she needed for this little project. Dal would kill her when he found out, but she was about ready to wring his neck for staying gone all night with no word to anyone, so they'd just have to square off and take turns at each other.

She drove through town in the throes of sleep. Not a car anywhere but hers. When she turned onto Dogtown Road, she cut the lights and drove along real slow, tires making crackly sounds on the gravel, like rain falling on a tin roof. The sky had gone from total black to an ashy shade as she neared SEFOR. The ball-shape of the reactor was outlined clearly, while the squat flat-topped buildings huddled around it were only shadows. Steering between trees, she drove as deep into the woods as possible and parked out of sight of the road. She pulled out the toolbox, added a bottle of water and a few small items from her backpack, stuffed it under the seat, crawled out, locked the Jeep, and stuck the keys in her pocket.

Remembering the hole in the fence, she grabbed the toolbox and flashlight, hunkered low so as not to make a silhouette, and scurried through the opening. At the padlocked door of the low-slung building, she set down the toolbox and opened it. She'd learned to pick a lock before she knew how to open a door with a key. One of her cousins was adept at it and had taught her. She got so good, she could open a locked door blindfolded. But damned if she'd tell Dal. Be just like him to arrest her for doing such a thing.

Because she couldn't think they would have hidden the diamonds on the grounds where anyone might accidently discover them, she opted for going inside for a look-see. It took about four seconds to open the lock and rattle the chain from the heavy metal door. She slipped inside, set the toolbox down.

The building had a smell all its own, one she wouldn't forget but surely couldn't describe. Dead, moldy, decaying stuff all mixed up with old oil, and an electrical odor like when you went around where electricity was being produced. Shadowy corners hid forms that might be machines of some sort. Unless they began to move toward her, which she hoped like hell they didn't. She touched the gun in her pocket, left it there for the time being.

From the article she'd researched, she learned there was only a small amount of residual radioactivity at the site, and it was safely stored. Hazardous materials that still remained were asbestos, residual sodium in and around the cooling system of the reactor, some lead in paint and PCBs in fluorescent lights. Nothing to worry about, really. The reactor itself was in the huge round ball adjacent to the cluster of structures, and she had no intention of going near it, which wasn't saying she wouldn't be exposed to something bad anyway.

If she hurried, she had time to give this building a cursory search before daylight. Maybe there'd be some places that would make a good hidey hole. The cleanup announcement released back in 2009 said nothing was actually done, the people at the college just discussed what had to be done and how much it would cost. When a price tag of twenty million dollars was determined, everything had come to a halt. The college couldn't afford that, and the government continued to drag its heels on paying the cost though it had originally ordered the cleanup.

Some research had been conducted out there until 1986, so there would've been minor activity around the site till then. After that, this would have made a very safe place for diamonds to lie in wait. That left a six year window between the robbery and the final closing of the plant. It didn't seem Mathon and Wesley could possibly have hidden the stones in the plant, so someone else had to. But who? And why was she so convinced they were here? She'd have to figure that out later. Now to follow her hunch.

Crap. The place was much larger than she'd thought. She'd overestimated her ability to do this. Flashing the light around the cluttered, massive room, filled with the trash of so many years, she nearly turned around and walked out. But she was here so might as well give it a go. Leaving the toolbox by the door to free up one hand for feeling around in hidden spaces while she carried the flashlight in the other, she moved slowly along the outer wall of the entire room, investigating anything that looked suspicious, including discarded metal containers. Her sneakers left scuffed footprints in dust that lay thick on the floor.

Turning the final corner, she noticed something sticking from between the sliding doors of a long heavy metal shelf that took up about twelve feet or so of the wall. The door creaked and groaned when she tried to slide it open. Wouldn't budge. With one finger, she flipped at the object. A piece of cardboard with a flap on it, like the top of a box. A quick search turned up a filth-covered metal bar. Hooking the thinner end of it between the two doors, she leaned all her weight against it and the door squawked and moved a few inches. One more try and it was open far enough to see the small box attached to the exposed flap.

Her hand fitted through the opening and she closed her fingers around the box. It wouldn't fit through the opening, but by shining the light on it, she made out something written on it. Goe... No matter how she twisted or turned or shone the light that was all she could see. Nothing else in the cabinet. Goe meant something, but she couldn't dredge it up from her memory. She finally gave up getting the doors open, and began another turn checking equipment, machines, tables, and some funny looking protuberances, large-capped pipes running up from the floor.

At last she moved on to the center of the room where all manner of office equipment was stacked. She poked in drawers and bins and locker-type containers like were found in gyms, all the while trying to remember what Goe could mean. Dust and cobwebs gathered in her hair and on her clothing, her hands were sticky from contact with dirt and oil-stained surfaces. Dawn poked its pale way through the window slats. She took a sneezing fit and had to stop while it wound down.

Standing in the very middle, she surveyed everything one last time with a final sweep of the beam, in case her eye would catch something, an ideal place, anything she hadn't checked. It was hopeless, yet she couldn't help remembering Mrs. Durning talking about pickup trucks unloading stuff in the dark of night some years back. Surely there would be some sign of what had been stored here then.

She stumbled, and the light temporarily climbed the wall and flashed on a grate along the ceiling. Possibly an air conditioner or heater vent of some sort.

Damn. What a perfect place to hide something. Who would ever go in there for any reason? Or even look in there. It was a well known fact that people seldom looked above eye level, even when searching for something. Wasn't she proof of that? If it hadn't been for the stumble and the light climbing the wall like it was pointing out the vent, she'd never have even glanced up there.

Heart pounding, she searched for something to drag against the wall so she could climb up and take a look. Tables were bolted to the floor, if there'd been chairs, they were long gone.

The chain on the outside door rattled and fell, link by link, to the ground, and she froze in her tracks, her racing heart pausing for a split second. Someone coming in? Or just the thing turning loose? Laughter, someone talking. Crap, she'd be caught. She searched frantically, tried to remember if she'd spotted a good place to hide. Finally, she shoved herself between two of the cylindrical towers until she was crammed into the darkness against a wall. Fingers fumbling, she shut off the flashlight and tried to still the hammering in her chest that made her head throb.

It wasn't until the footsteps started across the floor that she remembered leaving her toolbox at the door. And her car parked out back. Maybe they wouldn't think anything of it. Oh, sure. It was the only clean thing in this filthy place. They'd know it hadn't been there very long. They had to have seen her car. It was clear from where she'd left footprints on the dusty floor that someone was here. Hand on the gun in her pocket, she waited for them to track her passage round and round the building and into her hiding place. Daylight poked its way in, lighting all but the corners. They'd find her, and she had no place to go.

17
CHAPTER

Once Dal turned onto Dogtown Road with his rescued passenger, he radioed all the deputies that they could go on home, Mac was safe and in his custody. No one had seen Julie. Then he tried to call Jess. Voicemail. She must still be in bed asleep. He tried her landline. Same thing there.

About that time, Sam came on the radio. Told him about Tinker taking off and Jess thinking Julie might have called her for help. Now both women were missing. Well, damn it all. That meant a search for them. He'd give Jess time to get up, then he'd try her again.

"Mac, I'm going to drop you off at the station. One of the guys took your unit there yesterday. You need to go home and get some sleep. I'll go by and check on Jess. She's been without any protection all night long. Then I'll see if anyone has seen Tink and Julie. What a danged mess. Next thing we know, half the town will disappear."

"Okay, you check on Jess, I'll start looking for them women. Too much going on to sleep."

Dal nodded. "I got me a bad feeling this is all coming to a head, and we got no control whatsoever over what those morons do. If they hurt Jess, you won't have to worry about making room in the jail for them."

"Know how you feel, son, but don't do anything rash. Just find Jess, keep her safe. We'll catch them right quick. They don't exactly have a teacup of smarts between 'em."

Dal set a new speed record getting through town and out to Jessie's. His heart sank when he saw there was no Jeep parked there. A few lights were burning inside, but she could've left those on when she went in to work Friday. Still, he wanted to look around, so he parked, limp-loped across the yard, tried the knob but the door was locked. The spare key was still missing, so rather than take the time to pick the lock, he went around peering in the windows till he determined she wasn't there, then hurried painfully back to the car. While he wheeled the SUV around, kicking sod up from the wheels, he called Mac, told him what was going on.

"Tinker isn't home, either, and the family living there say they haven't seen her. Her car's not there." Mac sounded as frantic as Dal felt. "I've called everyone back in."

Dal went to the sheriff's office first, made his slow way inside, dropped into a chair behind his desk, dug in his pocket and dry-swallowed a Tramadol. The phone rang, and he reached to pick it up.

"Sheriff Richards, please," an official voice demanded.

"He'll be in shortly. This is Deputy Starr. Could I help you?"

"This is John Reilly. I wonder if I could come in and talk to someone about a missing person."

A sure-fire clue that John wasn't the dead body. Who could be missing now? Maybe the vic? But why had Reilly come all this way to report it? He knew something, that's for sure. "Yes, sir. Of course. Where are you now?"

"Just drove down from Kansas City. I'm on the square having breakfast."

"You're just across from the station. We're in the building in the center of the square."

"Perhaps you could join me, then," Reilly said smoothly.

Mac came pushing through the door, and Dal raised a hand, pointed to the phone. "Tell you what, Sheriff Richards just came in. I'll tell him. Hold on."

"Who is it?" Mac asked, sinking into a chair beside the desk.

Dal filled him in quickly, then added, "He lives in Kansas City and is a person of interest on our murder case. The two bodies? Interesting he drove all this way to report someone missing. Do you want to go on over and have breakfast with the man? I don't think I can walk another step for a bit."

Mac stood up, clapped him on the shoulder. "Sure. You're not supposed to be working the field yet, anyway."

"Keep me in the loop, would you, Mac? I'm worried to death about Jessie. And Tink and Julie, too."

"I am, too, and I will. You wait right here. I'll get on over there. See what he has to say. Advise him we need to question him as well. Better than waiting for him to finish eating and come over here. Take 'er easy for a while, would you?"

Frustrated, Dal nodded but didn't object.

Where the hell was Jessie? And he'd be damned if he couldn't help her when she needed him the most.

Mac had no more than disappeared into Grandma's when Burt Sample came barreling in the door. "Did anyone find Tinker?"

"Not yet. I hate to ask you this, Burt, I know you've been out all night, but could you take a quick run around town and see if you can find Jessie's Jeep or Tinker's little car? Take it you heard the call go out on the radio. I can't get out of this chair right now."

"Sure thing, Dal. You need me to take you somewhere first? The hospital or someplace?"

"Nah, thanks. I'll be okay. Just do this, would you?"

"I'll see what I can find. Sure hope those ladies aren't hurt." Burt hurried back out to his car and took off.

Dal pounded the desk with his fist. Cursed under his breath. If anything happened to Jess, he'd never forgive himself for this weakness he couldn't seem to shake. If she was somewhere hurt or in danger, he'd crawl to get to her, if he had to.

Jessie listened to the footfalls shuffling across the floor, coming closer and closer to her hiding place. She pulled out the gun and made herself as small as possible. Not sure she could shoot someone, she tried to think of a logical reason not to. Maybe this was only someone searching for the diamonds, someone who would pose no threat.

Or worse, it could be whoever killed John Doe with nothing to lose.

But Dal said one of them was a woman.

This sounded like men.

They drew near enough for her to begin to understand what was being said between the rhythm of footsteps and the clatter of apparatus being shoved around.

"I tell you, they're in here somewhere. I can't make out from Dad's old pencil scratches just where at they might be." That had to be Lennie, talking about a map his dad Mathon had left. "I'm some worried about that car out back. Don't appear to be no one in here, but shit, that's a nice car. Maybe they found the diamonds and went off with someone else. Keep a eye out, just in case they're still hangin' around here."

"Just how big would a million dollars worth of diamonds be?" This one she didn't recognize at all.

"Probably just a little pouch. Diamonds is really valuable for their size."

"What're we gonna do with 'em when we find 'em?"

"Sell 'em, lame brain." Lennie again.

"Do you know anyone who would buy them, no questions asked?"

Appeared to only be two of them, unless someone had nothing to say. During the discussion, they made a lot of noise opening and closing metal cabinets, including the one she'd tried to open. Obviously found nothing there or the little box meant nothing to any of them. They kept on turning over stuff, one of them kicked something that tumbled across the room, the din echoing throughout the building. So much noise that she didn't hear their conversation. When things quieted down a bit, the voices came through again.

"John finds out we found 'em and split, he'll kill us. You know that, don't you? I'm not *even* joking."

John? That had to be John Reilly.

"He don't need to ever find out. Soon as we lay hands on 'em, we're gone, far away from here, nowhere near Kansas City and that crazy family of his. The women's as nutty as the men."

Women? His wife was Delia Miller, but who else? He had a daughter. She could be involved.

"Well, your old lady is pretty tough. She's liable to lay us out with a two by four, we don't let her in on this." Evidently now referring to Sara, Mathon's widow.

"She don't never need to know, neither. We start sharing this out, they won't be none left for us. I do want to share with my kid. He ain't got much and his momma's dumber'n a turkey caught in a rain storm.

She'd just stick her nose in the air and drown." Talking now about Julie Crowe and their son, Merle.

Women involved, and it sounded like more than one. But not Julie. Must be Sara plus two connected to John Reilly. Jessie tried to make out more, but the two men had moved out of hearing, their voices fading to a mumble. That was definitely Lennie, following some sort of penciled instructions from his dad, one of the original diamond thieves, but she didn't know who the guy with Lennie was. A stranger, some kin of his or Wesley Miller's that no one knew about. Had to be close kin for Lennie to be willing to share. She settled back, realizing that they'd lost interest in looking for her when the discussion turned back to the diamonds. She'd just wait them out before searching that air duct.

Waiting became tiresome when it appeared they might hang around all day, poking and banging and kicking and cursing. Her stomach growled, her mouth dried out and her legs grew tired so she put the gun in her pocket and sank to the floor. Would they never leave? What was going on with Dal and Mac? And where the heck had Tinker got to? It was well into afternoon before the two finally banged out. But her relief was short lived, for the bastards dragged the chain back through the outer door handles, and she'd bet they fastened the padlock before leaving, too.

How much time passed, she couldn't guess, but finally she had to get out of hiding and stretch her bent, cramped legs. Before she could look in that air vent, she had to know if she was locked in. Not that it would help any to know, she just couldn't wonder about it any longer. She ran to the door, the place only lit by sunlight coming in through all those slatted shutters on the windows around the building. Both hands on the double steel doors, she shoved with all her might. Sure enough, they had chained them closed. How was she going to get out?

More than sorry she'd checked before looking in the vent for the diamonds, she fell to her butt on the dirty floor, opened the toolbox, and took out the bottle of warm water. Turned it up and guzzled half of it, then sat there a long while staring at the rust-flaked steel panels as if her gaze might magically open them. A glimmer of something lying in the dust on the floor caught her eye and she picked it up. A wrapper from a Hershey mini bar. Dark Chocolate. Same as the one she'd found earlier. One of the men must have been eating them. This hadn't been here very long.

Back to her problem. What did she care about them eating candy? Except she would've liked to have had some. Then, like a strike of lightning out of a clear blue sky, she remembered. The man who'd warned her had chocolate on his breath. Well, hell, who didn't like chocolate? Still it was like Dal said. There aren't any coincidences in a murder case. So one of those two men was the one she'd come in contact with earlier. Lennie or the stranger?

That didn't get her out of here. Okay, what she did have was tools, and the openings that appeared to be windows had no glass with metal slats across them like venetian blinds. If she could pry some of those loose, she could crawl out.

So, first, go find a bathroom. There had to be one in the building somewhere, and she couldn't wait any longer. Then get something to climb on and check that air vent. The suspense agitated her to the point of distraction even from her current problem of escaping. She had to check to see if the diamonds were hidden up there. Returning from a water-less bathroom, she spied a set of metal shelves leaned into a corner and dragged them under the vent, propped them lengthwise up the wall and climbed until, by stretching as far as possible, she could reach the bottom of the cover. She'd need a screwdriver to get it open, so back down to fetch one from her toolbox. In the oppressive heat of the closed-up building, her jeans clung to her legs and the tee shirt stuck to her back. She clambered back up and loosened the screws on the bottom corners of the frame. The metal came away with a shriek, dust sprayed into her face and down the front of the shirt. Choking and sneezing, she stuck one hand in to feel around. Clumps of hairy things that made her shudder, but she kept feeling as far as she could reach. The opening was about two feet by three feet, and if there were any diamonds in there, they had been tossed out of reach. She dug the flashlight from her pocket and took a look. Way in the back lay a cylindrical object that reflected bits of light. Lumps of indescribable stuff lay in piles, and they could be anything from rats' bodies to a bag of diamonds. Only one way to find out. Climb in there.

The idea gave her the jitters, plus she didn't see how she could do that with the rigging she had set up. First the cover would have to come completely off, so she'd need a ladder to reach that high. With a sigh that brought on another fit of coughing, she replaced the cover, turned the screws in good, and lowered herself to the floor. She dragged the shelves away so no one would be able to tell what she'd done.

Something familiar lay on the floor in front of the cabinet she'd tried to pry open earlier. It was a box. The name Goebel and a photo of a figurine on the outside. Her heart raced. Definite proof someone had used this place to store stolen items. She scooped it up, stuck it in her pocket.

Priority was to get out of here, get some help and come back to search properly. For what seemed like forever, she followed the walls, looking for a way out. The slats on the windows proved to be welded on the outside so she couldn't remove any of them. Another door was securely locked from the outside, chained and padlocked in the same way as the one she'd entered.

Then she slapped herself in the forehead. Her phone. Hadn't she put it in her pocket? Stuffing a hand down deep, she found nothing but the keys to the Jeep. Maybe it was in the toolbox. With her bad luck holding, it was probably in the console or car seat of the Jeep. A search of the toolbox answered that. The phone must be in the Jeep. She considered building a fire in the hopes someone would see the smoke, but there really wasn't much in the way of burnable materials in the building, and besides, she didn't have a match. And what if no one saw the smoke and came in time to rescue her and she choked to death? Bad idea all around.

Don't panic yet. Just don't. That order didn't work for long. Write a will, in case someone found her mummified body years from now. Tell her friends how much she cares for them. Especially Dal. A love note. Something for Tink, Parker, and Mac. Her best friends. All in her head 'cause she didn't have any paper. What a laugh, a reporter who leaves her stuff in the car. Sinking down against the wall by the door, she hugged her knees. Damn, why hadn't she pushed Dal into a corner, made him admit he loved her, told him she loved him. Couldn't face life without him. What would he say and do if she had the chance to say those things to him?

Her mouth dried, tongue and lips felt all crackly. She drained the water bottle. It was time to consider panicking.

Seated at his desk at the sheriff's office, Dal let the Tramadol kick in. Burt hadn't come back. He'd had time to drive all over hell and creation, had time to check in. Rising, Dal went out to the front office where Sam still manned the phones.

"Hey, Dal. Feeling better?"

"Yep, I'm okay. Have you heard from Burt?"

"Nope."

"Would you raise him on the radio and ask if he's had any luck finding Jess or Tinker's vehicles or any sign of them?"

He sank down on the bench in the hallway, elbows on both knees, chin propped in his hands, and waited till he heard Burt's voice on the radio.

"Tell Dal I found Jessie's Jeep. Just lucky too, would never have seen it where it's parked but fo—"

"Where is it?" Dal shouted, interrupting him.

"Out back of the old SEFOR plant, wedged into the trees. If the sunlight hadn't hit the windshield as I was passing—"

"Tell him to stay there." Dal hurried out the door. "Damn crazy woman. What the hell do you suppose she's up to now? Worrying everyone sick, going off on one of her harebrained searches. I'm going to tie her to a tree, so help me."

A woman pushing a baby stroller along the sidewalk turned and stared at him. He didn't blame her, he'd been nearly shouting a conversation on the way to the patrol unit.

He jerked open the car door and stopped talking aloud before she called the guys in the white coats, began to cuss under his breath instead. He was going to need help, so he got on the radio, contacted Sam and told him to tell Burt to see if he could round up any of the other deputies to join him out at the reactor plant. Mac was busy with John Reilly.

The rear tires of the SUV screamed, leaving black marks across the parking lot and into the street, startling some pedestrians who'd thought it would be a peaceful day to take a walk on the square. Boy, were they fooled. First he shouted at them, then he tried to run them down. Maybe he could issue a public apology in Jessie's paper.

Siren blaring, he raced out of town, did a slide onto Dogtown Road that kicked gravel and dirt up in a noisy arc, and in a few minutes, executed another off the road and through the trees to where Burt's unit sat near Jessie's empty Jeep.

He bailed out, nearly fell on his face, grabbed the door, then got his balance and loped as fast as he could to where Burt waited.

"I couldn't raise her anywhere out here, so figger she's inside some-where," the young deputy said. "Can't find Tinker. Real worried about her, too, but she's tough, ain't she?"

"Did you look for her?"

"All over town. She ain't nowhere. I sent out a BOLO."

"I meant Jessie."

"Oh, uh, no. Was fixing to when Sam got hold of me, so thought I'd wait for you to get here."

"Did you raise any of the other guys?"

"Only Wes, and he's looking for Tink. Hope that was okay, Dal. The others must've turned off their phones and went to sleep after pull-ing that all-nighter."

"Sure, Burt, that's okay. Keep trying to get hold of the rest of the deputies. When you do, you can follow me. I'm going inside this unholy place."

All Dal wanted was to get in there, so he took off, leaving Burt to catch up. He bent and slid through the opening in the fence and start-ed shouting Jessie's name. Hell, she could be anywhere in one of those buildings, in the woods on the other side of the reactor. Anywhere.

Goddamn it, Jessie. If you're hurt I'm gonna—

Loud hammering and shouting interrupted him in mid-thought, and he stopped, got his bearings, and headed toward the hellacious noise. At the back of the squat building, he located the door, started hollering to get her to shut up, but she just kept on banging and yelling.

Made it awful hard to concentrate, but he finally picked the padlock, yanked the chain from the two handles and swung the doors wide. Almost got hit in the head with the hammer she was pounding with, then took a body hit when she saw him and threw herself into his arms. He staggered backward, went down on his butt and her sprawled on top of him.

For an instant, neither of them said anything. She smothered him with kisses, smeared dirty sweat all over his uniform, and grit on his lips. Commenced to laugh, then sat up astraddle of him to concentrate on his features.

"You hurt? Did I hurt you?"

"Nope. What the hell were you thinking? You okay?" He sat up and brushed at the front of his shirt, then gave up and wiped his mouth. "You taste like a garage floor. We been looking everywhere for you. Is Tinker with you?" He peered around her, saw no one else. "I don't suppose you've seen Julie, either."

"I thought I wasn't going to get out of there. And after I may have found the diamonds." She tilted her head. "Wait. Tink isn't back yet? Does anyone know where she went? And Julie's still missing? What about Mac?"

"Okay, wait just a minute. Mac is okay. Tinker and Julie appear to be together. Or maybe they aren't. Can't find anyone who knows for sure. Figured Tinker was with you, but no one knew where you were, either. Found the diamonds, huh? Well, let's see if we can find these women before we worry about them. Give me a hand up, would you? I've about had all I can take of this desk duty. It's about to kill me."

She helped him up, and he leaned on her all the way to the fence, muttering under his breath.

"Dal, I'm sorry, I truly am. All night I didn't know where you were, was worried sick, too. So decided to get on over here and do a cursory search. Then Lennie and someone I didn't know came in and I hid, and when they left, they locked me in, not knowing I was there, of course."

By the time her tale of woe was finished, they had gone out the hole in the fence to see Burt trotting down the incline from the parked vehicles.

"Never mind. A rescue has been completed." Dal waved a hand. "Has anyone called in about Tinker?"

"Nope. Danged if I can figure out what's going on. I'm worried sick about that purty little thing. You got any ideas, Jessie?"

"Not a one. Did anyone look around her apartment? Maybe she left a note or something."

Burt turned and ran back to his car. "I'm headed out to help look, then." He took off, siren whining.

Dal swung open the SUV's door and plopped heavily into the seat. Jess gave him a frown. "I thought you were supposed to stay on desk duty, and here you are running around all over the place. First off God knows where in pursuit of outlaws, then—"

"I'm thinking, Jess, that you'd best be quiet as a little mouse about now. Unless you want me to handcuff you and take you in for trespassing."

"You wouldn't dare."

Dal unclipped a set of cuffs from his belt and stood. "Come on, come here. Don't make me chase you. Don't you run." He couldn't help but grin at her when her mouth dropped open and she began to back away.

"Don't you do it. You stay away from me." Looking half afraid he was serious, she ran to her car, leaped in, and started it, but when she went to back up, was blocked in by Dal's patrol car. "Dal, darn it. I need a shower and a drink of water. And I haven't had a bite to eat since supper last night. Please let me out of here."

In spite of everything, Dal couldn't help laughing. Lowering himself gratefully into the driver's seat, he started the SUV and backed out of her way. "You're lucky I don't add fleeing a law officer and resisting arrest to those trespassing charges. But I've got more important things to do. I'm going back to the sheriff's office. Want to see what John Reilly had to say. Hopefully, Tinker will have checked in and we can quit worrying about her. Julie could be in the wind if she's not with Tinker."

One leg up in the Jeep, Jess halted. "I thought Julie was with Mac. Wait, John Reilly? He's here? Those two talked about him and two women involved in this. I want to come."

"Seriously? Looking like that? Not to mention the charges pending against you." Dal shook his head, gestured at her dusty tee shirt and jeans, her cobwebby hair. "And what about you're starving?"

"You don't look much better. Come on, Dal. I can clean up in the ladies room, get me a Coke out of the machine."

"Okay, come ahead, then. But you keep your mouth shut and remember the rules. Shit, who am I kidding? But come on anyway."

She nodded vigorously. Climbed in the Jeep, reversed onto Dogtown Road and took off, headed for the sheriff's office ahead of him.

That woman would never change, but on thinking about it, he wasn't really sure he wanted her to.

While she steered the Jeep, Jess dug around in her backpack, came up with a bottle of water, set it between her legs, and screwed the lid off. The tepid liquid was sweet as honey to her parched throat, and she kept drinking until over half the bottle was gone.

Crap. She'd left the toolbox back at SEFOR. She hoped no one took it before she could get back into that vent and recover the diamonds.

At the sheriff's office, she ran inside, headed for the ladies room where she wet some paper towels and cleaned crud and wads of dust bunnies off her shirt and jeans, then splashed water on her face and hands and up both arms. Digging around in the backpack, she came up with a brush and cleaned the filth out of her hair. Unable to reach what stuck to her back, she slipped her arms out of the shirt, spun it back to front and finished the job. A quick brush of her butt and she called it good.

At the viewing window of the interrogation room, she switched on the sound. Dal came in, cast her a quick glance, then found himself a chair, cringing when he sat.

"When was the last time you saw your son?" Mac asked John Reilly, who leaned forward, elbows on the table, hands folded one over the other under his chin.

"I think it was a week or so ago. He said he was going to meet up with a girlfriend and they were going to Six Flags for a few days. So I didn't think much of it when he didn't come back right away. But then when time kept passing and we didn't hear any more from him, Delia asked me to see what I could find out."

Mac stared at John through squinted eyes. "So the first place you look for him is little ole Cedarton, Arkansas, even though he was going to Six Flags in Texas? I think you'd better come up with something better than that."

"Now you wait a minute. I come in here to report a missing person and you're treating me like a suspect in a crime."

"No, sir, you'd better wait a minute. As of this morning, you are a person of interest in a murder investigation. And I'd like to know why you thought we might know something about your son, who is missing."

"Murder? Who got murdered? I only arrived in town today. And as for my son, he had a thing for some woman who lives here, so it's just one of the places I'm looking for him."

"That sounds like a lie," Jess whispered to Dal. "I'll just bet he knew his son was on his way here, all right, but it wasn't to see a girlfriend."

He shook his head and put a finger over his lips, nodded toward the window.

"Sorry to say, sir, the man who got murdered fits the description you gave me earlier of your missing son, Rand. Is there any reason for him to get into it with someone here in Cedarton?" Mac hit the table with the flat of his hand. "Why was Rand here?"

John's face turned deep red, and he half rose from his chair. "I've already told you. You trying to tell me Rand is dead?"

"Sit down, sir." Mac's stern voice would brook no nonsense. "What I'm trying to tell you is we have a body that fits his description. We'd like you to make an identification."

John dropped into the chair. "What makes you think he's my son?"

Mac sighed. "You turn in a missing persons report. We've got a body fits his description. What do you think?" He paused a moment, gazed across the room. "Is your wife with you, Mr. Reilly?"

"Yes, she and our daughter, Claire. They're at the Cedar Creek Inn."

"Two women?" Jess said. "Lennie mentioned John and his two women. Sounds like the gang's all here."

On the other side of the window, Mac rose. "Before we go any further, then, sir, I'd like you to come with me to the morgue and tell me if the body we've got is your son. Would you like to call your wife?"

John stood up, a resigned look on his face. "No sense in putting her through that. Let's go take a look. I'm sure you're mistaken."

Jess headed for the door.

"Where you think you're going?" Dal rose, hesitated a moment before limping toward her.

Concerned about him, she tried not to show it and be in more trouble than she already was. "I'm going to follow them."

"Wait here. They'll be right back."

"I've got a story to finish Monday. I need to know if the body is John Reilly's son."

"I'll ask Mac to get you a release by Monday. This is still an ongoing investigation. I pushed it letting you sit in on the interrogation. You're not going to the morgue."

When he lowered himself gingerly back into the chair, she started toward him. "Dal, you okay? Need me to get you something? You're not even supposed to be running around all over the place."

"I got a release from the doctor to go back to work."

"Dal, excuse me, but that was for a desk job using crutches. You look like hell, release or no release. And you're supposed to be using those crutches, not hauling them around in your car."

"Back off, Jess. I've been up all night is all. Looking for *you*." He glared nails at her.

If she could have crawled under a chair, she would have. "Sure, throw that at me. Just the same, you sit right there. I'm going to go rustle you up a cup of coffee and some snacks."

"Appreciate it, Jessie." The corners of his mouth tilted enough to erase the glower.

At the snack machines out in the hallway, she fed the slots dollar bills until she had some Sun Chips, cookies, and two bottles of Coke.

Back in the viewing room, she dumped the armload on the table near Dal, sat next to him, and handed him a Coke. "Decided you needed sustenance more than a cup of black coffee. If you still want some, though, I'll be glad to go fetch you a cup."

"Why are you being so nice to me, Jess?" He ripped open a package of Sun Chips and twisted the top off the Coke bottle.

"Because you saved my life today, Deputy, and I'm grateful. And I'm also sorry. Not because you saved my life, but because I caused you so much worry. Besides, I'm usually nice to you."

"Well, make that sometimes nice to me and I'll agree." He dug in his pocket, took out a bottle of pills, and swallowed one with a swig of Coke.

She frowned. "Pain pills?"

He didn't reply, just gave her a dark look that said butt out and munched on Sun Chips, inhaling one bag and reaching for another.

If he suffered over all this, it was on her. He should've gone home to bed when he returned from his all night trek in the wilderness. Instead, he came looking for her.

She went to sit beside him to finish her Coke. He held out the last bag of Sun Chips like a peace offering. "Want these?"

"Nope, but I'll take some of those cookies."

He gave her one package, kept the other.

"Dal, I'm sorry… about today, and going out to SEFOR alone. I didn't mean to cause you so much trouble. When you didn't come back, I thought maybe I could get that job out of the way. I really do think I know where those diamonds are."

He touched his lips with two fingers. "Let's just keep that between us for right now. I'm going to ask Mac to let me talk to Reilly, but I'm hoping he can get Delia and the daughter to come in, too. I want them in the same room together. Did Lennie and his pal say where they were going when they left the plant?"

Had they? She frowned and thought about it a minute. "Something was said about meeting Merle. Oh, and taking care of that bitch, Julie."

"Lennie didn't take Julie and Mac. He was home while that was going on. I talked to him." His expression was puzzled. "But Sara wasn't home and the men at the Red Bird said Sara was a tough old gal. You don't suppose she is responsible?"

"Overpower Mac and Julie, set a fire, make a getaway, and take care of the vehicles? I can't believe one person could do all that. Especially not a small old woman."

Dal rubbed his face with both hands. "Nope, me neither. Besides, Mac said there was two of 'em besides Julie, and that she got away. Sam thinks the call Tinker got was probably from her. So what happened to the two of them?"

She shrugged. "I do believe that call came from Julie that summoned Tink away. She was excited, not upset. And Tink mentioned to me the other day that she knew Julie in high school, that they palled around before Tink went into law enforcement and Julie got in trouble. Said Julie wouldn't tell her who the father of her child was, and they sort of broke up their friendship over it. Said she'd like to see her, make up. So, if she did hear from her, she'd be pleased."

"I don't know. Maybe. Let's ask Sam if Tink said anything else before she took off." He started to get to his feet.

"Stay put, I'll go ask him." He did as she asked, not a good sign. If he'd messed up his back over this, she'd kick his butt. Well, maybe just chew his ass off for him.

She headed for the front office, waited while Sam took a call. When he hung up, looking perplexed and shaking his head, she flopped down in a chair opposite the desk.

"What's up?"

"I think the whole county has gone nuts. Someone just called, wouldn't leave their name. Said that two men had just stolen their brand new pickup and left this beat up old car in its place. Left a note saying it was a fair trade."

"What kind of an old car?"

Sam rifled through papers on his desk. "Well, that's what's crazy. It's the same car we have an APB out on. Owned by Sara Wells."

"Two men, huh? One ran off from my place and I couldn't tell if it was a man or woman. Small like Sara, and hair the same color, but dressed like a man. You don't suppose it could've been her, do you? At least, we know what the two who kidnapped Mac are driving."

"I reckon at this point anything is possible. Never heard of such a mixed up mess in my life, long as I worked for this place. And all over one tiny itty bitty diamond heist."

"Not so itty bitty, and I'm about to add to your woes. When Tink called in, did she say anything else at all about who called her or where she was going? Anything even remotely informative?"

"Let me think." Sam scratched his head. "Naw… wait a minute, she did say that it was funny how lost friends can turn up at the oddest times. Didn't make any sense to me, and sure don't tell us where she's at. Now, does it?"

"Maybe not, but thanks anyway."

Back in the viewing room, she found Dal finishing off the rest of the junk food and vowed to go get him something decent to eat as soon as she could get away.

"What'd you find out?" he asked.

"Two things. First off, got a report from a citizen that two men exchanged the car belonging to Sara Wells for their brand new pickup right out of their yard. So Sam has an APB out on it now. I have a hunch one of those so-called men is Sara Wells. An APB won't help much with all our deputies save two home asleep. Maybe the Staties will find them."

"And the second thing?" Dal prodded.

"Oh, yeah, Tink said before she left that it was funny how lost friends turn up at the oddest times. So, don't you think it's possible that Julie, not trusting anyone else, might have called on her friend Tink to help her out of this bad jam?"

"I suppose." Dal massaged his temples, a sure sign he was fighting a headache. "Still doesn't tell us where they disappeared to."

She moved behind him and began to rub the back of his neck. "Darlin', your muscles are tight as a drum. You need to go home and go to bed."

He relaxed under her touch. "Can't yet, but oh, God, that feels good."

She was still rubbing his neck when Mac returned, John Reilly in tow, his puffy red eyes the only sign he'd just identified the body as that of his missing son.

"I've sent Burt over to pick up Delia and Claire Reilly," Mac told them before shoving John into the interview room and closing the door.

"You look like hell, Dal. Why don't you go home?" he said.

"In just a while. I want to be there when you talk to the them."

Jess moved her fingers in circles on Dal's temples. If he didn't start taking care of himself, he would be back in that hospital in St. Louis, but there was nothing she could do about it. It would break her heart to see him disabled by his own stubbornness, and she wanted to stomp her feet and yell. But she just kept up the massage and hoped for the best.

She was still at it, and Dal seemed to feel better, when Delia and her daughter were escorted into the interview room to join John. The woman collapsed her head on the table when John spoke to her. The daughter, Claire, stared stoically toward the one-way glass.

Dal rose. "Okay, time to get busy. Reckon you can remain in here since Mac didn't say anything."

"Please be careful," she said.

"Who, me? I'm always careful." Weary green eyes gazed at her for a split second, then he was gone before she could voice her opinion of that statement, which was hogwash and bullshit. She settled in a chair near the one-way glass and made sure the sound was turned on. Dal was walking into his own private combat zone, and she hated every minute of it, yet could do nothing but watch.

The show was about to begin.

18
CHAPTER

Dal followed Mac and John Reilly into the interview room, closing the door behind him. Time to block the thoughts of everyone, at least temporarily. Get a feel for them first. He slid his gaze over each family member. Live participants were so much more easily shut out than spirits.

Delia was dressed in a brown pants suit that did nothing for her pale, make-up-free complexion and dull blonde hair that hung limp around her skeletal face. Claire was an exaggerated opposite of her mother. Dyed black hair curled and piled on her head, heavily made-up eyes, red lipstick that appeared as if she had been drinking blood. She wore a bright orange sleeveless sweater over a purple tee shirt, hems uneven and down around her jean-covered thighs. Though she had several facial piercings, her mother wore no jewelry except a wedding band. Both women were rail thin, as if they had been isolated on a desert island for a year. John was a bit hefty, wore a conservative short-sleeved shirt in pale blue and navy pants. His slip-on shoes over bare feet had tassels and his brown hair, cut short, was slicked down with something shiny. If they had money, it didn't show.

Each in turn glanced at Dal, then away quickly. Wary of his inquisitive stare that probed their thoughts. Interesting. None mourned Rand's death. Claire was so angry, he turned her off for the moment.

Mac indicated a chair for everyone, seating Dal to his right so both faced the three Reillys.

The elder Reilly clasped his hands together on the table, squeezing so tightly his fingers turned white. "I thought I asked you not to involve my wife and daughter."

Okay, now. Dal lifted his lips in a sardonic smile, ready to get to the heart of the matter.

Bitch better be careful what she says. John, staring at his wife.

"You told them not to tell me Rand was dead?" *You bastard.*

Dal shook his head against the unspoken and spoken words, then was sorry he did so. The headache raged back and with it the jumbled thoughts of all three.

He gritted his teeth, tried to keep a bland expression.

John leaned back, aimed a calm stare at Dal. His smile could be called a snarl. Something else going on there. Eyes gleaming with tears. *Rand, goddammit, I loved you. Why?*

I'd like to slit her throat… his too. This from Claire, the daughter.

Ever get my hands on those diamonds, I'm out of here. Let the two of them strangle in their own filth. An unhappy Delia.

Their violent memories flooded over him—threats, beatings, hatred toward one another that defied understanding.

Killed my brother… a couple of greedy butchers… all got out of hand… tried to stop them… I did… kick his fucking head in.

Phrase after phrase until he pushed back the chair and rose. Touched Mac's shoulder, then hurried from the room to lean on the wall outside and cradle his head in both hands. He needed these monsters in single file, not all at once.

Jess was there instantly, an arm around him. "I'm taking you home. Now. No ands, ifs, or buts."

He went with her because all he could see were lights slashing through his vision. All he could hear were those ugly words caroming around inside his head. A family gone berserk.

In the Jeep, he leaned back and closed his eyes, muffling the wicked thoughts. She reached across, fastened his seat belt, then started the car, moving slowly onto the street, then heading south toward the trailer park.

So unlike Jess to keep quiet, but she did and so did he. So accustomed to blocking her thoughts that it came naturally. He dare not invade her privacy in that way. Couldn't admit out loud that he was relieved to have her intervention, glad someone had stopped him before he spiraled out of control. All he wanted at the moment was his bed for at least twelve hours. He'd suppressed his own feelings in that room, wanted to shout and curse at people who could ruin their lives and destroy their family out of greed and violence. Yet they knew nothing of what true violence could do to someone. Kids with needles in their arms, Leann with a needle in hers. Alleys filled with dead bodies and someone in the shadows pulling a gun and filling him full of lead.

And those self-righteous non-humans ready and willing to assassinate their own flesh and blood over money.

He finally spoke, hoarsely. "They killed their own son, Jess. I'm so tired of the underbelly of humanity, I'd like to go live in a cave."

Her hand slid across the console, rested over his lying on the seat. "Dear God, who could do a thing like that? I'm so sorry you have to listen to crap like that. I wish you couldn't know what people are thinking."

"I do, too. I do, too." With his free hand, he scrubbed down over his face. "Maybe I ought to be doing something else. I thought here there wouldn't be—"

"You're worn out, Dal. Everything will be fine after you get some rest... some *sleep*."

"Thank you, Jessie. You're a good friend." He closed his eyes and said no more.

She didn't, either, just slipped her hand from his to steer into the long drive to his trailer. What was it the kids called a relationship like theirs? Friends with benefits?

When she rolled the Jeep to a stop, he didn't move, and she wondered if he were asleep. She hopped out, went around, and opened his door. He jumped as if startled, then put his arms around her, pulled her close. "Don't go anywhere, Jess. This isn't over. You could be in danger. Stay here with me. Tomorrow we'll finish this up."

"In danger from who? If they murdered Rand, what are the rest of this bunch gonna be up to?"

Without answering, he held her, and she leaned her head on his shoulder. His breath feathered her hair and she kissed his sweaty neck, not caring about anything but soothing him.

"Let's get you inside. I need to unfasten your seat belt. Could you turn loose? Give me the door key."

"In my pocket. Here." He patted but let her fish them out.

"Maybe I ought to take you to the hospital. I don't like the way you're acting."

"Nope. I'm just tired is all. Need some sleep. Should've listened to you." His arms fell away, and she got him out of the seat, encircled his waist, and guided him up the steps.

No sense in insisting, he wouldn't go. Not till he could no longer function at all, or the pain got too bad. Tough as he was, it took a lot to knock him down, so he must be putting up with mega torture and exhaustion.

In the bedroom, he collapsed onto the bed. "Call Mac. Tell him the dad killed his own son. Maybe Delia was in on it, but not Claire, though she knows. He'll have to figure out a way to prove it. Claire is fed up, so she might talk. Lennie and Sara were the ones after us. I think Mac can find the weapon Lennie used to shoot you and at me. Ballistics will do the rest. Oh, God, I'm tired. Just let me sleep, but stay here. Okay?"

"I will. Right now I'm gonna get you undressed." She took off his boots, managed to work off the belt with all its paraphernalia. He was already out and would probably sleep through the night. After some struggling, she peeled off everything but the white tee he wore under his uniform and his jockey shorts. She kissed his stubbled cheek, touched his face with the palm of her hand, and left the room.

She would remain there overnight, not because he told her she was in danger, but because she did not want to leave him alone. Hopeful that he still had some food left from her grocery run of a few days earlier, she went to the fridge. After building a ham sandwich, she took out a half-filled carton of coleslaw and a Pepsi, went into the living room, and plopped down in his oversized recliner to eat.

Between bites, she called Mac and left Dal's message on his voice mail. "We'll be here if you need us. At Dal's." She hung up.

Who could she be in danger from? Lennie and his unknown friend, Sara, her helper and Merle, were unaccounted for. No doubt halfway to Texas by now. It went through her mind like a brush of gentle wind that they wouldn't leave till they found the diamonds. Julie and Tink were unaccounted for as well, and that worried her some. If Julie knew where her son was, she would've gone straight to him. But instead she called her ex-friend Tink, who, soft hearted gal that she was, gladly went to help out. So where were those two? And what was Merle up to?

Unable to answer her own questions, she finished the sandwich and Pepsi, then climbed out of the chair, undressed as she headed toward the compact bath, turned on the shower, and waited till steam filled the room before stepping under the spray. It took a while to wash away the grit from her hair and body, but finally she stepped out, wrapped a towel around herself, dried her hair while sitting on the commode, then padded into the bedroom, shed the towel, climbed over Dal's inert form and was asleep literally as soon as her head hit the pillow.

Sometime during the pitch black night, he turned over, gathered her close, and nuzzled against her neck. Barely rousing, she curled up against him, went back to sleep.

Someone far away repeated her name, over and over. A dream, only a dream. A hand on her shoulder shook her, smacked her smartly on the cheek. "Dammit, Jessie, wake up."

"Stop that." She swung at the hand. Sat up, rubbed her eyes. Where was she? Where was Dal? "What? Who? Where am I?"

"Come on, Jessie. You're in your bed. Where'd you think you was? It's ten o'clock. Wake up. Get cracking." Whoever it was smacked her, first on one cheek then the other. Not Dal, he'd never do that.

Kicking and swinging her arms, she opened her eyes to peer into the face of a man she'd never seen before. Her heart thumped, her nerves tingled. She stared around at her things. All so familiar, the pictures of her grandparents, her parents, hanging on the wall. Mama's quilt across the foot of the bed. Her wearing a night shirt inside out. But this couldn't be.

"Who the hell are you? Where's Dal? I went to sleep at his place.

What's going on?" She shoved backwards on the mattress, halted with a thunk against the headboard. "What are you doing here?"

"You must've been dreaming, Jessie." He peered into her eyes. "You awake yet?" He thumped her forehead with the end of his index finger.

She jerked back. "Stop that. I know you. You were with...." She broke off before telling him she'd overheard him and Lennie in the SEFOR plant.

From the other room came voices in conversation. A male voice and a coarse woman's voice. Sara and the other must be Lennie. What the hell?

"Who's that in the other room?"

"Just some friends. You behave yourself and we'll be out of your hair in a few." He went to the door, jerked it open. "She's awake. You want her in there?"

Jess attempted to get off the bed and dodge around him, but he easily grabbed her, one hand clutching her hair, the other wrapped around her waist. He was big and strong. She kicked and tried to take a bite out of his arm, but stopped when he yanked her hair so hard tears spurted. How had they taken her from Dal's and brought her here without her waking up? And what about Dal? If he had awakened, he'd have fought.

Which meant they probably hurt him.

He dumped her onto the couch in the living room where Lennie and Sara stood. Merle was curled up in the corner on the floor asleep.

"What do you want?" She rubbed at the back of her head.

Sara, pale hair wild around her face, dressed in trousers and a flannel shirt with the sleeves ripped out, sidled over to her, got right up in her space. "You know what we want. You've been so forthcoming in your paper about them diamonds. I think you found 'em. Cops probably put you up to writing the story to smoke us out. Well, guess what? Won't work."

The light dawned, and Jess stared at her for a moment. "You're kidding. Right? In that case, they could be all around my house right now, which would mean you're smoked out. Bitch."

Sara drew back with her man-sized paw and slapped her so hard her teeth clattered. Stars danced in her peripheral vision.

"What's she talking about, Ma?" Lennie said, a whine in his voice. "Cops? All around us?"

"Shut up, Lennie. She's lying." Sara turned back to Jess who was still seeing flashes of light. "The diamonds. You got 'em, we want 'em."

A trickle of blood ran from the corner of Jessie's mouth, and she wiped it with the back of her hand. "Want away. I don't have them."

"In that case, I guess we have no choice. Give me your gun, Lennie."

"You're going to shoot me? What's wrong with you people?"

"Oh, not dead. I thought maybe another near miss might do. An arm, a leg. Bullet wounds can be quite painful. And who knows, I might accidentally hit a bleeder."

Jess gazed all around, trying to think. Someone was missing. The other man. Sara had to have to help taking Mac and Julie, Lennie had help searching SEFOR. So two strangers and only one here. A real mean son of a bitch, too. The realization didn't help her out of this situation, but it made her more afraid. The missing one might be with Dal, doing no telling what to him. Maybe they were going to kill them both.

"Oh, look. She's about to figure something out." Sara smirked. "For every bullet I have to put in you, one goes in him, too. And you really like that big handsome brute of a man, don't you, sweetie? Think women would know better, but they never do. Always fall for the bullies."

"And what do you fall for? Little girls?"

Sara swung the gun and Jess blacked out.

When she came to, the man who'd dragged her from the bedroom was the only one in the room with her. A warm trail of blood ran from her temple.

"Sara gets carried away sometimes. Likes to beat her skanks." He reached down and tucked a stray lock of hair behind her ear. "There now, honey. You and me are gonna have us a talk. I'm sure we can come to some arrangement without me having to kill you. There's lots of things we can do together, you purty little thing. Then you'll tell me where the diamonds are hid. We'll be on our way and you none the worse for wear."

The tone of voice and the look in his eye frightened Jess far more than Sara had done with the gun. Why didn't she just tell them where to look? Because, they would kill her as soon as they found them. She had to keep them from searching as long as possible and hope someone would show up or she could think of a way to escape. Chances of that didn't look good, though.

Dal opened his eyes and wished he hadn't. Felt like someone had hit him in the head with a twenty pound hammer. The bed, the room, everything whirled in a dark/light dance. He held on with both hands, but the whirling set his stomach to heaving. Closing his eyes didn't help, either. He still flew around in circles. Round and round went the man in the doorway, staring at him.

Dal's mouth worked but he had no control over the words that came out. Either he couldn't speak or he couldn't hear, or both.

Jess. Where was Jess?

If they hurt her, he'd hunt them down and kill them, slowly.

The man grabbed his arm. Got in his face. Moved his mouth, but the words were echoes that fell back upon each other so he couldn't make sense of any of them.

What had they given him? The taste was nauseating, he smelled something acidic, and his tongue felt too big for his mouth.

The man pulled him to his feet, but he staggered into him, got a hand around his arm and jerked as hard as he could. Laughter met his effort. "That all you got? You're so high you don't know up from down. Come on, come with me."

Barely keeping his feet under him, Dal staggered, bounced off the door jamb, hit a wall on one side, then the other.

"Jessie. What'd you do with her?" He thought he said that, at least. What came out was garbled and unintelligible.

"Sit, asshole."

Pushed, Dal staggered backwards, windmilling his arms, and fell into a huge chair. His chair. He embraced the comfort, hung on to the arms, planted his feet flat on the floor. If only he could regain some kind of stability, but the world continued to float amid wavering colors.

He had no strength, no sense of what was happening to him. All he could do was fear for Jessie's life. He tried hard to form each word, and must've at least come close. "Where's Jess?"

"You think about that when I ask you these questions. Answer them right and she'll be fine. Wrong, and I make a phone call, she dies."

With heavy concentration, Dal got the message, though some of the words floated away. Phone call, kill Jessie. He got that much, stared with bleary eyes up at the guy who wavered back and forth above him. A burly guy he could take if he wasn't high.

A gun, stuck against his head. "Where are the diamonds? Simple question. Think. They shoot her, I shoot you. Think, stupid."

He shook his head. Oh, god, that hurt. "Don't know. Don't know." It came out donno, donno, but the guy got the message. Cocked the gun.

"Once more." He lay down the weapon and picked up the phone, started dialing.

Dal flailed his hand out, but missed contact. "No. In SEFOR plant."

"We know that much, asshole. Searched the damned place. No way to know where they are. Two or three buildings, plus that big butt-ugly ball."

"No, no. Go in there. Die."

"Ah, so they wouldn't be in there, then." He still held the phone and Dal fixated on it, up to Burly's mouth and ear.

"Not in the reactor. No." His words and thoughts were coming a bit clearer. He understood one thing for sure. These people appeared willing to kill as many people as they had to in order to get those diamonds. And John Reilly in it up to his eyeballs, too.

"You can take us there. Where they're at?"

"No, no. I don't know." But Jessie knows. Yes, she knew where the diamonds were. Good god, Jessie. Tell them. Tell them. Who cares about the damned stones?

"I'll just call over there." Again he dialed, waited while the phone rang. Dal gazed at the vision of the gun floating around on the table. Could not lift either of his hands, though he stared hard and flexed every muscle to do so.

"She say anything yet?" Burly asked the phone.

Dal tried to shout her name, to tell her to tell them. No one could understand what came out of his mouth. He sure couldn't.

"Yeah, he's still high as a kite. That Special K is great stuff. Big as he is, I'd a had some trouble with him if not for it. But I need him to come down enough to take me over there. He knows something. Keeps yammering about the reactor being dangerous. I think that's that big ball. Probably rule it out as a hiding place. Tell you what, bring her, too. I've a hunch one or both of them knows where the stones are." He listened a while, with Dal doing his best to warn Jess. "Yeah, meet you over there. Around back, where we cut the fence the first time. And bring a dose of that downer. We can tape his hands behind his back, and we both got guns."

"What?" A pause while he listened. "Nah, leave them there. Make sure they're taped up good, tear the phones out, too. Shit, I don't care what Lennie says, that kid ain't getting a cut. Leave him there with his bitch of a mother and that bitch cop."

He stuck the phone in his pocket, picked up the gun, grabbed Dal under one arm, and yanked him to his feet. "Up and at 'em, Chief. We're going on a little trip."

With a shove, Burly propelled Dal toward the door. Misjudging his weight, he lost hold of him and Dal stumbled out onto the small porch and fell on his face in the yard. Pain zipped up his spine and out the top of his head. Darkness flowed over him.

When he came to, he was lying on his back staring up at the sky. And he couldn't move at all. Nothing worked. Someone was standing over him, talking into a cell phone.

"Yeah, shit. I can't move the son of a bitch. He weighs a ton, and he's out like a light." He listened. "Leave him? Hell no, I'm shooting him and getting it over with. She don't need to know till she shows us where they're hid, does she?"

"Hey, you." Ina Mae's shrill voice shouted from off to Dal's right.

He couldn't move his head to see her.

"I've called the sheriff's office. Drop your gun, or I'm gonna drop you."

"Lady, put that thing down. You won't hit me from there."

Dal tried to see what Burly was doing, tried to warn Ina Mae, but could barely even lift his arm.

"I said put it down." A huge bang slammed through the air over Dal and Burly yowled like a shot dog.

Ina Mae stood over him peering down, the shotgun at her side. "Honey, are you hurt? I called the sheriff. He's a coming. I shot the bastard. Always knew Herm's shotgun would come in handy someday. Kept it loaded too." She knelt beside him, laid a hand on his chest.

"Sweetheart, are you hurt?"

"I can't move. Leave me be and call an ambulance, would you?"

With a trembling hand, she dug the phone out of her pocket, dialed 9-1-1, and told them what was happening.

"Ina Mae, listen to me. Listen." His words weren't coming too clear, but she watched his lips and appeared to understand. "Some very bad people are coming. You need to go hide until Mac gets here. You understand?"

"Honey, I ain't about to leave you laying out here in the open, helpless and all. Are you shot? I got me more shells. I'll just load her up and wait with you. You're gonna be all right, I know you will. I don't see no blood."

She took his hand for a minute, then rose and dug two shells from her pocket. They were going to kill her if they arrived first. Jessie should be safe, since they thought she knew where the diamonds were.

"Ina Mae, please, at least go inside the trailer till Mac gets here." The Special K kept the pain down, but as it wore off, he'd be in agony. He'd been down this road before. He prayed he could stay conscious until this was over.

"Nope. I'm staying with you, by golly. Ain't nobody gonna kill my favorite tenant."

No sense trying to convince her. She wasn't moving. "Jessie is with them, be careful."

She patted his hand. "Don't you worry."

"Don't worry… don't worry… don't worry," followed him into a dark place filled with flashes of lightning that tore relentlessly up and down his spine to explode out his head.

Arms bound behind her back with duct tape, Jessie sat crunched up in the back of the pickup Sara had traded for her Accord. A big bald man sat in the club-cab, Lennie sat up front with his mother. Watching from the bed of the truck, staring at the familiar landscape flowing past, dread filled her. They were going to Dal's trailer, and the man on the other end had him well under control. They talked about something called Special K that she thought was ketamine, a horse anesthetic of some kind. They must have shot both of them with it while they slept. In all probability, they both fought back, but could not recall doing so because of the drug.

Obviously they hadn't used a very strong dose on her, because she felt pretty much over the drug's influence. But Dal, who was already on opiates, probably didn't fare so well, and him being bigger they'd have upped his dosage.

Just thinking of what might have happened to him drove her to tears. They'd taken Merle somewhere to put him with Tinker and Julie, who at least were still alive. Sara and Lennie discussed it, but didn't say where they were.

The truck slid sideways at the entrance to Hidden Holler Trailer Park and barreled across Ina Mae's little garden.

"What the hell?" Lennie yelled. "Does that old biddy have a shot-gun? Hell, duck."

Jessie did just that, hunkering down on the floor as best she could.

Sara slammed on the brakes and brought the pickup to a side-skid-ding halt. A shot rang out. Lennie had fired his gun through the side window. Jessie scooted her butt along the truck bed, hauled herself up, and tumbled over the tailgate.

She landed on her back, rolled as far as she could away from the vehicle, gathered her feet, and loped toward the creek and its protection of trees. Behind her, a shotgun blast bellowed, and she whirled to see the windshield of the pickup burst into a million pieces. When she finally looked toward Ina Mae, standing over Dal's inert form like a mother protecting her child, the woman was digging in her apron pocket for more shells. Jess changed directions, loped toward the two of them.

Her heart, already thundering, felt about to burst. She stumbled, almost fell, regained her footing, closed in on Dal. All was quiet in the pickup. Ina Mae trotted, calm as you please, toward the steaming vehicle and let go another double barreled blast that hit the side window and blew it to smithereens. Jess stopped watching and fell down beside Dal. With her hands trussed behind her, she couldn't touch him, so she leaned forward and put her lips against his warm cheek, then down to the hollow of his throat against the throbbing of his heart.

"Oh, Dal. Are you okay?"

He didn't move. No reply. She lay her ear on his chest. Breathing. Yes. "Please, please say something."

"Something," he murmured.

Breath whooshed out of her, relief so potent she grew dizzy with it.

Sirens. All over the place. Mac's car slithering and sliding, kicking up dust and clods of grass, ended sideways beside the battered pickup. And immediately behind him, the first responders in their yellow truck and an ambulance.

Mac reached her and Dal first. "Is he alive, girl?"

"Yes. Yes, he is, but he's doped and barely conscious. I don't see any blood anywhere. Mac, tell them about his back, don't let them move him without a backboard and a neck brace. Please, please." By then she was crying, snuffling, dancing around with her hands still taped behind her back.

"Sweetheart, let me cut you loose. What in the hell has been going on here? I get a call from Ina Mae that some brute of a man has Dal prisoner. Is that the brute laying over yonder?"

Jess took a quick look. "Never noticed, but looks like it. He's all covered in blood."

"I shot the bastard," Ina Mae said, running toward them, hauling up to gaze down at Dal. "Is he okay? Said he couldn't move after that son of a bitch shoved him off the porch. I shot that other'n, Sheriff, so if you gotta, you might as well take me in. He had a gun. I warned him, so it's self-defense. But you take care of Dal here." She ran from them toward the first responders and the EMTs, who had stopped to check on the people in the car.

"Leave them sons of bitches be and git on over here and take care of this deputy." It looked like they might be her next target if they didn't get a move on.

Mac took out his knife and sawed the tape off Jessie's wrists. She fell down beside Dal to touch his face and hold his hand and talk softly to him. It didn't matter what she said, she just needed to talk to him so he'd know she was there.

"It's his back," she told the first EMT. "He has this shrapnel in there, and I'm afraid... I don't know, but he's not moving. They shot him up with Special K, and he's on opiates for the pain, so be careful. Please be careful. If it moves around, he could be paralyzed."

"Ma'am, we understand, and we'll take good care of him. If you could just move so we can do that."

"Yes, yes, I will." She kissed Dal's cheek. "I'm right here, honey. Right here," she whispered, then moved away, but kept an eye on them. They placed a neck brace on him, then slipped a backboard carefully under his still form.

"I'm going with him, Mac."

"Go, I'll get this cleared up and be there soon as I can. Looks like Miss Ina fairly cleaned up around here."

"She sure is something. They may have to send Dal on up to Dr. Swinton in St. Louis."

"If they do, you go with him. He ain't got no business going through this alone. You hear me?"

"Yes, I hear you." If only she had time to hug Mac, tell him how much she loved him.

Instead, she gave him a quick smile and climbed in the back of the ambulance, wearing her inside out sleep shirt and no shoes. Then she remembered about Tinker.

"Would you go tell Mac that Tinker, Julie, and Merle Crowe are trussed up somewhere? It could be at my place or Sara's. He needs to get some deputies looking for them."

The EMT leaned out the door and spoke to one of the first responders, who took off toward Mac. The EMT pulled the ambulance door shut and they were off. She sank down beside Dal and took his limp hand in hers. He had not responded to her at all since the one word, but she kept hoping it was the ketamine and not his injury that kept him knocked out.

They had been at the hospital an hour when a doctor finally came out to talk to her. "You Jessie, kin to the deputy?" he asked.

She nodded, because he had no kin and it was the only way she could find out anything. Besides, she was getting pretty good at lying about being his kin.

"Okay, he's stabilized, is moving around a bit. We've sent him to get a CT scan and some x-rays just in case, considering his history. Glad we had that on file here."

"Are you sure he's okay?"

"Seems to be, and he's spitting mad. Said something about little old ladies and shotguns upholding the law just ain't right." The doctor grinned and shook his head.

Jessie chuckled. "Sounds like Dal."

"Tough as a goddamned boot. We find anything that necessitates it, we'll Life Flight him to his doctor in St. Louis. I imagine you'll go with him?"

She nodded, mute and shaking.

"Don't worry now. As soon as we put him in a room, I'll send someone to take you to him. He's asking for you."

"He doesn't have anyone else." The sadness of that statement rocked her. At one time, she'd been alone in the world. But no more. And never again was he.

She sat in a chair staring at the floor when feet stepped into her line of sight. "Miss West?"

She jumped to her feet. "Yes, that's me. Is he okay?"

A stout male nurse grinned at her. "Looks like it. Come with me. I'll take you to his room before he rips down the walls and comes looking for you. He's a mite disconcerted at the moment. Thinks you're being held prisoner and we have to let him go rescue you. Don't worry, it's the drugs." The nurse trotted ahead of her. "Might be good to hurry."

Down the hall something crashed to the floor making a dreadful clatter, a familiar voice shouted a few choice curse words that made her cringe.

The nurse skidded to a halt at an open door, gestured Jessie to enter, then scurried away.

She stepped through to see Dal, standing with his back to her in the center of the room in a hospital gown that stood open to reveal his fine butt. A bedpan and aluminum pitcher lay on the floor in a puddle of water and a burly attendant hovered nearby.

Jessie ran to him. "Dal, what the hell are you trying to do, tear down this hospital?"

Fist in the air, he turned. "Jessie? I thought you… you're okay?"

"Of course I'm okay, you doofus. You need to lay back down before you hurt yourself."

"Yeah," the attendant muttered. "Or someone else."

She giggled like a school girl and tiptoed through the water to Dal's side. Taking his arm, she guided him to the bed, whispered in his ear. "You're mooning all the pretty nurses."

"Doubt it's anything they haven't already seen."

Several of them fluttered away from the open doorway, their laughter echoing in the hall.

Once he was settled on the bed, the attendant left and she sat beside him.

"Tell me what happened." His tone had quieted somewhat.

So she repeated a blow-by-blow description.

He shook his head. "That's downright embarrassing, being rescued by an old lady with a shotgun. Hell, cases aren't supposed to end this way. The hero is supposed to bull his way in and rescue the girl. Even in books and movies that's the way it goes. So what went wrong? There I am, laying on my face in the dirt while she corrals a big bully, then proceeds to shoot up the rest of them, rescuing you? Well, hell, Jessie. I believe I'm mortified."

She laughed so hard she collapsed on his shoulder.

"It isn't funny, woman. Not funny at all."

"Oh, yes it is, Dal. Besides, books and movies may end that way. This is real life, and believe me, shit happens in real life. Stuff you never read in books or see in movies. Admit it, if you'd been awake you'd know just how funny it is."

19
CHAPTER

The next morning, Dal insisted she tell him the story over again, from start to finish, or at least the part where he lay on his face in the dirt. She obliged, giving him a short version.

"You should've seen Ina Mae. She was like some Wild West gunslinger. Saw that guy shove you off the porch, got her shotgun, and took over. After she filled him full of pellets, she turned on the rest of the gang and blasted their truck into pieces. And there I am, running for my life. Luckily, she didn't kill anyone. They'll all live to stand trial, but there was a lot of pellet picking to be done at the emergency room."

He let go with a laugh that filled the small room. Then stopped, stared at her. "Wait, what about Tinker? She's not hurt, is she?"

"She was in quite a state, but she recovered. They found her along with Julie and Merle trussed up in the fruit cellar at Sara's. In the dark. I guess Julie had her hands full. She'd called Tinker after the fire to come help her get away before Lennie got a hold of her and Merle. She had managed to escape from Sara and her friend after they left Mac where you later found him. I'm not clear on exactly where Lennie and Sara found them, but they did. Trussed them up and tossed them in that dark dungeon, as Tink put it, but you know how she exaggerates." She laughed and it sounded so good he joined her. A lot of that going around lately.

"Oh, and one more thing. Mac relayed how John Reilly confessed after his daughter tried to claw his eyes out while they were putting the whole family in holding. Told how for years he used the old building at SEFOR for storage of the stolen items till he could ship them out to buyers. That was the reason he bought the land adjacent to the plant. Guess he'd been heading up those gangs on a small scale till he moved to KC, then he really got going. That's what that box I found was. Something left behind from one of those stolen Goebel figurines included on the list from Harrison PD. Guess he stopped using the place when he moved up in the world. He has some old wholesale storage buildings in KC now. The police up there raided them after Mac got in touch. Turned up a lot of stolen stuff that hadn't been shipped out yet."

"Did they ever find the diamonds?"

"Not yet. I think I know where they are, though. As soon as we get you home, let's go check it out."

He grunted. "Sounds like a damned fine idea to me. Including the getting me home part."

"Doc says you're good to go first thing tomorrow."

"Wonder who will claim the stones. Mr. and Mrs. Vandergriff are both dead. Maybe they had kids."

She hauled him home the next morning, listening to him bitch all the because she didn't take him straight to the sheriff's office.

"Not gonna do it, Dal. Mac would have a fit and put *both* of us in the cooler. He says you'd better behave yourself."

Once he was settled in the trailer, she told him she had work to do. "But if you need anything, just holler. And if you don't stay right here, I'm fixin' to sic Mac and Tinker on you. From what I hear, your job is safe, but no chasing bad guys for a while yet. Now, how would you like to meet me tomorrow morning out at SEFOR? We'll take Burt with us for the heavy lifting."

All the while she talked, he stood before her, arms crossed over his sexy six-pack, a wide grin on his face.

"What're you laughing at?"

"When did you get to be so danged bossy?"

"You sure are gorgeous in that tee shirt. I might change my mind and stay here. Just to look after you, of course."

He gestured with both hands, palms up, fingers beckoning. "Come on. I'm up for it, if you don't mind the pun."

"Getting sassy on me, aren't you?" She stepped forward, crawled her fingers beneath the shirt and over his tightly muscled stomach to his smooth chest. "Remember, you asked for this."

"Wait." He leaned down and nipped at her ear with warm lips, sending chills all the way to the bottoms of her feet. One arm then the other snaked around her waist, lifted, and walked her into the bedroom.

"My goodness. That hospital rest did you a world of good."

"I asked for it. Now what do I get?" His eyes glistened.

With a low laugh, she skinned his shirt over his head, and he did the same with hers, burying his mouth between her breasts while he undid the bra and let it fall to the floor.

Warm strong hands spread over her backside, holding her so close his muscles rippled against her belly. Nibbling his way to one nipple, he teased with lips and tongue, setting fire to her skin. Heat from his breath branded a path down across her belly button while his fingers unsnapped her jeans and slipped the zipper down. His hot kisses trailed after the waistband he lowered ever so slowly. Taking his time, lower and lower, tasting with tongue and lips. The hands that cupped her butt lifted her and he lay back on the bed, his mouth and tongue sending her tumbling toward the stars. Orgasms cascaded through her like a cataclysmic blast, stealing her breath and vision. She clung to him to keep from falling away into eternity.

Rolling her to his side, he pulled her hands down to his belt.

"Now, lady. Take off my pants."

Scarcely able to speak, she gasped, "Give me a minute here, okay?"

"Thirty seconds. I'm about to bust something."

One hand spread over the tent in his jeans, she pulled the zipper down one set of teeth at a time while he moaned.

"Oh, don't be such a baby. You know you like it." Zipper at half-mast she massaged his erection, then tucked her fingers under the waistband of the jockey shorts, tongue following along.

He groaned. "Come on, Jess. You're killing me here."

"Thought you liked foreplay, tough man."

"Mount up, or you're gonna see one angry Indian on the warpath."

"In due course, my beautiful brave." She placed her mouth where her hand had been, bit gently through the denims.

"Oh, God, woman."

Slowly, she lowered the jeans and shorts, nibbling down one leg, then the other. A bite on the inside of his thigh made him holler.

"You still up for this, my big strong warrior?"

"If you don't do something soon, I'm gonna need CPR."

"In just a minute. I want you to do that thing you did with your tongue again." She straddled one leg over him and scooted forward, then rose to her knees. "Come on, please, pretty please?"

He threw himself back onto the pillow. "I think I have a headache. Maybe we ought to stop."

He sounded so serious, she actually thought he meant it. She touched his temples with her fingertips. "Dal?"

"I'm kidding. Umm, you are delicious." Tasting, groaning with pleasure, he sent her once more flying off into a bright ecstasy.

"Now, woman. *Now.*"

She slid ever so slowly along his stretched out body onto the stiff erection until he slipped inside her and held him that way, tightening and relaxing her muscles. He grunted and rolled onto his back, lifting her, then ramming into her over and over, both collapsing, exhausted and sated.

Several minutes later, her fingers walking around over his twitching belly muscles in after-play, he let out a long sigh. "Curl up here next to me and stay the night. Please don't go anywhere. I need to hold on to you."

Tempting as that was, she sat up, crossed her legs and studied his weary features. No good mentioning that though, she kissed his cheek, then said, "Much as I'd like to, I'd better not. You need your space so you can burp and fart and spill your coffee across the floor and tear all the covers off the bed when you turn over. And I need some quiet time."

"Okay, but you don't know what you're missing. All that sexy farting and burping. So I'll see you tomorrow? What time?"

As tasty as he looked, she had to get out of there fast before she changed her mind. So she hollered the time, pulled on her jeans and shirt, picked up her shoes, and high-tailed it out of there.

The next morning, Burt followed her and Dal to SEFOR with Mac's blessings. It was time to wrap this up. The bad guys, mum about the diamonds, were all awaiting hearings in cells at the county jail. John and Delia Reilly would be charged with fraud, transportation of stolen goods out of the country, and murder of their son, Rand. By cooperating with the prosecuting attorney, Claire was free on bond. Sara, Lennie, and their two cohorts, both from Hot Springs, faced charges for a long list of burglaries, robberies, assault of a sheriff's deputy, kidnapping, and assorted other charges. Mac swore he would see they were also charged with attempted murder for shooting Jess.

The PA was also considering attempted murder charges for Lennie's warning shots at Jess and Dal. Jess was pretty sure she could identify Sara as being the one who ran from her house after leaving the warning on the mirror in lipstick. The kicker was, of all things, something about chocolate candy wrappers at the crime scenes. Turns out Lennie left a nice print on the inside of the one found where the shooter had stood to shoot at Dal. Jess remembered the smell of chocolate on his breath, plus he left another wrapper at SEFOR. Merle admitted to killing Jasper Long, and would go to Juvenile Detention until his eighteenth birthday. Julie planned to move into Sara and Mathon's house where she promised her son a room when he got out.

All was well once more in Cedarton. At least for the present. How long it would stay that way was anybody's guess.

By the time her update to Dal finished, some recited while they tromped from Burt's SUV to the hole in the fence, they were standing at the back of the SEFOR property. Burt held up the cut fence while Jess ducked under, then waited for Dal. It was a warm morning, with a slight breeze rustling through the trees and whipping a cloud of dried leaves across the concrete tarmac. A mockingbird perched on top of a light pole singing her heart out.

Jess glanced up at the crystal blue sky, then shifted her gaze to the tall Cherokee lawman. He'd lost a little weight from his ordeal, but was putting it back on in all the right places. She winked at him, then laughed gaily when he flashed that dimpled grin.

"Ready to break in?"

He nodded. "Forge on."

"How are we supposed to get in this place?" Burt looked at Dal, who shrugged and glanced at Jess.

"Ask the reporter. This is her gig. Do you have a key, ma'am?"

"Nope." She reached in her backpack and pulled out her lock pick kit. "But I've got this."

"I believe this might be against the law," Dal said.

"Nope. Burt has a warrant, don't you?"

He nodded. "Pick away, girl."

Inside, she set her pack down. Dal raised a brow.

"This time around, I won't be caught without water, a phone, my recorder, and camera. In case we're locked in."

Both Dal and Burt laughed.

It was a good day, a great day. They were going to find those hidden stones, Jess knew it in her bones.

"Lead the way." Dal tucked his fingers in the back pockets of his jeans and waited for her to head out. "And I guess you know what's going to happen to you if you don't find those stones, don't you?"

"No, what? I just said I thought I knew where they were."

Dal snorted. "Yeah, now you're trying to renege."

"Come on, I'll show you. Burt, can you find something to climb on and reach that air duct?"

"Oh, no, the old hide it in the air duct. I don't believe this, Jess."

Dal stared up at the vent. "Are you serious? Hadn't any of those jokers watched movies or TV lately?"

"Well, I have. You just wait, you'll see."

Burt banged and crashed around for a while, then showed up dragging an actual ladder. "Will this do?"

"Looks like it." The men's expression told her that they were humoring her. They didn't expect to find anything in there. There'd be a long spell of teasing to endure if they didn't, but she couldn't help but believe she was right.

Burt leaned the ladder against the wall and scrambled up. Dal and Jess watched him for a while, then Jess said, "You might need this," and held up a screw driver.

"Thanks so much," he said, came back down till he could reach the tool, then headed up again. He soon had the cover removed, dirt and wads of dust bunnies raining on them, and dropped it straight down. The clatter echoed from wall to wall in the empty building.

"Now you have to crawl in there."

"Aw, Jess, come on. You do it, you're smaller than me." He pulled the flashlight out of his belt, clicked it on and poked it toward the vent. "I don't see nothing anyways."

"There's lumps of all kinds of things back there. One has got to be the diamonds. No one has found them anywhere in this place. I looked. Lennie and his pal looked. Go on, get in there. You'll see. I'm smaller, but you're much more agile than I am.

"Agile? I'm agile? Never thought I'd have to pay for being graceful."

"Not the same thing. Dal, you tell him. You're his boss?"

"Hell, no. I'm not anyone's boss. This is between the two of you. I'm neutral. Just call me Switzerland."

"Traitor, you just wait. Go on, Burt. Don't be such a sissy. They're only lumps of rat shit, nothing alive."

"Lumps? Shit? And so you deduce a bag of diamonds from that?" Burt continued to grumble but he went in headfirst, body then feet disappearing into the dark hole. The echoes of his boots banged, crashed, banged, shoving him along. Then silence.

"What do you reckon he's doing?" Dal peered up toward the dark hole.

"Awful quiet." She took his hand. "You feeling good?"

He glanced at her. In the gloom of the building, lit only by bands of sunlight coming through the window slats, his eyes glistened a forest green. "Yep. Good as gold. Don't worry about me." He was silent a moment, then said quietly, "You're the best friend I've ever had. You know that? You do stuff for me, you don't hassle me... well, not too much. And best of all, I don't feel lonely any more. You and Burt, Kathy and Dave. Mac. You all make me feel... well, settled. Safe."

His words touched her in unexpected places. He wasn't one to get all feely touchy. Kept his emotions buried pretty deep, so it meant a lot to her, him telling her that. "We love you, Dal."

He cleared his throat. "Okay, enough of this. First thing you know, we'll be hugging and crying. Hey, Burt, you okay in there?"

"I'm coming out."

"Did you find them?" she yelled.

"Just wait a minute." A cough, a sneeze, then laughter.

His feet emerged, then his legs, and he felt around with his toes till he found the ladder rung and scooted out, bringing great wads of dust and dirt with him. He shut off the flashlight, stuck it back in his belt, and came down the ladder. Under one arm, he held a well battered stainless steel thermos which he handed to Jess.

"Here," he said, shaking the thing. Something inside rattled. "Could be a handful of rocks, from the sound of it, but at least it ain't rat shit. You get to look first."

She took the thermos, the kind people carried around before they started carrying plastic bottles with nipples on them. Truck drivers had this kind of thermos 'cause you could knock them around and they never broke. Plenty of truck drivers around this place delivering stolen goods after the plant closed down. A thermos left lying around, a handy place to hide stuff.

The top was stuck pretty good, but she finally screwed it off, then unscrewed a stopper. Moving to a nearby table, she poured the stones out. Burt shined the flashlight on the glittering pile. One large glistening diamond caught and reflected the light. The rest, small crystals cut from rocks like those found along the roadside around Hot Springs.

"What the hell?" Burt said. He grabbed the thermos, turned it up and shook it. A tightly folded piece of paper fell to the floor. He bent and picked it up, opened it.

Left you one for your trouble. Let it lead you where you're going.

It wasn't signed, but it was dated. June 1986.

"Son of a bitch." Dal stared at Jess a moment, then laughed. "Almost thirty years ago. Around the time this place shut down for good. Reckon who has them by now?"

"Question is, how'd they get from the 1980 robbery and arrest to this guy? I'd guess they're long gone. Sure would like to figure out who took them, though." Jess held the single flashing diamond in the palm of her hand, moving so it caught the light. "Beautiful, isn't it? Wonder what it's worth?"

Dal held it between his thumb and forefinger. "Let's have it appraised. Maybe we can find out for sure if it's one of the Vandergriff stones. At least it can lead us that far."

"Or we could just put it in our pocket and forget we found it."

For a moment, a frown creased his forehead, like he might halfway believe her, then he grinned, pulled a small plastic evidence bag from his pocket and sealed the stone inside.

"Could be this stone will tell its own tale. But I have a hunch I'd like to follow up. 'Cause I think I know who put it in that vent and what went with the other stones."

All the way back to the car, Jess ragged Dal, trying to get him to give her at least a clue as to who he thought wrote the note, but he just grinned in that way he had, so that his dimples flashed on and off.

"Did you get a message from the spirit in the thermos, or what?"

"Nope, just putting two and two together, and it finally all makes sense. Well, almost all of it."

"Come on, tell me. I won't breathe a word till you say so, I promise."

"Just you hide and watch, hide and watch," he told her.

Burt laughed at the two of them. "I'm going to take you guys back and let you hassle this out. Tink's waiting for me. We're going out to the swimming hole this afternoon."

After Burt left them at Dal's place, he and Jess loaded up in his SUV and he started the engine.

"Where we going?"

He just shook his head, and took off, heading up Sugar Mountain.

At a mailbox marked only with an address and no name, he turned in. A long narrow rocky track wound its way deep into the woods to reveal a new log cabin. One of those that came in a kit and was put together on site. A new Corvette sat in the driveway.

"Who lives here?" Jess said.

"You remember the guy who found the blue Falcon in the woods a few years ago? The car I crawled all over looking for clues?"

"Marcy? Alvin Marcy?"

"Yeah, that's him."

"He lives here?"

"I thought you knew. You said you talked to his wife."

"Yes, but I never came out here. I talked to her on the phone. She was supposed to have him call me, or I was supposed to call him. I forget now. Anyway, we never spoke. Then I forgot about it when all hell broke loose."

"Uh-huh."

"You telling me he…?"

"Want to go in with me when I question him? Gotta keep your mouth shut. Just sit there and look like you know something. Take notes or something."

"You bet I want to go with you." She zipped her fingers over her lips and dug her notebook and a pen from the backpack.

He shut off the engine and they both stepped out. A barking dog approached and Dal talked it down in his melodic voice, then headed toward the massive front porch. The dog followed along, tail wagging.

A woman came to the door before he knocked, peered at him through the screen. "Help you, Deputy?"

"Alvin at home? We need to speak to him. I'm Deputy Dallas Starr. This here is Jessie West with *The Observer*. I believe she spoke to you a while back about that old Ford Falcon your husband found in the woods. He was never able to get back to her, and I just have a few things to clear up before we close this case."

The woman's dark eyes slid in one direction, then the other before meeting Dal's steady gaze. The dog licked his fingers hanging at his side. She slipped a glance downward.

"Git on off the porch, Sandy." She didn't open the screen or invite them in. "He's not here right now. I could have him call you if you'd leave a card."

"Where's he at, Mrs. Marcy?" Dal's voice cut away from its gentleness.

The plain woman licked her lips. "I don't rightly know."

"Oh? Is your husband missing?"

"Of course not. I'm just not sure where he went to this morning."

"Well, ma'am. I tell you what. When he does get back, you tell him for me that if he doesn't come in to the sheriff's office first thing tomorrow, I'm putting a warrant out for his arrest. Could you do that?"

She jerked her head up to stare at Dal. "Whatever for? Alvin hasn't done nothing."

"Well then, he won't mind coming in for a chat. Now will he?" He touched the brim of his silver Stetson, then turned and crossed the porch, Jess trailing along behind. Made her feel kind of like that dog, following him with her tail wagging.

Once settled in the SUV, she asked, "How in the world did you figure out he took the diamonds?"

"Pretty simple. He found the diamonds stuffed away in that car, sometime before 1986. Remember ole Herb Nelson reported seeing Mathon Wells and Wesley Miller coming to get gas. They didn't have anything with them when they were arrested soon after that, and the stones weren't found out at Old 41, so it figures they had to have left the stones in a safe place. That car had been driven deep into the woods. Wouldn't nobody see it there for God knows how long. Marcy didn't report the Falcon in the woods till a few years ago, but he found it before 1986, else how did the diamond get in the vent back there? Sam told me Marcy worked there for a few months before the place shut down that same year. All that dust and stuff. Figured no one would put it all together. He's worked at a sawmill most all his life and lived in a four room house. He's got a teenage son who turned up with a Corvette for his graduation gift last summer, and several years ago they built that expensive house. Told everyone his wife inherited money."

"So Mathon and Wesley left the diamonds in that old car. How'd you figure that out?"

"The steel thermos was a clue. Back in the eighties, everyone carried them. They'd become a great substitute for those lined in glass that broke when you even banged them. But the best one was that Alvin Marcy worked at the SEFOR plant until 1986 when it closed down. He figured it was time to be a good citizen and turn in the car. But he stuffed that one diamond in the vent back before the plant closed. It'd be a good joke when someone found it, which they'd surely do once the plant was torn down."

"But why did he leave a diamond in it? Why not just the crystals?"

He glanced at her. "That was the fun part of it. It proved someone had gotten away with the diamonds. If they were never found, why then folks would assume they were forever lost wherever Mathon and Wesley hid them. I think Marcy couldn't stand no one knowing someone had ended up with them."

"Wait a minute. What about the directions Mathon left for Lennie?"

"That one only Alvin can tell us."

Alvin Marcy turned up the next morning at the sheriff's office, wearing overalls and ratty looking work boots, his skinny neck the kind of dirty that's been there so long it won't wash away. His hair hung in long greasy strings clotted with dirt.

Dal escorted him into the interrogation room and sat down opposite him at the table, crossed his arms over his chest and leaned back to stare in silence at the man.

Who this son of a bitch thank he is?

Dal smiled and tapped the table with his knuckles. "You lose something, Alvin?"

"Don't reckon." *And wouldn't tell you if'n I did.*

Dal dug in his pocket, tossed the plastic bag holding the diamond onto the table.

Alvin's eyes widened, then flashed. *So they finally found it. Wondered how long it would be. Keeping my mouth shut. How in hell he figure this out? Won't say nothin'. Cain't prove nothin'.*

Grinning great big, Dal said softly, "Don't be too sure of that. Did you wear gloves when you used that thermos? Or wipe your prints off?"

Sheeit, man. Don't do it.

For a second Dal wasn't sure what that last sentence meant, till Alvin leapt forward, head-butting Dal in his midsection and knocking him backward. He scrambled to his feet before Alvin could pin him down, twisted the skinny arm behind his back, and slammed him up against the wall. Handcuffs out, he snapped them around the one wrist, had the other one pulled down and cuffed. Alvin tried to kick him in the shins and Dal threw him to the floor, knee in his back.

"I'd just stay down, if I were you," he said close to the man's dirty ear. "I'm not breathing hard yet." While holding him on the floor, Dal read Alvin his rights.

"How in the hell did you figger this out?" Alvin gasped out the words when he finished.

"You should never have built that fancy house. Couldn't resist, could you? But when you bought the kid that Corvette, that pretty well did it. A man who's spent a lifetime living hand to mouth doesn't suddenly have enough money for such as that."

"Hell, I waited all them years so no one would suspect anything. Just spent it in dribs and drabs otherwise. So my family didn't go hungry. If she hadn't wrote that story and got everyone all stirred up."

"No, Alvin. Let's face it. If you hadn't put that diamond and note in that old thermos just to show off, you might have got away with it. Tell me one thing, though. How in hell did you send Lennie and that Reilly bunch off in the wrong direction with that so-called treasure map from Mathon Wells?"

Alvin grinned, showing teeth tinged green from lack of brushing. "That Lennie don't exactly connect the dots all the time. Hell, he'd have me over to his place for a beer now and again. After she wrote that story, it was easy to slip the note and map into one of those boxes stacked off in the corner of their trashy house. Then start talking about how if I was Mathon, I'd a left something behind for him, just in case.

"It wasn't no time till he was tearing into all that junk his daddy had saved back in case it might come in handy someday. He couldn't help but find it eventually. Still, I never figgered anyone would find that thermos till the place was torn down, and the way it looked, it would be another twenty years."

Dal stared at Alvin. "What I can't figure out is why you wanted Lennie and them looking for the diamonds in the first place."

Alvin chortled. Dal couldn't remember the last time he'd heard someone chortle. The man's eyes blazed with glee. "I just got bored and wanted to see what would happen, that's all. Ole Lennie and them always have been a weird bunch."

Not as weird as *you*. Dal wanted to say the words aloud, but it wouldn't do any good. People never did tend to see their own weirdness, only that of others. "You got two men killed with your games, you asshole. And I'll see you're charged with it, too. Doubt you'll ever get out to enjoy that beautiful house."

Jess sat on the other side of the one way mirror, taking notes ferociously. Dal would have nothing to do with the charges, but Alvin didn't know that. He was not very happy. Once the PA brought charges, he would be even less happy.

What a strange story this would make. As always, in agreement with Dal, she would not mention his ability to pick up on people's thoughts. He still wasn't completely sure he could trust her with that knowledge, and while she enjoyed teasing him about it, she would never, ever tell anyone.

Most everyone knew how he solved crimes by communing with the spirits involved in the violence. That was enough to keep folks telling stories from now on.

Beyond the mirror, Dal placed a legal pad and pen in front of Alvin and asked him to write it all down from the very beginning.

Jess made a note in capital letters. ***WHAT WILL ALVIN BE CHARGED WITH?*** He didn't steal the diamonds, though he took them from who did. That must be against the law, but she wasn't sure which law. The value was enough to make it a felony. Maybe after the fact.

She waited outside interrogation till Dal came out. Alvin followed in handcuffs, Tink shoving him along, a huge grin on her face.

"Well, looks like that's over." He took her hands in both his. "I think it's time I kept my promise to take you dancing."

"When and where?" she asked.

Tucking her arm through the crook of his elbow, he led her toward the exit door. "I'm thinking I'll surprise you. But here's a clue. Wear something Western."

"We're going line dancing? Are you sure you're up to that?"

"Second guessing me already." He laughed and did a little forward backward shuffle. "Eight o'clock Friday night."

She leaned her head against his arm, warm and strong through the uniform shirt. "It's a date. Maybe afterward we could watch a movie and eat popcorn."

"And after that?"

"I guess that depends on whether a body turns up or not." She grinned wickedly.

"Even if it's only an alligator?"

"Well, you know how it is out here in the boonies. Not much happens in a small town."

"Bite your tongue," Dal said, and twirled her into the curve of his arm.

The radio on his belt crackled his name.

"Guess I'd better get that."

She raised her shoulders in an exaggerated shrug. "Might as well, they'll find you, no matter where we go."

The voice said something about a raven flying out of an attic carrying something she couldn't make out.

"A raven? Are you sure you know the difference between a raven and a crow?"

"Why does it matter? I need help catching the blasted thing."

"Well, they're bigger and they make a different sound. Did you know a raven's tail is short whereas a crow has nice long feathers in its tail? Now you take the American crow, he has only three feathers in his tail while...."

Chuckling, he held the phone away from his ear. "He hung up on me."

Velda Brotherton writes from her home perched on the side of a mountain against the Ozark National Forest. Branded as *Sexy, Dark and Gritty*, her work embraces the lives of gutsy women and heroes who are strong enough to deserve them. After a stint writing for a New York publisher, she has settled comfortably in with small publishers to produce novels in several genres. She enjoys reading mysteries, but it never occurred to her she could write them until Dal Starr and Jessie West emerged from her background in the newspaper business, and the *Twist of Poe* mysteries were born.

Facebook: Author Velda Brotherton
Twitter: @veldabrotherton
http://www.veldabrotherton.com

www.ingramcontent.com/pod-product-compliance
Lightning Source LLC
Chambersburg PA
CBHW031031030726
47497CB00004B/1093